HEALING HEART SERIES

LOVE, Michael

GINA A. JONES

Black Rose Writing | Texas

This is a work of fiction. Names, characters, businesses, places, events, and incidents are either the products of the author's imagination or used in a fictitious manner. Any resemblance to actual persons, living or dead, or actual events is purely coincidental.

ISBN: 978-1-68513-584-3
PUBLISHED BY BLACK ROSE WRITING
www.blackrosewriting.com

Printed in the United States of America
Suggested Retail Price (SRP) $25.95

Love, Michael is printed in Minion Pro

*As a planet-friendly publisher, Black Rose Writing does its best to eliminate unnecessary waste to reduce paper usage and energy costs, while never compromising the reading experience. As a result, the final word count vs. page count may not meet common expectations.

PRAISE FOR
LOVE, MICHAEL

Love, Michael by Gina A. Jones is a poignant reflection on first love, first heartbreak and dealing with betrayal. Jones draws you in with the well-crafted and relatable characters she created through her own personal struggles, lending a realistic emotional journey that the reader shares.

—USA Today Bestselling Author Andrea Smith

LOVE,
Michael

PROLOGUE

After

"The board was cleaning Michael's office a month ago, and we found this." I tremble and grab my coffee as she pulls something from her purse. Through the tremors, coffee splashes over the rim, causing the hot liquid to run down my fingers. But I'm too nervous to reach for a napkin and begin with slow sips.

She hands me the envelope, and I freeze when I see my name scribbled across the paper. "I think you should read what is in this letter," she says.

Setting the cup down, I wipe my hands on my jeans and reach for the envelope. My heart races, and I slowly tear open the seal and pull out the letter.

Dear   _Jill,_

CHAPTER 1

Now

I swing the veil and watch as it slowly floats over my daughter's perfectly styled French twist. It falls in slow motion, and the years flash through my mind like old family films. The positive pregnancy test that changed our entire life. The ultrasound looked more like an *alien* than a baby—telling us she was a girl. Although, I couldn't see anything. They've become so advanced. The significant gender reveal parties involve Mom and Dad with bouncy houses and ice cream machines.

The day she was born, I couldn't believe she was real—and mine: her first birthday party—cake all over her face. What was supposed to be a special day...well, it wasn't. But I made sure to make it memorable for her.

Her first day of school. I think that's when she learned about divorce. I picked her up from school, and she wanted to enlighten me that some moms and dads live together. At that moment, I realized she never remembered her father and I ever being married. And I don't know if that's a good thing or bad. Probably good.

Her first crush was Davy Wells, who lived across the street. Summers grew from playmates holding hands to kissing in the dugout during travel league. I thought he was the one until we stayed up all night eating ice cream and using up an entire box of Kleenex as she cried, reliving the horrid scene of catching Davy with Rachel Matthews in bed at a party.

My chin quivered uncontrollably at her high school graduation. Although I was not too fond of the fact she was leaving for college in a few short months, I was so proud of her and me—we made it. *Alone.*

My voice chokes as my throat tightens. "Monica, you are such a beautiful bride."

"Oh, Mom, don't start." Through the veil, I can see her eyes welling up. "There's no time to reapply my makeup." I pull the sheer veil over her head and touch her cheek. Rapidly batting her eyes, she looks up, forcing the tears to dry up.

"I'm sorry. You know I can't help it. That's what, as a mother, I'm supposed to do—cry at every event in your life." We laugh out the tears and reach for the Kleenex box. Cautiously, she dabs under her lashes and then turns to admire her bridal reflection.

"I wish you had a wedding dress, Mom, so I could wear it today."

It's times like this when I feel guilty about how things ended. "I know, but...we just didn't have a wedding."

"But, do you ever wish you had? Didn't you have those dreams of planning your wedding when you were a little girl?"

That look she is giving me drains my whole existence. Of course, I wanted that-- the white dress, the music, the doves, the first dance as man and wife. I would have loved to have someone look at me with tears as I walked down the aisle to become his wife, thinking how beautiful I looked. "Yes, honey, of course I did. But we didn't plan things very well, and now it doesn't matter because I get to experience it with you, the person I love more than anything. *This* is what makes me happy, Monica." I straighten her veil, standing behind her as we look at each other in the mirror.

"You look beautiful, Mom. I think you're going to steal my day." We laugh, and I give her a wink.

"I'll let you have a little thunder."

"I love you, Mom."

I wrap my arms around her from behind and take her in a long hug. This day will be the last of only her and me. It hurts, but it feels so good for her to have this. A man who loves her to death. A man who stood in the rain, begging her to talk to him after he drove *two hundred* miles after a fight one night on the phone. A man who tells her what his babies will look like with such a beautiful mother. A man who will stand with tears in his eyes as she walks down the aisle to become his wife. "I love you so much, Monica."

The door opens, and Chelsea, her bride's maid, pops in her head. "Hey, I think the photographer is ready to get pictures of all of us brides' maids."

"Okay. Just give me a minute with my mom."

"Sure, no problem. Jill, you look smokin' hot. Just a warning, my Dad is going to be all over this," she says, running her finger up and down in my direction. She smiles and then shuts the door. Chelsea's dad has been begging for a date—and it doesn't help that Monica gave him my number.

"Mom, are you sure it doesn't bother you that...*Dad* is here? I never expected him even to come. Let alone…"

"Yes, it shocks me too. No, honey, it doesn't bother me. It's what you wanted, and I'm just happy your father has been thinking of someone other than himself for once."

"It's strange, you know—having a man walk me down the aisle who I haven't seen since I was three. Are you sure *you* don't want to walk me down the aisle? It's always just been you and me, Mom. Please don't think that he will ever take your place."

"Oh, honey, don't think that. This is what every daughter should have—her father giving her away on her wedding day. It's perfect—exactly how I always wanted it to be for you."

"Because…you didn't have a wedding?"

"No, because you deserve it, baby. And besides, he could never take my place." I smile and kiss her cheek.

She looks at me and then at her reflection in the mirror. She presses her lips and gives me a sweet smile. "No one will ever take your place, Mom."

"You look perfect. Now, let's go take those pictures," I say, leading her by the hand.

Monica wanted a rustic wedding, so six months ago, we found this beautiful historic round barn, which leases out for weddings—for a hefty price. It's late spring—the end of June- and trees burst with luscious green leaves. Cherry trees explode with white blossoms, and the winding creek fully crest its boundaries. It's a gorgeous sunny afternoon, and all the bridesmaids are perfectly polished.

The photographer poses the girls around the cherry blossom trees and snaps several pictures. Next, we move to a bench set along the creek's edge, and he poses the bride on the court with the bridesmaids behind. Monica then insists on several pictures of just her and me. Her smile is genuine, and I couldn't be happier for her. I wonder how that smile would look when it's time for her to pose with her *father—a stranger.*

There are a few sillier poses and sentimental ones. Then comes the big moment—her father walking her down the aisle. Will anyone even know who he is?

We rush back inside, careful not to let the groom spot his bride. As I walk past the reception hall, I stop. Servers work like busy little bees, setting white linen tables into stellar perfection. I gasp at each table's array of silver buffets and floral arrangements. One would think this is an affair for royalty. My insides ache with happiness to think this is all for my daughter. I swallow the lump burning my throat and return to the bridesmaids' area.

"Did you think he saw me?" Monica squeals from giddiness. I'm so happy for her to have this moment—this day in her life. She deserves all of it.

"No, he didn't see you, Monica," Chelsea says, arranging her veil and straightening out the long train of her dress.

"Mom, did you like the poses? How'd they look?" She, indeed, is beside herself.

"I loved them, Monica. I know I'm going to want each one." I smile and help Chelsea with her dress.

A knock on the door startles Monica. "Oh God, oh God, oh God," she says, her hands fanning her face. "Something's wrong. He didn't show up. Oh, God. Mom, how could he do this to me?"

"Monica, calm down. Jordan would never leave you at the altar. He's crazy for you."

"Not him, Mom." Her eyes fill with panic, and I realize the dread of abandonment is behind that look.

Chelsea cracks open the door. "It's just the photographer."

"Your father has requested pictures with you and your mother," she says. My head swings around, thinking I didn't hear correctly.

"What? Are you sure that's what he has requested?" I ask. I thought Michael would surely be bringing a date, or whatever he calls them these days.

"Yes, ma'am. Are you Jill?"

"Yes."

"Then I need you and the bride to come with me."

I squint my eyes in Monica's direction as she shrugs her shoulders. Why would he want me in his pictures? It's been over twenty years since we've seen each other. And now, I'm suddenly assessing my looks. Why would I care? I'm sure that, with his lifestyle, he's aged horribly: late-night parties, closing down the bars. I shake my head and inwardly yell at myself. *This is Monica's day—not yours, Jill.*

We follow the photographer onto the lawn, where she assures us that the groom and the groomsmen are all back inside. As she leads us across the garden, I see a man standing with his back to us between the cherry trees. *Michael?* When we are a few feet away, he turns around. *I was wrong.* He's still just as handsome as the day he left us. He's a little thinner than I would expect, and his hair has just the right amount of gray at the temples to give him that *distinguished* look. And he still has that perfectly square jaw, I remember.

"Jill," Michael says, reaching for my hand.

I hesitate, feeling awkward. Is this a joke? Is there going to be some *bimbo* half his age calling out his name the minute I take his hand? Even though I'm ten years his junior at thirty-nine. Yes, that's what this is all about. He wants to rub in my face how he's still *got it*, dating women half his age.

"Wow. You haven't aged a bit. You are just as beautiful, Jill."

Me? Is he talking to me? "Ah...thank you, Michael. That suit wears you well." *That suit wears you well*? What the hell? "I mean...you look nice, too." I take his hand with the expectancy of a firm handshake, sealing a business deal, and freeze when his lips gently press a kiss on the top of my hand. Desperately, I try to look past his deep blue eyes, which are looking up at me through his lashes. It's a look I do not recognize—not from him. It's sincere. And a bit of something else I can't put my finger on. I slowly pull my hand back and begin fussing with Monica's veil. "Doesn't Monica make a beautiful bride?" I say, bringing the attention to where it should be. Monica's smile is almost devious.

"Yes, she is a gorgeous bride," Michael says, his eyes slowly moving from me to his daughter.

"So, you want some pictures of...the three of us? Or..."

"Please," he says. "Yes, I thought..." He trails off, and we both know why. He takes my hand and pulls the three of us together. "Whatever you think is best. I want lots of pictures," he says to the photographer.

Lots? Well, he is the one paying for them. And that's another topic.

For Monica's sake, the photographer poses us in several positions, and I only hope I don't look stiff or bogus. After ten or so snaps of the three of us, Michael suggests some of only he and I. Again, I look stunned, but I try not to overly show it, and I suggest they would be nice for Monica to have. However, when Michael wraps me in his arms, I know the look on my face only shows confusion, so I purposely don't look at the camera. I hear the camera click several times, all while I look past Michael, over to the creek, and when I stare down the front of his chest, he kisses my forehead just as the shutter flashes.

"Perfect," the photographer says. "It's like you never knew I was here. I think you're going to love these pictures."

What? I thought she was messing with her camera. We never posed. "Are you sure? I mean…I was waiting for directions from you."

"Do you want me to take some more?"

"Oh no, it's fine. I shouldn't be looking at the camera anyway," I laugh. Lord knows what my expression must have looked like. Michael still has his arms around my waist, and I look into his eyes and see that unrecognizable expression again. *What's that look all about*?

"I better go check on Monica. She's a nervous wreck—although everything is smoothly coming together," I say, breaking from his hold. He smiles and tucks his hands in the pockets of his trousers.

"I'm glad. I want everything perfect for our daughter…and you, Jill."

I swallow and fight back the urge to ask him the big question—the *thirty grand* he has dropped on this wedding. Monica only reached out on Facebook. I'm sure Michael used it more as a dating site and asked if he would attend the wedding. The next thing I knew, Michael told her the sky was the limit. He also is paying for their honeymoon in Paris.

"Michael, thank you for making Monica's dream come true. And I don't mean all the money you have spent. I mean…yes, that is amazing too. But, just being here for her on this day. Well, it means the world to her."

His blue eyes soften, and he blinks a few times. Are those tears he's fighting back? "It means the world to me, too, Jill. You don't know how much."

I find it hard to break from his sincere gaze. And so I nod, smile politely at him, and turn back inside. I'm about to open the door, looking back at Michael. He has his back to me and seems to be pondering over the beautiful countryside. I watch him walk to the creek and bend down to gather water in his hand. He lifts his hand and watches as it spills back into the stream. He turns and spots me watching him and smiles. I quickly turn my head, rush inside, and smack right into Chelsea's recently divorced father.

"Hey, Jill," he says, grabbing me lightly by the arm, "Looks like you got the wedding jitters."

"Ah, just a little," I laugh, pulling my arm from his embrace. "I need to go find Monica." I break from his hold and rush down the hall.

"Better save me a dance," I hear him holler. I roll my eyes and return to the bridesmaids' room. Opening the door, I shut it and lie against the cool wood.

"Mom, are you okay?" Monica walks over and looks at me with concern.

"Oh, yes, honey. I'm fine." Her eyes scan my face, searching for whatever has come over me, but I don't want anything to take away from her day. "Hey, it's just about time," I say, taking her in my arms. "You're going to be a married woman soon."

Another knock on the door, and I hear Michael's voice. "Monica," he says, and I slowly open the door. His eyes shine as he looks at his daughter. I've never seen that look, either. He holds out his elbow, and she graciously takes it. "I know we have a few minutes, but may I have a moment alone with you as just my daughter before you're someone's wife?"

Her chin begins to quiver, and I touch the small of her back. This will be the last time I see her before she belongs to someone else. "I love you, Monica." She turns and kisses me on the cheek, and I watch them leave the room as father and daughter—a precious sight I never thought I'd see.

CHAPTER 2

Then

A car honked as Tammy and I pushed through the school doors. My brother was picking me up today, and I was hoping he would forget. So much for that. I held my hand, gesturing that I saw him, but to give me a minute. He only honked again. Asshole.

"I would take you home if I didn't have to be at work right after school," Tammy said, flipping my brother off. Another long honk. "What's his problem?"

"I don't know, but I better get going before he embarrasses us even more. See you tonight at the game," I said as I walked down the sidewalk and to the curb where his car awaited. Bending down, I glared at him through the open window. "I just walked out, asshole. You didn't have to lay on the horn for everyone to hear."

"Just get in. I have to see a friend," he said, putting the car in gear before allowing me to get in. Quickly, I threw my bag into the back seat and climbed in just before he took off.

"Who's the friend?" I asked.

"A buddy from college recently just took a job here and is renting an apartment. I haven't seen him since graduation."

"Well, can't you drop me off at home first?"

"Can't. I told my buddy I would be there at 3:30. There is no time to drop you off. Just stay in the car and listen to music or something."

"Well, how long are you going to be? I need to shower and stuff before the game tonight."

"Why the hell would you need a shower before a football game?" he said and hit the gas, knocking me back into the seat.

"Scott, watch it," I said, struggling with my seatbelt. He seemed to ignore my dilemma and sped down the highway. I reached for the stereo button and turned the dial, searching for something good to listen to.

"Keep your hands off."

"You told me to listen to some music, and I sure the hell don't like your shit," I said. The only thing Scott listened to was that head-banging crap. He smacked my hand, and I punched his arm in retaliation.

"Stop it. You want to cause me to wreck?"

"Fine then. I'll wait until you leave the car. And you can't expect me to listen to your devil music." He looked sternly at me, then his eyes returned to the road.

"You better not leave it on that country shit," he said. I stuck out my tongue and then pushed back into the passenger seat, crossing my arms. "Oh, real mature, Jill. Are you seventeen or seven?" I ignored his response and turned to watch out the window for the rest of the drive.

Twenty minutes later, we were pulling into an apartment complex, and Scott parked next to a silver Corvette. "*Swee...eet,*" Scott said as he exited the car. "Looks like someone is doing alright." I started to get out when he told me to stay in the car.

"Then give me the keys."

"Why?"

"You said I could listen to the radio. I need your keys for that." He tossed them through the window, landing on the driver's seat. "Hey, how long are you going to be? I could come back and get you."

"I don't know."

"But, I'm going to the game tonight. Twenty, thirty minutes—what?"

"Just stay there and wait. I won't be that long."

I grabbed the keys and started the ignition. When he was out of sight, I changed the radio station to country music. He'd better not be very long.

Glancing around, I noticed the place looked new. I was surprised that a just-out-of-college guy could afford such a situation. And was that his Corvette? I didn't remember my brother having any rich friends from school, but I didn't know any in college.

I rested back and listened to Garth Brooks, *Friends in Low Places*, and hoped he'd be back by the end of the song. No such luck and another thirty minutes passed, and I was now royally pissed at him for bringing me along. The game started in an hour, and I still needed to prepare. I wanted to blow the horn but didn't want the embarrassment of others looking at me. Thinking about entering the building Scott went into, I still wouldn't know which door to knock on. *Shit.* I was forced to wait, pressed my eyes shut in anger, and continued listening to the radio.

I must have dozed off and opened my eyes just as *Amazed* by Lonestar was playing. I looked into the eyes staring down at me. "Hey Jill, this is my buddy, Michael."

"Hi, Jill."

I slowly sat up and hoped I didn't have drool running down my chin or my mouth hanging open from my small catnap. "Ah, hi," I said, my voice croaking. *Crap.* My mouth *was* hanging open. The song was still playing, and I sat up. I wanted to pull down the visor and check my reflection in the mirror because Michael was *gorgeous with* glassy, deep blue eyes and a perfect square jaw that screamed *all things, man.* Beautiful hair tossed around his perfectly shaped head. He was wearing *those* kinds of jeans. The type that looked like you just threw them on but probably paid a million dollars for. He wore a Ball State, faded T-shirt that his body wore like art. There wasn't a flaw about him.

"What the hell is that shit on my radio?" Scott protested.

"Why didn't you bring your little sister up?" Michael asked as Scott hit the radio button, silencing Lonestar.

"She was fine in the car," Scott said as if I was a pet waiting on my master.

I was slightly disappointed when Michael called me a *little sister*. But there was no denying it. If Michael was a friend of Scott's, then he was older than me.

"Would you like to come up? Get something to drink before you leave?" Michael asked while looking at me, not Scott.

"No, thanks," Scott answered for me. "She wants to get to the football game." Now, I looked even younger in this gorgeous man's eyes.

He squatted down, met my face through the opened window, and smiled politely. "It was nice meeting you, Jill. Next time, don't let him make you stay in the car." He winked and tapped his hands on the car door before standing back up. *Next time?*

I tried not to show how my eyes racked up his long, muscular body—glaring too long on those jeans before falling deep into his blue eyes. I needed to speak, but my mouth couldn't form a word. Eventually, my reverie was broken by Scott's loud voice. "Good to see you, man. And next time, I won't have my little sis in the car. Today, she had no choice. See you tonight?"

Michael was still looking at me when his gaze broke to answer my brother. "Yeah, you can show me around this area. What's a good bar?"

"Tossi's is pretty swank. Or would you rather have a dive?"

"No dive. Had my share in college."

"Tossi's it is then," Scott said, returning to the car. He started the engine, and Michael gave me a wink as the car pulled away. All I could do was smile shyly with my head bowed. *Idiot, show him how you're nothing but a shy schoolgirl, Jill.*

"So, you went to college with Michael?"

"Just two years. Michael was completing his master's when I began as a freshman," Scott said as he drove out of the apartment complex.

"Where's he from, and why is he here?"

"Why the sudden interest in my friends?" he asked sarcastically.

"Not a huge interest." I was interested, though. "It's just that you never mentioned him before. He doesn't look the type to travel in your circle."

"And what's that supposed to mean?"

"Well, he seems nice…well-mannered." Attractive was on my tongue because most of Scott's friends were not. But I didn't want to hear the backlash and the teasing, and most of all, him telling Michael that I thought he was hot, which sounds so cliché. And then they'd both get a kick out of how Scott's little sister has a schoolgirl crush on Michael.

"Go ahead and say it. You think he's hot."

"You know how dumb that sounds coming from your mouth? I don't even use that word." Though, I did in my mind. "Yes, he's a nice-looking gentleman."

Scott laughed. "Now that sounds even dumber. Nice looking gentleman," he mocked, raising his voice to sound girly.

"Okay, attractive," I said.

"Well, whatever. You're definitely not Michael's type."

"I never even considered…" I stopped mid-sentence and said, "And what is his type… and what's wrong with me?"

"Michael's type is anything he wants; you are ten years younger than him. So, there is nothing you have that he would want. He has been banging professors' wives behind their backs and several other cougars. And a few moms who pretended to be visiting their sons in college. Oh, yeah, he's well-mannered and well fucked."

"Just…shut up," I said, turning the radio station back to country music.

"And…Michael hates country music."

I grabbed the knob, and before I turned up the volume, I said, "Sounds like you have a man crush on him the way you idolize and know so much about him." I cranked the volume, sat back, and folded my arms, giving him a quizzical look.

He pressed the button, shutting the radio off. "What the hell does that mean?"

"Why would you know all that stuff? Is that all you guys do—kiss and tell?"

"No, Jill. It's called bragging. And Michael has plenty to brag about."

I didn't particularly appreciate where the conversation was heading and didn't want to think of Michael that way. But I guess Scott was right. The man had looks that would get him anything. And why did I think it could be me—Being a seventeen-year-old senior in high school was even more ludicrous. It would be years before I could find a man who looked like Michael. After all, I was just at the beginning of my senior year, and college was more than a year away. Michael was already out of graduate school and on his way to success. Though, I didn't know what he did for a living.

"What does he do? Where does he work?"

"Still obsessed, are you?"

"Just making conversation."

"He's a contracted engineer for Whirlpool."

Whirlpool just happened to be located here in St. Jo, Michigan, and it was a place where everyone wanted to work after graduation. "But his T-shirt said Ball State. Isn't that located in Indiana? How'd you meet him at Michigan State?"

"I told you. He completed his graduate study at Michigan State."

"So, he's from Indiana?"

"Still not obsessed? Yes, he's from Indiana."

During the remainder of the drive home, I didn't ask any more questions about Michael, but what seemed like a chance meeting would turn into a life in which Michael would come and go for the rest of my life.

CHAPTER 3

Now

The last of the bridesmaids and groomsmen take their places, and Jordan's face is everything I wanted at Monica's age. The glassy smile in his eyes tells me how much he loves my daughter. How much he wants to be here and be her husband. That *'I can't believe she's mine'* look on his face.

Sometimes, I worry that Jordan is more into this relationship than Monica. Not that she doesn't love him—she does. Jordan is just always the one making plans for them. Like the time he was planning their honeymoon. He came over with honeymoon brochures of the Poconos. Monica didn't seem impressed, and I could tell Jordan was hurt. I knew the feeling all too well and talked with my daughter.

"Monica, Jordan seems bothered by your lack of interest after he showed you the brochures," I told her. I remember she stood up from the bed where we were both sitting after Jordan left and told me her valid concerns.

"It's not that, Mom. The Poconos look beautiful, and I'm happy with wherever Jordan wants to take us on our honeymoon. It's just...well, when I saw all those heart-shaped bathtubs and large, walk-in showers, it bothered me."

I wasn't catching her drift and approached her concern as motherly as I could, yet not wanting to step on toes or be the intruding mother. But I wasn't sure why it bothered her.

"Is that what married people do? Always bathe together? Will I ever have privacy?"

I pressed my lips, forcing the laugh that was about to come out. But then it hit me. Monica never remembered Michael and me much being together. Even at her age, she hadn't a clue about how married people interacted. The guilt of Michael and I's relationship and failed marriage had once again defined our life and how the past still played a role in my daughter and I's current life. And no matter how much I told myself, 'We're okay. We're a family, just you and I. It was at those moments that I questioned everything. But I never questioned having her.

"No, of course not, Monica," I said. "You will still have privacy. I don't think Jordan wants to know all your business. And…I think he will want his as well." Knowing now, she worried about going to the bathroom before him and those special times of the month. It was not precisely a silly concern. Even back in the day, I thought I'd die if Michael ever saw me use the toilet—*number two* or saw my panty liners under the bathroom sink, which was foolish because Michael didn't care or see anything about me.

The music starts, and we all stand. What is it about those first few choruses that bring goosebumps and well the eyes? Today is justified. But I haven't been able to withstand those feelings at any wedding.

The doors open and…I can't breathe. My heart bangs against my chest, and I must take a breath. Inhaling deeply, I let the air out of my lungs slowly, controlled. I look back at my daughter walking down the aisle—with Michael.

I'm a complete mess now, and I must dry it up if I intend not to miss a second of this wedding. Oh, my. She's perfect. The perfect bride and Jordan's tears are running down his face. His head moves side to side in an almost disbelief of her beauty. This moment is nothing but celestial. If I die and go to Heaven now, my whole messed up existence with Michael was worth it. How can a feeling this wonderful, this joyful bring such a painful, happy sense in my heart? And to see and know that Michael is here witnessing this moment with me escalates that feeling. I'm not sure how he feels now. After talking with him no more than twenty minutes ago, I noticed something different about him. But I don't want to ponder it because Michael will always be that ache from the past. I don't wish to mess up my future. Me and Monica's future.

Dabbing my eyes, I smile at Monica as she looks at me through her veil, arm in arm with her father. She looks so happy. *So, perfect.* Then I look at Michael, wanting to give him a, 'thank you for being here' glance, and spot that strange look again in his eyes as he looks right at me, *right into me.*

I swallow a lump down and fix my gaze back to Monica. A million thoughts are running through me, and I worry the chatter will begin as soon as the music stops. *Who's that man walking Monica down the aisle? That isn't Scott. Didn't Monica's dad run off a long time ago?*

I look at Scott, whose words were transparent about how he felt about Michael being here, let alone walking her down the aisle. Six months ago, Scott was going to be walking Monica down the aisle. It took many talks and begging him that *this* was Monica's day, not mine. But still, he was outraged.

Scott slowly looks at Michael and Monica with tolerance in his eyes. I mouth, *thank you,* and he nods. However, this wedding has only started, and there's the whole reception thing yet to be done— *with alcohol.*

The preacher asks who gives this woman to be with this man, and I hold my breath.

"Her mother and I," Michael says and looks at me. I nod with a smile, and he hands Monica to Jordan. He glances again and sits on the other side of the church. I catch my breath before sitting down.

Jordan's family watches as Michael sits beside them and looks at me. They are wondering why he's on the groom's side. Well, one would have to ask my brother.

"Scott, please behave and don't make Monica feel guilty," I said one day when he visited me at work.

"He has no business being here or at my niece's wedding."

"He's her father, Scott."

"How can you even call him that? I've been more of a father to Monica than…him," he said disgustingly, not wanting to mention Michael's name. I didn't blame him. He had been there for Monica. Dad and doughnut day at school. Field trips I couldn't make. Her first father-daughter dance in Girl Scouts.

All in all, he'd always been the one picking up the pieces. Pieces that Monica and I would still stumble over from time to time. How could I not understand his feelings for this? I did, but I had to make him know it wasn't about us, he and I. Or even Michael. It was about Monica and her day. Despite how we both felt. And to be honest…I felt differently. Shocked and…*happy,* Michael was doing this for his daughter. And that also made me feel guilty. No matter how far Michael was from our lives, his ghost was always around the corner, lurking in those unexpected moments. And this was one of them.

"I'm telling you, Jill, I don't think I can be there with that piece of shit in the same building as me. I don't think Mom and Dad will be there either."

"Did Mom and Dad say that?"

"Jill, I haven't told them yet because I don't want to be the one to bring bad news. But, yes. I'm sure that, once they find out, they won't be going to Monica's wedding either."

Dad had just suffered a heart attack two months earlier, and Monica thought we should postpone the wedding until after Dad's rehab. My father had also been a surrogate father to Monica for the times Scott couldn't commit. And once again, Michael was becoming that thorn in my family's side. But no matter what he'd done or how they felt, Michael was still part of Monica's family.

"You know, it would have been better for you if…he would have died."

"Scott," I protested. "You can't mean that?"

"Jill, what he did to you and Monica is unforgivable. He deserved to die."

Those truthful words coming out of Scott's mouth were no different than when I thought it. But I never said it out loud. Because it was true, and death probably would have given me closure. With Michael, my heart was a revolving door, swinging round and round. Though his heart was shut to me, I could never accept it. And now, he was back. But not for me, and I had to get a grip on my emotions. I hoped no one could see that *hope* in my eyes once again. And I was lying to myself. The day Monica told me she'd reached out and found her father on Facebook, I was seventeen again.

"Look, Jill," he said remorsefully, "I'm sorry it had to come out that way. It's just that I'm afraid it will be another one of his no-shows. And then what?"

"No, Scott, you're right. But Monica has her heart set on this."

"That's my point, Jill. I watched you go through hell many times. I want to spare my niece the pain you went through."

He was right. The hell Michael put me through ate me alive, and the only way I survived it was to forgive him for something he was never sorry for. I didn't know which was worse. And now, I was going to ask Scott to do the same.

"That's because I put it behind me. Behind me," I said, throwing my arms over my head. "Can you do it just for one day, Scott? For Monica? I'll do my best to keep Michael away from you."

He rested his hands on his hips and bowed his head in defeat. I knew the feeling. He took a deep breath and said, "Okay, but he doesn't sit on our family's side."

He left that day, and I hoped it was settled; Michael would walk his daughter down the aisle. I went into the bathroom, locked myself inside the stall, and cried. All I ever wanted was to love and be loved, and in the process, I was destroyed for wanting that. I never understood how it was such a bad thing. Indeed, there were worse things one could do to someone, and bad things had been done to me. But, I had learned that wanting passion and romance was distasteful and a waste. The worst thing you could ask of another. *'Let me love you.'*

Shaking my head, I return to the present. This wedding forced back the pain of the last two decades. No, I haven't let it go, according to the trembling of my body and the ache in my heart. But to hurt Monica or to tell her that her father was not welcome would ten-fold that. And I have done my best to protect her from my pain.

"We are gathered here to bring together this man and this woman in holy matrimony," the preacher says, asking for a word of prayer. Before I bow my head *like an idiot*, I look again at Michael. He hasn't bowed his head yet either and stares at me. I don't want to watch, but I do, and try as I may, read what's in his eyes. Are the last two decades running through his head? What has life been like for him? I'm sure it's been nothing but ski vacations in Aspen. Sunsets on the beach in Aruba. European sabbaticals when he can't *cope* with life. But then I realized those are all *romantic* things, and Michael was anything but. And I'm sure there's a line of women who thought of romance when the *Handsome Michael Danforth* took them away to someplace exotic. All their dreams went down the toilet the minute he dumped them at the airport once the vacation was over. At least I got a wonderful daughter out of it.

Yes, I smile at Michael and bow my head.

CHAPTER 4

Then

The look on my face was that of seeing a ghost when Tammy parked in our driveway. We were returning from the football game, and even though I couldn't tell you who won or lost, Tammy was now up to date on the whole *Michael* incident.

"Wow! Whose car is that?" Tammy asked as we both looked at the Corvette in my drive.

"I'm pretty sure it's Michael's car. That was the car parked at the apartment where Scott and I went today."

"The Michael?"

"Ah, yes." Why was he here? I thought he and Scott were going to Tossi's.

"Awesome! Now I get to see him in real life," Tammy said as she rushed from the car and bee-lined to the door. I was nervous and wanted him here…and not wanted him here.

I opened the front door, and there he was. All gorgeous and standing in my living room. He turned and looked at me, and then the smile on his face melted my heart. Just his smile affected me, and I didn't know why. Plenty of people smiled at me. What about him made me feel…*special* when he did? It felt like his smile said, 'It's you.'

Tammy stood with that ghost look, and I had to say something before everything I told her was written all over her face. I bumped her with my foot and said, "What are you guys doing here? I thought you were going to Tossi's?"

"We will be. I'm just waiting for Jen," Scott said. Jen was Scott's girlfriend who worked twelve-hour shifts at the hospital and didn't get off until 9:00 at night.

"Hi, Jill. Nice to see you again," Michael said, and I introduced him to Tammy.

"Hey. Good to see you, too. This is my best friend, Tammy," I said, hoping my voice was at a standard octave.

"Hey, Michael. You're going to love April," Scott said as they walked out of the living room and into the kitchen. "Don't say anything to Jen, but I think she is smokin' hot."

April! He was fixing Michael up with Jen's sister, April?

I was glad they turned to leave because I'm sure the look on my face was full of disappointment. What was I thinking? To him, I was just a schoolgirl crush. And April was closer to his age and smokin' hot. But I tried to act all approvingly and joined their conversation.

"April's nice," I said, following them into the kitchen. Scott grabbed two beers from the fridge and handed one to Michael. "You'll like her. I heard she's a good nurse."

Scott then nudged Michael with his shoulder, and with a raised brow, I knew what that look meant—a hot nurse in a uniform, playing doctor. Michael gave a small laugh, which I knew meant he agreed.

"That's what I plan to do after graduation," I said, continuing my 'I'm okay with you and April' conversation.

"Oh yeah? Where're you planning to attend school?" Michael then asked.

I went to the fridge and pulled a coke for Tammy and me. "Michigan State," I said, handing Tammy her coke.

"Great university," Michael said, and my mind went to all the women he probably had sex with. I was processing all that talk of him in my mind.

I was about to elaborate more on my interest in nursing when I heard Jen from the front room. "Scott?"

"Yeah, Babe." He made the shush sign with his lips—a warning not to say he thought April was hot before they walked in.

Jen walked in and went to kiss Scott on the lips. April followed behind, flipping her dark hair and looking at Michael with her *blow-job eyes*. She always looked like she was looking up at you, even if you were shorter, her eyes slightly crossed in that sexy way. Tammy and I practiced that gaze but always laughed at each other with crossed eyes. However, April did it; she had it mastered.

I could tell Michael was impressed with what he saw, and I witnessed him mold into his MO of seduction. He took in a deep breath. His hard chest rose, showing all of its glory in that shirt he was wearing with those jeans, and he tilted his head and held out his hand.

"You must be April?"

"That'd be me," she answered as if it were a game show. "And you must be Michael." *Duh*, I thought and tried not to roll my eyes. This would be the first of many to come.

I hated that Michael's beautiful eyes were all over April, and I was now invisible in the room. I tried to think of a diversion to grab Michael's attention again. But all I could say was, "Have a great time."

I didn't want them to have a great time. I wanted Michael's sexy smile on me and not looking into April's blow-job eyes. But as I watched them walk out the door, my eyes fixated on his perfect ass in those perfect jeans, and I opened my can of coke to have it blow up all over me. *How ironic.*

•   •   •   •   •

Friday night had ended as it had started—obsessing over Michael. It was Saturday evening, and as much as I wanted to hang out with Tammy and set a plan to run into Michael accidentally, it was my weekend shift at Delanie's—the local pizza shop—a job I took so that I could be where all the guys hung out after games. However, I spent most of my time in the kitchen with frizzy hair and a sweaty face from the pizza ovens.

Tonight, we were short on drivers and heavy on cooks. So, I jumped to take the next few deliveries across town—anything to get out of that hot box. I grabbed the top three pizzas, now boxed and in their thermal carriers, and loaded up my car. I had the pizzas stacked in order according to the address for delivery and looked at the name and address for my first delivery—Roe, 217 High Street.

After delivering the first pizza, I was off to the second address—Smith, 305 Oak Street. Luckily, it was only a block over. After counting my tips and stashing into my purse, I looked at the address of the last pizza. Danforth, 213 Chamberlain Dr., Apt B.

Oh, no way! But yes, it was. I wanted to run into him accidentally. But not wearing a pizza dough cover T-shirt that smelled of sweat and onions and with my hair frizzed into oblivion. There was no time to return to the Delanies and fix myself up. I had to face the music. I would see Michael in this pitiful, ugly state—reeking of pizza.

Parking outside his apartment building, I saw his Corvette parked where it was the day I came with Scott. At least now I knew which apartment was his—213. But now, I didn't want to go in. Maybe I would set the pizza in front of his door, ring the doorbell, and run. And that's what I should have done. But that didn't happen.

I opened the door to go into his apartment building, and there he was, unlocking the door to his apartment and about to walk in when he turned and saw me.

"Jill?"

"Ah, hey, Michael," I said, acting surprised like I wasn't just here yesterday. "Here's your pizza."

"Wow. How nice to move to a new city and know the girl delivering your pizza. Come in. Let me get you your tip."

I walked in, feeling lower than ever. I went from my *friend's little sister* to *the pizza delivery girl*. I didn't know which was worse. But I did accomplish one thing—I accidentally ran into Michael.

He tossed his keys onto the counter, and I looked around his place. It was nice, but also bare, as he had just moved here. Maybe his stuff was in transit. One couch sat along the wall in the living area next to a stereo with huge speakers and two barstools in front of the kitchen bar. I walked over, placed the pizza on the counter, and removed it from the thermal.

Michael pulled out his wallet from the back pocket of those perfect jeans and handed me fifty. Reaching into the change bag, he then said, "No. Keep the rest as your tip."

Even though I was elated to receive a forty-dollar tip, I couldn't let him do that. "No, please. I have the correct change."

"I'm sure you do, but I want to leave you a forty-dollar tip since you're Scott's little sis." He wasn't going to take no for an answer and went to turn on the stereo. "I bet you're a Shania Twain girl," he said, sliding a CD into the player. The song began, and he came over and took my hands. "Have time for a dance before delivering the next pizza?"

"Um, you're my last," I said as his arms wrapped around me, and, the next thing I knew, I was slowly dancing in Michaels' arms as Shania sang, "*You're Still the One.*"

I wanted to look pretty. I wanted my hair not to look like a frizzy rat's nest. I didn't want to smell like pizza. But one thing I knew, I liked being in Michael's arms.

He sang along with the chorus, and I looked into his gorgeous blue eyes and smiled. I hoped since I was looking up and centering in on his eyes, that maybe I had that perfect blowjob stare that April had mastered.

He held his forehead to mine and gave me that smile I remembered the day before. "You're so cute, Jill," he said. *Cute.* Like pretty...*cute*? Beautiful...*cute*? Or, just how cute a puppy is? But I felt it was a little more than just cute. After all, I was in his arms.

Shania sang on, and we were both singing along. It was fun and romantic. I forgot that my hair was a mess, pizza dough was on my T-shirt, and I smelled like pizza and sang along with Michael and Shania.

The door opened, and I heard someone say, "Awe, aren't you two cute." It was April, and she was walking in with a bottle of wine. "I picked up Cabernet," she said. "Did you get the beer?"

"Yes," Michael said as he let go from around my waist and walked over to where April stood in the kitchen.

I went to grab the pizza thermal on the counter and watched as Michael kissed April's cheek. "And the pizza is still warm. I'll open the wine if you want to grab some paper plates in the cabinet," he said.

"Hey, Jill. How are you?" April asked.

"I'm good. I was delivering your pizza for tonight. You guys have a nice night," I said, walking to the door like Charlie Brown, my head mentally bowed.

"Tell Scott hi for me," Michael said, and I stepped out and shut the door.

Before I left the hall, I could hear them talking from inside.

"What the hell were you dancing with her for?"

"Why? Are you jealous?" I heard Michael tease. I pictured them having a great laugh once I shut the door. How he just wanted to humor the little pizza girl and give her a little dance. Like the unpopular girl, you ask her to sit with you and then embarrass her by spilling milk on her pants.

I threw the thermal bag into my car and returned to Delanie's.

CHAPTER 5

Now

The low hum of chatter fills the reception hall, and I listen for any word: *Who was that man who walked Monica down the aisle?* Everything seems to be performing flawlessly, and I pray that when the bar opens, so does this reception.

I spot Michael hanging around alone in a corner across the room, and I'm surprised he's here. Nobody said he had to stay after the wedding, and he has fulfilled his daughter's request to walk her down the aisle.

His eyes cast to me, and I'm not sure how to respond. In a way, I wished he would never have come because this day should be all about Monica and Jordan, not Michael. But she is his daughter, too. Maybe I shouldn't give him such ownership—since he never stuck around and bailed by the time she was three. Then that voice whispers: *This is what your daughter wanted.*

The low hum quiets when the officiator grabs the mic and announces the wedding party's arrival. "Ladies and gentlemen: please welcome Mr. and Mrs. Jordan York and their groomsmen and bridesmaids." The music begins with a catchy beat as each groomsman carries a bridesmaid to the wedding party table. After each is seated, Jordan carries in his bride, Monica, as the crowd whoops, hollers, and cheers. Goosebumps invade every inch of my body as the tears sting the back of my eyes. She is happy. I am delighted. And I look at Michael and see happiness in his eyes for once. He genuinely wants to be here.

I walk over to our family's table, where Mom and Dad, Scott, and now wife, Jen, have already been seated. I look to Scott for any rebuttal and force a smile. I then say *thank you*, and he presses his eyes open and shut, showing his tolerance level.

"Wasn't Monica just beautiful?" I say, breaking the ice and avoiding the white elephant in the room.

"Lovely," Mom replies.

"I hope this cost him an arm and a leg," Dad says, jabbing at the white elephant.

I inhale a deep breath, grab the rolled-up napkin on the table, and squeeze it as my only means of therapy. "Dad, let's not get into this now. It's Monica's day, and this is what she wanted."

"You're her mother, Jill. You were supposed to sit her down and tell her no."

"Dad, she is an adult. This is her wedding—her day. Please…"

"Arthur, let's not make a fuss," Mom defends me. For how long, I don't know. She has always let Dad have the upper hand.

"Well, it's not right," Dad says, turning to Mom. Mom wraps her arm around his—a gentle touch that calms him whenever Dad voices his status quo. "I'm just making my opinion known. I'm allowed to, at least."

"Yes, dear. We all know how you feel—there's no denying that." Mom rubs Dad's shoulder, letting him have his *moment*, then switches topics for a quick save. "Don't forget. I've changed your cardiology appointment to Tuesday instead of Monday." I'm sure it's to remind Dad of his still *delicate* situation. I let out a cleansing breath and repeat with another.

Dad turns back and says under his breath, "It's bad enough what we all had to go through back then." And there it is. The shame of how their seventeen-year-old daughter got herself pregnant and disgraced the family. Though, it's impossible to get *yourself* pregnant. However, as I took on the responsibility of motherhood, Michael got to go on with his life as a successful person with all his priorities in order. *What a big sack of shit.*

"Dad..." I stop, remembering his heart condition, and excuse myself from the table before causing him to have a third heart attack. And I'm sure in his eyes, and I was probably the cause of his heart disease in the first place. And not the pork rinds and five pounds of bacon he ate weekly. Or the twenty years he used to smoke. "I'm going for some fresh air." Grabbing my purse, I walk out of the reception hall, forcing composure in my steps.

I look for the nearest restroom and throw myself in before the heavy sob that's been building in my chest releases. Opening a stall, I lock the door and let it out as silently as possible. *Fuck!*

After having my silent pity party, I tear off a piece of toilet paper, wipe it under my eyes, and discard the mascara-soiled tissue down the toilet. My shoulders lift with another refreshing cleanse before stepping out of the stall and assessing my *sorry-ass* state in the mirror.

Now red-eyed and puffy, I pull out my compact and attempt to cover the sadness of the last twenty years.

God, Stop it. You and Monica have had a great life. And there's still more to come. When thinking of Michael, two things always correspond with the thought. One, he ruined my life, and two, if he hadn't come into my life, I wouldn't have Monica. What a twisted way to live for the last twenty years. And I must admit, my life with him out of the picture improved. No more 'Oh god, what will I find going through his pockets?' Or phone calls from a woman who enlightened me about how she was *taking care* of my husband. The weeks he went on business trips, instead of spending those times relaxing with my baby daughter, planning trips to the zoo or walks to the park, my mind was consumed with what I knew he was doing and physically searching for the next clue in his infidelity. It was exhausting being his wife. I should have praised the day he said goodbye. No more consuming my thoughts and controlling whether I was to have a good day or not. And here I am, giving him the power again. *Damn it.*

Breathe. Exhale. Smile. 'Show Michael how him walking out, did you a favor,' I say to myself and walk out of the restroom.

"Michael," I say, shocked.

"Are you okay, Jill?"

"Ah, sure. Just an emotional time for me. My daughter is getting married and all." Please don't let him think he has anything to do with my state. "I told myself, over and over, no crying at Monica's wedding."

"I think that's what you're supposed to do," he says, wiping under my eye with the pad of his thumb. "Cry…at your daughter's wedding."

His touch alone puts me on high alert, and I pull out all defenses to walk away. "That's right, Michael. *My daughter.*" I push past him and focus on the music thumping down the hall.

I will not let him destroy this one day for me. And maybe Dad and Scott were right; Michael has no right to be here. He made that clear many years ago.

The staff is now serving the food, and Monica gives me a desperate look as I walk in. *Get it together, Jill, for your daughter's sake.*

I put on my best motherly, prideful smile and walk to her. "Mom? What's wrong? Did something happen?"

"No, Baby. I just had to freshen up my face. Can't hold the tears back." She relaxes with a smile, and I kiss her on the cheek.

"Well, we were waiting for your return. We are going to toast, and I want you here."

"Oh, good. Now, keep that smile on and enjoy this day. I love you, Monica."

"I love you too, Mom." I tap her on the hand and return to the family table. Dad is now engrossed in his food, and Mom looks up with an apologetic look in her eyes. Scott has that *'I told you so'* look in his.

The sound of clinking as the best man stands and makes his announcement. "At this time, the bride's father would like to make the first toast."

Oh. Shit. What the hell would he even have to say?

Michael walks to the wedding party table, and the best man hands him the mic. Through the soft background piano music and the clinking of silverware, I hear my heart pounding and watch Michael pull a piece of paper from his suit. He begins to speak, and his voice cracks.

"Monica, let me start by saying," he chokes and breathes to start again. "I'm sorry for being absent from your and your mother's lives." The silverware clinking stops, and now only the soft piano music fills the room. "It's a regret in my life daily. I have missed out on so much, and there's no excuse I can give. Despite what you feel, there wasn't a day when I didn't think of you. What did you look like, and if you had a boyfriend? If he treated you well." Scott clears her throat. "And…I know I don't deserve to be *here* on your special day. Because I never had any hand in any of it. When you contacted me to walk you down the aisle." He chokes up and presses his hand to his mouth. "It was a second chance. A chance I know I don't deserve. But I will tell you one thing: I will never miss out on any chance you give me to be with you."

A hushed sorrow echoes throughout the room, and even though I want to hear every painful word that is coming out of Michael's mouth, I wish he'd stop.

"Monica, you are as beautiful as I knew you would be. And when I look at you, I can't believe the life I missed with you and your mother," he says, looking over at me.

Where's this coming from? This man is not Michael, as far as I remember. Michael was incapable of emotions. And to be adding me into his apologetic-toast-speech? Do I want this? I mean, I do. Just, maybe not here. He hasn't even looked at the note in his hand.

"I…I'm sorry for everything. And though you may not think so, I love you, Monica."

Monica stands, now in a full-on cry, and goes to hug her father. "Thank you. Thank you for coming today and wanting to be a part of this," she says but doesn't tell him she loves him back. How could she?

He asks her to remain beside him and looks at his note. "I would also like to make a toast to your husband." She nods and wipes her eyes.

"Jordan," he says—his voice choked, "Jordan, make sure that wherever you go, hold your wife's hand. Show everyone that you are her man. And not because she's incapable, but because she's your wife, always open her car door. Take her on long weekends, even camping on the beach. Sit by the fire and look into her eyes. Tell her everything you love and appreciate about her. Surprise her with small gifts for no reason. Let her know that, one day, while mowing the yard, you looked over and saw her tending her flowers and felt how lucky you must be."

He's speaking in past tense and looking right at me. My mouth is agape, and I feel lost in a tunnel. No, this is not the Michael I remember. All these things are what I wanted him to do. And even on a simple request, he ridiculed and rolled his eyes when I suggested them.

Michael continues and watches me with glassy eyes. "When you look out the window and see the first snow, grab your wife, bundle up, and make a snowman together. Do this every year as your tradition. Make every day a new celebration for you and your wife. Save every champagne cork and write the occasion. Go back each year and read them to each other."

I'm shaking, and I'm not sure how to feel. On the one hand, it's everything I've ever wanted to hear from Michael. But on the other…, *it's Michael.* The Michael who hated all those things. The Michael who made me feel guilty for getting pregnant. The Michael who looked at me one day, a day I will never forget, told me he couldn't do *this* anymore. And when he said *this*, he meant Monica and me. We weren't a family to him. We were reduced to pronouns—*this*.

CHAPTER 6

Then

"I don't know. It was just weird," I said to Tammy. It had been a week since the *pizza delivery dance* with Michael, and we would spend our day at the mall this Saturday. The homecoming dance was in a week, and even though we didn't have dates, we were shopping for the dance—new dresses.

"And then he stopped when blow-job eyes walked in?"

"Yep. Pretty much."

"So, you think they're a thing now?"

I answered her and didn't know why I needed to explain this even to myself. Michael was ten years older, just a friend of my brother's, and I was only a senior in high school. But still, the feeling was that I had just lost the love of my life, and it ached in my heart. "Well, they had pizza and wine together. And apparently, she's been staying at his apartment."

"April is such a whore," Tammy said, and I had to agree. But that was why she got any guy she wanted. And maybe I shouldn't be so jealous. But I was. He was nothing special to her and had already grown a place in my heart. Was this just a schoolgirl crush? But I felt it was more profound, even if the dance was meant for me. Something about Michael would change who I was and who I would become.

"Can you believe she acted jealous after I left? I heard her ask Michael why we were dancing." Even if it was just a tease, it did elevate my private status with Michael. *She was jealous.*

"Hey, let's stop talking about this. Let's get some dresses picked out," I said, pointing to the 5.7.9 store.

As I pushed through the rack of dresses, the question was always there. *Would Michael like me in this?* I needed to remind myself I was shopping for a high school dance and not a hot date with Michael.

"What about this dress?" Tammy asked, pulling out a black button-down dress, thigh-length and white pock-a-dots. It was cute, but I focused on something *sexy* for Michael. She could tell by the look on my face that I wasn't feeling it. "Okay," she said and placed it back onto the rack.

I then came across a pink, sleeveless t-shirt dress and showed it to Tammy. Her eyebrows raised as I put the dress up to me. "Turn around," she said and grabbed the dress. Pressing the dress on my backside, she said, "barely covers your ass. Is that what you're going for?"

"You're right. Let me look at the black dress again." She pulled it out, and I thought of a way to *sex it up.* Fishnet stockings and high heels? Of course, I had never worn fishnet stockings, but the grunge look was coming from Seattle. Mixing it with black combat boots, we could get away with it.

We both grabbed a dress; I the poke-a-dot one, and Tammy the plain black and headed back to the fitting rooms. Sharing one room, we stood and assessed our pre-grunge look. After, we would hop over to the Hot Topic and complete our look with fishnet stockings and combat boots.

Looking in the mirror, I wished I had Tammy's long, silky, almost black hair. Mine was just as long but very blonde. And the summers, living in the sun, didn't help. The summer golden-California girl look had passed, and winter dark and gloomy was now the rage. My long, wavy curls were no longer in style, and there was no way I would ever get that silky, straight look. With my large blue eyes, I could give that darkness with some heavy liner. Everything about me was wrong, and thinking that Michael would be attracted to me was crazy. I was too young, too blonde, and out of his league.

We paid for our dresses, headed to Hot Topic, and found our fishnet stocking and black, shiny combat boots. After that, we grabbed our favorite Chinese food and sat in the middle of the food court.

"Are we still going stag?" Tammy asked.

"I plan on it. It's a thing now, you know. Don't need a date for a dance," I tried to justify, but the truth was that neither of us had a date. But it was still a week away, and the chances of being asked, asked by someone we wanted to go with were probably not going to happen.

"How should we wear our hair?" she asked, and I thought how perfect her hair was.

"What do you think about me dying my hair black?"

"Why?" she exclaimed.

"Because I hate it, blonde. It's so…80s. It's almost 2000, and black hair is in."

"Since when?"

"Ah, since Nirvana."

"I believed Kurt Cobain had blond hair. And didn't his wife…what's her name?"

"Courtney Love."

"Yes, Courtney Love," Tammy said and drank her Coke. "Man, it's such a shame what happened. I loved that song. What was that song?"

I laughed. *"Smells Like Teen Spirit,"* I said.

"Yeah. That song. What does that even mean?"

"I think it means how our generation will someday be in power," I said. Years later, people learned that the song was dubbed an "anthem for apathetic kids" of Generation X, and the band grew uncomfortable with the attention it brought them.

As I took a drink of my Coke, Tammy said, "So, would you have sex with Michael?"

I choked. "What? Why would you ask that?"

Tammy and I had many sex partners…in our minds since we were both still virgins. David Charvet, Joey Lawrence, John Stamos. So, for her to bring up Michael as one of them was a fair question and should not have startled me. *But it did.*

"Oh. My. God. You have."

"No!"

"Then why are you so flustered with the question?"

She was right. It did fluster me. Because ever since I'd met Michael, my hand had slipped into my panties, getting myself off to his perfect face every night.

"Do you think he would be great?"

He was in my mind every night. I shrugged, "Probably."

"You know, we always have these visions of how great it would be with a certain guy just by how he looks. But what if they weren't?"

She was right again, but it would be with Michael. I just knew it. I laughed again. "Like we would be great, never having done it before, and to judge how good they would be. Well, now we sound shallow." And we liked to pride ourselves as not.

As I took another bite of my shrimp with lobster sauce, I froze when I saw Michael standing at the Chick-fil-A counter. Suit bags were draped over his shoulder, secured with one finger, as he reached around to grab his wallet from his back pocket. Tammy must have noticed the look on my face and swung her head around.

"Oh my God. Is that him?"

I couldn't answer because I was still frozen at the moment and watched him return the wallet into the pocket of *those* perfect jeans on that *perfect ass.*

"That is him. Holler at him."

"No."

"Why not?"

"I don't know," I said and did my best to hide behind my large cup of Coke.

"You want me to?"

"God, no."

He turned around with his food tray and was now searching for an open table. The food court was packed, and we did have room at our table. But I was still too shy to yell his name. "Act like you don't see him," I said.

"My God. He affects you tremendously," Tammy said, and then, while I could die on the spot, called out his name. "Michael!" He looked around but still didn't see us. "Over here," she yelled again. He then spotted us.

I straightened up from behind my large Coke and smiled at him. He looked relieved and began our way. I was afraid he could hear my thoughts, which was impossible, but it had to be written all over my face.

"Hey, girls. Thanks for coming to my rescue," he said as he laid the suit bags over the extra chair and set his tray on the table.

"No problem," I said as casually as I could. But my insides were screaming, *yes, yes, yes.*

"Jill," he said and then looked at Tammy. "I'm sorry, I can't remember if I got your name last time I saw you."

"Tammy," she said and held out her hand.

"Michael." He shook her hand, and I watched Tammy's eyes glisten with a tease to mine. She darn well knew his name. But, in my defense, I feigned ignorance.

Michael sat and began unwrapping the foil of his sandwich. "What are you girls shopping for today?" he asked.

"Dresses for the homecoming dance," Tammy said. "What's in the bags?"

"Work clothes. My new job at Whirlpool has a dress code—slacks and ties. So, I picked up a few suits."

He was hot in a T-shirt and those jeans, but thinking of Michael in a suit sent alarms down low, and I feared that horny look was all over my face. I knew Tammy could see it.

"So...homecoming," he said right before taking a bite of his Chick-fil-A, then returned to its foil. As he chewed, I watched his lips move in action. Michael even made chewing look sexy. Grabbing a napkin, he wiped his mouth and then replied. "Wish I could go back to those days."

Thinking of Michael in high school as a young student played a whole other side of him. Football star. Class president. Most popular. And then recalling what Scott said about him sleeping with teachers, professors' wives, and friends' moms invaded the thought as fast as it came. But was I any different? Fantasizing what it would be like to sleep with him?

"Yeah. The dance is next week," I said, searching for words. I was now speechless and couldn't think of a topic. So, I continued to watch him chew. He smiled at me through his chewing lips, and of course, I shied away and grabbed my Coke.

"Since you are here, Michael, we were discussing what to do with our hair and could use a guy's opinion," Tammy said. He wiped his mouth again as he looked her way and took another bite of his sandwich.

"Shoot 'em," he said after.

"Jill wants to color her hair black. What do you think?"

I panicked as he slowly looked back at me and intently studied my face. Yeah, I wanted him to notice me but not see every flaw in detail.

His hand smoothed across my cheek and then to my hair, where he placed it behind my ear. "Do not mess with this perfection. You have beautiful hair and gorgeous blue eyes. A natural beauty." His words were genuine and honest; they meant more to me than he knew. Shyly, my eyes blinked while I searched for security at his compliment. But now, I was more doubtful and confused. Was he attracted to me? Or was he only being nice to the little sister?

I should have said *thank you*. I should have said: *You think so?* But stupid me only grabbed my fork, picked at a shrimp on my plate, and said, "Oh…I don't know."

"It's always the really pretty ones who think that," he said, and maybe that doubt decreased a little. I went from pretty to *really* pretty.

"So, that's a no then?" I heard Tammy from across the table and was happy for the distraction.

"A definite no! You don't change a thing, kid. Stay just the way you are." *Kid?* And just like that, Michael reduced my doubts to irrational thoughts. For me to think he would be attracted to me as a woman—that was crazier than thinking I was going to marry John Stamos.

CHAPTER 7

Now

You can cut the tension with a knife as Michael hands the mic back to the MC. Three sounds echo in this reception hall. The soft *ah*. The whispers of *He really shouldn't be doing this here*. And my heart banging against my ribcage.

Scott's face is angry, and I'm too shocked to say anything.

"Well, that was a bunch of horse shit," Dad says, making no bones of his feelings. Mom again sends me her apologetic look, pressing her lips and rubbing Dad's arm.

"Oh, how much could you have heard, Arthur? You don't even have your hearing aids in."

"Well, I heard enough, and what I did hear was a bunch of horse shit."

"Dad's right, Jill. It sounded like bullshit to me. I'm heading to the bar," Scott says, throwing his napkin on the table. Jen shakes her head with pity and swallows a smile at me as she follows him. She gestures that she will handle Scott.

Through all the commotion, I missed the toast from the best man and maid-of-honor and wrap my head around all the chaos. I need to get to Monica and see if she's okay. Maybe what Michael said and *did* was too much to take. Though maybe his speech lasted a minute, I feel hours and years have passed. And I've already lost too many.

Dad returns to his plate after Mom cuts his meat, and I stand to get myself a glass of wine. *I will make it a double.*

I look at Monica and see that she is laughing and talking with her party at the table, and she seems okay. I move to the bar on shaky legs. Scott and Jen are still in line, and I delay my destination.

"Jill, the wedding was just beautiful." Mom's noisiest neighbor, Barb, has *purposely* run into me to ask about Michael. And to tell you the truth, I don't even know why she's here. Barb gave Monica piano lessons, like *forever ago*. She insisted to my mother for an invite.

"Now, that man. Is he…?"

"Yes, he's Monica's father. Excuse me," I say and continue to the bar. The line has only grown, so I cut to the front when I see Chelsea's dad ordering a bourbon. "Hey, can you make it two for the bride's mother?" I toss my hair and throw a begging smile.

"Hey, Jill. Make it two," he says to the bartender.

"Thanks, Jerry."

"You got it. Now, you're mine on the dance floor."

My insides cringe, but not as much as when I rehash what occurred a few minutes ago. I will dance with Jerry till the cows come home if it means avoiding my family. *And…Michael.*

"You got it, Jerry," I say, reaching for the bourbon the bartender sets before me. Taking my first sip, I invite the burn down to my empty stomach and say a prayer I don't fall while walking over to Monica. "Thanks," I say and attempt the journey across the room.

"Don't forget about that dance," I hear him holler. Without looking back, I hold up my drink as my *sure won't* gesture.

I only make it halfway when I'm stopped by…*Michael. Quick. Game on, Jill.*

"Jill, are you okay? I wanted to talk to you before the toast, but you hurriedly walked away."

How dare he ask if I'm okay! Of course, I'm not OK. I want to scream and say, *what the hell was all that*? I want to take this glass of bourbon and throw it in his face. But I'm going to need every drop to get through this reception.

"Yeah, I'm fine. Just mother-of-the-bride jitters. Nothing you would understand." *Yes. First jab. Now, walk away, Jill.*

"Jill…

"I'm needed at the bridal table, Michael. So, if you don't mind."

His eyes search my face and then softly relent. "Sure. Okay. Talk later?"

"Ah," I breathe, sounding more annoyed and exhausted. "Maybe."

I walk away, trembling more than ever, and it's a struggle to keep the bourbon from splashing out. I take a hefty swallow once I reach my destination, which seems to have been a journey. I *need to calm down.*

Monica looks up and recognizes the apprehension on my face. The bourbon has yet to kick in. She tells Chelsea to excuse her and walks around the table.

"Mom, are you okay?" she asks, and I watch her eyes move to the glass in my hand. "Did…did Dad upset you?" For her to see me with hard liquor is probably alarming.

"Ah…well, I wanted to make sure you're okay…after Michael's speech." I still struggle with your *father.*

"Wasn't it moving? I mean, to think after all these years, he's regretful."

And that's Monica. The ever-forgiving daughter that I raised. I think I bestowed all the forgiveness I wanted to believe I was capable of onto her. Yet, my inner self was anything but. Internally, I was a hypocrite.

"Yes, it was moving all right. I just wanted to make sure you weren't upset."

"Of course not, Mom. Unless it upsets you." Her eyes alter from pleased to anxious.

What can I say? It did upset me. But I don't want her to feel bad. "No. Although, it was a shock. Wasn't quite expecting that." She relaxes with a sigh, and I rub her cheek. "Okay then, I won't take up any more of your day. Enjoy yourself, Baby," I say, hoping my smile is genuine. Then, I kiss her on the cheek.

She takes both my hands in hers. "Thanks, Mom. You've made my day perfect." Her words assure me that I have done my best to keep the past suppressed, almost non-existent to her. I will always be the wall that protects her from the hell Michael put us through all those years ago. That is why she has no problem with him being here—*another one of Michael's bullets.*

She returns to her wedding party, and I take another cleansing breath before returning to the family table. Scott and Jen returned with their drinks, and Mom cleared Dad's plate. I know she will get up to get Dad's after-dinner coffee, so I head over to the coffee bar area and wait. Just like clockwork, she gets up and leads this way. I don't think Dad has poured himself a cup of coffee in fifty years.

"Mom, how's Dad?" I ask.

"He's okay. He needs to say his peace, and then after that…" She swishes her hands, not finishing her sentence, and reaches for a cup and saucer. "Don't worry about your father, Jill. I got him covered. Jen's doing her best with Scott. You focus on Monica and yourself," she says. Like I haven't been doing that for the last twenty-four years.

"Thanks, Mom. Apologize to Dad for me, will you?"

"Jill, you have nothing to apologize for. Besides, he's probably forgotten the last twenty minutes. He just wants his coffee now." She lays her hand over mine and smiles before taking Dad his coffee. I know it also had to be hard for her back then, dealing with Dad and all. Sometimes, I don't know what would have been worse. Her marriage to Dad and keeping him content and anchored while working and raising Scott and me? Or, my horrible marriage to Michael.

Feeling it's safe to return, I walk back when Jerry, Chelsea's dad, stops me.

"The DJ is playing one of my favorites." *Don't Stop til You Get Enough*? "Time to return the favor."

"Ah, what the hell," I say and down the last of my bourbon. Setting the glass on the nearest table, I burst for the dance floor.

Apparently, the song must be a favorite for all the forty-and-over as the crowd closes in.

By the song's end, the bourbon has kicked in and is doing its job. I am no longer on pins and needles and dancing away with Jerry. Or, it could be a false sense of security from the alcohol. For safe measure, I thank him for the dance and make a beeline for the table.

As I sit, the lights dim, and the DJ begins announcing. "At this time, I would like all married couples on the dance floor." That leaves me out.

Jen pulls Scott out to the floor, and Dad argues when Mom tugs on his arm. "Oh, come on, Arthur. You must work off some of that bread you should have avoided." He huffs and gives in to Mom. Together, the two slowly make their way to the dance floor. I watch and then feel the smile press on my lips when they dance to Alan Jackson's "*Remember When.*"

"If you were just married today, please take your seat," the DJ says. Of course, Monica and Jordan are the only couple to leave the dance floor, and the song continues for a few more choruses. "If you have been married for five years or less, please take your seat." About two-thirds of the couples leave the floor. Alan Jackson sings on. "If you have been married ten or less, please take your seat." The only couples left are the late thirty and forty-year-olds—and Mom and Dad. A few more reductions and Mom and Dad are the only ones left. The crowd applauds as my parents steal the dance floor, moving small circles in each other's arms. I wonder how it could have all worked for us—Michael and me. Even through all their pesky little fights, I watch the two of them look into each other's eyes and know it was all worth it—something I will never have.

Across the room, I spot Michael looking over at me, and I turn away. What did he need to talk about? Feeling that uneasiness rounding itself back, I get up and walk to the bar for wine. I order a glass of cabernet and then attempt to mingle and vanish in the crowd.

"Jill," a husky, low voice says from behind. Turning around, Michael stands only inches from me.

"Yes, Michael? What is it?" I say and take a sip from my wine.

"I would love to dance with the mother of the bride."

What? Hasn't he done enough damage just by being here? My family will have a cow if they see us dancing. That was one topic they drew the line on—the father and daughter dance. Monica agreed to dance with her grandfather. Also, she couldn't think of a song representing her and Michael's relationship. "Really," I state, "you're here for Monica, not me."

His eyes relentlessly take my verbal punch. "Please. And we could talk?"

"What is it you want to talk about?"

He doesn't seem to have an answer, so I use this time to get in a few of my own words. "Sure, Michael, just let me finish my wine, and then we can dance and *talk.*"

"Thank you," he says and walks away. *What the hell?* I laugh. "Fucker," I say under my breath and tip back the wine. Typical Michael. He was always disappearing.

The song ends, and the DJ announces that the next song has been requested. I start to walk away when Shania Twain's *"You're Still the One"* begins.

Before I can convince my feet to move, Michael is back and holds out his hand. *He's the one who requested this song?* Setting my glass on the nearest table, I take his hand cautiously. The wine hasn't done its job, and the minute our hands touch, stimuli of the last twenty years invade every part of my being. It's good. It isn't good. It's confusing. It's…back. Like cancer, you thought you had beaten.

He moves us to the dance floor, and I hyperventilate when his arms wrap around me. I tell myself it's the thought of what everyone will think, what my family will remember, not how I feel in his arms.

I feel him looking right at me as I try to look past him and into the crowd. "I thought this would be the perfect song for us," he says.

My eyes slowly find their way to his, and I let the last twenty years come out. "What! Have you ever listened to the words, Michael? *Looks like we've made it.* We didn't make shit. It was hell and the last thing you ever wanted: marriage and me and Monica. You couldn't do *this* anymore."

He listens to my chastisement and quietly says, "I know. I'm sorry."

"You're sorry?"

"I wanted to dance with you, and this was the first song we ever danced to. Remember when you delivered my pizza?"

"Yes, Michael. I do. I remember everything. It was painful. It was exhausting. And I barely lived through it. Please, don't remind me of those horrible days."

"I know. I cause you so much pain, Jill."

The dam breaks, and it all comes flowing out. "What the hell was that up there, Michael? All that talk about what a husband should do. You hated all those things. What? Did you compile a list of all the things I wanted to do? All the things you refused to do with me? All the things you did that broke my heart and made a speech out of it?"

"Yes."

"*Yes?* You're the last person to be giving *husband* advice. Oh my God, Michael. You put me through hell, and after you left, the hell didn't stop for me. Oh no. You went on your merry way while I got ridiculed, talked about, lectured on our failures. All everyone saw was how it was all my fault."

"Nothing was ever your fault, Jill. Nothing. It was all me."

"Well, it does no good now. Twenty years later, and I'm still considered the *community's failure.*"

"I'm sorry."

"*Sorry.* That's all you have to say? Sorry? You know what? This dance is over." I push back and break from his arms. "*I* can't do *this* anymore."

The song fades as I walk away and dash to the bar. The sound of *scratchiness* and *mic squeal* feedback quiets the room. "Two bourbons, please." The bartender sets them down, and I throw one back and chase it down with the other. Then, the sound of Michael talking into the mic.

"Can I have everyone's attention, please?" I turn around. Oh no. Michael has taken the DJ's mic. "For those of you who don't know me, my name is Michael Danforth, and I was married to Jill, mother of the bride. Together, we made a beautiful daughter, Monica." I hold my breath. *Can this day get any worse*? "And…and what happened in our marriage is my fault."

The room is dead silent, and I turn back to the bartender. "Make me another."

CHAPTER 8

Then

It was the following Saturday, and luckily, I didn't work in the kitchen at Delanie's because tonight was the homecoming dance. It was a warm day for September, and I was washing my car in the driveway, wearing cutoff shorts and a black tank top. *"This Kiss"* by Faith Hill was playing on my radio when I heard a motorcycle coming down the street.

I was squatting and scrubbing the tires when, from under the car, I saw that the motorcycle had pulled into our driveway. When I stood, I saw it was…*Michael.* Oh, shit, I thought. I was a mess, and I hadn't even showered. Quickly, I looked at my face in the side mirror, only to confirm that I was a mess. My hair was loosely knotted on top, and I had no makeup on my face. Why couldn't he show up four hours from now—when I'd be sexy-grunge?

"Hey, Jill," he said, swinging his leg off the bike, "Scott here?"

"No. I'm not sure where he's at."

"You got a new bike?"

"Yes, I was wanting to show it to Scott. But hey, since you're here, I have something for you."

"Me?"

"Yes. I saw it the other day, which made me think of you. So, I had to get it."

Me? Something made him think of me? What on earth could it be?

He unbuckled the saddlebags and pulled out a plastic bag. "Here, for you," he said, holding the bag.

I dropped the sponge into the bucket of water and walked around the car. Why did I have to look like a mess every time in his presence? His smile was how I remembered—reserved for me. At least, that's what I liked to believe. I opened the bag and pulled out a T-shirt. "Read it," he said. Unfolding the shirt, I read the caption. ***Blondes Are the Prettiest***.

I was dumbfounded and looked at him in disbelief. "Ah…thank you, Michael."

"I was hoping that by the time I saw you again, you wouldn't have colored your hair."

He remembered our conversation at the mall—me wanting to dye it black and how he told me not to mess with perfection. *And he thought of me.*

"Well, since Scott isn't here, you want to go for a ride?"

"Ah…sure," I said and looked down at myself.

"It's not too cold. But grab a jacket," he said, hopping back on the bike. I turned off the key to my car, silenced the radio, and ran inside for a jacket. Throwing on a light denim, I stopped by the hall entry mirror and worked like crazy to fix my hair. But it was useless, and we were going for a motorcycle ride. My hair would only get worse—and I didn't care. I was going for a ride with Michael. I then ran back, changed into the T-shirt he bought me, and ran out with the denim jacket in my hands.

"It fits," I said, completing a circle with my arms up.

"Looks great on you. Shorts are cute, too," he said. But this time, when he said the word cute, it sounded different, and I felt the word sexy behind it.

He leaned the bike over, and I climbed on after wearing the denim jacket. "Ready," he said, and I had nowhere to put my hands but around his waist. He started the bike, and we took off.

I was in Heaven, pressed against Michael, my arms around his waist and the wind tossing my hair wildly around. Through the reflection of his side mirrors, I watched his rugged, handsome face staring straight ahead in pure perfection. There wasn't anything about

Michael that wasn't all man and *gorgeous*. His square jaw was peppered with dark shadow, his lips pressed in a straight line, and his dark glasses made his face even more handsome. I was in all my glory, and he was to me, *all things man*. The man I dreamed I would marry and have his children. Even at seventeen years old, I knew Michael would somehow be a significant part of my life. It would take years to figure out just how major his role would play havoc on my life.

The motorcycle slowed at the end of our street, and he leaned to turn the corner. I pressed into his back and tightly squeezed my arms around him as the bike sped up and drove through town. I wanted everyone to see me with him. I enjoyed this day, this moment, to last forever. And…sadly, it did. For each night after I closed my eyes, his image in that mirror and us on his bike repeated in my heart. I was forced to watch, rewind, and watch over and over. And each time, it became worse.

Michael circled the town a few times and then stopped at the drive-in. "Do they have great Coney dogs here?" he asked. Was Michael asking for future reference? Or were he and I going to eat together? Like a date?

"Yes, they're pretty good," I answered and did not attempt to dismount the bike. Just in case he was asking.

"Awesome. Would the prettiest blonde like to join me for Coney Dogs?"

I wasn't in the least bit hungry and wasn't sure I could eat a Coney dog in front of Michael, but I wouldn't miss the chance of being with him. So, I said, "Sure, sounds great."

He leaned the bike over, and I slid off and tried to fix my now tangled hair. I also pulled my shorts from the crack of my ass. Michael kicked down the stand and parked the bike before dismounting. Even though I knew I looked like a mess, I felt like Princess Diana walking beside Michael at the picnic table. I sat first, and my heart leaped when he sat beside me and not across. His leg was touching mine, and the thought of moving a little crossed my mind. Did he want his leg touching mine? I left my leg where it was, making Michael decide to move. *He didn't.*

April's (blow-job-eyes) younger sister Amy worked at the drive-in and came out to take our order. I hoped she would tell April that I was here with Michael—sitting next to Michael and riding on the back of Michael's motorcycle.

"Oh, hey, Jill," Amy said, surprised to see me. And I knew it was because I was with Michael. "What can I get you guys?"

"This pretty blonde tells me you have great Coney dogs," Michael said, wrapping his arm around my shoulders and pulling me into him. I tried not to appear stiff and act natural. However, my body shook with excitement. For one, I was in Michael's arms. Two, Amy would tell April, and three, everyone was looking at us.

I smiled into Michael's eyes when he looked down at me. I still couldn't tell what his true intentions were. Was I still just the cute little sister of a friend? Or was I becoming something more to him?

"Two Coney dogs," Michael said, and Amy took the order. Michael's arm was still around me when she walked back inside. Amy turned around and looked at us again. *Yes*, she was going to tell April.

"Does April like to ride?" I asked, and he moved his arm.

"Who?"

Who? "April. The sister of Scott's girlfriend, Jen."

"Oh. April. Um…I don't know." I was happy he didn't know because he never took her for a ride. "I'll find out tomorrow, though," he said, and my moment in Michael-cloud-number-nine deflated like a balloon. But why hadn't he remembered her name?

"So, you two are hanging out then?"

"Yeah, I guess she has Sunday off and said she'd stop by. I'll ask her then."

I breathed in slowly, trying to regain the oxygen that left my lungs as my balloon cloud fluttered away. "Well, make sure you remember April's name," I said, faking a small laugh.

Amy returned with our Coney dogs, and I thought maybe I would casually mention that she was April's *younger* sister. Before she turned to go back inside, I said, "Hey, Michael, Amy is April's other sister." I was hoping there would be a look of panic on his face. Afraid that April would find out we were together. But it didn't seem to matter.

"Is that right? Now I see the resemblance in those gorgeous eyes of yours. I love April's eyes," he said, and I was sure it was because of the *blow-job-look*. "Tell April I have a surprise for her tomorrow."

Mentioning Amy was April's sister had only backfired, and I was now angry with myself. I was delusional again, thinking that maybe Michael was romantically interested in me. I grabbed my hotdog when Amy asked if I was still attending homecoming tonight.

"Yes, Tammy and I are still going."

"Oh, that's right. You two were shopping for the dance last week when I saw you at the mall. Well, we better eat up so I can get you back in time to pretty yourself up for your date."

"Who are you going with?" Amy asked, and I wished I had a date to throw it in Michael's face. Though I don't think he cared.

"Um, Tammy and I are just going alone."

"What?" Michael said with a mouthful of Coney dog. "I can't believe you don't have a date."

It hit me wrong, and I was going to defend my dateless ass. "You think I couldn't get a date," I said sarcastically. "Tammy and I chose to go stag."

"Oh, I see. That's cool. I respect that—you don't need a date or boyfriend to define you. I find that honorable in you upcoming girls."

He respected my wishes, which were only lies. The truth was, I wanted a date. I wanted a date with him. I wanted him to be my boyfriend, and now he would think I would never be interested. No matter what I said or did, I was losing.

"If you wanted a date, I'd happily take you to the dance. I have nothing going on tonight."

Was he asking? I stopped chewing and forgot how to swallow. What should I do? If I said yes, he would know I was lying. Because I didn't think I could compose the excitement running through me. Also, Tammy would be mad and think I was ditching her and our plans. I so did want him to take me. No matter what his reason was—a favor for brother's little sister, or maybe because he was interested in me. And he was asking in front of Amy, which meant April would find out.

"But that's cool. I understand," Michael said and went back to his Coney dogs. The opportunity was over, and I had lost my chance. If only I could go back in time—the last five minutes. I'd be going with Michael on a date. I slowly swallowed my food and gave the worst thank you ever.

"Well, thanks for asking." I hoped he would ask again and I would accept his offer with some hesitation. But not too much.

He looked at his watch and then crammed the rest of his Coney dogs in his mouth. Now, on anyone else, it would seem appalling. But not on Michael. He wiped his face with the napkin, stood, and reached for my hand. "I better get you home."

I took the last bite and then took his hand. "Yes," I said, but I wanted to stay with him and do…whatever. The dance was no longer my priority, and I even thought of telling him I would skip it and hang out if he wanted. Then, I thought of Tammy.

He started the bike, and I climbed on, wrapping my arms again around his waist, and loved the warmth between us. The motorcycle was loud, and everyone watched as we pulled out and took off down the street. Maybe when we got home, I would change my mind and say he could take me.

He pulled into our drive, and I climbed off. "Thanks for the ride and the Coney dogs."

"Hey, no problem. Have a great time with your friend at the dance," he said and winked as he pushed the bike backward out of the drive and took off down the street. I listened as the sound of his bike became faint and felt the ache in my heart. I missed him and couldn't understand why he possessed my soul.

Mom was in the kitchen when I walked in and hollered. "Is that you, Jill?"

"Yes, Mom."

She came walking out with a towel in her hands. "Where'd you go? Tammy called about an hour ago. She sounded urgent and wanted you to call her back right away."

"Did she say why?"

"No. I just said you weren't around, and I would have you call when you got back. Where'd you go? Your car was in the drive?"

"Michael stopped by. He was looking for Scott and gave me a ride on his new bike." She eyed me suspiciously, and I knew what that meant. "We just went to the drive-in." Her look didn't change, and she was already reading the look on my face. "He wanted to get Coney dogs. That's all. It's not like we ran away to get married." As soon as I said it, she knew how I felt. I could never hide my true feelings with her. "Whatever," I said and went to call Tammy back.

"Hey, Tammy. Mom said you called?"

"Yeah," she said, and I could tell something was behind it. "Okay, here's the thing." *I knew it.* "I know we said we would go stag, but Ryan Foster called and asked if I would go with him." Ryan Foster was the guy she had a crush on since the third grade. I knew she wanted to go with him but feared I'd be upset. I thought the same thing when Michael asked if he could take me. How ironic. "So...do you mind?"

"Um, actually, I was asked too...by Michael." However, I was stupid and turned him down. Maybe I could call him?

"NO!"

"Well, he did ask. If I had known Ryan called you, I would have accepted. But no, that's great. Go with Ryan. Maybe I'll call Michael." But I didn't have his number, and Scott wasn't home.

"Are you sure?" I could tell she felt bad for asking, but this would give me an opportunity or more of an excuse to accept Michael's offer.

"I'm positive. We will throw this party down tonight when you walk in with Ryan and me with Michael. Let's do it." And that was all it took. She squealed and hung up the phone. Now, how do I get hold of Michael?

CHAPTER 9

Now

My head pounds as I attempt to crack open one eye. Oh, God. I think I'm going to puke. I'm in bed and don't know how or who put me here. What did I do last night? *Monica!* Did I ruin the wedding? What the hell happened?

I try to sit up and immediately regret it. The room spins, my mouth fills with saliva, and I fall back onto the bed. When I slowly open my eyes again, I spot my dress and bra neatly folded and laid across the chair in the corner. Indeed, if I were that incapacitated, wouldn't my clothes be strewn across the floor? Picking up the covers, I see I'm in a T-shirt. One I remember but never slept in. Why would I put this on?

I breathe a massive sigh and bring one arm across my face, shutting out any light and focus on last night. Monica walking down the aisle with Michael. *Check.* The reception and Michael's toast. *Check.* The dance with Jerry: *Don't stop until You Get Enough*—check. The dance with Michael—*You're Still the One.* (Ha). *Check.* Fight with Michael. *Check.* Michael grabbing the mic and announcing to the entire wedding party that he is to blame for our failed marriage. *Big...check.* After that...three, maybe four bourbons? I'm not sure. Oh God. I don't even remember Monica and Jordan leaving. We were going to light lanterns and throw rice as they drove away to the airport. Was I there? I need to call Monica and see if she's okay. Did they make it to the airport? To Paris? Shit! I deserve this for allowing Michael to come to his daughter's wedding. Why didn't I listen?

Taking a deep breath, I notice the smell coming from the kitchen. "What is that?" My voice cracks, and my mouth is dry as cotton. Yep, at least four bourbons.

I roll cautiously out of bed. What time is it? I search for my phone, which is always next to the bed on the nightstand, and find it's not there. However, a glass of water and a packet of Alka-Seltzer is. Shit! I don't even know where my purse is, let alone my phone. *God!* Please. Please let it be on the table, and let my phone be inside. But what about my car? Did I drive home last night? Focus, Jill.

I place my feet on the floor and challenge myself to stand. I'm weak and shaky, but I must find my purse and phone. Okay, I'm up. Now, I walk across the room and open the door. Easier said than done. But, at a snail's pace, I make it and, with caution, open the door when the smell hits me. *Pancakes?* Is someone making pancakes in my kitchen? Mom. Yes, Mom is here, and before she lectures me about whatever I did last night, she is first preparing me breakfast.

Stepping out of the room, I mentally prepare my defense but come up with nothing. I'll accept my punishment; hopefully, life will go as usual.

"Look, Mom. I'm sorry about…" I stop when I find Michael standing shirtless over the stove, holding a spatula. This has got to be a bad dream. Maybe I should go back to bed. He's not here, is he?

"Hey, good morning, Jill. I've got you some greasy food prepared. How are you feeling?"

I'm speechless and try to form words. "Michael…what are you doing here?"

"I'm here to help you recover this morning. Lord knows you've helped my sorry drunk ass many times. I left a glass of water and a packet of Alka-Seltzer on your nightstand. Have you taken it?"

"Ahh…no. I…why are you here?" I ask again and then remember I'm only in a T-shirt. *Standing in front of Michael. Michael, making pancakes and…shirtless.*

"Here, let me get it for you," he says, moving past me to the bedroom. When he returns, I watch him open the packet and drop both pills in the water. "Here you go. Drink up."

Taking the glass from his hand, I bring it to my mouth and feel the cold bubbles burst up my nostrils. Oh, God. This is real. This is happening. I get about six swallows down and set it on the counter.

"Nope. The whole glass, Jill," he says.

"I…" Before I can protest, he presses the glass to my mouth and forces me to finish the Alka-Seltzer.

"That's a good girl," he says, rinsing the sink glass. "Do you feel good enough to eat here, or do you want me to bring you breakfast in bed?"

Now I know I am dreaming. Michael would never make me breakfast in bed. Not in a million years. Let alone take care of me if I were sick. So, I walk out of the kitchen and back to my bedroom. "So, in bed then," I hear him say. He's not here. It's all a dream.

I pull back the comforter, crawl into bed, and cover my head. The seltzer begins its job, and I burp a few times, allowing my stomach a little reprieve and closing my eyes. But it wasn't Michael who made it for me. Right? And that wasn't Michael standing in my kitchen, shirtless. Right? And why would he be shirtless? Why am I in this T-shirt, and who folded my clothes neatly? Mom did. I was having delusions of Michael.

"Here you go, Princess." And Michael would never call me princess. Who the hell is here? I throw off the comforter and see Michael standing over me with a food tray. I press my eyes tightly shut. Open. Nope, he's still there, and I close them again. "You feel good enough to sit up?" Opening and closing my eyes does not make the image of Michael disappear.

"Michael, why are you here?" I ask, pushing myself up. As he leans over, setting the tray of pancakes and sausage links down on the nightstand, a necklace dangling from his neck catches my eye. It looks like the necklace I bought him in high school.

"Here, lean forward," he says, grabbing the other pillow, and I have no choice but to let him place the pillows behind my back. "How's that?"

"Ah…okay, I guess." He then sets the food tray over my lap and smiles at me.

"Alka-Seltzer working?"

"Somewhat. Michael, what happened?"

"Jill, just eat first, and then we can talk," he says, heading to my bathroom. He returns with a washcloth and presses it to my face.

"Why are you doing this?"

"Because I want to take care of you, Jill."

"Now, stop it," I force out, having had enough of this nonsense.

"Jill, whatever you're thinking, everything that happened in the past. Just put it on hold for a few minutes and eat so you'll feel better. Then…we'll talk." That sincereness is again in his eyes—the look I didn't recognize from the wedding. So, I look away from his pleading face and slowly pick up the fork. "You want orange juice or milk?" he says, walking toward the door.

Now, with a mouth full of pancakes, I answer, "Milk, please." He walks out, and I wrap my head around what happened. *My purse and phone!* He returns with a glass of milk, and I ask. "Where's my purse?"

"Do you need it? It's on the kitchen table."

"No, just making sure I had it." I take a few more bites of the food and drink down the milk. It's cold when it hits my stomach, and I immediately feel better. I can only handle one bite of the sausage.

Michael sits in a chair in the corner of the room and watches me. I study his physics and think about him twenty years younger. He is a little thinner, his chest hairs glisten with silver, and his middle is a little softer than I remember. Gravity does not discriminate as I think about my own body and then remember the T-shirt I'm wearing.

"Who took my clothes?" I matter-of-factly state.

"I did, Jill."

"What?"

"Jill, it's not like I've never seen you naked. I'm impressed."

"Michael…" He was impressed? I roll my eyes and attempt the sausage, now that the milk has helped my stomach, and avoid his stare. Why is he staring at me? "Where's your shirt? We didn't…"

"No, Jill, we didn't. I'll tell you about my shirt when you're finished eating."

Wanting to know the truth, I pick up the tray and hand it toward him. "I'm finished. Talk."

He gets up from his chair and takes the tray. "You're sure?"

"Yes. Talk."

"Let me take this to the kitchen, and then we'll talk." He walks out with the tray, and I dash out of bed and into the bathroom. I pee, flush, and then look at myself in the mirror. Oh, good Lord. Definitely five bourbons. I think and then wash my hands and face. Grabbing the bathrobe hanging on the back of the door, I throw it on and fluff my hair—stupid. I rush out to find Michael, smacking into him at the doorway.

"Let's talk out here," I say, looking up to him.

"Okay," he says and does not attempt to move. So, I have no choice but to brush against his chest, walking out of my bedroom and into the living room, where I sit on the couch. Tucking my legs and covering my knees, I tighten the robe around me. He then walks over to the fireplace and runs his hands lightly over the portrait hanging above. Monica's senior picture in high school—one with her and I hugging in a field, sunbeams in the background. One of my favorites.

"That was one of her senior pictures," I say, wondering if the portrait that hung there twenty years ago comes to his mind. And even though I have forced myself not to think about that night, I do.

"I love this one. I have a copy of it," Michael says.

"What? How?"

He pulls out his phone and shows me his screen saver. It's the same picture. "I saved it from her Facebook. I have many more, too," he says, scrolling through some of his photographs. I can see what he's thinking from his gestures, smiling warmly and nodding as he periodically shows me a picture. It's not like he's traveling down memory lane because none of those are his memories. They're ours—Monica and me.

"Why would you save pictures of Monica and me when we are not part of your life, Michael?" It's more of a reprimand than a question.

"Because that's why. I missed out on a life with you and her."

As much as I want to boast, I bite the inside of my lip. "That was your choice, Michael. Please don't accuse me of being one of those exes who never sent you school pictures or other life events. And this is not what I want to talk about. How did you and I end up here in my house?"

He puts the phone back into his back pocket and takes a deep breath. Next, he comes and sits next to me on the couch. I pull myself in and wrap the robe tighter under my legs. "You were drinking…a lot."

"Because of you," I defend.

"Yes. Like I said, it's all my fault."

"Michael cut the shit. What did I do, and how did we end up together?"

"After my speech, I stopped counting the number of times you went to the bar. I tried to talk to you. But after you began yelling, I backed off—not wanting to cause another scene for you." I close my eyes and cover my face. "You didn't…you just…disappeared."

"Where did I go?"

"Out. I followed you outside. You went and sat on a bench next to the creek, and I stood next to a tree so you couldn't see me."

"So, I didn't dance naked or throw stuff at you?"

He chuckles. "No, you didn't."

"Oh, thank God. Then what?"

"You began crying hysterically. That's when I came and sat next to you. But you yelled at me and started to walk away. I pulled you back, afraid you might hurt yourself, and sat you back down. I told you that I would leave you in peace. But I only stayed near, watching out for you. Later, I followed you to your car, where you fell asleep. You never noticed me climbing into the passenger side. When I saw Monica and Jordan come running out, I woke you and helped you out of the car."

"I kind of remember that part."

"Yeah, I wiped your face with my handkerchief and said, 'Come on. You don't want to miss this.' I grabbed a lantern, lit it, and we both held it until it floated away. I helped you walk to the wedding car, where you kissed Monica and Jordan goodbye. I held you around the waist as we waved our goodbyes. She called this morning. They arrived safely in Paris around nine this morning."

"Oh, good."

"I helped you back to your car where you thought you would drive home. After you punched me a few times, you passed out, and I put you in the back seat, found your keys, and drove you home." Of course, he knows where I live. We used to live in this house—before he walked out. "Your cell was ringing this morning. It was your mother. I answered and let her know you were sleeping it off."

"What!"

"Should I not have done that?"

"Ah…Michael…never mind. Did she sound mad?"

"No. Your mother wanted to see if you were alright."

"So, you drove my car, unlocked my door, and…took off my clothes, put on the T-shirt, and put me to bed?"

"And put you in the shower."

"What? Oh, God."

"You puked all over the sidewalk, Jill. You missed your dress but covered my shirt. I put it in the wash if you don't mind."

Taking a deep breath and mentally recalling the image of what he just said, I pull up my knees and drop my head. "What happened after I showered?"

"After we showered…"

"We?"

"Jill, you puked all over me. And you were too drunk to stand up. I didn't want you to fall through the glass door." The image of Meg Ryan in *When a Man Loves a Woman* comes to mind. "You leaned against me. I washed you while holding you with one arm to wash myself. Found that T-shirt and put you to bed."

"Where did you sleep?"

He hesitates and reaches for my face, gently laying a finger under my chin. "Next to you." I look into his eyes. That look is back again. "We slept, Jill. That's all."

"I can't believe this. I've ruined Monica's wedding."

"No, you didn't. Everything was perfect, just like she wanted it to be. I made sure you didn't do anything to embarrass her or you. I promise, Jill."

I drop my head again and start to cry. Michael pulls me to him, but I push away. "Michael, just go away. Thanks for bringing me home…and…and taking care of me. But I need you to leave."

"I don't think you need to be alone right now." And that's all it takes.

"What the hell do you know about being alone? It never seemed to bother you before. You couldn't wait to run out that door."

"I know. I'm so sorry, Jill."

"Sorry?" I jump up and pace back and forth. No. No. Don't let him get to you, Jill. "Michael, I was wrong about letting you come here for my daughter's wedding. I should have listened to Scott and Dad. But I didn't. I thought I could handle this. But obviously, I can't. For years I have fought against the shit you put me through, and now it's back."

"Jill, please," he says, standing and trying to comfort me in his arms.

"Stop it," I yell and break from his embrace. "You know, the night you left, I stood at this window until the sun rose, waiting for your headlights to pull into the drive. I was hoping that, by some miracle, you'd come back. Maybe you'd changed your mind about wanting Monica and me in your life. But as the sun rose, shining on my face, I knew you never would. You told me that you never planned to marry the day you married me. So, what did I expect? And in some ways, it was a relief. I should have been glad it was finally over. Like death is a blessing as cancer is slowly rotting away life." I wipe my face and turn to look at him. His eyes are full of sorrow, tears, and pain. Somehow, it's lifting—something I've always needed to say to him. It's a bit of a closure. "Thank you for bringing me home and caring for me, but I want you to go now." I turn to walk back to my bedroom and stop at the doorway. "Thank you for finally leaving us," I say and close the door.

I sit on the bed and pull a tissue from its box on the nightstand. I cry in silence and hope Michael doesn't walk through that door. The sound of the hall closet opens where the washer and dryer are kept, and I hear the dryer door slam shut. He must be getting his shirt. I then listen to him talking in the living room. He must be on his phone. A few minutes go by when there is a light tap on the door.

"Jill, I've called an Uber to take me to get my car. Please tell me you're okay."

Shit! Of course, I'm not okay. He just conjured up the last twenty years of my hell. "I'm fine. Goodbye."

I hear the front door shut and wait a few minutes before exiting the bedroom. Cracking open the door, I see Michael is indeed gone. My feet step on something, and I bend down, picking up a piece of paper on the floor. It's a note.

Dear Jill,

I know I didn't deserve to walk our daughter down the aisle. And you are right about me never being a part of her life. I know the pain that I have caused you all these years, and sorry will never fix it. My coming here was not to hurt you again; it was a chance to see you, see our daughter, and see what I have missed. In some ways, it was punishment for myself, and in the process, I hurt you again. There's a lot I would like to tell you, Jill. Please see me again so we can talk. I have no plans to return to Seattle, and I currently rent a house here in town. Here is my number. Please call me. I need to talk to you.

847-555-1415

You are still gorgeous. Thank you so much for allowing me to participate in our daughter's day.

Love, Michael

CHAPTER 10

Then

Scott still wasn't home, and I needed Michael's number. Maybe he was at Jen's. But would he even give me his number? I picked up the phone and called Jen's apartment. Hopefully, April wouldn't answer. But then, I could ask her. Yeah, probably not.

Jen answered. "Hello?"

"Hi, Jen. Is Scott there?"

"Yes, hold on." I heard her cover the phone and yell Scott's name. "He's on his way. He's out front fixing the brakes on my car.

"Thanks." I heard the phone set down, and soon, Scott picked it up.

"What's up?"

"Well, I need Michael's number." I cringed.

"Why?" I knew it.

"I…I do. That's all."

"Tell me why."

Why was he making it such a hassle? But I did need to think of a reason. "He was just here on a motorcycle, and I think he dropped something."

"Like what? Just tell me, and I'll call him."

"Okay. I want to call and see if Michael wants to go to the dance with me." There, I said it. But, of course, he began laughing.

"Stop laughing. He already asked, and I said no. Now I'm changing my mind."

"You're kidding."

"No, I'm not. Now, are you going to give me Michael's number?"

"Fine," he said and read out his number. I copied it down and hung up. Now, I needed courage if I was going to call him. I looked at the time and saw it was three hours before the dance. Hopefully, he went straight home after dropping me off.

I dialed his number and panicked when his answering machine went off. "Hey, you've reached Michael Danforth. I'm not here. Leave a message."

I waited for the beep and cleared my throat. "Hey, Michael. Jill here. Um…if your offer still stands for the dance, I would like to take you." Saying I'd take him made me feel like maybe I felt bad for turning him down. "So…"

"Hey, Jill. I just walked in. What's up?"

"Oh, Michael. I felt bad after you asked me to go to the dance. And since you gave me a ride on your new bike, I would like to take you to the dance. As a thank you." It was a lie, but I didn't want to sound desperate.

"Sure. What time should I pick you up?"

In my mind, I was jumping up and down, doing my happy dance. "Um…six?"

"Perfect. I'll jump in the shower and be there at six."

"Awesome. Thanks," I said.

"No problem. See you later," he said and hung up. I couldn't believe it. I was going to the dance with Michael. I was the happiest girl alive. Little did I know that my whole life would change and that my life as a young teen would never be the same. I should have never let Scott give me his number. I was too young to understand that Michael would affect everything in my life. And by the time I was old enough, it was too late.

I wasn't sure I wanted to dress grunge and searched my closet for something sexier. But nothing screamed sexy. So, I wore the dress I bought and borrowed Mom's black stockings and high-heeled shoes. I was surprised she had high heels and let me wear them.

At six o'clock, the doorbell rang, and my stomach jumped. Mom called from downstairs, and I stared in the mirror. My hair was down, and I tried to blow it out straight. Stepping out of my room, I walked as gracefully as possible in the heels down the steps. Michael was waiting by the front door, dressed in a suit. God, he was gorgeous, and I pictured him dressed for work, remembering the suit bags at the mall. Michael smiled at me, and I thought I saw a spark in his blue eyes. Did he see me differently?

"Hey, kid. You sure clean up," he said. It wasn't the most glorious compliment, but to me, it was everything. Michael was looking at me, and I felt unique and pretty in his eyes.

"Hi. You look great, too. One of the suits you bought?"

"Yeah, it is. On its maiden voyage—just for you."

Just for me.

He was holding a box. "I wasn't sure what color you were wearing. So, I went with a red rose. Can't go wrong with roses," he said as he opened the box. Inside was a single rose corsage with baby's breath. He took my hand and placed it around my wrist. I loved the feel of his hands on my skin. They were well-manicured and strong-looking, with an expensive-looking watch on his wrist.

He even took the extra time to buy me a corsage, and I had nothing for him. "I'm sorry," I said. "I wasn't expecting this and didn't get you a boutonniere."

"Not a problem. I got a pretty girl on my arm," he said with a wink, lifting his elbow. I wrapped my arm around him just when Dad walked in. I looked at Mom to soften the situation. After twenty-some years, she had the technique down.

"Arthur, this is Scott's friend Michael. He's making sure Jill gets to the dance safely. It's better than two young girls going alone." She stressed the alone part.

Michael held out his hand. "Nice to meet you, Mr. Hudson."

Dad stared at Michael's hand and then shook it. "And you'll make sure she gets home safely." It wasn't a question.

"Of course, Mr. Hudson."

Dad gave Mom another look and then retired to the front room, where his clickers were set next to his chair. "Ten o'clock," he yelled from the room.

Michael smiled down at me. "Yes, sir," he said, and we walked out the door—me on his arm.

His Corvette was parked out front, and my already Michael cloud number nine was elevated to hyperdrive. I was arm-in-arm with Michael, going to the dance in his Corvette. What else could a girl want? I could die happy now, all because of this moment. I couldn't know then what heartbreak would be in store for me.

He opened the door and helped me inside. The car was just as grand inside as out. Black leather seats that shined and smelled of luxury. Once in the driver's seat, he kissed my hand. My eyes widened, and I wondered if he would kiss me on the lips by the end of the night.

"Which way, my Princess?" he said and started the car.

"Take a left at the end of the street and then another left. The school is ten blocks from there."

I couldn't believe I was here, here with Michael, and the smile on my face never left the entire ride there. Soon, we were pulling into the school, and I couldn't wait for everyone to see us together.

He opened the car door, and as we walked together to the school, I tried to remain calm, like this was an everyday incident. But the smile on my face said it all. I was in Heaven.

Once inside, Tammy spotted us and waved us over. She, too, was not wearing combat boots. I took Michael over to where Tammy and Ryan stood and felt everyone's eyes on us. It was my red carpet moment. I didn't know that someday, I wished these same eyes would stop looking at me.

Tammy did her best to compose her look. But underneath, I knew she was screaming: *Holy Shit! You are here with Michael.* "Michael, remember Tammy; this is her date, Ryan."

"Nice to meet you, Ryan," Michael said, shaking Ryan's hand. I loved watching Michael interact with my friends and see his adult business side. While most guys in my class wore nice jeans and a polo,

Michael was stellar in his suit—tie, cufflinks, and a shiny watch to set it all off. He was a cover for GQ magazine—and I was falling hard.

"So, you guys want to get some soft drinks and find a table before the DJ starts?" Tammy asked, and I felt a little embarrassed that all we could have were soft drinks. Michael was a man who drank beer and wine, and I wanted to fit into his world.

"Would that be okay, Michael?" I asked.

"Sure, whatever you girls want to do."

Eyes followed us to the soda bar, and I felt intimidated by all the attention I was getting with Michael as my date. Especially when he wrapped his arm around me, I pushed that feeling away and wrapped my arm around him. He looked down at me with a smile, and I thought he liked it just as much as I loved his arm around me.

We ended up with white sparkling grape juice in champagne glasses, and I felt more to Michael's level—though it contained no alcohol. Even though I was in a gym decorated with pink and white balloons, I fantasized I was a princess at a ball, and Michael was my prince.

"To the class of '98," Michael said, raising his glass, and we all clinked them together. He was a good sport, and I feared maybe he would feel out of place. But I hardly doubted Michael would feel out of place anywhere. He would always be the center of attention, no matter where he was.

We found a table, and Michael pulled out my chair. Ryan had already sat before Tammy, and she gave him a look, warning him that he could learn some manners from Michael. Everything Michael did made me feel special, and these would be the things I would only look back on and realize none of it was real. I would learn that human nature can behave briefly but not for a lifetime.

The DJ began with the announcements, and the lights dimmed as the music started to play. He began with a few pop songs, Madonna, and I hoped Tammy wouldn't mention how I loved Madonna. I knew Scott hated her, and probably so would Michael. But before I knew it, my shoulders were already moving to the beat.

"I think someone's ready to dance," Michael said, taking me onto the dance floor by the arm. Again, all eyes were on us because we were the only ones on the floor. I soon lost my reserve and fell into the rhythm, dancing with Michael and his moves. He was a good dancer, and I had only danced with friends or alone in my room. He made it fun, and soon, I was just as comfortable as alone dancing in my room. Tammy pulled Ryan to the floor, and the four of us were the main spectacle, and it was also just what the party needed. Because after that, the dance floor filled up. All because of Michael.

We were about to return to our table when Shania Twain's *"You're Still the One"* started to play as the first slow-down song. "Hey, they're playing our song, Kid," Michael said, pulling me into his arms. It no longer bothered me when he called me kid; maybe it was just his way of warming up or breaking the ice. He held me closer this time, and I lay my head on his chest. It was broad and warm and firm and all man. I closed my eyes and listened to the beat of his heart and Shania's voice. I knew that from then on, here is where I wanted to stay—forever. And a part of me always did. The part I was never able to get back.

The song was over, and as we walked to our table, Tammy wanted to use the restroom and asked me to go with her. I excused myself from Michael, and we left for the bathroom.

Our walk there was all cool and calm, but our excitement exploded when we hit the bathroom door. "Oh my God. Oh my God. I can't believe this night," she said. Her voice was a few octaves higher, and her exuberance was contagious.

"I know. Having Ryan and Michael is much better than going stag. I mean, is God shining down on us tonight or what!"

We were giddy and in all our glory. It was too bad it was our last year in high school because tonight would have set the level for all our school days. But one thing was sure: we were set for the rest of our senior year. More so than I would ever know.

Andrea Felky and her mean girl minions enclosed us when we exited the restroom. She was the girl who was voted for everything—

even if she wasn't participating. It had much to do with being the only Asian in our class. We needed to treat her extra special and make her welcome. But ironically, she was born and raised right in St. Jo.

"So, decided to bring your cousin, Jill? Or is he your uncle? Because he sure looks old enough," Andrea snidely remarked, and the rest of the minions stood around with their arms folded.

I wanted to say something clever but couldn't think of a thing. That's when I heard Michael from behind. "Neither. Jill walked into my apartment one day with a pizza, and I thought: 'Who is this beauty?' I couldn't let her leave until I had a dance with her." He looked at me, stretched his arm, parting the mean girl minions, and reached for my hand. "Do you remember that, Jill?"

God reached down, gifted me some nerve, and replied, "A day I will always remember. And, whenever we're together, they play that song." Even though Michael thought it would benefit the minions, it was the truth. I will always remember that day and wish it never happened.

CHAPTER 11

Now

I hit the shower, eager to get to work this morning. The last twenty-four hours have been a kaleidoscope of past and present, colliding with one another and trapping me in the crosshair. When Michael said he had no plans of returning to Seattle and was renting a place here, the walls I built around my little world became too thin. I spent all of Sunday inside—fearing I would run into him. I need the distraction of work to keep me focused. Or unfocused, I should say.

I'm about to start the water when I hear my cell phone from the bedroom. Hoping it's Monica, I run out of the bath and snatch my phone from the nightstand. The hospital reads on the screen.

"Hello, this is Jill."

"Hi, Jill." It's my supervisor. "Due to low census, I'm calling you off today. Looks like you get that extra day you wanted three months ago."

Three months ago, I put in to have the Monday off after Monica's wedding, thinking I would need the extra time to unwind. However, due to new circumstances, I want to go to work today. "Well, I can still come in."

"Low census. You know the policy," my supervisor says, and yes, I was up on rotation to get it off.

"Well, let me know if anyone calls off. I'll come in."

"Are you sure, Jill?"

"Yes. Monica's off and…I could use the distraction to keep from worrying about her."

"How'd the wedding go? All went off without a hitch?" she asks.

"Ahh…yes. Thanks for asking."

"Well, have an extra day to recuperate. See you tomorrow."

"Yes, goodbye," I say and set the phone back down. Well, shit. I do not want to become all agoraphobic, locking myself inside all day.

I walk back into the bathroom, remove my jammies, climb into the shower, and ponder what to do with myself. Monica's gone, I'm called off work…and Michael is somewhere in this town. Why?

Now showered and wrapped in a towel, head, and body, I move to the closet and throw on a pair of leggings and a tank top. I also grab a pair of black boots and an open loose sweater to throw on after hair and makeup. My cell rings again. "Now what?"

Walking back to the nightstand, I see the hospital displayed once again.

"This is Jill."

"Well, you got your wish. Tammy is not feeling well today. Are you sure you want to cover her? It's your turn to be off."

"Tammy? Did she say what's wrong?" Tammy was at the wedding. She seemed fine. Perhaps it's just a bug.

"No. Tammy sounded exhausted. We have three a.m. outpatients scheduled. After that, there was nothing in ambulatory surgery. I can schedule you for half a day."

"Yes, I will come in."

"Thanks, Jill."

Back to the closet, I remove the leggings and tank, throw them into a bag with the boots and sweater, and jump into blue scrubs. Since I will be only working half a day, I will get my grocery shopping done after. And I hate being seen in scrubs in public. I might as well be in sweats. After I dry my hair, I throw on some makeup, take a deep breath, and walk out the front door—ready to face my day.

Pulling out of the drive, I grab my phone to call Tammy and see if she's all right. I press the home button and say Tammy's name. It rings through the speakers, and she answers, sounding weak and tired, just like my supervisor said.

"Jill?"

"Hi, Tammy. I'm going in to cover you. Are you okay?"

"What? It would be best if you didn't have to cover for me. They said Linda was up."

"I asked to go in. It's not a problem. I prefer not to be home alone today. Are you sick?"

"I guess. Just tired and old. I'll be in tomorrow," Tammy says, but by the sound of her voice, I doubt it.

"It's a low census at the hospital, and I'm only going in for half-day. Can I bring you anything?"

"No, it's fine. Ryan's staying home today."

She must really be sick. "It's not a problem. I'm going to the store anyway."

"I'll let you know later, okay?"

"Ah…sure, okay. Get some rest, Tammy. I love you."

"I love you too, Jill. Thanks." I end the call and pull into the parking garage, parking in my usual spot, and head inside the hospital.

Dr. Stine is standing outside my station and looks up from his clipboard when he sees me. "Nurse, could you page Dr. Buck to cover my morning rounds? I just got called to OB. A patient of mine has gone into labor." He looks at his watch. "Her contractions are one minute apart."

"Yes, doctor," I say, picking up the phone to page Dr. Buck. Why he couldn't do it himself is beyond me. One thing they didn't teach in nursing school was how to become the doctor's at-work wife.

"Thank you, Jill." He hands me his clipboard with a list of his patients, walks away, and stops.

"Oh, how was the wedding?"

"Good…beautiful." Is he asking for a reason?

"Sorry, we couldn't make it. Please tell Monica we wish her the best," he says, walking to the elevator.

"I will. Thank you, Dr. Stine." The elevator closes, and I breathe out a sigh of relief. With all that has happened, I was unaware he and his wife didn't show. I haven't heard anything from those there about my state of being. Like I said, I locked myself inside yesterday. Mom called and asked if I had heard from Monica. I told her yes. And that was because Michael told me she called. Why hasn't she called me?

I page Dr. Buck and then head to Ambulatory Surgery on the fourth floor, where two patients had already been brought in for post-opt. According to admissions, only two more are on the schedule, which will put me out of here by 1:00 and give me time to stop by the grocery and pick up something to make Tammy—perhaps chicken soup or potato.

"How're you feeling? I'm going to put this on and check your blood pressure. It will go off about every fifteen minutes," I say to my first patient, who slowly nods with half-closed eyes. "The doctor will be in later and read your results to you. You feeling okay?" She nods again and rests her eyes. "Good. I'm going to put this call button in your hand. You press it if you become uncomfortable." I say and smile down at her. She nods again as I check her vitals before tending to my next patient.

I have been a registered nurse at Lakeland Health this month for sixteen years—the only hospital in St. Joe. I have worked myself up from bedpan duty and sponge bath duty until I transferred to Ambulatory Surgery. I have wanted to become a nurse since my first year in high school, and even for that, I must give credit to Michael. As much as he has fractured my thoughts of true love, I owe him this.

After setting up the following few patients on the monitors, I head back to the nurses' station and text Tammy.

Are you feeling better? I'm stopping by Martin's when getting off. What can I bring for you? If she's sleeping, I hope my text doesn't wake her. But then I see she read it and wait for her response.

No need. Ryan just left. Thanks for covering.

Her text is short, and I can't help but feel something is wrong. Is she mad at me? Perhaps the way I disappeared at the wedding. She did help me plan everything and was my only support when I told her Michael was attending. Shit! I wish I could remember more.

Dr. Buck is standing next to the nurses' station when I return. "Good morning, Jill. My wife enjoyed the wedding. She wants me to ask you for information about The Round Barn and their wedding details. Our son has just popped the question."

"I'd be happy to send her the information. And congratulations on Barren's engagement."

He looks up from the clipboard, not very enthused about the idea. "I feel they are rushing it. He's just completed his grad school. He hasn't even started his residency yet."

Dr. Buck comes from a long line of doctors dating back to his great-great-grandfather, and now Barren, his only son, has followed suit. "Well, I am sure Mrs. Buck is excited to finally have a girl in the family."

"Yes, she is. And she will probably be running her off by overtaking the wedding plans. You know how she can be."

"She's been a blessing for all the events here at the hospital," I say. Dr. Buck's wife runs many charities in the community and the many benefits of the hospital sponsors. But then again, men seem to take all the work behind the scenes for granted, making them appear essential and successful in their careers. I should know.

"Yeah, you're right. Please let Dr. Stine know I've completed his morning rounds. And signed to release his patient in 213."

"Yes, doctor."

"And...email my wife the information for The Round Barn," he says, placing his pen in the pocket of his lab coat and handing me the clipboard.

I smile. "Yes, I will."

"Have a good day, Jill.

"You too, doctor."

He walks away, and I recheck my phone, hoping Tammy has sent a message. When I see she hasn't, I send another text: *Chicken or potato soup?* I wait for her answer, but nothing appears. So, I slide the phone down into my scrub pocket and head back to Ambulatory Surgery.

Due to a few late arrivals after surgery, I finally clock out at 1:30, grab my bag, and head to the restroom to change into my packed clothes. Now to the grocery store. I think potato.

The sun shines heavenly through the row of trees, now full of new leaves, as I drive down Lake Shore Drive—and still, nothing from Monica, which only adds to my worry. But she is on her honeymoon, and calling her mother is probably the last thing on her mind. But still.

After parking my car and entering the grocery store, I grab a cart and pull out my list, adding Tammy's potato soup items. I also write soppin' bread for soup—nothing like carbing it up with comfort food when sick.

I push through the aisle, heading to the produce first to select the best potatoes. I grab a few and struggle to open the damn plastic bag.

"Excuse me. Do you have a great recipe for chicken cacciatore?" I freeze. *Michael.* He's behind me. I slowly turn around, and both potatoes fall out of my hand and drop to the floor. They roll right to his feet, and he picks them up, brings them over, and reaches for the bag I'm struggling with. He licks his finger, slides the bag open, and drops in the potatoes. "You see, I used to know this girl," he hands me the bag, "and she used to make me the best chicken cacciatore. I haven't had it since." There is a long pause as we stare into each other's eyes. "Hi, Jill."

"Hi, Michael. Look it up on Pinterest. I'm sure they have plenty to choose from," I say, pushing my cart down the aisle.

"I don't want plenty to choose from. I want yours," I hear Michael say as I walk away. I ignore his comment and turn to the next aisle. I'm shaking and now confused about what I have come for—my list. I look down and see I can check off potatoes. He pulls his cart next to mine as I'm groping for a pen in my purse. "Could you help me? I don't want to get home and not have the right ingredients. Or better yet, how about we get the stuff together and go to your place, and you can show me how? I'll grab a bottle of red…"

"What? Michael! You are not coming to my house to make chicken cacciatore."

"Okay. Then come to my place, and I'll make you chicken cacciatore. But, either way, I need your recipe."

"Michael, I'm not going to your place… And why are you staying here?" I lift my hand. "No, don't answer. I don't care. Now, if you excuse me, I'm making potato soup for my best friend, who is sick." I walk away and consider the items in his cart—green zucchini squash and chicken breast. "It's yellow squash. And use chicken thighs. They're much more tender than breasts," I say and walk on with my cart.

"Thank you," he says. I ignore him and turn the corner.

I focus on the rest of my list and dash to the U-scan, hoping I don't run into Michael again. So far, success. My groceries are bagged, and I'm going to my car. But once I'm there, no such luck. He's right behind me.

"I made the exchange, but I still need the recipe. Could you please take a picture of it and send it to me? I left you my number." He stands there, looking helpless, with two bags in his hand.

"No, Michael, I won't do that. I don't want you to have my number." I'm surprised Monica hasn't given it to him. Probably the lecture we had after she gave Jerry, Chelsea's dad, my number. My phone rings inside my purse, and I see Monica's name when I pull it out. I can't get to it fast enough. "It's Monica," I say with excitement. "Hey, Baby. How are you?"

"We're fine, Mom. Oh, Paris is amazing."

Michael bends down and yells into my phone. "Hi, Monica."

"Was that Dad? Are you two still together?"

"What? No. He just ran into me at the store. I'm at the store. *Leaving*," I say to Michael and climb down into my car. I shut the door, and he looks at me through the window.

"Put him on. I want to thank him again for the honeymoon."

What? Err. I open the door. "Monica wants to talk to you." He motions the bags, and so I put her on speaker. "Go ahead. I have you on speaker. He's standing right here."

"Hi, Dad. Paris is gorgeous. Jordan and I want to thank you again."

"You're welcome. I'm so happy it makes you happy," Michael tells his daughter.

"So, you two hanging out?" she asks.

"No…"

"We're going to make your mom's famous chicken cacciatore tonight," Michael says, smiling at me.

"NO. No, we're not," I say, giving Michael a stern look. "He was just asking for the recipe. Tammy's sick, and I'll be making her soup tonight," I say, directing it toward Michael.

"She's still sick?" Monica asks.

"What do you mean, still?"

"Yeah, she left the wedding early. She said she wasn't feeling well. She couldn't find you and told me to tell you." *She did?* "Sorry, I forgot to tell you when you and Dad lit the lanterns." *He did help me with the lanterns.*

"Oh, honey. It's not your fault. It was your big day. I should have been paying more attention." I raise my brows to Michael. "Well, I'll be seeing her tonight. I'll tell her you told me."

"Okay. Love you, Mom." She hesitates. Is she going to tell Michael the same? "Tell Dad bye." And that's a no. Michael presses a weak smile.

"Bye, Baby. I love you." But by the time his words are out, the call ends. I don't think she heard him. I don't know how to feel about this. This is Monica's emotional department, and I hope it wasn't just to get the trip to Paris. Is that why she had Michael come to the wedding? But I can't think about that now. I need to check on Tammy.

I get back into my car and watch Michael as he walks away to his car—a black Toyota 4Runner. He smiles and waves one last time after his groceries are inside. I give him a little wave and then pull out of the lot.

Once home, I waste no time making the soup and find my best crock to pour into. I wrap the warm bread in foil and head back out the door. Tammy lives only blocks away so that the soup will remain warm.

Ryan answers the door, and I hand him the basket with the food. "She's been sick since the wedding?"

"Come in, Jill. She's still in bed."

"Did she catch a bug at the wedding? Monica told me she left. I wish I would have known."

"She hasn't been feeling well lately." He places the basket on the counter.

"Ryan?" I hear Tammy call from the bedroom. Ryan walks to the hall.

"Yes, honey?"

"Is that Jill?"

"Yes…"

"I'm here, Tammy. I brought you potato soup," I call down the hall.

"Ryan, tell Jill to come in," she says weakly.

I look at Ryan, and he nods. "Thanks, Jill. She'll love this. I'll bring her some. Go ahead."

I nod and walk to their bedroom. Tammy is sitting up in bed, face pale with reddened eyes. She looks awful, but I don't want to tell her that. "Tammy, you look a bit under. How long have you been sick? I'm sorry I missed you at the wedding." I shake my head. "Michael…"

"Hey, how's that going? You two were getting along great. Please tell me it wasn't just for Monica's sake."

She has no idea that I can't remember a damn thing. And despite her condition, she will get a kick out of it. "Tammy, I don't remember anything after Michael's speech—second speech." She laughs, and it's the release I need after the last few days.

"Oh, please tell me more. I could use some cheering up," Tammy says, pushing herself against the headboard. Not caring if she's contagious, I sit down next to her.

"I woke up, and Michael was in my kitchen making pancakes. What the hell happened?"

She laughs like it hurts, and Ryan brings in a bowl of soup. "Here ya go, Babe," Ryan says as he sets a tray over her lap. Up to eating?"

"It smells wonderful. Thank you, Jill." She takes a small bite and then says, "Go on. I need to hear the rest." I look up at Ryan. "Could we have a moment?" she says to him. He kisses her on the forehead and smiles before leaving the room.

"Hey, you sure you're okay?"

"Don't deflect. Spill it. Tell me about the great make-up sex."

"There was none," I say. Tammy eyes me suspiciously. "Michael swears, but I guess we did shower together." She stops with the spoon in her mouth and looks at me. "I puked all over him," I say before thinking. "Sorry." But she takes a bite anyway.

"After three kids, nothing shocks me anymore, Oh, Jill. It's delicious."

"Well, it should be. It's your recipe." Tammy was destined for culinary but somehow went to nurses' school with me. I guess we're inseparable.

"Hey, speaking of recipes, I ran into Michael at Martin's, and he wanted our chicken cacciatore recipe. He was determined to come over and make it." She widens her eyes with a spoonful of soup.

"And?" she says after swallowing.

"No way."

"No way you didn't give it out, or no way he's coming over?"

"Both," I say. "I'm here, aren't I?"

She smiles. "Yes, thank you."

"So, how long have you been feeling like this?"

She takes another bite of soup and smiles again at me. After taking a deep breath, she looks me in the eye. "I have Leukemia."

CHAPTER 12

Then

I left the dance that night with my head held high and Michael on my arm. The minions watched with mouths agape. Tammy and I high-fived each other as we walked out through the door. It was only 8:00, and I didn't have to be home until 10:00.

"So, what are you in for now, kid?" Michael said as he helped me back into the Corvette. He could call me a kid as much as he wanted. I didn't care; somehow, I felt it was a unique pet name reserved only for me.

"I don't care. Anywhere, but back in there or home," I said as Michael closed the door.

Once he was in the car, he asked, "You hungry? We could go back to my place and call in a pizza."

Hanging out with Michael at his place sounded like an excellent idea. But pizza didn't. "How about we stop at the grocery and pick something to make?"

"You're sure? I'm not much of a cook."

"I don't doubt that," I said, feeling more comfortable around him.

"If you don't mind. I buy, you cook," Michael said.

"Great. You like chicken cacciatore?"

"I've never had it."

"Well, you're in for a real treat. Tammy and I have perfected our recipe, and it's to die for."

He smiled, and his eyes gleamed with happiness. I was happy, too, and felt something special starting between us. At seventeen, everything has magic. And magic is only an illusion.

As we walked through the grocery store dressed to kill, I felt like one of those sexy celebrities caught out in public, doing everyday things with all the looks we were getting. I loved it. Michael pushed the cart as I threw things in to make the chicken cacciatore. The smile on my face never waned. Nor did his. In my mind, we were not only celebrities, shopping for dinner, but married too. Every so often, his name for me would switch from kid to dear. And even how he used the word, *You're such a dear to do this.* It still felt like a term of endearment.

Our menu was complete, and he paid with his credit card at the checkout. I felt so grown up, and what would be a hassle for most was a Mardi Gras for me. I couldn't wait to make Michael dinner and sit across the table with candles, wine, and music. I would do my best to give him all the attention. He would never want another. I already knew I was in love. But love doesn't come even; I learned that the hard way.

Once we returned to his car, he said, "This will be fun. No one besides my mother has ever made me dinner." I was already on a great start to winning Michael's heart. I was going to be the first to make him dinner. To be the first girl to make him dinner made me happy.

I had Michael light the candles he had bought, stating it was necessary since we were eating Italian and he had opened the bottle of wine. He would have purchased sparkling grape juice, but I told him natural wine was okay and that Tammy and I have wine sometimes. Her mother would allow it when we made our gourmet cuisines as long as I spent the night. But I doubt I would be spending the night with Michael. I would have to pop in some gum before Michael took me home.

He didn't have any Italian music, so we settled on an instrumental channel on the radio, and I loved how he involved himself on our special night. Why things like this could never last will always be a mystery to me. I didn't know that loving, wanting, and pleasing someone would become the last thing anyone ever wants. Like it was the worst thing you could do for them. Yet, this is what I wanted in return, and I didn't know about vulnerability at such a young age—letting someone see that all you need in your life is the other person. And trusting him not to hurt you would become a reality.

The table was romantic, with candles, wine glasses, and paper plates. "Look how you even make my paper plates look posh with your amazing cacciatore," Michale said, pulling out my chair. He took the seat across and lifted his glass. "To your to-die-for-cacciatore…Jill," he said my name with hesitation, and I wasn't sure why. But then, when I saw the look in his eyes, I couldn't deny there was something there.

"Thank you." I clinked his glass and sipped the wine. I watched his reaction when he took the first bite. Through his chewing, his smile radiated superbly. He began talking with a mouthful.

"Wow, this is the best thing I've ever tasted." I was pleased that I could make him happy with something so simple.

We finished our dinner. I found some leftover Chinese takeout containers and stored the rest of the cacciatore in Michael's fridge. Afterwards, we sat on his couch. He took off his suit coat, pulled his tie off with a '*swish,*' and dropped it on the side of the sofa. He unbuttoned his shirt just below his chest, and my eyes raked over his exposed skin as he topped off his wine. I still had some left and knew I shouldn't, but I lifted for a refill anyway. "Not much more, kid," he said, topping my glass halfway.

It was quiet as we drank our wine, and I wondered what he was thinking. I wanted to ask him what this was. Was I still just a friend's kid sister? Or was I gaining a place in his heart?

He set his wine on the stereo speaker and turned to face me. His look was different and soft, and I tried to discern its meaning. "How old are you, Jill?"

I thought he knew how old I was. But then again, it never came up until now. "Seventeen," I said like it was no big deal. Why was he asking now?

"Does your brother know you're with me tonight?"

"He knows I took you to the dance." I was splitting hairs. Because Scott didn't know we had left early and that I was alone in his apartment. I wanted to ask if April knew he went with me tonight but didn't want her to obstruct our night. But I did want her to know.

His hand came toward my face, and he cupped my cheek. "You are a beautiful girl, Jill. Never think that you aren't." He smiled, and it was different from all the smiles he had given me in the past. There was sweetness, curiosity, and…fear. Perhaps he saw more in me than a young girl with a crush. But even at that moment, I knew it was more than a crush for me.

Before moving them to my lips, he considered my eyes for the longest time. "Have you ever been kissed before, Jill?" I thought of my first year in high school when Tommy Sommers and I made out on the church hayride.

"Only by a boy. I've never kissed a man before," I said, looking sincerely into his eyes. And I hoped his asking was an invitation. Because I wanted this man to kiss me, I wanted it more than anything. And at that moment, his look told me he did, too.

"You want to kiss me?"

I nodded. I couldn't speak. Because if I did, I was sure to ruin the moment.

"Come here," he whispered. I leaned closer, and he wrapped his arm around my shoulders. My heart was pounding against my breastbone, so much I could hear it. He leaned down and pressed his lips gently onto mine. It started with a small kiss, and he pulled my lips into his. When I began to open my mouth, he moaned. I felt something so combustible inside me. I was dizzy and full of what must have been lust or love. I couldn't tell because I had never felt like that before. My hand came to his face, and I gently rubbed it with curiosity. He then covered it with his hand and pulled away. My eyes were closed, and he smiled down at me when I opened them. "Was that different?"

This time, I could speak. "Yeah," I said, all breathy.

He gave a small chuckle. "I'm flattered. Don't think anyone's ever responded like that from a kiss." His finger traced down my cheek. "Just wish you weren't seventeen. Or the little sister of my friend."

Even at that moment, it didn't seem to matter that there were obstacles in our way. Because it meant he did have feelings for me. Romantic feelings. And in some way, those obstacles seemed to make what we had even hotter: forbidden.

He turned around, reached for his wine, and looked at his watch. The reality that I had to be home at 10:00 was slowly creeping in, and I searched for a reason to call and see if I could stay longer.

"I could call and say we are helping with clean-up at the dance and stay longer."

He shifted his body and said, "Jill, I promised your father I would have you home at 10:00. I don't want to be on his bad side." I smiled down shyly like I did whenever my parents lectured me. "Besides, how will I get another date if I didn't honor your father's wishes?"

Another date? He did consider us on an actual date. And at that point, I loved his chivalry. He wanted to remain loyal to my father out of respect to see me again. How could I argue with that?

"You're right. It was just a suggestion. Thank you for wanting to honor my father." Respecting my father showed me he was a real man, not a boy. Most guys Tammy and I hung out with always asked us to lie and stay out longer. Occasionally, we did the *'I was staying with her, and she was staying with me'* trick and stayed all night at some guy's house who was a friend of a friend. But the house was full of people we didn't know, so Tammy and I slept in a friend's car. It wasn't fun. We got away with it but never did it again. And now, Michael was changing my view of responsibility, and I needed to be more grown up and trustworthy.

He finished his wine, and I took another sip, forgetting it was in my hand. I was happy I didn't spill it in his lap with the heart-melting kiss. "So, how long have you worked at the pizza place?" He was changing the subject and was still interested in my life.

"A year. I want to find something else. But with school, finding something part-time that works with my schedule is hard. During the summer, I work more hours."

"How much do you need—money-wise? If you find something to fit your schedule?"

I didn't understand why he was even interested. But I said, "I make at least $75 to $150 weekly. Depending on tips. I mostly work in the kitchen. That night I brought your pizza, our driver didn't show."

"Would you like to work for me?"

Work for him? "What do you mean?"

"Whirlpool has put a lot of hours on me, and I could use someone to clean and run errands. I would pay you $150 a week. It can fit your schedule. And now that I know you're a superb cook, I could use that too."

He was serious. I could be with Michael every night. "Sure," I said with the excitement of a child at Christmas. "I would have to give Delanie's notice." I tried to bring it down some.

"I understand. So, you want the job?"

"Yes."

He held out his hand, and we shook on it. "Let me know your last day at Delanie's, and you can start immediately."

"Okay. Awesome. And thanks."

"No, thank you." He looked again at his watch and made a sad face when he saw it was 9:30. *A sad face*! He did want me to stay. He reached for my wine glass, so I finished what was left and stood when he took them to the sink. "I'll try and have them cleaned before you start," he laughed. He rolled the cuffs of his sleeves as he walked back. Then, he reached for my hand and placed a small kiss on top. "Thank you for allowing me to escort you to the dance and the wonderful chicken cacciatore, my Lady. But your chariot awaits."

"Thank you for taking me. I had a wonderful time," I said with a curtsy.

He grabbed the keys from the counter and placed his hand on the small of my back as we walked out to his Corvette. As he helped me inside, the smile on my face felt as if it would last forever as I watched him walk around and climb into the driver's seat. He started the car and slid a CD into the player. When Shania began singing, *"You're Still the One,"* our eyes met for a second. I knew right there and then the girl I was before I knew Michael would never be the same. Worlds change when eyes meet. And change isn't always good. And I was too young to sense the danger a smile or a glance could hold.

CHAPTER 13

Now

Leukemia. NO! This is not happening. Not to my best friend. My rock. My other half. Tammy is the only stable thing in my life. She was there when Monica was born. Through all the affairs, when I cried myself to sleep and when Michael left. And when Michael came back.

"How? When did you find out? There's a mistake." I'm in complete denial and will not let this happen to her.

Tammy inhales a deep breath as if the situation warrants no grand explanation. "Last week," she says and exhales.

"And you didn't tell me? Why not?"

"Jill, I didn't want to ruin Monica's wedding."

"Are you kidding me? Can you stop being so unselfish, just for once? My God, Tammy. And work? You've never missed any work except for today."

"Come here," she says, holding her arms out for me. "Calm down, Jill."

"Calm down! Oh, Tammy," I say and hold her tightly to me. Through my crying, she rubs my back as if I'm the sick one. As always, she gives me comfort in my darkest times. But it's me who should be comforting her. I'm such a selfish bitch. "Please tell me this is all a bad joke. Something to distract me with Michael's return."

"Okay, it's a bad joke," she laughs.

"How can you laugh?" I push up and hold her face. "We'll get a second opinion. We'll travel the world."

Her eyes still hold that assuredness she has given me my whole life. The strength I needed. My Tammy strength. I can't be without her.

"We did get a second opinion. Leukemia."

"Now what? What do we do now?"

"I start chemo this week."

It's absolute the minute the word chemo comes across her lips, yet she says it as if she's talking about the weather. My existence begins fading away. Dammit. She needs me, and all I can do is worry about myself.

"Where? I'm going with you." Though we both work at Lakeland Health, it's not at the top of cancer research.

"Woodland Cancer Center," she says. "But Ryan has already scheduled to take me."

"Good. I've heard nothing but the best about Woodland. And I don't care if Ryan is taking you. I'm coming too."

She laughs. *Actually,* laughs. "You're just trying to hide from Michael."

I pull the covers down and climb in with her. "Tammy, I would go through a thousand Michael traumas just to make this all disappear." I kiss her cheek. "We're in this together. I'm stuck to your side."

"Please, I'm going to need my space," she teases.

"Too bad. I hope Ryan doesn't mind the couch." She smacks my arm. "And don't worry about the girls. I will get them off to school. No worries."

"Jill, I'm not dead yet."

"Don't say that! I meant while you're going through chemo. Oh, I'm going to shave my head."

"Why?"

"You know…to show support while you're going through this. And we can pick out wigs together. It will be like shopping when we were teens. Except for this time, I get to be the straight-haired brunette, and you can be the curly blonde. I will donate my hair to Locks of Love and make it a wig for you."

She runs her hands through my hair. "Well, make sure they cover up the grey." She laughs, and I kiss her again on the cheek.

"Gray, my ass." And that's Tammy—my rock.

"Jill, don't shave your head. I don't think I could stand to look at your ugly, bald head." We laugh. We cry. But one thing is for sure. We're in this together.

Ryan walks in, and the stress on his face lightens maybe a few degrees since Tammy has confessed to me. Walking over, he grabs the box of tissues and pulls one out for both of us. After I blow my nose, I ask, "Do the girls know?" Ryan drops his eyes.

"We're telling them tonight," he says.

Tammy and Ryan have three girls—fourteen, twelve, and an *oops* at six. They wanted Hailee to be a boy, but Tammy and I were destined to have girls. Casey and Callie are the best older sisters and, without a doubt, will help their mother. Tammy and I always talked about how we'd raise our children together, but with Monica being much older, she babysat the two older girls when she was a teen.

"Do you want me here when you tell them?"

"We…kind of want to do this alone," Ryan says. I look at Tammy, and she nods her agreement.

"If the girls come in and see you here…us crying, it will lead to the worst in their minds. We want to break it gently. Explain what I have and why I'm starting chemo."

I don't even want to ask about the percentages the doctor talked about. She will get through chemo, and our life together will go on. "Okay, I understand. But please call me if you need anything or if they need anything. I will arrange my schedule at the hospital."

I kiss her again and hold her face close to mine. "I love you, girl."

"I love you too, Jill."

I get up from the bed, and Ryan takes my place beside his wife. I look at the two of them. They made it. And Tammy will make it. "Hey, Ryan. What do you think about Tammy having my blonde curly hair? I'm going to donate it to her."

His eyes squint, investigating the loose bun on my head. "Make sure to color the grey."

I laugh. "Kiss my ass, Ryan."

•   •   •   •   •

I watch the flame dance from the candle across the room and pray for Tammy. I never turned on the radio all the way home, and I've been sitting in silence at home. *Leukemia.* As shocked as I am, it still is surreal to me. And that's because I refuse to believe it's happening. But as a nurse, I know science has come a long way with cancer treatment. I must remain positive.

I wonder if they've told the girls yet? How are they taking it? Maybe I should call. I know they wanted to be alone. But after?

My phone sits on the counter, and as I get up, thinking I need to call, the doorbell rings. That would be the girls, and they know Tammy needs me. I rush to the door and fight with the locks to quickly open. Michael. He's standing on my doorstep holding out a pan of chicken cacciatore.

"I don't know. It's missing something, and I need you to taste it."

Without warning, I begin to cry—hard and drop my head into my hands.

"You haven't even tasted it yet. That bad, huh?"

"Oh, Michael. Tammy has Leukemia."

"Oh, Jill. I'm sorry," he says and steps inside. He sets the pan on the counter and then wraps me in his arms. I don't protest, and that's because I'm numb. I cry into his chest, and once again, the past and present slam into each other. "When did she find out?"

"Last week. Tammy didn't tell me until today. She didn't want to ruin Monica's wedding." I'm angry, and the foul language pushes up from deep down. "Can you fucking believe that? She didn't want to ruin my daughter's wedding." I choke out more cries, and Michael listens, looking deep into my eyes. Everything feels like an illusion at this moment. He holds my face in his hands, his thumbs wiping my tears, and that look in his eyes. What's going on?

"Come here," he says, leading me to the couch. He sits and pulls me next to him. He holds me close, and I feel robotic. I should be telling him to get the fuck out. I should say to him he never should have come. I should tell him to shove his cacciatore up his ass. Yet, I am—lying on his chest and so glad he's here.

"Oh, Michael. I can't believe this," I whisper, and when I do, the use of his name feels foreign on my lips. I haven't used or said his name in years. And now, it seems to be dropping out of my mouth redundantly. I can't remember a time crying in his arms. And that was because I was crying in Tammy's arms for something Michael did. This moment feels oddly strange.

He slowly rubs my arm up and down as his lips place tender kisses on my head. This is the same Michael who made my pancakes in bed just the other day. The Michael, I didn't know.

"Why are you here, Michael?" I don't look up and lay lethargically on his chest.

"For this."

I don't accurately comprehend what he means, and I'm sure Tammy didn't tell him first so that he'd come and hold me. But I'm too exhausted to argue at the moment. However, I can't let my guard down, not around Michael.

"Did you know she left the wedding early because she was sick?"

"Yes."

"She told you?"

"She told us."

"Us?"

"We were in your car…after…"

"Yes, after I got drunk. And that's your fault. But go on."

"I'll accept that," he says. "Tammy said she'd call you. You tried to get out of the car, and when she noticed how fucked up you were, she bent down and hugged you through the window and told me to make sure you got home safely. I promised her I would."

"Oh, God," I say and break from his side, standing up from the couch.

"Have you eaten, Jill?"

"No, Michael. Nor do I want to. So, take your cacciatore and go home. Wherever that is."

"Jill, I don't think you need to be alone right now."

"What the hell do you know about what I need? Or even care. It was never a problem in the past. I needed you years ago. And…I learned you were the one thing I definitely didn't need." I walk over to the kitchen counter and look out the window. The streetlight is on, and suddenly, I'm back there. That night watching and waiting for him to come back.

I hear him get up from the couch and walk close behind me. "I'm sorry, Jill." He touches my shoulders, but I shrug away. Through the reflection of the dark window, I see his hand still held above my shoulder. I turn around.

"Well, sorry or not, you never came back. And I should probably thank you." His eyes look guarded. "Because finally, I realized that no matter how much I loved you, it wasn't what you wanted. And it took a long time to figure that out."

"Jill…"

"You know what else I figured out, Michael? The entire time Monica and I were *so* in your way, making you feel miserable, it was exhausting being your wife. You never had to do anything to prove how much you loved me or our daughter. Because you didn't. Yet I drained myself daily, showing you love. No one ever gets tired of being loved. They get tired of waiting, assuming, hearing lies, and saying sorry and hurting. How could I prioritize someone who didn't value me? In the end, Michael, I didn't know who I hated more, me or you."

His eyes glass over with heavy tears. "I'm sorry." His words are faint. "All you ever did was love me, and all I ever did was hurt you." A big tear drops down his cheek and onto his white shirt. I watch the color darken from the wetness and know I am not crying.

"And so, once I overcame that, I had to overcome the fact that you left us for something better. And I couldn't figure out what that would be. And there I was, making you a priority in my thoughts. So, I will ask you, Michael, because I want to know. What was better than our daughter and me?"

"Not hurting you anymore."

CHAPTER 14

Then

I wasn't scheduled to work at Delanie's after school and had given my two weeks' notice. Tonight, I was going to start my job for Michael. He said whenever my schedule allowed, and I was bursting at the seams to start. Concentration was at a loss; all I could think about was him. After dropping me off at home, he gave me a key to his apartment, and I wore it on a gold chain around my wrist. I wanted everyone to see and ask me about it. Feeling it and watching it dangle from my wrist instilled the reality that something was special between us. It was a symbol that he had won the key to my heart. I wished I had something to give him. I wanted him to wear something that meant *'me'* whenever he felt or saw it. Giving him my class ring felt too juvenile since he was ten years older. I thought about buying him a necklace with some medallion and engraving, 'Love, Jill' on the back. Tammy and I would go to the mall this weekend, and she'd help me pick it out.

The PA came on to give the end-of-day announcements, and my legs bounced eagerly. When the principal dismissed the school, I was out the door and to my car. I was heading to Michael's. I called him the night before and told him I'd be there. He said he worked until 5:00, meaning I had time to freshen my makeup or fix my hair.

As I pulled out of the parking lot and onto the street, those romantic feelings of driving home to my husband once again entertained my young heart. Later, it would no longer be a dream, and the pain in my heart would prolong the journey.

I pulled into his apartment complex and parked next to where his Corvette would be parked when he got home. I unlocked the door, walked into his apartment, and into the make-believe world I had created. It had only been three days since he kissed me on that couch, and my destination for his love began. I walked over and took a seat, remembering the moment. It was real—that kiss and his sound when he kissed me. I wanted this job to be more than just cleaning and running his errands. I wanted to cook for him and care for him. Be there to make his bad days disappear—if he had bad days.

My eyes spotted a note on the counter, and I went to read it.

Dear Jill,

Thanks again for taking the job. Feel free to use the stereo or anything you can find in the fridge. There's a box with some money on the dresser in my room. Use it to buy anything you need to clean. The vacuum and other cleaning items are in the small hall closet. I will work late tonight, so if I don't see you, have a great night. Hope to see you soon.

Love, Michael

My fingers caressed over the words: *Love, Michael.* I stared until my eyes burned. I wanted to make sure I didn't see things. It wasn't my creative imagination. He wrote: *Love, Michael.* I held the letter to my chest and smiled. I went to his room and stopped at his unmade bed. My hand smoothed down the sheet, and I wanted to feel and smell where his body slept. I lay down and squeezed into his pillow. I breathed in his scent—manly soap and cologne. I rolled my face in it like a dog rolling in something terrible. I wanted his scent all over me. I wanted it on me long after I went home. Everything I smelled refreshed my senses, and I was back three days ago on that couch where he kissed me.

The smile on my face was forever embedded, and I thought I would have to learn to turn it off. *Later, I would have to learn how even to smile again.*

I got up and went to the little box on his dresser, where his note said the money was. I thought about wanting something nice for dinner while waiting for him to come home from work. I wanted a reason to stay longer and be here when he returned. After that, I checked the closet for cleaning supplies. He had everything I needed, and they had never been open. I wouldn't need to buy anything.

I went to the kitchen and checked his refrigerator. Yes. The chicken cacciatore was gone, which meant he finished it and hopefully thought of me when eating. I thought of him when I felt and saw the key hanging from my wrist. Of course, I didn't need anything to feel about him.

I popped in a Faith Hill CD, cleaned his bed, scrubbed the bathroom, and vacuumed the apartment. There was no need to polish the furniture, such as end tables, because he had none.

It was 5:00, and he'd be home soon. I wanted to make him a steak dinner. But I didn't know how he liked his steak.

His phone rang when I was about to grab the money from the box and head to the grocery down the street. An answering machine next to the phone clicked on.

"Hey, Jill. This is Michael. If you're still there, pick up."

He wanted to talk to me. He was thinking of me. Looking in the mirror, I saw a bright smile when I picked up the phone. "Hi, Michael."

"Good, you're still there." My heart fluttered. He wanted me here.

"Yes, I was about to leave for the grocery store." He interrupted me before I could ask him how he liked his steak.

"Great! That's what I was calling about. Your cacciatore was impressive." I bit down on my lower lip, giddy with all sorts of feelings. "Take the money in the box and make another pan if you can." I was more than excited. He had the same thoughts about me—having me here and dining together.

"Sure, not a problem," I said, glad I didn't miss his call before I bought him a steak.

"Great. April is coming over for dinner, and I want to impress her."

My heart sank as I watched my expression in the mirror of his dresser. I never saw anything sadder. He wanted to impress April. And he wanted me to make dinner…*for him and April*—blowjob eyes. My mouth remained open, speechless. I knew if I spoke, it would come out all wrong, and he would know how upset I was. And maybe I should have because all I could say was, "Okay."

"Great. You don't mind, do you? Might require you to stay a little longer."

By now, the tears were so welled up in my eyes that I couldn't even see my reflection in the mirror. I felt my nose begin to run, and I couldn't sniff it, fearing Michael would know I was crying. I inhaled a deep breath as quietly as I could and responded. "No, it's fine."

"Thanks, Jill."

"Ah hah," I said and hung up the phone. By now, snot and big, watery tears were dripping down my face. What was I thinking? He had no romantic feelings for me. But what was that on the couch three nights ago?

I went into the bathroom, dried my eyes, and blew my nose. I flushed the paper down the toilet, not wanting Michael to find my snot-dried tissue, and then angrily snatched the money from the box; it fell to the floor. I went to pick it up and found wallet-sized photos that were also inside the box that I hadn't seen before. They were of all girls—high school photos. They were all very pretty, and I turned them over to read what they wrote on the back.

Michael, never forget Montauk. I won't. Jenny.

I read another.

Michael. I've been in love with your eyes since 1st grade—Love Rochelle.

What the hell went on in Montauk? Where was Rochelle now?

Michael, Thanks for taking my virginity, Love, Pam.

I threw the pictures back in the box, set it down with force on the dresser, and left for the grocery store.

As I shopped for their dinner, I passed by the medication aisle and stared at a bottle of ex-lax. I picked it up and thought about adding it to the chicken cacciatore. How much would it take? I threw it in the cart and headed to the checkout. Standing in line, I heard the person in front ask for the receipt, and then I knew Michael would see it if he asked. So, I took it out and laid it on the shelf next to me.

I had another cry on the way back, and once I was at the apartment, I prepared the cacciatore with a deep heaviness in my heart. How, just three days ago, I was on Michael cloud number nine. Michael played music, lit the candles, and poured the wine as I cooked. And now, he was going to be doing it all with April. And I knew after, he would fuck her. Just like the girls in the box. Jenny, Rochelle, Pam, and the rest of the girls' pictures that I didn't read.

The oven dinged, and I pulled the pan out onto the stove, wrapping it with foil. The front door opened, and Michael walked through it. "Wow, I could smell it as soon as I exited my car. You're such a doll, Jill."

I couldn't even look at him. I was furious, hurt, and heartbroken all at once, and he would be able to tell by the look on my face. "It just came out. Depending on what time…April gets here, it should be plenty warm," I said and went to gather my things.

"The apartment looks nice too." I didn't respond and headed for the door. I felt him watching me from behind.

"I'll call you when I have a free day. I still have a week left at Delanie's," I said, opening the door.

He knew now something was wrong and hesitated before responding. "Oh…kay. No problem. And…thanks for making dinner."

"Yeah," I said and shut the door behind me. I got into my car and drove out of the complex. I was only a block down the road when I had to pull over. I couldn't see through the tears burning my eyes, and I laid my head on the steering wheel and cried.

CHAPTER 15

Now

I walk in with two coffees as the nurse hooks Tammy up to the chemo pump. Her port had already been surgically implanted—another secret she kept from me. "Here you go, Ryan," I say, handing him one cup.

"Thanks, Jill."

Setting my coffee on a nearby table, I grab my bag of goodies and sit next to Tammy on the bed. "What is it? Christmas in that bag?" Tammy jokes, still taking all of this with a grain of salt.

"I put together some items to help you get through this. And Ryan, I got a few things for you too," I say, pulling out car magazines, Hot Rod and Car Craft. Ryan has restored a few cars, and I thought it might also help him.

"Thanks again, Jill. And thank you for coming today," he says, taking the magazine.

"Ryan, I will be here each time," I tell him, pulling a sack of ginger candy from the bag and handing it to Tammy. "This is to help with nausea. And here are some iTunes cards. Guess what we're going to do?"

"Buy music?"

"Close," I say and pull out two sets of earbuds. "We're finally going to listen to *Fifty Shades of Grey*"—together."

She laughs. "Oh my God. You're serious."

"You know I am. Everyone in the book club wants to read it, too. They won't admit it. Well, we will listen in private."

"Ryan, you want a set of earbuds?"

"Ah, no thanks. Go right ahead. If I listen, it will be Fifty Shades of Puke."

"Whatever," I say and reach back into the bag. "Here's a BPA-free water bottle to keep ice water in. They say your mouth can get dry during chemo. Also, I ordered some already prepared meals to be delivered for my work days. I was going to hire someone to come and clean, but I don't want you to be exposed to anyone who might be sick. So, I will do my best to help the girls out. And here is some moisturizer for your hands and feet. They dry out as well."

"Wow, Jill. You're amazing. I love you," Tammy says, and I brush her hair back. I can't help but think about when her hair will begin to fall out.

Ryan sets in with his coffee and magazine, and I download *"Fifty Shades of Grey"* to my iPad. As the book is loading, I pair both wireless earbuds to the iPad. Tammy's chemo IV begins to drip, and I distract her by handing her the earbuds and telling her to put them on. "You ready? The book has been downloaded."

"Let's go for it." She smiles bravely at me, and I start the audible, snuggling up beside her. I take her hand when the audible begins. "This is Audible. *"Fifty Shades of Grey"*, by E.L. James. Read for you by Becca Battoe—chapter one. I scowl at myself with frustration in the mirror. Damn my hair—it just won't behave, and damn Katherine Kavanagh for being ill and subjecting me to this ordeal. I should be studying for final exams, yet here I am, trying to brush my hair into submission. I must not sleep with it wet. I must not sleep with it wet," says the narrator, and I burst with laughter.

"Oh, my God. This book is awful," I say as we both begin laughing.

"Yes, but *awfully* good." Ryan looks up from his magazine, and I see the sigh in his smile. He needs me here just as much as I need to be here. Ryan has always been an excellent husband to Tammy and has never let our close friendship be a problem in their marriage. Even when Tammy spent countless nights with me, talking me off the emotional wall, I was about to jump off. At times, I felt death would be better—for me. How selfish of me to think that while she's here hanging onto hers.

Though he's a good husband, Ryan is quieter and more reserved about his feelings, and Tammy has always accepted that. He's complacent with what they have, and over time, I find that maybe satisfaction is better than passion. Passion has two meanings. Once you have it, you can't live with anything else. And two, passion can kill. Life and death are the two things that drive it, so being stuck in between can feel safe. And *safe* is comforting. But not passion.

Chapter One finishes, and Tammy pauses the book. "How many hours is this?"

"I think fourteen."

"I think they might find a cure for cancer by then. I don't remember even talking or thinking like that in college," Tammy says.

"Me either." But I was married and raising Monica at the same time. Maybe I could have been an Anastasia Steel, and in some ways, I was. I tried desperately to get Michael to love me on some level. But to him, we were in a situation, as he called it. Not a real marriage and my ideal of marriage has been fractured ever since. It scares me that I may never find out or reach a level of complacency.

"I'm going to get more coffee. Can I get you girls something?" Ryan asks.

"I'm fine. But can you get Tammy a bottle of water? And here," I say, handing him the bottle I bought, "find some ice too, and then pour the water in here."

"Sure," he says, kissing Tammy on the cheek before he leaves.

She pulls the earbuds out. "Thanks for the audiobook, Jill. But now that Ryan is out, I want to talk about Fifty Shades of You and Michael."

"What? Why? Didn't I rob you enough of your life back then? I'd rather not."

"He came to see me yesterday."

"He what? Why in the hell would he do that? He has to know how you feel."

"He came to thank me and apologize. He brought a small vase of white daisies and told me how sorry he was about my cancer. He seemed deeply concerned and understanding. Wanted to know if there was anything he could do or if I needed a good cancer doctor."

"Wow. Are you sure it was Michael? Because I've had these delusions, too," I say with a tease.

"I know. It was weird. Yet, it is comforting. Michal thanked me for being there for you after he left and before." Before is right. Life during Michael was hell. And if it wasn't for Tammy and all her love, I don't think I'd be sitting here in this bed with her. Michael time-stamped my life. Everything became pre-Michael, during-Michael, and post-Michael. "So, I take it he has been back since the after-wedding-pancake-breakfast since he knew about the cancer?"

"Yes, he showed up Monday night after I left your house. I was crying—praying for you, and strangely, he showed up."

"And...?"

"He held me. I cried in his arms."

"Kind of like I held you when you cried in my arms over him."

"Huh," I say under my breath. "Yeah. But then my sanity returned, and I lashed out a few things I thought I buried."

"What did he say? After you unleashed on him?"

"Nothing. Michael stood there looking at me, and I watched a tear drop from his cheek. It was the saddest thing I think I've ever seen. The whole time we were together, I wished some emotion would have affected him. And when it finally did, it hurt."

"Why do you think that?" she asks, pulling out my earbuds.

"Maybe because part of me knows how it feels."

"Know how what feels?" God, why is she doing this to me? I'm supposed to be here for her. And here she is, lecturing me about my feelings.

I glance from her to the IV chemo drip, and I now use it as a distraction. "What does it feel like? When the...poison goes in?"

"Jill, do not deflect from this. This, too, shall pass. Tell me."

"What it feels like when someone wants your love."

She smiles, and I feel I have answered her correctly. We can then get off the subject. "Michael wants your love." She doesn't say it as a question. She just…says it.

It's quiet, and I need to say something because that has caught me off guard. "The one thing Michael never wanted was my love. And why would he want that? After all these years. You think he just woke up one day and said, "I need Jill to love me."

"Because he loves you."

I shake my head. "Tammy, what are you doing? I think that chemo drip is going straight to your brain. There are three words Michael could never say—*I, love, and you.*"

"Are you going to start singing The Avett Brothers now?"

"Do you want me to sing? Because I'll do anything to drop this subject."

She laughs. "Oh, God, no. Please. But you answered your question. You said you know how it feels to want someone's love."

"I said, someone. I didn't say Michael's."

"Stop splitting hairs, Jill. We both know how you ached for Michael to love you."

"Ached—past tense. People change. I've changed."

"And maybe Michael has changed."

I think of the pictures he wanted of us all together at the wedding. Of us alone. The kiss on my forehead. The photographer never asked us to pose like that. Was Michael acting on his impulse? The toast. The Dance. The…

"Well, even if he has, which Michael never would, wouldn't this be the time where I say, 'It's too late. You missed out.'"

"Is it too late?"

"Of course, it's too late."

"Why?"

As she looks at me intently, I can't come up with a reason. I'm single after a failed attempt to marry a few years ago. And though we've never discussed the real reason, I default to my fear of failure as an excuse. And how Monica was my focus. But now, she's gone on with her own life.

Ryan walks in with his fresh coffee and the water bottle for Tammy. I'm so relieved. "Sorry, it took forever. I couldn't find any ice maker."

"Thanks, Honey," Tammy tells him and pops the top to take a drink. "Ah, you're right. My mouth is parched."

Twenty more minutes go by, and her drip is empty. After a few light beeps, the nurse comes and unhooks her IV. She tells her not to exert herself and that the chemo will begin to make her tired and drained. Knowledge, we both as nurses know.

Ryan sweetly walks with his arm around her waist, and I open the car door. I climb into the back seat, and he drives us back to their house. "The food in the crockpot should be done. Just set it to warm, and it should be fine until the girls get home," I say.

"Thanks, Jill," Ryan tells me, and Tammy thanks me too.

"Call me. I'll be home all night," I say and head to my car in the driveway. I watch Ryan guide her through the door and think of my parents. After Dad had his first heart attack and the way Mom fussed over him. For richer or poorer, in sickness and in health. It does exist for some, and I know in my heart for me…it never will.

•　　•　　•　　•　　•

A black 4Runner is parked out front of the street when I pull into the drive and hit the garage door opener. *Michael.* I can't tell if he's sitting inside due to the dark tint, and I decide to ignore him and close the garage door once inside. That should make it clear.

Walking into the kitchen from the garage, I find him standing at the table. The lights are low, candles softly flicker, soft music plays, and something smells terrific.

"What are you doing here? And how did you get in?"

He's in nice jeans and a white button-up shirt with rolled-up cuffs. A key hangs from a leather band around his wrist when he lifts his hand. "You never changed the locks."

"That's because I knew you'd never be back."

"I'm here now, Jill."

I throw my purse on the counter. "Yep. That you are, so answer the next question. Why?"

"You took care of Tammy, and now it's my turn to take care of you." Did Tammy put him up to this? Is that what all her Michael talk was about?"

"How is she?"

"She's okay…for now. The chemo will eventually take its toll."

"It's nasty stuff," he says. "Why don't you go take a bath, and I'll set the table for us when you return."

"Us?"

"Yes. Us. Me and you. You and me. Michael and Jill," he says, walking toward me.

"This is unbelievable—first you, and then Tammy's cancer. I don't know how much more I can take. Not counting Monica clear across the world. And why did you have to send her to Paris?"

He steps in front of me, and I can smell his manly cologne scent as he reaches out and gently brushes my cheek with the back of his fingers. My eyes catch the key dangling from his wrist. "Because that's where she wanted to go, and I wanted to make her happy."

"No, I think you wanted to make me miserable."

"You're tired and stressed. I have your bath waiting. It should still be warm."

"What? How'd…Never mind. I am tired, and I do want to soak. And by the time I get out, this apparition of you will be gone. You're just a ghost who has decided to come back and haunt me."

"Do you believe in ghosts? Because they say, all ghosts are wanted and are the imagination of the one being haunted."

"And for that reason, I don't believe in ghosts. And who said that anyway?"

He smiles and gives a small laugh. "You're still so cute. Take your bath. I'll keep dinner warm."

"Unbelievable," I say, walking past him and to my bedroom. "Maybe I don't believe in ghosts, but I do believe in demons," I holler back.

"Or maybe I'm an angel."

"Far from it," I yell, shut and lock the bathroom door. Turning around, I find that Michael has indeed filled the tub. But what's more shocking are the rose petals floating on top of the water, the candles on the side, and a glass of wine set along the edge. "What the hell," I whisper.

I strip off my clothes, step inside the tub, and sink shoulders deep, closing my eyes. When I open, I reach for the glass of wine and see a card under the glass. Setting the glass back down, I take the card and read what Michael has written on the other side.

Dear Jill,

You are a genuine and wonderful friend for being there for Tammy. She will need you; in return, you will need someone to care for you as you do. Let me be that someone. I wish I could turn back time and make it undone. I swear that I will make it up to you. If you give me a slight chance, I will prove that it will be one of the best decisions you'll ever make. I was once your rain. Let me now be your umbrella.

Love, Michael

"Oh…God."

CHAPTER 16

Then

It was my last day at Delanies, and Michael called to see if I was coming this week to clean. I thought of quitting already and staying on at the pizza shop. I didn't want to give him any indication I was jealous of him and April. But I was, and it wasn't just jealousy. I had a wave of righteous anger. He gave me so many mixed feelings. I still wore the key on my wrist—I don't know why. I guess because it was the only tangible thing I had of him. And I wore the T-shirt he bought me as much as possible—even slept in it.

His apartment was a little messy when I showed up, and all I could envision was him and April having crazy sex while hanging from the chandeliers—even though he didn't have chandeliers. Whenever I picked up a pillow or some article of clothing, I was afraid of finding a bra or panty that belonged to April. I even thought about leaving a pair of my panties hidden down inside the couch, hoping April would see them and they'd have a big fight.

There was another note on the counter, and I was less than excited to read it.

Dear Jill....

Even starting his letters with *Dear Jill* sent mixed feelings. If he felt nothing but a friend, why not just begin with Jill?

Dear Jill,

Sorry, the place is a mess. I hoped to see you sooner, but I understand your commitment to Delanie's. Plus, I miss your cute face around the place. Hopefully, I won't be late, and we can do something together. I say get a pizza, but you're probably sick of pizza. If it's not too chilly, maybe we can take a ride on the bike and get some Chinese. Just call me at work. My number's at the bottom. Let me know what you're up for. See you soon.

Love, Michael

And why did he have to sign *Love, Michael* to his notes? It drove me crazy. Michael's number for work was written on the bottom, but I wasn't going to call. Just clean and get the *hell* out before something with April popped up, crushing my world again.

And how dare he think I had nothing planned on a Friday night— like I had no friends or even a boyfriend. *And I didn't have plans.* Tammy was babysitting, and I didn't have a boyfriend. But maybe I could make one up and make him jealous. But would he say something to Scott, blowing my cover? I would think about it. But when would the subject come up? 'Oh, by the way, Michael, I have a boyfriend.' But then he would wonder why I took him to the dance. I decided not to ponder on it and finished cleaning his apartment.

I washed his dishes, swept his carpet, and made his unmade bed. I didn't want to lie on it because all I could see was him and April having sex all over it.

The phone beside his bed rang, and I almost picked it up. The answering machine clicked on, and just like last time, Michael was calling me. "Hey Jill, if you're still there, please pick up. It's me, Michael."

Yes, Michael, I know it's you, I thought. But I continued to look at the phone.

"I hope I find your cute little face when I get home. I missed having you around. Well, I hope I don't miss you; that's all. Bye."

Why would he continue to talk after I didn't pick up? Did he know I was listening and intentionally would not pick up? Did he know I was…hurt? It's not like I would see his machine flashing and check his messages. He knew he had hurt me. I was mad, yet I didn't want jealousy to be part of the issue.

I finished putting away his laundry and took out the trash, and when I was walking back inside, I heard his Corvette come into the parking lot. Shit! I wanted to be gone by the time he was home. Now he would know I purposely avoided his call.

"Hey, no wonder you missed my message. I called, hoping you'd still be here."

The garbage can was still in my hands, and it was a good cover. "Oh, yes. Must have just missed your call." I turned and headed back inside. "Everything is done. I also unloaded your dishwasher. See you next week," I said, picking up my purse on the counter.

"Hey, wait a minute. Would you like to hang out tonight or do something? Did you read my note?"

"Yes, I saw your note. Goodbye, Michael." My hand was on the door when he spoke again.

"Jill, are you mad at me? Have I done something? Did…did the kiss scare you off?"

I froze. There was so much I wanted to say, and now was my chance. The words were rolling around in my head, but I couldn't begin or form how to answer him. "Jill, let's talk. What have I done?" Walk out the door. Walk out the door.

"No, nothing's wrong." My voice was high, and my words were fast. I started to open the door when he came up from behind and pushed it shut, holding the door so I couldn't open it.

"Hey, let's talk. Something is wrong."

"I don't want to talk, Michael." Without any control, I began to cry, and I hoped he couldn't tell. But there was no hiding it from him. He put his hand on my shoulder while still holding the door shut. "Let me go. I'm fine."

He turned me around, and I covered my face, not wanting him to see me cry. He tried to pry them away. "Jill, are you mad at me for kissing you? I didn't mean for it to scare you. I won't do it again, I promise."

"That's the point, Michael. I don't understand what the kiss meant. No, it didn't scare me. That's not why I'm mad at you."

"So, you are mad at me. And the kiss...I don't understand it either."

"Then why did you kiss me?" Michael's eyes locked with mine, both of us searching for answers the other couldn't give.

"Because I wanted to." And it was the best answer he could have given me. He could have said, 'Because you asked me too.' He could have said, 'You looked like you wanted me to.' But he said, 'I wanted to.'

"You wanted to kiss me?"

"Yes," he whispered and wiped my tears. "Did you want to kiss me?"

"Yes."

"Then why are you upset with me?"

"You confuse me, Michael. The first time I came here, with the pizza, you danced with me, and then he took me on motorcycle rides, taking me to the dance. The kiss. The notes with *Love, Michael*. Am I reading mixed signals? In one minute, I think maybe we will have something special, like I could have something with you. And next, you have me making dinner for you and April. I mean...what the hell? Is this some sick, cruel joke you and April are playing with me?"

"Oh, God no, Jill." He held my face and wiped my tears with his thumbs.

"Then what is it? Because I'm getting baffled. Do I see things that aren't there?"

"You're right," he said, and I still didn't know what he meant. "You want to know how I feel about you?" I nodded as he still held my face. "I'm shamefully attracted to you. I can't help it, but I am." My eyes widened. I wasn't making things up in my head. He was attracted to me. "I try to keep it innocent, but when I'm around you, I can't help it. I keep thinking you'll slap me or tell me to stop, but you don't. And I'm not saying it's your fault—it's mine. I should know better because you're only seventeen. I shouldn't have hired you to be here alone. I know it was wrong, but I did it anyway."

"Oh, Michael." I fell onto his chest, and he held me tightly. His arms felt strong, but I felt his entire body shiver underneath. I scared him.

"God, Jill…you're beautiful. You're young; you're my friend's little sister. It has all the hallmarks of a disaster. And yet, that makes it even more enticing. I know I should keep my distance. But I can't."

I should have run right at that moment. I should have said he was right and needed to keep his distance. I should have taken his words as a warning. But I didn't. And everything he said only made me want him more. I would someday look back, wish to undo this moment, and run out that door. Because I didn't know that one day, all he said would turn out to mean nothing anymore.

He kissed me—hard. No one had ever kissed me like that before, and this is what passion must have felt like because my own body reacted without thought. My hands went in his hair and down his neck. The crisp collar of his dress shirt only heightened my desire for him. I saw him as ambitious, successful, accomplished, and reckless. Wasn't that what stirred desire? Judging all the romance books I had read, I was now in my own romance book. And didn't they all have a happy ever after? It was the most pivotal time of my young life. I only saw one thing—Michael and me forever. What could ever change this feeling we had right at this moment? It was too strong. *Too desirable, too wanted. Too wrong, and I didn't care.*

He picked me up, and my legs wrapped around his waist. I felt his hands squeeze into my bottom, and the ache inside me was a pleasure, desire, curiosity. I was on a new adventure, and Michael was my guide.

He walked us to his bedroom, and I didn't care if he and April had sex on his bed. I should have, but I didn't. He laid me down and remained on top of me. His body was heavy, and I loved every ounce I felt on me. He moved his hips, and I felt his stiff erection. That took my breath away because it was scary and excitable, as he was hard because of me.

The kissing was out of control, and I was dizzy. I was out of breath yet in bliss. He reached up my shirt, moving his hands under my bra. My breasts weren't big, maybe a large B, but he made them feel heavy and swollen.

He stood, and I was afraid he was going to stop. Part of me wanted him to, and part wanted him to go on. He began loosening his tie and unbuttoning his shirt. I considered stopping this during the process, but when I saw his bare skin, I couldn't. My young and curious instincts went to his chest, and I touched it and kissed it. I loved his scent—his Michael scent.

He pulled off my shirt and took off my bra. I was exposed from the waist up and not in the slightest shy about it. He made me feel sexy, beautiful—older. Once his shirt was off, he climbed back over me, and we began moving our hips, pushing into one another's groins. It was different than when I masturbated. So much different. I was so hot and wet down there. I didn't know if we would go farther or continue with the heavy petting and rubbing. But then he began to speak, and his voice sounded like a challenge to get out. "Should we stop? Want me to stop?"

Without thinking, I said, "No." With my response, he moaned and kissed me harder. I felt him reach and open the nightstand drawer; his hand fumbled inside, searching. He did this all while still kissing me passionately.

He broke our embrace just for a second to look down inside the box he pulled from the drawer—condoms. "Shit," he hissed. The box was empty, and he threw it back inside. He looked at me, torn.

"I'll go to Planned Parenthood," I said. With that, the passion took on a whole new level, and this was going to happen. He stood and removed his pants, along with his briefs. His penis was much bigger than I imagined—or any penis for that. I had never seen one in real life. I knew they grew with arousal; I didn't know how much.

My eyes widened, and he became concerned. "Jill...is this your first time?"

"Yes."

"Fuck," he said. Not in anger, with arousal. I was as much a fantasy to him as he was to me. He reached for my jeans, and I helped with the removal. My panties came off inside the jeans. I hoped they weren't my period-stained ones. I always used the same ones during that time of the month. But somehow, Aunt Flow would show up uninvited when I was wearing new panties.

He climbed back on me, and his penis was hot to the touch. He was out of control—I was out of control. If this was my first time, somebody needed to take the lead. "Michael…I'm scared. Will it hurt?"

"Yes, just for a bit. You want to stop?"

Part of me wanted to. But I feared he would never want to see me again. "No, but will you go easy?"

"Of course, Baby." I was his baby now. No longer the kid. I loved the sound of it. I felt his penis push against my opening, and I tensed. "Shh, it's okay. I'll take it slow." Would he push in all the way? I didn't know how this worked. Would it go in? Would it fit?

He moved side to side, his penis entering me a little at a time. I felt the stretch inside me. He pushed in a little farther and looked at me. "This, okay?"

"Yes. It burns a little." He kissed me tenderly this time and circled his penis inside me without going deeper. Was it *all the way* in? I felt I didn't know my vagina at the time and that he would know it better. He was in control, and I felt better about what we were about to do.

He inched in a little more each time through the kissing and touching. He was gentle. I trusted him. Eventually, he began to move faster, and his breathing became rapid. I felt like I was splitting inside. It hurt. It felt good. I was a jumble of nerves and emotions. My heart was bursting, and my vagina was beginning to feel something I'd never felt. I was having an orgasm from way up inside. From this place, I never felt an orgasm when doing it myself. It was intense and unique. Even through the pain, I felt euphoria beyond what I thought possible. This feeling I was experiencing was what a real orgasm feels like. Had I been having fake orgasms with fake sex? There was a difference. Or was it because it was Michael? Was it different for him—being with me?

He began pushing harder and faster, and we both started to scream for some reason. Then I felt his penis throbbing, pulsating inside me. His body went limp, and all his weight lay over me. He was out of breath. I was out of breath and struggled to breathe with his weight on me.

Finally, he rolled off me, and I took a deep breath. It was real. It had happened. He covered his face and said, "Ah shit. What the hell did I just do?" Was he already regretting it? Why? He turned his head and looked sincerely at me. "I'm sorry, Jill. Are you okay?"

Why was he calling me Jill? I thought I was now his...*baby*. "Yes. Are you mad at me, Michael?"

His hand moved to my face and smoothed my hair away. He smiled, and his eyes crinkled at the corners. "No. I'm mad at myself. That never should have happened."

It hurt when he said that. I didn't want him to have regrets. Bad regrets about me. "Why? I wanted it to happen. And...I wanted it to happen with you. I thought about making love to you for a long time." However, I'd only known him for weeks.

"Really?" He traced my face with his finger. I could smell his cologne. "Why?"

"Why? Because." This was it. I was going to confess my love to him. "Because I love you, Michael."

"Oh, Jill. Don't say that. You'll go to college, meet many new people, and forget all about this old guy." He gave a small laugh.

"No, I won't. It will always be you, Michael." It hurt that he couldn't see us together forever at that moment. I couldn't see anything else.

"I'll remind you of that when I see your beautiful face and gorgeous body flaunting me when I'm an old man, begging to have all your attention because all the young guys now hold your interest."

I rolled over with my head in my hand. I considered his eyes and saw them more beautiful than I remembered. "That will never happen."

He pulled me onto him and hugged me tightly, and my head rested on his chest. "Oh, Jill. You don't know how much you turn me on."

And at seventeen, I thought that was love.

CHAPTER 17

Now

Stepping out of the bathroom, I know Michael is still waiting for me, so I pull on a tank top with flannel shorts. During my bath, I thought about what Tammy said. Michael may have changed. How I knew what it felt like to want someone's love. Had Michael and I switched roles? And now, I was in the driver's seat? I thought of his comment the night we first made love—well, had sex and took my virginity. "I'll remind you of that when I see your beautiful face and gorgeous body flaunting around me when I'm an old man and grey, begging to have all your attention because all the young guys now hold your interest." Were there younger men who wanted my attention?

Food is on the table. Michael stands from his chair and holds his hand when he sees me walk out. "Just took it out of the oven." I don't take his hand and take the chair across. He walks back and pours the wine. "How was your bath?" he asks, pouring wine into his glass.

"It was nice. Thank you."

He looks up, his brow quirks. "You're welcome."

"What did you make…in my kitchen?" I add.

He pulls off the cover to a silver platter centering the table. "Fruited pot roast." The aroma wafts from the steam, and I smell a hint of plum. A savory hunk of roast is covered with carrots and potatoes. I'm impressed, and I should probably say so.

"This…looks amazing."

"A recipe I learned from an old friend." I'm curious who that might be but don't ask. I've known nothing about Michael's life since he left for Seattle. I had to make it that way—stop the consuming. Yet, here he is in my dining room.

I take a bite, and it's to die for. "Tell your friend it's delicious."

He smiles. "I would, except…they're dead."

My mouth stops mid-chewing. "Oh, I'm sorry," I say with a mouthful.

"It's okay. I'm glad you like it. The plums give it a hint of sweetness without overpowering."

"Yes, I thought I smelled plums."

We continue to eat in silence. The light music plays in the background, and Michael smiles at me occasionally. I smile back only out of politeness. I will have to make him leave after dinner. "This was nice of you, Michael. I'll get the dishes so you can get going."

"I'll do the dishes. You relax." How can I relax with him in my house?

I change the subject. "Have you heard from Monica?"

"Yes. She called while you were taking a bath." He must have noticed the look of panic on my face. "She called your phone first. Then mine."

"Oh. You didn't tell Monica you were here, did you?"

"I think she figured it out when I told her you were in the tub."

I drop my fork. "Dammit, Michael. What is she going to think?"

"Jill, she's an adult. She can think what she wants."

I pick up my wine and eye him coldly across the table. I watch the candles reflect and flicker in the glassiness of his eyes. I'm trying to read him. What's he thinking?

He continues to watch me as I sip more of my wine. I set it down but hold the glass against my chest. "Why aren't you going back to Seattle?"

"Because I'm in love with you, Jill."

The thumping of my heart vibrates the wine in my glass, still held to my chest. I can't look away from Michael's haunting stare. How now? After all these years? I ignore his response and say, "Tammy said you went and saw her."

"I did."

"Why?"

"To apologize…for the cancer and everything else."

"Well, everything else I can see. But you didn't give my friend cancer."

"No. I didn't. But I know how it can be," Michael says sadly, taking his wine and breaking the stare. I think of his earlier comment—his friend who is dead. Cancer? "Did you read the card in the bathroom?"

I inhale and answer. "Yes." But that's all I say.

"And?"

I give him an emphatic look of disbelief. "Michael, I'm all out of chances. I've used them all up on you."

"I understand. But I'm not giving up." He's serious. What the hell is going on? Has he forgotten the last twenty years and what he put me through? *He's not giving up?* He couldn't give an ounce of trying back then. I must know.

"What have you been doing all these years in Seattle?"

"Trying to forget about you." Trying? Is he kidding me?

"Well, try became one of your signature words. 'I'm going to try, Jill. I'll try to be a father. I'm trying, Jill.' Like it was such an effort to love us." I get up and pour more wine. He slumps in his chair and watches me as I parade around the dining room, glass in hand. "How'd you think it was for me? I was a young wife and mother, and you were impossible to live with. Yet, it was you who had to try. I wasn't even grown up yet. How do you think it was for me?"

"Awful."

"Yes, Michael. It *was* awful. Why would I want that again?"

"It wouldn't be like that. I want to love you the way I should have back then. I want to do everything I took for granted when you asked. Because you wanted to do them with me, I'd do anything to return that time."

"You hated that time. You told me I was crazy. All my crazy thoughts of us doing romantic things and fighting for a chance to have your attention—how I wanted to live in a storybook. What was so horrible about that? I wasn't asking for the moon. I was asking for your love. And all I ever got back was, *I'm crazy.*"

"Yes. The times you harped me to do things with you and Monica drove me up the wall. I did make fun of your crazy, little storybook life you saw in your head for us. Yes, I did call you crazy." He stands and walks near me. "And you know what?" He softens his voice and says, "I'd give anything to have *crazy* back."

It's what I've been waiting to hear all these years, yet I'm still so angry. And giving in to Michael on his first attempt doesn't sit right with my bitter heart. I could never wrap my head around Michael and wondered why he had to make our life so confusing. That one person that, no matter how much he hurts me, I fight more to have his love. I struggled for years—he doesn't get one day.

"You're the crazy one now, Michael. That ship sailed a long time ago. You taught me that life isn't a book with special moments filled with love and happy-ever-after's. And it took me a long time to figure it out. But I did figure it out. Once you were gone, I learned not to define myself as something you didn't want. But as something you could have had. And once I didn't have to compete with the entire universe, my world came into view. And I no longer saw you as something I was reaching for. Life is a balance between holding on and letting go. My heart finally let go of you, and I could hold onto myself."

He nods and presses his lips, and I watch his eyes blink with sadness. He knows I'm right. He knows I was crazy for him. But he turned my crazy love into a mockery of a delusional world I created for myself. "You're the delusional one now, Michael. Do you *really* expect me to let you jump into my arms when you spent every minute of our life together, throwing me out of yours?"

"No. But as I said, I will not give up on us as long as I have breath. Yes, I'm crazy; crazy for you. But I'm not delusional. For once in my life, everything is so clear. I love you, Jill. As far as the universe— you're mine."

I can't take the look in his eyes. Guilt burns in my belly, eating its way up like a monster with sharp teeth. I'm right, dammit. I am.

"I know what you're thinking. And you're right. I don't deserve the life you wanted for us. But I will die trying. I'm not giving up. I know you're calloused to the word."

"Michael, thanks for dinner. But you need to leave. Leave this town and return to Seattle or wherever you came from. It will be a useless cause to stay here. If you never give up, I will have no choice but to build higher boundaries."

He steps away. "Let me do the dishes before I leave."

"No, Michael—now."

He steps forward and kisses me on the cheek. "I'll leave tonight. But I won't be leaving town. Never, Jill. Tell Tammy I'll be thinking of her."

"I will. Thank you."

He walks to the front door and looks at me again before opening it. "So sorry for everything. Get some rest. Bye." He walks out, and when the door clicks shut, I press my eyes. I had to do it. I must protect myself. I've worked too hard.

Walking over to the door, I hear his Toyota leave and turn the lock. Shit! I forgot to ask for the key.

•   •   •   •   •

Despite everything last night, I slept like a baby. I think it was the therapeutic, emotional baggage I dumped on Michael—closure. There's a pep in my step this morning as I walk into the hospital with new resolve. Tammy is going to be okay. Michael will get the drift and leave. And Monica called early this morning. She and Jordan are back from Paris, and I can breathe. Tonight, they will be celebrating dinner in their new home. She'd ask me to come by and join them. I couldn't be happier.

Walking to my station, I find a vase full of pink and white carnations sitting on the desk. Curious, I read the name *Jill*. Of course,

Michael. I won't keep them, but it will brighten a patient's room. I might as well read the card before throwing it away.

Pulling out the card, I find I was wrong. The flowers weren't from Michael. They are from Tammy and Ryan.

Jill,
We love you,
Tammy & Ryan

Feeling stupid and angry with myself, thinking they were from Michael, I place the card back into the slot and text Tammy. *Love you too. How are you feeling today?*

Tammy: *Not bad. I'm a little tired. How's Michael?*

Me: *You are in trouble.*

I send the text and feel the smile pressing at the corners of my lips. Tammy's only response is the *'what'* emoji.

Before sliding my phone back into my scrubs pocket, I quickly text Monica.

Me: *What should I bring tonight?*

Monica: *Your seven-layer salad. Jordan's making spaghetti.*

Me: *Thumb-up emoji.*

I finish with three Ambulatory patients, clock out two hours early due to low census, and head to my car. One rose lies across my windshield, and a note awaits me under the wiper.

Jill,
How was your day? Tell me everything about yourself that I have missed. I really want to know. I'm crazy in love with you. I will never give up on my fairytale life with you.
Love, Michael

CHAPTER 18

Then

Tammy was the only person I told that Michael and I had sex, and she was now eager to lose her virginity to Ryan. We did take pride in still being virgins, but we always said if the right guy came along, that's who we would lose it to. Since mine was with Michael, I was glad that Ryan would be hers.

It had been a month since Michael and I had sex for the first time. Now we had sex every time I came over. I enjoyed it more each time, and he taught me things about myself I didn't know. For example, when I sat on him, I was in control, and my orgasms were stronger. I hadn't the need to masturbate because nothing compared to the real thing with Michael. He'd bought more condoms, and we used them each time until the birth control that Tammy and I got from Planned Parenthood would kick in. I hadn't started mine yet because I was to start the last day of my next period. Tammy had started hers when she had her period.

I couldn't wait to spend my first paycheck on Michael. I picked out a manly necklace at the mall with a gold nugget flatted on the backside. And I did what I had wanted to do. I engraved: Love, Jill.

Michael was eager to get home on the days I came, and he wouldn't work over. He would leave me a sweet note telling me how he missed me and couldn't wait to be together. Michael signed all his notes—Love, Michael. I would have dinner ready and jump into his arms when he walked through the door. Music would be playing— love songs I picked out for us. He called me his beautiful secret, but soon I would turn eighteen. We wouldn't have to hide our love. In some ways, hiding our secret love was exciting. But I wanted to shout it to the world when April came around. A few times, we would fight over April. But he swore nothing was happening, and I had to believe him.

Around our third or fourth time, he wanted to teach me oral sex, and I was a little reserved. But once he showed me how it felt, I enjoyed that just as much. I loved the way he moved his hands in my hair when I went down on him, and many times, I would look up and hope I had those blow-job eyes that April always made look so sexy. His eyes would roll back, and I knew I was doing right, pleasing him. He would tell me how unbelievable I was and that he loved the way I made him feel when we had sex. Michael said he was glad I was his first because he could teach me all the things he liked, and I was on a sexual journey of self-discovery with him as my teacher.

I loved to watch the necklace I bought bounce off his chest when I rode him on the couch. The way it would hang down and bounce on my face when he made love to me on top.

Sex was amazing, and I loved it. And I knew it was because I had such an excellent and handsome teacher. I couldn't get enough of Michael, and once, he told me the same in one of our passionate lovemaking. "I can't get enough of you, Jill."

It was Friday night, and Tammy and I were doing one of our *'I'm staying with her; she's staying with me' things*. I was going to spend my first night with Michael, and she and Ryan had arranged a place to stay—some older friend of Ryan's with his own place.

When the door opened, I was on my highest Michael-cloud-number-nine, preparing lasagna and a Greek salad. I was playing Lonestar on his stereo "Amazed" because it was the song playing on the radio the first time I saw Michael. It couldn't have been more perfect. I ran over and jumped into his arms.

"I couldn't wait to get home." We kissed in between sentences.

"I couldn't wait either." I kissed him.

"I thought about you all day." He kissed me.

"Really? You're always on my mind," I said and gave him another kiss. Our playful banter would continue every night. But there was never the *I love you* spoken. I wanted to say it. I had tried to say it. And many times, it was on the tip of my tongue. But I was going to wait until after he said it first.

"It smells great. What are we having?"

"Lasagna, minus the garlic bread." He questioned me with a look. "I didn't want to have garlic breath." True, I knew that the sauce had garlic in it, but it wouldn't be as strong as what garlic bread would have been. "And Greek salad," I said.

He carried me across the room and said, "You're going to make somebody a great wife someday." Why would he say *somebody*? I wanted to be his wife.

"I don't want to be somebody's wife," I said, and before I could get out 'because I want to be your wife.' He said….

"Smart girl. Marriage is overrated." How would he know? He wasn't married. I didn't respond anymore on the subject, and we finished dancing to Lonestar. I was still in his hold, my legs around his waist.

"I'm going to shower first before we eat, okay?" he said as he began to unknot his tie.

"Sure. Everything is ready." We kissed, and he left for the shower.

Later, he returned in jeans and a T-shirt—the Ball State T-shirt I remembered him wearing that first day. I would always shower when I first arrived, and sometimes, we would shower together after sex.

I loved how he looked in wet hair and would run my hands through it. I could touch him now, as much as I wanted. Because he was mine and I was his. I wonder if he ever got jealous of guys from school that I would sometimes talk about. If he did, he never showed it. But the minute April's name would come up—it took all my power not to blow our cover. Once, after our lovemaking, I asked about the girls in his box—the pictures I found. He told me they were just friends from high school, and he hadn't seen or heard from them since. I asked him about Montauk, and when I did, he slowly turned around and asked how I knew. That's when I confessed to reading the back of the pictures.

"Montauk," he said with a smile, and I could tell it was something special. I became jealous. I tried not to show it.

"Well? Are you going to tell me?" I asked.

We were still lying on the bed, naked, and he said, "What do you think of when I say this apartment?" I thought of him and said: Michael. "How about this bed?" My answer was still: Michael. "Hmm," he said. "What about me and you and this bed?" When I thought of him and me in this bed, I thought of us—having sex. Then it hit me.

"That's where you lost your virginity," I said.

"And hers, too."

It now angered me that I didn't have someone in my past to make him jealous. But when he told me I was special because he was my one and only, I was glad I had never been with another.

He poured the wine, and we sat at the table. Candles warmed and flickered with every meal, and music set the room's cadence. It was always romantic, whatever song was playing. We only watched TV a few times—most of the time, we spent having sex and holding each other afterward. I was in love. We were in love. And tonight, I was going to say it no matter what.

After dinner, we set the dishes in the sink, and he chased me to the bedroom. "This is what I've been waiting for all day," he said, picking me up and throwing me on the bed. I giggled and began to undress. He pulled off his shirt; his naked chest was always more than I could take. I sat up from the bed, crawled to him, and looked up with my blow-job eyes. I had mastered it, and each time I did it, he said, "Oh, Baby."

Unbuttoning his jeans, I had become less shy and felt secure in being the aggressor. He liked it when I would take him in my mouth, and I loved giving him that look when he watched me. His hands would squeeze in my hair, and he would moan and breathe heavily. I liked the way I affected him.

"I want to be inside you, Jill," he said, pushed me down on the bed, and took off his jeans. Before putting on the condom, he went down on me, and his tongue lapped and circled the area he called my clit. I never heard that name before. But when he said it, it sounded raw and dirty, and I liked it. He could make me come several times, and he said that it was rare that I had been the only woman who had multiple orgasms with him. I tried not to think of the other women when he said that and focused on the compliment he meant for me. I gave him credit because I could never make myself come twice.

I came hard, and he began to climb me and said, "I want to fuck you." His voice was harsh, and I could smell my arousal on his face. His penis, now his cock or dick, he wanted me to call it, pushed inside me. Penis sounded too much like a health class, he once had said. I stopped him and told him to grab a condom.

"Jill, aren't you on the pill now?"

"No, I haven't got my period yet," I said. I had told Michael about when the nurse at Planned Parenthood said to start taking them. And even after that, use condoms for another month. And we had used condoms for a month. For once, I wished my damn period would come.

He gave a disgruntled sigh and reached for the drawer, pulling out the condom. He wasn't happy having to stop and put it on, and I hated that it killed the excitement. But then, seconds later, we continued as the hot lovers that we were. In a way, I liked the fact he didn't want to use condoms and told me he wanted me like our first time—raw, spontaneous. He said it's like that first high you can never get back. But for me, it was better each time because I was learning about him and sex and myself.

He didn't come until I came again. He would watch my face and tell me to come. And I think it was in the way he commanded me to come that excited me, and then I was done. As soon as I said, 'I'm coming,' he would smile big and tell me, 'Yes.'

We both came, and he fell on top of me like he always did when he was on top. I loved the time it gave me to pet his hair and caress his back. He kissed me down my neck and my breasts. Sometimes, he would fall asleep, and I would feel his heart beating as it slowed down from our passionate love. We created this passionate cloud, and I wanted to stay—here under Michael's embrace forever.

We fell asleep for maybe twenty minutes, and when he woke, he picked me up and carried me to the shower. Though he showered before dinner, it had become part of our lovemaking ritual. I wished he had a tub so I could lay against his chest. But we would take turns washing each other. It was the most romantic thing one could do for another after lovemaking. I was thankful he wasn't one of those *'wham bam, thank you ma'am'* guys. He took pleasure in touching and washing me after our hard lovemaking. I loved how the water would run down our bodies and into our mouths when we kissed. Everything with Michael was enhanced, and life was abundant with pleasure. Nothing would ever be mundane in our lives. And how true that would turn out to be.

After our shower, I would wear one of his T-shirts or sometimes wear the shirt he had just taken off from work. It smelled like him and work, and I imagined how his office would smell. I asked him if he would take me to his work so I could see his office and what he did. "I'll take you tomorrow. No one will be around. Maybe we could have sex in my cubicle."

"You don't have your own office?"

"Nope. Not yet. Hopefully soon. But Whirlpool is just a stepping stone for me."

I became worried he was going to leave. Would he take me with him? "What do you mean? Are you moving up in the company?"

"I'll work up to as much as I can. Until then, I'll always be looking."

"Where did you want to go? You just got here."

"My sites are set on Boeing."

"The airplane?"

"Yes. Aviation or aerospace is my true interest." I couldn't blame him. Big jets and rockets would always be more impressive than washing machines or refrigerators.

"Where's Boeing? Where's it located?"

"The headquarters are in Chicago." Chicago wouldn't be that far from here. I could take the train and see him until we could be together forever. Depending on when he left. "But I want to work in aviation engineering, and that's in Seattle."

Seattle? "When would you go?"

"I need to get at least a year with Whirlpool first." I was then relieved. I would be out of high school and could attend college somewhere in Seattle. I would need to start looking at their nursing programs.

"So, you're spending the night with me, huh?" he said teasingly, wrapping me inside his towel.

"Want me to make you breakfast in the morning?"

"I want to fuck you in the morning," he said. I didn't always like the term he used when addressing our lovemaking, but when we were in the middle of sex, and he said it, it did turn me on. I kissed him on the lips and pulled on his dress shirt, which he had taken off before his first shower. "I like you in this," he said, kissing me tenderly. I almost told him I loved him then.

As he was pulling on briefs and night pajama pants, he asked, "Why haven't you started your birth control pills yet?"

"I haven't had my period yet," I said, and even my periods were something I could discuss with him without embarrassment.

"When are you due to start?"

I tried to think because I had no reason to keep track of them. I was always regular, and when it was time, I just started. "Any day now. But if it doesn't start by Sunday, I'll start taking the pills."

He walked over, dropped to his knees, tucked his head under the shirt I was wearing, and kissed me down there. "And please don't make me wear a condom for another month. I love this pussy," he said.

I wrapped my hands around his head, entrapping him under the shirt. "And I love you," I said it. If he loved my pussy, that meant he loved me. Right? He didn't move from under my shirt, and I feared what that meant. Maybe he didn't hear me or was thinking about his answer. But that was one thing I learned at seventeen: to tell someone you love them and waiting to hear it back is like listening for an echo that never comes.

CHAPTER 19

Now

After leaving the hospital, I make another run to the grocery store. I'm unsure if I have all the ingredients for the seven-layer salad to bring to Jordan and Monica's. I'm so excited to see her and can't wait to put my arms around her and Jordan. I hope she has lots of pictures of Paris. I'm shaking. I'm so excited.

I park and sprint to the doors as heavy rain falls and splashes from below. I'm soaked and breaking my rule—never wear scrubs in public. But I wasn't expecting the dinner invitation, or I would have packed clothes. Oh, well. Anything for Monica.

Grabbing a basket instead of a cart, I head to produce and slip on the wet floor. "Jill?" I look up, and there is Michael, standing in the wine section, holding a bottle of red. He returns the wine on the shelf, runs over, and helps me. "Are you okay?"

Dammit! "Yes. My shoes are wet from the rain. I'm fine." His arms are still around me, and I look around to see who else witnessed my embarrassment. "I shouldn't have been running."

Still in his arms, he retrieves the basket from the floor. "Was anything in it?" he asks, looking around the floor.

"No. I just got here. I was heading to pick up some fresh lettuce for dinner."

"To Monica and Jordan's?"

What? Don't tell me he knows about it. "Yes, she called this morning—invited me for spaghetti."

"Me too. I'm bringing wine. Isn't it red that goes with pasta?"

I stare at him incredulously. "Yes," I say, and my demeanor sounds broken.

"We can go together. I'll pick you up."

"No, Michael." I regain composure from my silly slip and rip the basket from his hand. "Excuse me." I'm cautious about taking my first step and then gradually working up to a swift pace.

"It's not a problem. I'd think it'd be great to go together…Jill," he hollers as I carefully flee away. I need to find another grocery store. However, Martins is the only one in this town. And dammit. What's Monica trying to pull? I shouldn't go. But I want to see her. Well, shoot. Maybe he will be different with Monica and Jordan around. Michael will have to put his emotions on hold. It was never a problem when we were married. And besides, he'll have to feel like a complete outsider during the conversation—knowing nothing about our last twenty years.

I squeak through the aisles—wet shoes and gather the rest of my items. I don't spot Michael at any checkout. So, hopefully, he's left, and I run through the U-scan and back out the door. The rain is still coming down in sheets, but I run for it, only to stop as soon as I get to my car. Or what used to be my car.

"I'm sorry, ma'am. Is this your car?"

"Ah…yes. Oh, my God!" The front end of my car is smashed and mangled, with one headlight hanging out and the other down on the ground. But the jacked-up 4x4 pulling away from my car is just fine. "What the hell happened?"

"I'm really sorry, Miss. I didn't see your car back there."

"Well, of course not. Why in the hell do you have to have such a big truck? It's Michigan, for peat's sake. Not the Alaskan Tundra."

"Can we exchange insurance cards?" he asks.

"Why would you need mine? Your truck is fine." He pulls a small piece of paper from his wallet, now drenched from the rain. I reach for it, and my groceries spill out of my bag. "Dammit."

"What's happened?" I'm covered with an umbrella and look to find Michael.

"He totaled my car. Oh, God!"

"I'll take care of this, Jill. Go sit inside my car." His Toyota runs beside us while he picks up the fallen groceries and then leads me around the other side. "Are you okay?"

"I am. My car's not." He gives an understanding smile and wipes the wetness from my face.

"Stay here," he says and closes the door. Before walking back, he pulls out his cell. A police car arrives in less than five minutes and takes down the report. Michael returns to get my license and the information needed for the report. And then, a tow truck shows up. Like he said, he took care of it.

"Your car is being towed to Stafford's Body Shop. Not sure if they'll total it."

I lay my head against the window and cover my face. "Oh, God. Now, what am I going to do?"

"You can use my car." I give him a look that says, 'Are you serious?'. "Or, I can take you everywhere."

"Oh. You would love that," I say condescendingly.

"I definitely would." His smile is genuine.

"You caused this to happen."

"What? I made that truck back into your car?"

I eye him suspiciously. "I can't prove it. But somehow, you're involved."

He laughs. "Jill, you're too cute. You know that?"

I'm soaked to the bone; my hair is wet, and I'm still in scrubs. And Michael says I'm cute? Now he sounds like high school Michael. "Just take me home," I sigh and lean my head against the window.

We pull into my drive, and he says, "I can just stay here while you get ready to go to Monica's."

"No. Why would you?"

"Because you don't have a car."

Great. I have no choice now other than to ride together. "Fine," I say, remembering I forgot the garage door opener. "Shit."

"What?"

"My…" I'm about to say when my garage door begins to open.

"Here. I grabbed it when getting your registration."

"And when were you going to tell me? Never mind." I reach for the groceries in the back and run into the garage. And when I do, he pulls his Toyota inside."

"Why didn't you wait?" he says, getting out of the car. I don't answer and go inside, dropping my groceries on the counter.

I quickly shower, change into a blue tunic T-shirt dress, and run some gel through my hair. It will be curly tonight—no time for a blow-dry and flat iron.

Michael semi-prepared the salad with a large bowl of lettuce, with the other ingredients neatly set on the counter. "I started it for you. Wasn't sure of the rest," he says with his head in the fridge.

"Just make yourself at home in my kitchen, why don't you?"

Shutting the refrigerator door, he glances up to say something but then stops. "Wow! I like that dress on you."

I should thank him, but don't and begin with the salad. While I'm chopping this and mixing that, he continually wraps me in his arms and whispers sweet sentiments in my ear. It's weird and uncomfortable. I turn around with the knife. "Watch it."

He smiles and backs up with his hands in the air. "Can't help it," he says.

He winks, and before he can catch me smiling, I turn around and say, "Be useful and wash the dishes. No woman ever shot a man in the back for doing dishes."

"Yes, Ma'am," he says in my ear and kisses my neck. It's all too weird.

•　　•　　•　　•　　•

Monica's smile is all too diabolic as Michael and I walk through the door together. "My car was totaled," I say, walking straight to the kitchen with the salad.

"Oh my God. Mom, were you hurt?"

"No. I wasn't even in it. Come here," I say, taking Monica in a big hug and repeatedly kissing her cheeks. "I don't want to talk about me. I want to know all about Paris."

Michael walks in behind me, and Monica breaks our embrace and runs to hug…him. I feel a bit resentment. But wait until there's nothing he can join in with the conversation. "Hi, Dad. Paris was wonderful. Thank you for everything. Jordan and I loved it."

What I'm feeling inside is torn. I've always wished Michael had a relationship with his daughter. But it's also hurtful how he dropped in after all these years and trumped me. But, like I said—just wait.

We have our dinner, and afterward, we take our wine out on the patio. Monica says she has something for each of us. She leaves and returns with two Shutterfly albums. "I had these made," she says with the most wishful smile. I open the book, and my heart melts seeing her wedding pictures. It stops short when I come to the pictures of Michael and me together. To anyone else, we look like a couple in love—held in his arms, his lips resting on my head. I turn the page, and we are holding each other on the dance floor. I look up and spot him looking at me with the warmest smile I've ever seen. I close the book and say, "Monica, these are…very thoughtful of you. You and Jordan look beautiful."

"And so, in love," Michael says but looks at me.

"I hope you like them."

"I do," I say and reach to kiss her cheek. I get up to refill my wine, but Michael intervenes and tops off my glass. I look up and catch his eyes. "Thank you."

"Mom, what are you going to do about your car?"

"I can pick you up tomorrow for work, Jill," Michael says.

"Oh, Mom doesn't work on Fridays," Monica informs him, and his eyes show a bit of disappointment.

"I don't know if they'll total it. But I need to get a rental by tomorrow."

"I can take you wherever you need to go," Michael says.

"I'm sure you could. But I wouldn't want to interfere with your plans." He only smiles at me. I want to ask more about Paris, but that only involves Michael. So, I bring up another topic. "Your old piano teacher was at the wedding. Did you notice her?" Michael has no idea how beautifully Monica plays the piano.

"Mrs. Reese? No, I didn't see her." My eyes slide to Michael as I take another sip of wine.

"She didn't know who Michael was. Sorry," I say, looking at Michael. "I'm not used to you being in the room." Bam! Take that.

"I'd love to hear you play, sweetheart," he says. "I've listened to a few of your recitals on Facebook. You're very talented."

"Thanks, Daddy."

Daddy? How long have they been corresponding?

Throughout the rest of the evening, the conversation is surprisingly comfortable, and Michael is fully engaged. He doesn't seem lost on any topic and appears genuinely interested. He's...happy. Involved, and it's...weird. I don't know what I'm feeling or how to feel.

I'm ready to go and tell Monica and Jordan thank you for dinner and that everything was beautiful. Michael does the same. We kiss our daughter goodbye and leave for Michael's car. He smiles when we get into the car, and I give him a polite smile his way. Then, I fake a fuss with the seatbelt. That only backfires when he comes to my rescue and buckles my belt. "That was wonderful. Wasn't it?" he says, inches from my face.

"Yes...I suppose it was." I try desperately to ignore him, but he remains with us face-to-face. I have no choice but to say, "Michael, what are you doing?"

"Gazing into the most gorgeous eyes I've ever seen." Again, I'm speechless and search for another tactic. "I need to get home."

"Which home? Mine or yours?"

"Mine."

"Then I'll stay with you."

"No, you won't."

"Then you stay with me." Before I can say no, his lips are on mine. I don't move and let him kiss me. I don't know what has come over me. But I must make it stop.

"Please, Michael. Stop." But that only makes his kiss more intense. For a second, I'm back in high school, feeling that lightheadedness and heaviness in my chest. Without a thought, my hands are in his hair, and I hear that moan from deep down inside him, like I heard when we first kissed on his couch.

"Come home with me, Jill," he says without leaving my lips.

"Michael, I can't." I'm losing air, and my lungs are about to crash.

"Please. I love you, Jill."

Why is he doing this? But better yet, why am I letting him affect me this way? "If I do, will you promise to stop this?"

"Maybe I'll stop pressuring you, but I'll never stop loving you. Just come home with me. And let's see what happens. If it all goes bad, I promise to take you home. Please?"

The kissing hasn't stopped, and the conversation is spoken on our lips. I can't reason with Michael's lips all over me for a second. "Yes. Fine."

"Thank you," he says and gives a few more reassuring kisses before starting the car and leaving. I hope Monica and Jordan weren't watching. But then I remember the dark tint on his windows.

He holds my hand tightly in his and drives with the other, glancing over every so often with lovesick eyes. He hasn't said a word, lifts to kiss my hand repeatedly, and rubs his face with it. The rain is still beating on the windows, and the wipers screeching across the window is the only indication that this is not a dream. I should stop this. I need to stop this. But somehow, breaking this silence would almost be like purposely destroying art. Something is building and driving this moment. It's scary, exciting, and beautiful.

He pulls into a drive that must be his and doesn't even bother with the garage. He races over, pulling me out of the car. He doesn't yet set me down—carries me to the door. We are soaked, and as he fumbles with the lock, we kiss like it's our last day to be alive.

The door opens, and he carries me in, kicking the door shut with his foot. Setting me to my feet, I grope with the buttons of his shirt as he lifts my hair and kisses my neck. My dress is pulled over my head, and I'm grabbed firmly in his arms. Neither of us wants to break this moment. I fumble with the belt of his pants. He picks me up and carries me to his bedroom. Once there, I must stop. But once he starts kissing and massaging my breasts, I can't.

Somehow, he has removed his pants, and I'm too drunk on lust to have even noticed as he pulls my panties down off my legs. Within seconds, he's on me, and I feel his swollen erection that I couldn't see in the dark. "I love you, Jill. I love you, Jill," he says over and over. It's like he's still trying to convince me. I can't stop it. I'm too far in and feel him enter me.

"Ah, Michael," I cry out. I say it without thought. I say it with pain and anger and…love. But it can't be love.

"Come first, Jill. Please, come for me," he begs, almost demands. "I've missed you so much." He's crying. He thrusts into me hard, and he's…crying. "I'm so sorry for everything. I need you, Jill. I need you to forgive me. Please." His chest heaves with each thrust and each sob. It's the strangest thing and yet the most erotic.

I'm about to come and force myself to say the word. "I…forgive you, Michael."

"Ah, yes," he breathes into my ear. His hot breath runs down into my being. I come and strangle out his name.

"Michael." He knows I'm coming. He knows the sound I make and the way I move. He knows because he taught me.

He loses himself and comes hard like it was our first time again. He rides his orgasm out slowly as he kisses me tenderly. "That's not how I had it planned, but I'm not sorry," he says as we both come up for air and slowly come down. And when we do…where do we go from here?

CHAPTER 20

Then

Positive! NO! It couldn't be. We only had unprotected sex one time—
the first time we had sex. And I got pregnant? I couldn't believe this
was happening.

Once I told Tammy that I still hadn't started my period and hadn't
started my birth control, that's when it hit me—us. Our eyes widened,
and we ran to the drugstore.

My hand trembled as I stood with the stick in my hand, staring
down at the plus sign. Tammy was talking, but I couldn't hear her. I
was in such shock. What were my parents going to say? What would
Scott say? What would Michael say?

"Jill? Jill, talk to me. What are you going to do?"

"Ah...Oh, God. I can't believe this. I never even got a chance to
use the birth control pills. How could I have been so stupid for this to
happen?"

Tammy braced my shoulders, forcing me to look at her. "Jill, it
takes two to make a baby. Why didn't Michael use a condom the first
time?"

"He was out...and things were happening so fast." Everything was
crashing down. I no longer looked at our first sexual encounter as a
romantic, heat-of-the-moment, epic love, world-changing, heart-
stopping happenstance. It was world-changing, alright, but in an
entirely different direction.

"Are you going to tell your mom?"

"Should I tell Michael first?" I was looking at Tammy for answers.

"How do you think he'll take it?"

"I don't know. Michael has never even said he loves me. He loves sex but has never said the actual words to me. Even after I told him I loved him."

I walked over to the bed and threw myself down. "Oh, God, what's my father going to say? No one knows I'm seeing Michael. That makes things worse. And he's ten years older than me."

"Well, at least he has a good job. He already has his master's degree. He'll be able to support you and the baby."

"He doesn't even like marriage. He's made some derogatory remarks about it." I rolled over and covered my head with the pillow. "Tammy, what am I going to do?" I cried.

She rubbed my back with loving caresses as I cried into the pillow. How I wished I could go back in time. Stop everything and make Michael wait. But would he have waited for me?

"I think you should tell Michael first. It's his baby, too, and then you both can decide together. You made this baby together; you'll solve it together."

The more she said baby and ours and together, my heart softened a bit, and the other side of reality flittered inside me. Michael and I had made a baby. We were going to be parents. And this would be something that would forever connect us. Would this make him love me? Would he be able to say the words? I still loved him, and even with this tragedy, I think it made me love him even more.

"You're right. I'll tell Michael tonight," I said and sat up. She wiped my tears; that was the first time Tammy kissed my cheek. We hugged; even if I didn't have Michael, I would always have Tammy.

•   •   •   •   •

I was sitting on the couch, biting my nails, and waiting for Michael to come home from work. Everything felt different than it had been when I'd been waiting in the past. I'd be scared one minute and feared how this would all go when I told him. The next minute, I'd be elated with happy thoughts of Michael and I becoming a family. Our little family and I would feel a smile forming on my lips. I started to picture baby stuff lying around—toys, bottles, blankets, and diapers. I saw Michael on the floor, cooing baby talk to our child. Would he want a boy or a girl? I had already formed a happy-ever-after story, but it would depend on Michael. And that was my first mistake.

He came through the door, and the look on my face stopped him in his tracks. I saw the fear in his eyes like he already knew. But he couldn't have. Only Tammy knew, and she wouldn't tell a soul.

"What's wrong, Jill? Have we been found out?"

That's what his look was for—fear that someone had seen us together. But I was not too fond of that look either. Maybe if he looked as if he was glad—we didn't have to hide it anymore. But it wasn't. And what I had to say wouldn't make it any better.

"I'm…pregnant, Michael."

He didn't move from the door. It was still open, and I feared he'd run out and never return. "What!"

"I took a pregnancy test this morning. It's positive."

Finally, thank God, he shut the door and covered his face. "Fuck!" That is what he said. Fuck. Not, 'We'll make it work. It'll be okay. I'm going to take responsibility for our baby.' Nope. Just fuck.

I began to cry harder, and he never came to comfort me. I needed him, and he never came. "Michael, what are we going to do?" I needed him to answer. I needed him to hold me.

"I thought you said you'd go to Planned Parenthood."

"I did. That's where I got the birth control pills. We got pregnant the first time."

"Oh no. Not we. You got pregnant. You should have prepared for this." He was preaching at me as if it was all my fault. Was it? Did I seduce him? No more than he seduced me with his kiss and mixed signals—which turned out to be signals that he did want me. "You said you'd go to Planned Parenthood. I took that as you'd get an abortion if you got pregnant. After that, I took on the responsibility of using condoms until you got on the pill."

"But, Michael?"

"Don't *but* Michael me. Have the abortion, and I'll pay for it. That's me still being responsible."

My anger rose, and I stood from the couch and began screaming. "You're the responsible one? You're an adult. Twenty-seven years old, Michael. I'm only seventeen."

"What the hell does that mean? Is it all my fault? You're nothing but a fucking prick tease. Flaunting your sweet ass around me like candy. What the hell did you think I'd do?"

How dare he. But he was right. I did flaunt myself. I did want him to notice me. This fight was when it all began, and Michael instilled doubt in my head. "Stop it. I loved you. I still love you, Michael." I was crying and screaming my love for him. But his never came for me.

"Jill, sex isn't love. It's just fucking and having a good time. Don't confuse it." I fell to my knees, waiting for him to pick me up and apologize. I'd be waiting for a long time.

He stomped past me, and I heard the bedroom door slam. Even though I knew all this was not good, I was relieved he didn't storm out and drive away. But it was his place, and it meant I was to leave.

I slowly got up and looked at the apartment door, then his bedroom door. Two doors, two choices. Either door I chose would alter my life forever, and I picked the wrong door.

I walked to his bedroom door and cracked it open. He was lying on the bed, staring up at the ceiling. Part of me felt sorry for ruining his day. I used to be the reason for the bright smile on his face, but it wasn't exactly like I was having a grand time. I would spend the next few years convincing myself that I could make him happy again, and my happiness would sit on the shelf.

I waited for him to tell me to come in. I expected him to look at me and hold out his hand, and I'd come to lay on his chest. He did turn his head and glanced at me. We stared into each other's eyes, and I saw an entirely different person. What had happened to us in the last month? We used to be glued to each other. We used to laugh and sing and kiss each other. Would we ever get it back? Or did it end here?

"Michael?" I whispered. He turned his head away, and I knew what it meant. There were no more mixed signals. He didn't want his baby or me. It was clear. I was on my own, and before I walked away and shut his door, I said, "I'm at least going to ask my mom." I needed to hear him say one thing, just one thing before I left.

"About the abortion? Jill, don't tell her. It will just disrupt everyone. It only needs to concern us." For once, he had included himself.

"Maybe she'll think I should give the baby up for adoption."

"But then she'll still know. You say you love me, right?"

His question gave me hope when he asked. "Yes, Michael, I do."

"Then don't tell anyone. I could get in so much trouble with you only being seventeen. I could lose my job. My career would be over."

Guilt is a powerful motivator, and he was right. Either way, he would need his job, especially if I had the baby. "Well, I'm going to tell her. I have no choice. She won't want me to have an abortion."

"What about you? You'll be eighteen soon, and you can make your own choice. This baby is going to affect you too, Jill."

We were having a real conversation now, discussing it out loud. "Why can't we keep the baby—raise it together? You have a good job."

"Jill, I didn't work hard to get a good job. I want a career—a future. I never saw or planned marriage or kids in it. If you tell your parents and keep the baby, I'm going to have to marry you."

My heart stopped. Michael was giving us options. He was considering marriage—and me and our baby. Sure, even though he said, 'have to marry,' we could get back to us again. It would be the same. He would see that. I would be the best wife ever. And I would be a great mother—mother to his child.

"I'm going to tell her," I said and left his apartment.

•　　•　　•　　•　　•

There I stood at the justice of the peace, holding Michael's hands and looking into his eyes. His left eye was black from where Scott had punched him. All the commotion of the last few weeks would be worth it once they pronounced us husband and wife, and I'd be Jill Danforth. Dad told me how ashamed he was of me and that I should go live with his sister and come back after I gave the baby up. Mom cried for hours, saying how she wanted so much more for me—not to end up like her. Was she not happy with us—Dad, Scott, and me? Scott and Michael were no longer friends. And the only people at my courthouse wedding were Tammy and Ryan as I stood in my best dress—not white or even a wedding. Mom said it wouldn't be proper since I was pregnant. We had all taken the day off school, and Michael took a half day from work. Afterward, he would drop me off at the apartment and return to work. How romantic.

We were officially man and wife, with no rings. Michael said it was just a piece of paper, and rings were unnecessary. But I still wanted one. When the lady said, "You may kiss the bride," Michael gave a quick peck on my lips, and I stood there with my eyes closed, thinking there would be more. I was wrong. Tammy hugged me, and we left the courthouse, and that was it. I was married…and I was Michael's wife. Somehow, I thought it would feel differently.

He dropped me off at our apartment and went back to work. Tammy stayed and helped me unpack my stuff. I didn't have much to add that would dress it up. Because let's face it. I was a teenager, and my décor was posters, shoes, and purses. And even then, I didn't have much. But I was determined to make Michael a good wife—and I was going to have his baby. Maybe someday, he'd love us.

Nighttime came, and Michael still wasn't home. Tammy left hours ago, thinking we'd want to be alone. The dinner I prepared, chicken cacciatore, was now cold, and the candles melted away. I couldn't drink the wine and drown my sorrows because I was pregnant. I cried and went to bed—alone.

A loud crash awakened me, and the sound of Michael hollering. "Honey, I'm home." His words slurred, and he was yelling at something he fell over. I sat in bed, waiting for him to enter the bedroom. Finally, he appeared, and he reeked of smoke and alcohol.

"Ah, there she is. My little wife." His eyes were half-closed, half-opened.

"Where have you been?" My voice had anger, but I kept it low. He struggled to get his clothes off, and I got up to help. He fell, and we both went to the floor.

"I was celebrating," he slurred.

"Celebrating?"

"Yup. Guys gave me a bachelor party. And now I'm so fucking horny. Man, there was this stripper, and she was so fucking hot." He laughed between his words, and I tried to push him away. "So, now I want to fuck my wife. Come here. Kiss your husband."

"Get off me," I yelled.

"Oh, don't be like that. You won't be one of those wives, are you?" I pushed him away and went to the couch. I thought he would go to bed, but he came out. Even in his drunkenness, he picked me up with anger and brought me back to the bedroom.

"Leave me alone, Michael."

"You wanted to get married? Well, this is marriage, dear." He removed his belt with force and threw it across the room. I crawled up against the headboard and told him to stop. He removed the rest of his clothes and then came at me. "Take off your clothes, or I'll rip them off."

"NO! Michael, stop it." It didn't matter because, within seconds, he had my T-shirt off, jerked my panties down, and was on top of me. I held my legs shut, but he pried them open with his knee. We hadn't had sex since I told him I was pregnant, and this was going to be the first. And it was our wedding night.

He was now inside me, and for the first time, I hated it. He kissed my mouth, and I tasted cigarettes and whiskey. "You're a fucking prick tease," he said as he rocked in and out of me. I began to cry, wanting my simple teenage life back. I would even sacrifice the Michael I knew before to forget this moment.

He came in a few seconds, but it felt like a lifetime. When he satisfied himself, he dropped on top of me and passed out. As I tried to get out from under him, he puked all over the bed. I went to the couch and curled up in a ball, rocking back and forth, and cried uncontrollably. I wanted to go home. I wanted my mom. But I was now committed to the drunk, passed-out man in the bedroom—*my husband.*

CHAPTER 21

Now

I wake next to Michael as he sleeps peacefully beside me, and I carefully slide off the bed, dress, and tiptoe out of the room. We fell fast asleep after the lovemaking, and I regretted what happened last night. Why did I let myself fall into his trap?

The sun is coming up, and I glance around his living room. This place does not look like someone who moved in a week ago. His place is furnished, thoroughly lived-in, and fully decorated with pictures of Monica...*and me.*

I walk over and pick up a framed picture of me strolling on the beach of Lake Michigan. Monica took this of me last summer. I looked down and watched the waves move in and cover my feet. I felt so at peace that day. Monica and I spent the day together, planning her future wedding, and I was proud that she would never know about the wedding I had. I wore a string bikini top and a white lace cover-up wrapped low on my hips. My skin was freshly sunkissed, and the sun shone on my face, with just the side of my profile showing behind a straw beach hat.

"That's my favorite." I turn around and find Michael standing in the doorway of his bedroom. "What were you thinking when that picture was taken?" I don't answer. "Where were you going?"

I set the picture down and look for my purse. "I need my phone. I need to go, Michael."

"Monica said you weren't working today. Why do you need to go?"

"Because, Michael. Last night never should have happened. Why do you have all these pictures of Monica and me, and where did you get them?"

"Monica's Facebook. She permitted me."

"When?"

"When I asked."

I can see I'm not getting anywhere, so I turn to leave. "Did I leave my purse in your car?"

"Yes. But I went out and brought it in. It's in the kitchen."

"When did you do that?"

"Last night, as I watched you sleep."

"How…never mind," I say, looking for my purse in the kitchen. I find another picture of Monica and me together on our vacation to Hilton Head. She was still in high school. I look back at him, pointing at the picture. "This one's old."

"Yes, but it was still on her Facebook."

I spot my purse and dig for my phone. I can't call Tammy. I'm sure she's not feeling well. *Not Monica.* I don't want her to know about this. I decide on an Uber and open the app only to find my phone is dead. Dammit! "You have a charger?"

"Yes. You can use my phone if you need to make a call."

"Could you call me an Uber?"

"Jill, please don't go. Spend the morning with me. I'll make you breakfast. We'll talk, and then I'll take you home…if you still want to go." Why's he so…melodramatic, looking at me with those…eyes?

"Michael, I don't want breakfast. I don't want to stay here. I want to go home to my house—now. As far as talking, this never happened. Monica is not to know about this. It will never happen again, and it shouldn't have happened last night." I don't believe this. After all these years, how did this happen? "I should have never agreed for you to come and walk Monica down the aisle. It was stupid, and I'm ready to wipe this whole thing from my life." As I keep talking, he keeps walking closer with that desperate look in his eyes. The look I didn't recognize at the wedding. "What are you doing, Michael? I said I was ready to go home. Call me an Uber, or I'm going to start walking," I say and notice the picture above his fireplace, now with the sun shining through the window. It's a large canvas of him and me—the one with him kissing me on the forehead from the wedding shots. "What's that doing there?"

He turns. "Isn't it beautiful?"

"It's weird, Michael. That's what it is. What are you? Obsessed?"

"Yes. I'm obsessed with you." He says with no regard. No hesitation. "Not psychotically obsessed. More like…I love you, obsessed. I'm still legally sane."

"No, you're not. You're crazy. You are crazy if you think I'm falling for this. I think it wasn't enough for you to have ripped me open, torn out my heart, filled me with fallacies of a family, and then took off. Oh, no. Somehow, you found out that I got over you. We became just fine, so you're here to finish the job."

"Good. We're talking. I'll put some coffee on." He smiles, pulls the blinds up over the kitchen sink window, and makes coffee. "Wow! Look at the gorgeous sun out there. Let's not waste it and spend the day at the lake."

"Don't you have a job or something to get to? A woman? A…life?"

"No. Just want to be here with you."

"Oh, now I get it. It's all starting to make sense." He looks at me, smiles, and quirks his brows.

"What is?"

"What's going on? You don't have a job. You think you can sleep with me because I'm a sure thing, park your dick at my house until you're back on your feet and some piece of ass comes around. And then zip, you're gone."

"Ouch. That bad, huh?" He sets out two cups. "But you're wrong." He opens a drawer, pulls out a magazine, Forbes, and thumbs through. "That's my company. I can run it from here," he says, handing me the magazine.

Danforth Jet Center. Lead by pilots for pilots. The company is a supplier for Boeing, providing pilot service between Seattle and Gary.

The company is rated as a Fortune 500 company, with Michael Danforth as its owner and CEO. "Well, you finally capitalized upon the mile-high club. I'm not surprised."

He hands me a cup of coffee. "I deserve that. Let's sit outside in the sunshine while you chastise me more."

"Dammit, Michael, I'm serious."

"So am I. I'm sure you have a lot to say. And I need to hear it." I follow him outside to a patio, where he pulls a chair for me. "For you."

"I need to stand."

"Okay, I'll sit," he says and takes the seat. "Spill it. Because I need to hear, and you need to get it out so we can go on." Why's he so agreeable? It's taking all the pleasure out of it.

"Okay. Let's talk about our wedding night." I've struck home. His eyes glaze with sadness, and his chest slightly chokes. He's about to cry.

"Yes," he whispers. "I will always hate myself for that night especially. I've done a lot of wicked things to you, Jill. But that…" He can't finish and covers his mouth with his fist.

"I was just a little girl. Younger than Monica." He chokes. "I can't imagine having something like that happen to her. You were my husband. You were supposed to protect me. Take care of me. Love me. But you didn't. You…." I don't finish. His heavy sobs say it all.

"You had your career. You made it, and I was there taking care of you. I never complained about wanting more out of life. I just wanted you to love me. Love us."

"I know," he whispers. "I never got to experience those things and finish my adolescence. Yes, I became pregnant, and I had to become responsible and grow up overnight. You had your time. Yet, I was the one who suffered."

"I know." His eyes never sway from me as he takes my verbal lashing. I'm shaking, and my words are full of rage and sadness. I don't know if it's helping or hurting me. But now is my time to get closure.

"All I wanted was to make you happy, and I thought that would win me your love. My God, Michael. For you to think that you were the miserable one. After all, my efforts were pointless, and I never gave up. Not once, Michael, did I ever give up. Who left, Michael?"

"I did. I did, and I'm so sorry for the life I gave you and Monica. I know I can say it until I'm blue, but I will never stop saying it."

I turn away. I can't look at Michael's sorrow and don't know why. I should be enjoying this. Finally, I get to say it to his face and not my therapist, who I stopped seeing years ago. At this rate, I'll see her again if I don't get away from him.

He wraps me in his arms from behind and cries in my hair. He's trembling—it's pitiable. He's taking this to heart. Maybe it's his age—losing time and testosterone. "Please forgive me, Jill. Please let me know if I can have another chance. Please tell me we can start again. I promise you everything. My love. The moon. The Stars. Our happy ever after."

We're both crying. My insides ache. Buried hurt for the last twenty years is surfacing—all the pain and sadness and wondering why. I need this. I need this closure, and then I can never see him again. I will sleep like a baby—no more nightmares of the past. The air will smell better. The sun will shine brighter, even on cloudy days. Food will taste better, and life, in general, will be better. I can finally look him in the eyes and tell him the pain he put me through, and then walk away like he never existed.

"You want to hear something that is so messed up?" His eyes are red, and inside, I feel his soul hurting. I don't know why. "Do you remember the last time you used the word *try* that day?" He says nothing but continues looking at me with red, watery eyes. "I was having a happy day…and happy days were hard. Because it meant holding my breath and living on hope, and it would always come crashing down. Bad days had no surprises—no waiting for the floor to drop." I sip coffee and hold the cup close to my chest. "It was after your office Christmas party…the moment in your car." His eyes lighten a little with the thought. "That night, we came home, and you told me you wanted to try and how you messed up so much. I held my breath. I wanted to believe you. On a whim, you took us to Florida on vacation. As much as I tried to enjoy us, I was holding onto hope. You took us to the ocean—the beach. You picked up our daughter…" My lungs ache with pain, and it's a struggle to get my words out. "You set her on your shoulders and walked on the shore. I sat back and just watched with happy sadness. You must have been pretending to fly because you held out your arms, and she did the same. Your white shirt was blowing in the ocean breeze, and Monica's sun-kissed, baby blonde hair tossed around her little shoulders. I watched this tableau of love and wished I *really* had it. I wished…I wished you could have seen how beautiful you were with her on your shoulders. Because maybe then, you would want it. Want us."

"I love you, Jill. I want you. I want us. I wish I could go back and do everything right this time."

"And what would right be, Michael?"

"Give you a wedding. Surprise you with an engagement ring. Watch you walk down the aisle to me. Be there when our baby girl was born. …love you." He takes the cup from between us, sits it on the table, and returns, holding both of my hands. "I'm not the same man, Jill. I want to walk with you in the summer sun. Make a snowman with the first snow of winter. Sit by the fire on cold nights. Sleep on the beach with you."

"I don't think I can do that, Michael. Because I don't think those things exist. Life's not a book. You taught me that. I had to learn to live on faith. Not hope. I can't take that chance."

He holds me. We both cry, and I'm becoming numb. Do I have anything left? Is this it? Am I empty? Empty of Michael?

He holds my face and kisses my forehead, cheeks, and lips. Do I feel him? Or once I empty it all, do I fade away? What's next? "I need to go, Michael. Please, take me home."

He presses his forehead on mine, and his eyes search with longing. "I'll do whatever you want. Just don't shut me out completely. Please." I don't answer because I don't know how. I stare into his sad gaze.

He walks back inside, his shoulders holding the weight of the world. I've never seen a sadder exit as he looks back one last time before disappearing inside. I return to the kitchen, gather my purse and phone, and wait in his car.

I don't look at him when he gets in, and I turn my head and look out the side window. But that doesn't stop him from holding my hand. And…I don't stop him. Am I testing myself to see if I still feel?

"I remember that day. Monica was wearing a little red dress with polka dots. She said, "Let's fly, Daddy. Let's fly." I turn and look at him. He's staring straight ahead. "She wanted to fly with the seagulls because she thought they were angels. She wanted to fly to heaven and see the angels." I watch a tear run down his cheek and feel an ache of guilt. He did remember.

He starts the car, and we continue holding hands until we reach my house. He hasn't let go. And I'm not sure I want him to. There are more questions I want to ask. And so, I do something stupid. "Would you like to come in—so we could talk some more?"

"Thank you," he says, kissing my hand before letting go.

We head inside, and I make another pot of coffee. It is a beautiful morning; maybe we should spend the day at the lake. Maybe. Or perhaps it's my guilt thinking for me.

I pour the coffee and suggest sitting on the back patio where the sun rises on the horizon. Nothing has been said about what happened earlier, and I think he's waiting for me to start.

"Michael, did you ever marry…again?"

"Almost."

Maybe this was the person who died—the one with the pot roast. I don't want to ask, but I need to know if he *wanted* to marry this woman. "The woman I found you with?"

"No, Jill," he quickly says. "It wasn't her. It was a woman I worked with from Boeing. We traveled together and shared the same projects. I thought it was time. Time, I should…commit."

I get up and begin to leave when he stops me. "It's none of my business. I don't need to hear it." He grabs my arms, and I pull away hard, knocking myself unbalanced.

"Please, I would like for you to know."

"Know what, Michael? How you wanted to marry another woman? No, I don't need to know. I've always known that you never wanted to marry me."

"I couldn't marry her because she wasn't you. All I did was compare her to you. And in the end, she couldn't take it anymore. I failed again."

"Why? Why would you do that, Michael?"

"Because I would wake up and she…she would still be in bed."

"Stop it! I don't care to know."

"I missed the smell of morning breakfast you would make. I missed the smell of your fresh shampooed hair, how it would fall on me with your morning kisses and the little notes written on the fridge. I missed the smell of the fabric softener you used or how you would tell me how handsome I looked right before I walked out the door. I missed seeing Monica held on your hip as you cooked dinner or did your homework. I missed the way you served my plate, and you would tell me the stove was hot and not to touch it. The way you made every season special with its décor, celebrating each one. The smell of cucumbers in the summer. The smell of cinnamon in the fall. And Christmas. You made Christmas so magical."

There's hesitation, and I don't know what to say. Because Michael never acknowledged any of those things. He just appeared frustrated and unhappy.

"She was none of those things. And when I would bring them up why she didn't do those things, it would end with a fight about you. She'd tell me she was above being a mousy little wife. And that would make me angry, and I would defend you. Eventually, I found her stalking you on Monica's Facebook. She then saw the beautiful, loving wife I had left and wanted to know why. When I told her that I made the biggest mistake of my life, she left, and I never saw her again. You taught me what a wife is and does. What love is."

Through the tears, a cynical laugh escapes me. "Well, that makes two of us, Michael. I was also almost married again. But you taught me what it's like to have a husband—and I couldn't make that mistake again. It's a shame because he was a wonderful man. He's now married to someone else and very happy. And once again, I lost because of you. You have left me with a bad taste in my mouth and a fractured heart. Not broken, I won't give you that much credit. My heart only beats for one now—myself. It's too risky to take on more. I can't be that person you remember. Because I thought that person was why you left us."

CHAPTER 22

Then

As I sat and cried, I thought of my mother and how she cared for my father, even when he was selfish and self-consumed. My father would apologize in his way, and life would go on as usual. Sometimes, I would overhear my father telling his friends he'd be nothing without her. And at times, he would confess this to her: Is this how it worked? Was it my responsibility to take the brunt of things and focus on his happiness? Someday, Michael would say he couldn't live without me.

I took a deep breath, swallowed back my tears, and went back to the bedroom where Michael lay naked, passed out in his vomit. As I looked at him, it was a disgusting sight, and I could no longer see the beautiful Michael I fell in love with. I had said a vow, though, for better or for worse. I didn't think it would start like this on my wedding night.

"Michael," I whispered. He moaned, and I lightly shook his shoulder. "Come on, Michael, let's get you into the shower. He didn't fight me as I walked him to the bathroom. He was heavy, and I struggled to hold him up as I stepped into the shower. He leaned on me, his head on my shoulder, and I let the water run over us both. "Michael, can you lean against the wall? I'm going to wash you now." His eyes strained to open as he peered at me through bloodshot slits.

"Jill?" he mumbled, and I wasn't sure he knew where we were.

I leaned him against the shower wall and lathered his body with soap. Before I could finish washing him, he slid down and sat on the shower floor. "Come, Michael. Stand up. Let's rinse you." I couldn't get him back up, so I unhooked the portable shower head. I sat on my knees and washed my husband like a pet—lifting his arms and rubbing his hair. He would try to speak a few times, and I couldn't tell if he was grateful or becoming more annoyed.

I pulled him from the shower and walked him to bed, but I needed to change the sheets. I leaned him against the wall, where he slid to the floor, sat while I put new sheets on the bed, and threw the soiled ones into the wash.

Pulling him up, he fell to the bed, and I covered him with a clean blanket. Would he remember this in the morning and be grateful?

•　　　•　　　•　　　•　　　•

I needed to be at school at 8:00 a.m., and Michael was still passed out in bed. I had already showered, blow-dried my hair, and stood over my husband, contemplating how to wake him. I was still furious but desperate for his love. He was not only my husband now but the father of my unborn baby. And despite what happened last night, I wanted us to work.

I bent down and kissed his cheek. "Good morning. I know you don't feel like it, but you must eat to feel better." When Scott came home a little hungover, he would beg me to fix him greasy food and pancakes. He said it helped with nausea. After that, I would make him pay me or tell Mom and Dad. "Are you going to work today? I can't miss class again. I have a test."

His eyes cracked open, and he looked at me like a stranger. "Jill? You're here?" Did he remember and was surprised I stayed? Or did he forget we were husband and wife?

"Yes, Michael. I have your breakfast ready. Can you get up and eat before I leave for school?"

He rubbed his face and moaned. "Oh, God…I feel like shit." Was it from what he did to me? Or just the hangover? "But something smells good."

"Yes, it's your pancakes. Come and eat, so you'll feel better." There was a long pause as we stared into each other's eyes. Mine was full of sadness, his bloodshot. Despite all he had said and done, I wanted to kiss him. I wanted him to know that I still loved him. And so, I gently kissed his lips. As I moved away, his look was sorrowful.

I left the bedroom and waited in the kitchen. I was gathering my books when Michael came walking out, wearing only a pair of shorts. I looked up from my bag and waited for him to speak first. I wanted to hear he was sorry. I wanted to hear he loved me.

I pointed to his plate, and he moved slowly and took his seat. After packing my bag, I poured him a large glass of milk and set it in front of him. He looked up, and I waited. But nothing ever came, and he began eating.

I went to the medicine cabinet, grabbed a packet of Alka-Seltzer, poured a glass of water, and took it to him. Again, he just looked at me, and I wanted us to talk. But I didn't know how. Dating was fun. Hanging out was fun. Why was this so hard? Because I had learned that, all this time, I was the only one falling in love while Michael was only having fun. But it was me taking care of Michael, and it wasn't fun like it had been. Would it ever be again?

I started to walk out the door when he finally spoke. "Jill...I'm very sorry for last night. It will never happen again." I began to cry, and so much emotion came over me. I did the right thing last night. I stayed and helped him. I was a good wife, and I wanted him to know it. "Do you have a few minutes before you have to leave?"

I closed the door and went to sit next to him. I didn't care at that point if I did miss class. My husband needed us to talk. "I've been thinking about us," he said, and I waited. "It's not exactly what we wanted. I get that." I did want to be married to him, but I didn't want it to be like this. "After you graduate, I want you to enroll in college and get your nursing degree—like you said you wanted. I will stick by you and make sure you graduate. After that, we'll go our separate ways—divorce. And people will think we couldn't make it work. I owe you that much."

My heart broke in two, and I felt the bile rising in my throat. My hands shook to the extreme, and I felt like a giant hole had opened. I was falling into it. What would life be like for us if he was only sticking around until I graduated college? What about our baby? Had he even thought about our baby?

"You'll have your degree, able to support yourself. And I will pay the required child support. It's not what I wanted. It will set my goals back, but I won't have people saying I never paid my child support. People get divorced every day, and no one looks down on that. Not paying child support is a different story. That is my arrangement for us."

Arrangement. Our baby and I were an arrangement. He couldn't even say his child; he said his child support. He had no attachment to me or our baby. We were something that sidetracked him from his goals, which was what the sorrowful look in his eyes was for. It wasn't for raping me. It was because his goals were set back. And I wasn't one of them. What about my goals? Maybe I should have told him how much I loved him before I finally said it. Perhaps I should have never told him I wanted to be a nurse. He couldn't love me, so he would help me become a nurse—our arrangement.

I was in shock. I couldn't say anything and got up to leave for school. I got to the door and stopped. I went back, kissed Michael on the cheek, and said goodbye. "That's in case I never see you again." Something my mother always did when she left the house—just in case she was killed in a car wreck. But I didn't think it would matter much to Michael. But I did it anyway.

•   •   •   •   •

The looks I received at school felt degrading and shameful. I went from goody-two-shoe-Jill to whore of the month. It didn't matter that Michael was my only and that I was married. I was no better than the girls who gave blowjobs on the fan bus. I could hear the whispers as I walked through the halls, and even some teachers would roll their eyes in disgust instead of congratulating me on my special day. In the past, I walked these halls with pride and my love for Michael elevating my day. I was confused about how everyone was okay with sex, but as soon as they found out you're pregnant, it was a big taboo. Hello, people—that's where babies come from. And everyone only talked about the girl. No one ever talked about the guy who got the girl pregnant. His social status remained untainted.

Tammy stayed close to me all day, deterring any remarks, and would speak up. I wanted to tell her about last night, but sadly, I didn't want her to think ill of Michael. Given my earlier thought of the guy and his untainted status, I was just as much a hypocrite. I tried to keep Michael's good image.

But what about me—had what I'd done been so terrible? Was it wrong to love Michael and want to have a life with him? I didn't trap him. I just stupidly got pregnant. And when I thought of it that way, I felt I would be a terrible mother. I became confused between love and sacrifice. Was I sacrificing myself to love Michael and our baby? Or was Michael sacrificing his goals for us? Were they the same? I began to look at my parents differently and wonder what we had. Did they want that?

I did love Michael. I knew this because it hurt so much. And I was confused about whether it was the love that hurt or the love he would never have for me. My eyes stung with tears, and as one ran down my cheek, I realized the answer. Both.

•　　•　　•　　•　　•

The principal gave the last announcement, ending the day. Now, it was time to go home and be a wife. Before, it was a school-girl fantasy, but now it felt differently. Part of me was happy. I was going home to Michael—my husband. But knowing he wasn't having the same feelings weighed on my happiness. No more would he walk through the door with a smile, and I would jump into his arms as he spun me around. Would I ever hear: *I couldn't wait to get home?*

I pulled out of the school parking lot, remembering the smile on my face when I was going to Michael's. Now, it all felt different. It was home, and I was married to a man who didn't love me. I was going to have his baby. Oh, how does the fantasy feel much different from reality?

Once I was home, I decided. I would fight for Michael—for us. I would show him my undying love if he were willing to put me through college. I wouldn't use the excuse that we were an arrangement. We were *real*—and could be real. It would be like it once was. There was no reason why he couldn't be happy and love me. And once our baby came, he would love our child, too.

I would make chicken cacciatore for dinner and hoped it would spark the fun we had our first night together. We would make love and talk about names for our baby. I wouldn't mention what happened last night, so he would never have to feel bad. He would see me as his wife who loved him unconditionally. Maybe he had a note waiting for me at home, telling me how much he wanted to try, and we were more than an arrangement. With these thoughts, I hit the gas with anticipation and eager to get home and make my marriage work.

A note awaited me, and I smiled, knowing my wish had come true.

Jill,

Don't think you must be here when I get home. Our arrangement goes both ways. If you want to hang with your school friends, I won't object. I won't take away your freedom, so I don't expect you to take away mine. You're free to come and go. I don't know when I'll be home, so don't wait up. Or, stay with your friend Tammy. And what happened last night will never happen again.

Love, Michael

I dropped to the floor and cried. Did Michael not know the severity of what happened last night? Did he think we just had sex, and he meant he never wanted to have sex with me—ever?

At seventeen, I wasn't in a marriage. I was in…an arrangement. And no one ever prepares you for that.

CHAPTER 23

Now

"Oh my God. I can't believe she signed the contract. Even after he said, 'I don't make love. I fuck. Hard.' Who says that? She thinks she loves him?" It's Tammy's third chemo treatment. I couldn't come last week since I was covering her spot at the hospital. And today, I worked half shift and ran here as soon as possible. It's good to be here with her, laughing and listening to *"Fifty Shades of Grey."* I feel we are teens again, and sadly, it's her cancer that has ported us back to this closeness. I will never take friendship for granted again.

I stop the audio and pull out the lotion I bought for her feet. "It's lotion time," I say, pulling up the covers and removing her skid-free hospital socks.

"Remember, I'm ticklish." With this, I can't help but run my finger quickly up the bottom of her foot. She jerks it away. "Jill! You're awful. But I love you."

I begin rubbing and massaging the lotion on her feet. She closes her eyes and lies her head back. Ryan didn't come today, and I told him no worries because I already had dinner ready for him and the girls.

"That feels so good, Jill." I'm happy to be giving her some pleasure. She'll feel like she has the worst flu for the next few days. "Now, back to Fifty Shades of You and Michael," Tammy says, still relaxed back with closed eyes.

I continue with her feet, moving up her legs and thinking of Anastasia. People do wonder how you could love someone who can't love you back. I understand it all too well, and listening to the audible brings back that desperate feeling of wanting that love. I haven't told her about my stupid moment—Michael and my one-nighter. I try to brush her question under the rug. "There's nothing to tell." I've kept my distance, dodging his happenstance appearances—grocery store, my morning walks on days off. And since my car's destruction, no flowers have been left on the windshield. Michael now leaves the flowers and notes on my front porch, along with notes always signed Love, Michael. "Give me your other foot," I tell her and pull off her sock.

"Jill, you're avoiding my question. Please tell me. I might not have much time left."

I smack her foot. "Don't say that." She laughs, and I run my finger up her foot again. "I've been avoiding him. I have to, Tammy."

"Why do you have to?"

"My God, you were there. You know how he was."

"*WAS.*"

"What's that supposed to mean?"

"You don't think he's changed? We're listening to this book, and if I get the chance to finish it, I'm pretty sure this Christian guy will change."

"Michael and I aren't fictional characters written into a happily-ever-after. And what do you mean not to finish? Stop talking like that," I say and lightly smack her foot.

"I'm realistic."

"No, you're not. It's not about you and not about Michael. You'll be fine, and Michael will be onto…whatever Michael does." I finish with her feet and struggle to get her socks back on. "How's that feeling? Better?"

"Yes, thank you."

I sit back on the bed beside her and place the earbud back in. "Next chapter."

She pulls them out. "No. Next chapter of you and Michael."

She's grave, and it scares me somewhat. "Tammy, why are you persistent about this? Weren't you the one who told me to leave him several times?"

"Back then. This is now."

Back then, she told me to leave him. But I wouldn't. He wouldn't care if I went, not because he forced me to stay. "Remember when you had to get me back from Seattle in one piece? Do you want another repeat of that?"

"Just think about it. Michael is older now. He sees things differently."

"Differently how?"

She presses her lips, stalling on my question. "Kind of how I see things now," she says, and I know where she's going with this. "Things of the past, they don't matter anymore. One thing does. To let go of the hurt and live the rest of your lives together, being happy. Even now, with Ryan and me. Since the cancer, it's like we see each other differently—precious and not here forever."

"Stop it. You'll always be here."

"Jill, we're all dying. Some of us have a fast pass getting there." How can she talk like that? Is she giving up? Here I go with the tears, and I'm here for emotional support. She's so much stronger than me.

"So, you think I should give Michael a chance? Is that what you're saying?"

"I think you should be open to what he wants to give you." The minute she says what he wants to give me, something opens. And I see it differently. Maybe it's not what he wants; it's what he wants to give me.

"Are you trying to get rid of me? Am I hanging around too much?" I tease, grabbing her hands and kissing the tops.

She looks at my hair, eyeing it quizzically. "Weren't you going to shave your head? Or is that off now, so you look good for Michael?"

"You're not going to stop, are you? Do you want it shaved? I'll shave it tonight."

"No," she laughs. I have enough *ugliness* to look at, going through this. Seeing you and your gorgeous blonde curls brightens my day." Her eyes soften, and she studies me for the longest time. "Please, stay perfect. Stay beautiful, stay…Jill."

"Oh, honey. I will always be me, and you'll always be you. We'll always be us."

· · · · ·

As I'm about to get into the rental car, my cell rings with a number I don't recognize. My gut tells me it's Michael as my finger hovers over the accept button. I think of Tammy and people changing—wanting to be loved. What Michael wants to give me, I tap the accept button.

"Hello."

"Is this Jill Danforth?" It's not Michael.

"Yes, this is her."

"Hi, this is Robert from Stafford's Auto Repair. Your car is ready to be picked up."

"Oh. Um…what's the damage? I haven't yet received a check from my insurance."

"It's paid in full. It would be best if you came to pick it up. We're open until 6:00."

"Paid in full? How?"

I hear the shuffling of papers, and then he responds. "Michael Danforth signed it."

Michael. "Well, thank you for calling. I'll be there in about twenty minutes."

"Yes, Mrs. Danforth."

"That's not Mrs.…." The call goes silent. Well, I wasn't planning on going anywhere after work. So, I'm breaking my scrub rule again. Oh, well. It's just a body shop. I start the rental, pull out of the hospital parking garage, and head to Stafford's. I'll have to find out the cost, write a check, and have Monica give it to her father.

Before heading to the body shop, I quickly called Monica to see if she would pick me up at the Avis Car Rental and then drop me off at Stafford's.

I dropped off the rental, and Monica is outside waiting. "Hey, Mom," she says when I enter her car.

"Hi, Honey. Thanks for picking me up. Are you back to work now?"

"Yes," she says disappointedly. "Kind of hard to get back in the swing of things after Paris."

As much as I love my daughter, she has no idea how lucky she has it with Jordan—to have a honeymoon. "Yes, well...I'm sure the honeymoon is continuing now that you're home. You look so happy, sweetheart."

"Yes, I am, Mom. What about you and Dad?" I don't like what she may be insinuating.

"What about us? There isn't anything." She eyes me suspiciously before turning her look back onto the road. What has he been telling her? Hopefully, it's not about our one stupid moment last week.

"I mean, are any old feelings rekindling?"

"Rekindling! There are many feelings, but I wouldn't call it that." Michael never had feelings for us in the first place. "He's made various comments, apologizing for the past."

"And?"

"And that's it. Turn here," I tell my daughter as we near Stafford's.

"Mom, I know where Stafford's is. You're ignoring the question."

"Monica, there's nothing to discuss. Right now, I'm more concerned about Tammy."

"Yes, I'm sorry, Mom. How's she doing with the chemo?"

"Mentally, I think she's remaining strong for my sake. But physically, I see a decline."

"Will she be okay?"

"Of course. I refuse to think otherwise."

She pulls into the lot of the body shop, and I see my car parked out front. "Oh, hang on, and let me write you a check for your father," I tell her.

"A check? Why?"

"They called and said Michael paid the bill."

"Why don't you give it to him? I don't know when I'll be seeing him again."

"I'm sure it will be before me, Monica."

"Mom, if he came here to pay for it, he probably doesn't want to be paid back."

"No, it's because he was the body shop's only contact. He took care of the arrangements. So now, I need to pay him back."

She huffs. "Fine. I'll wait."

After I receive the keys and the receipt, I write a whopping check. I'll need to transfer the money and give it to Monica. "Be sure he gets it soon."

"Yes, Mom."

"Okay, love you. Thank you for picking me up," I kiss Monica's cheek. She leaves, and I hope it's straight to Michael's. I inspect my car, which looks brand new, and then drive home.

As usual, another bouquet, another letter.

Jill,

How was your day? Your car should be done. I hope you enjoy my flowers. I owe you many and regret I never brought you any in the past. I regret a lot of things, Jill. I'm leaving my number again, just in case you misplaced the last note I wrote. Please call me anytime.

Love, Michael

I smell the flowers and think of Tammy, Monica, and Michael again. I should thank him for paying and that Monica has his check. Pulling out my phone, I take a deep breath and press his number.

"Michael Danforth," he answers.

I pause. I could end the call now; Michael would never know it was me. But what if he calls my number back? I won't answer.

"Jill?" he questions, and his voice is soft.

"Ah…hi, Michael. I wanted to thank you for the car and that Monica has a check for you. She should be on her way to your place. That's all. Have a nice evening…"

"Jill, don't hang up. I'm so happy you finally called."

"Well, it was just to let you know that I don't expect you to pay for the damages…"

"I don't want the money. I want to see you. Can I see you, Jill?"

Dammit. Why's he being like this? "I just got home. I'm tired. I'm going to check on Tammy and…"

"She's fine. I just talked to her."

"What? Why?"

"To see how she is doing. Why else?"

"Oh, okay…good. I'm just going to relax and…"

"I'm coming over, Jill. Have you eaten?"

"No, but I…"

"I'll be there soon."

"But, Michael…" The call goes silent. Dammit! I should have never called.

Shoving my phone back into my purse, I walk inside and drop it on the counter. Scrubs! I hit the shower and change into a sundress— modest in front, a little showy in the back that's opened down to the small of my back. I even made sure to paint my toenails. Why?

The doorbell rings as I walk barefoot to the living room and meet Michael at the door. He holds another bouquet of sunflowers and a bottle of wine. "Hope lasagna will do," he says, pulling out a box of frozen lasagna. "Picked it up on the way."

"It's fine. Thank you." He hands me the cold box, and I turn around. "I'll preheat the oven."

"Wow. That dress."

I know, I think to myself with a wicked smile. "Just got out of the shower, and it's the coolest thing I have for such a hot day," I say casually. What am I doing? I hear him place the wine and flowers on the counter and then feel his warm hand glide across my bare back, followed by a kiss on my shoulder.

"You make it gorgeous," he whispers in my ear.

Ahh. "Did Monica bring you the check?" I ask, moving away.

"Yes. Here," Michael says, pulling out my check, torn in two. "I told you I'd take care of it."

"No…"

"Shh," he whispers and places his finger over my lips. "No discussion about it."

"But…"

"Ah. None."

I excuse myself to grab water for the flowers and open the lasagna. "And thank you for dinner and the flowers. It's not necessary."

"It is to me," he says. I try to look away from his pleading eyes, and my heart is saved when a knock on my back door breaks the moment.

"Jill?" Alan, my next-door neighbor, pops his head in. "You home, Love?"

Michael gives me a discerned look. "My neighbor," I say. "Yes, Alan. Come in."

"Hey, Love. Kyle and I…Oh. Hello," Alan says, all wide-eyed. "I didn't know you had company. That's great. The more, the merrier. Movie night. *The Lake House*," he says, making a heart shape over his heart.

"Alan, this is Michael…Danforth."

Alan places his hands on his hips and inspects Michael with charming eyes. "You're Monica's father. Oh my God. It's so nice to meet you."

Michael holds out his hand. "Yes, I am."

"I'm Alan. My husband Kyle and I live next door." Micheal's eyes trace back to me before returning to Alan. "Nice to meet you. Glad you came to movie night." Alan turns to me. "How's Tammy?"

"As well as to be expected," I say.

"Good. Well, I won't keep you two. The movie starts at dusk. Bring wine, and all will be fine," Alan, my sweet neighbor, says, waving his hands as he walks back to the door. "Bye, Love. Nice to meet you, Michael." The door shuts, and Michael smiles with questioning eyes.

"Yes. Alan and Tyler are my gay neighbors. They entertain the block with wine and movie night. They host on their back patio, projecting onto their back shed. It makes a great outdoor theater. They're the best neighbors anyone could have, and the block loves them."

"The movies or them?"

"Both." He smiles and wraps his arms around me like it's all-natural. I feel myself tensing and break away to open the wine. "It'll be a while before dinner is ready. I'll open and pour the wine."

As I open the wine, Michael traces small circles on the exposed small of my back, and I chastise myself for wearing this dress. It's doing what I wanted. Yet, I am tense.

"Here you go," I say, handing him a glass. I take the other, and he holds it for a toast.

"To Tammy."

"Yes, to Tammy," I say, and we sip. "So, have you ever seen The Lakehouse?"

"No," he says and pulls me into his arms. "Is it a romantic movie?"

"Yes. So, now's your chance to run." His hand is warm on my back, and I consider his eyes, waiting for his response. "I know you hate all those sappy, lovey movies." Nothing. He continues smiling into my eyes. "Hallmark…ish." That should do it.

"I couldn't think of anything I'd rather do than watch them with you."

"Oh, come on, Michael. I know better."

"And so did I…now." He moves slowly to my lips and gently kisses me. My arms are around his neck when we finish the kiss. I don't know what's happening.

"Why don't we sit on my patio? We can see and hear the movie from there while waiting for the lasagna."

We move to the patio and sit with our wines. We're quiet, and Michael watches me with that smile. The movie lights up the yard, and the music settles as the perfect ambiance. "I forgot how much I loved the soundtrack to this movie," I say.

"You're beautiful, Jill."

I try to look away but can't. Michael sets down his wine and takes mine. "Please, I want to dance with you right here." I take his hand, and he holds me in his arms. My heart slams against my ribcage, yet I feel relaxed. Paul McCartney sings *'This Never Happened Before'* as I lay my head against Michael's heart. He kisses my head, and I squeeze my arms tighter around him as we dance to the song's cadence. I don't know how this is happening, and I'm not sure I care to know, but I'm enjoying this moment because this has never happened before.

I need a tactic. A tactic to come back to my senses. "Michael?"

"Hmm?"

"Tell me more about this woman you were going to marry." This subject will strike a nerve and open my eyes. My heart can be easily deceived, but not my mind.

He lifts my chin to meet his eyes. "She didn't have these beautiful blue eyes. She didn't have this perfect nose," he says, kissing my nose. He traces my cheek. "She didn't have these perfect high cheeks or this soft skin." He squeezes me tightly. "She didn't have this beautiful body." He traces my heart. "She didn't have this beautiful Jill heart." He takes my hand and gently rubs my open palm down his cheek. "She didn't make me feel this way when she touched me."

My eyes blink with confusion and lustful sedation—it's genuinely distracting. How does Michael master something that repels my feelings and directs them into drawing me to him?

"You want to hear more?" I can't answer but stare into his eyes. "She never made me feel like I wanted to make love to her the way I want to make love to you right now." I'm speechless, and he picks me up and carries me into the house. How do I stop this?

He puts me down on my feet once we reach my bedroom. "I never wanted to remove her dress like I want to remove yours," he says as he pulls my dress off. I'm in a complete hypnotic state as he strategically places kisses over my naked body. He steps to the side and begins to remove his clothes. "I never undress, thinking how good it will feel to be inside her, like it's going to feel when I make love to you, Jill." He picks me up and lays me down, crawling over me and opening my legs with his knee. "She wasn't you, Jill," he says, and I feel him enter me. My chest heaves, and I whisper his name.

"Michael."

CHAPTER 24

Then

It had been six months since I became the wife of Michael Danforth, and ever since, my life has been draining into a cesspit of sadness. My baby had grown inside me, yet Michael hadn't once acknowledged my tummy or any baby-related questions. It was Tammy or my mother who visited with me at my prenatal appointments, and I found out I was having a baby girl. I never told Michael, hoping he'd ask. I even took my old job at Delanie's back.

Once, I was a teenage girl working at a pizza shop, delusional with dreams of Michael and our life together. I was a married woman working in a pizza shop, living in a nightmare with Michael.

He wasn't ever physically abusive again, but emotionally, he hadn't touched me since, not even in a loving way. Sometimes, he came home, and sometimes he didn't. I feared he had other women, and deep down, I knew he did. But if I didn't pry, it wasn't real.

Despite his lack of love and emotions for the baby and me, I continued loving him. I woke him every morning with a kiss after I showered and dried my hair. Michael's breakfast was cooked, and just so I could touch him, I would help button his shirt and tie his tie. Before he walked out each day, I told him how handsome he was and that I loved him. I never heard it back.

I was making a special chicken cacciatore dinner tonight and planned to tell Michael he was having a daughter. It was hard to include words such as our baby and our daughter because he made me feel so alone in all of it. I wanted us to return to where we were before I became pregnant. I knew there would be no moment of bliss filled with joy, kissing, and hugging. But I wanted him to express something. Did he even care what he was having? And maybe it would all be a lost cause—if he didn't come home. Nonetheless, I carried on with my loving wife duties and hoped someday I could look back and say it was all worth it.

I had also turned eighteen since we married, but he didn't even know my birthday. Tammy and I celebrated alone at the apartment—because it was a no-show night for Michael. The following day, he asked who the birthday cake was for. When I told him, Micheal wondered why I never said anything. He didn't remember what I told him in the past, before getting pregnant. I was hoping for a little something. But nothing. He did say under his breath, 'Should have said something. Maybe we would have gone out.'

So tonight, I hoped to get an extension for my birthday and even made another cake—chocolate with butter pecan frosting. It was Michael's favorite—not mine. And since it was Wednesday, he was sure to come home. It mainly was Fridays and Saturdays he didn't.

I wore a long, black tunic dress that hugged my baby bump. I was small for six months, and the lady at the store told me I looked darling in it. My hair was up with a few curls that wisped at my shoulders. I looked…beautiful. And with my baby girl inside me, I felt special. I just wanted Michael to see me this way.

The candles flickered, and music played softly in the background. I stood next to the table when the door opened. Michael came home.

"Why are the lights off?' he asked, setting his briefcase down.

"Hi, Michael," I said softly, lovingly. He looked at me, the table, and then back at me.

"What's going on?" he began to remove his tie when I joined him at the door.

"Let me," I said, unknotting his tie. "How was your day?"

"Fine, I guess." Was he going to say I looked pretty?

I kissed his cheek and said, "I missed you." He began with the arrangement talk.

"Jill…don't…"

I stopped him. "Shh. Just listen. Remember when you said you wished you would have known my birthday and that maybe we would have done something?"

He inhaled. "I don't know…maybe."

"Well, let's redo it. I've made chicken cacciatore and your favorite cake." His tie was off, and I began to unbutton his shirt. I placed a small kiss in the well of his throat and felt him swallow. I wanted him to hold me. I didn't want him to think I feared his touch. That we could start our wedding night over, and maybe all this time, he thought I was wary of sex because of what happened. I was taking a stand and going to win my Michael back—my husband.

"Jill…you don't have to do this. Just let me know if you want something for your birthday, and I'll pick it up tomorrow."

"I don't want something else, Michael. I want dinner with you," I said, looking into his eyes. There was remorse there; maybe I could use it in my favor. "Have dinner with me, and I will tell you what I want for my birthday." He looked over at the table and back to me. "Please. And I found out what the baby is today." His eyes widened a bit. Was he eager to know?

"Oh? So, you know if it's a boy or girl?" he asked. He…asked, and it was the light I needed to brighten the visions I so wanted for us.

I smiled into his eyes. "Yes." He seemed…intrigued. I was happy. Was I winning my husband? I led him by the hand to the table. "First let's eat, and I'll tell you." He sat, and I moved to the chair across. I watched his eyes watch me.

"You…look pretty."

I gasped, and I could feel my heart skipping beats.

"Thank you, Michael." I served his plate and poured his wine. As I did, he watched me with captivating eyes. Maybe he thought I didn't want to try, and after tonight, we would be happy in love. I was allowed to go on with our marriage and become a family.

After a few bites, he said, "I really would like to know." Was he referring to us…or the baby? I needed to know more how he really felt and wanted to set the record straight.

"Michael, I want you to know. I'm willing to work on our marriage. I realize it came as a shock to both of us and I understand how you must have taken it at first. But that doesn't mean I love you less." His eyes never wavered from me, and I felt a shift in our favor. "I will stand by you in your career and any decision you make on that," I remember his longing for Boeing and moving to Seattle. Maybe if he knew I was willing, and not a threat, he would let down his guard and love me.

He looked down at his plate and back at me. "Thank you. And like I said, I will see that you get your degree in nursing." I smiled and thanked him before taking a bite. Something had shifted. We were exchanging positive inclinations, and I was hopeful. I wanted to tell him about the baby. Would he be upset it wasn't a boy?

"So, how do you feel about having a daughter?" I said it and held my breath. He stopped with his fork and set it down.

"We're having a girl?"

I was still holding my breath. "Ah huh." He smiled, and his eyes became glassy. I bit my lip, waiting for more. "I know most men want a boy…"

"A girl. Wow…I just…wow."

It was *real* to him now. He was going to be a father, and he was having a daughter. Yet, I needed to know how he felt. "I know you weren't happy when I first told you, but how does having a daughter feel?"

"It…it feels different," he said. Different good or different bad? He got up and came over to me and bent down. My breath hitched, and the tears were already forming in my eyes. I had done the right thing. I had fought for us and won my husband.

He pushed my chair back and touched my pregnant belly. It was the first time he had touched me. My heart was in melt-down mode, and he laid his head on my lap. Had it finally become *real* to him?

He began to cry, and my hands smoothed his hair. He did love me. He just didn't know how. He then looked up, and I saw the hurt and pain in his eyes. He tried to speak but each time would break up. I cupped his face and told him it was all right. To say what he needed to say.

"It…it was easier to just stay angry. Go on with life and not think about it," he said. "But now, now when I think of a little girl…looking up to me to care for her…I…" He couldn't finish and cried on my lap. I told him how much I loved him and how happy I was to be having his daughter. He took my hands and looked longingly into my eyes.

"Jill…I know I haven't been a husband. And I've done…done things…." I wonder what other things he had done, and I didn't know if hearing that he had other women, I could take. But at that point, I knew it was true. But I had had my moment and love was working its miracle in this doomed relationship. "I'm going to try, Jill. I can't promise it will be easy for me. But I will try."

I didn't like how it was an effort for him to have to try. But it was a progression, and I was willing to accept any effort he was willing to give. I felt now would be a good time to ask him what I wanted for my birthday.

"Michael," I sniffed and wiped my eyes. He looked at me with heavy tears. "For my birthday, I would like a portrait taken of us. A girl at school is studying photography and has asked if we would like some pictures taken. She has a whole portfolio of expecting parents, and I would really like some of us."

"That's what you want?"

"Yes."

"Okay. Just tell me when."

My smile couldn't have been any bigger. "Really?"

He held my hands, and it felt so reassuring. "Really."

"Thank you." Just then, the baby kicked. "She's moving. You want to feel?" I placed his hand over the area, and she kicked again. She was kicking for us. She felt my joy, and it was her way of telling me that I too had finally acknowledged her. I had been so consumed with gaining Michael's love, that I hadn't taken the time to think of her. But it was all changing now—for all three of us.

I stood so he could feel more of my belly and I kissed his cheek. He kissed back, and when his lips found my lips, everything I had been through with us had been worth it. My love brought us together.

He wrapped me tightly, and the kissing became...sexual. His hands were under my dress and we were becoming lost in his touch. It had been so long, and I was falling in love all over again. He picked me up and carried me to the bed. Our bodies pressed into each other, and I felt him growing hard. Our breathing was heavy, our kisses were hungry, and everything in life had happened to get to this moment.

He pulled off my dress and sucked hard on my nipples. They had become tender, but the ache was pure pleasure as his tongue massaged the soreness. "God, you've grown," he said, noticing how my breasts had become engorged with the pregnancy.

"Michael," I cried out his name, fearing he thought I would want him to stop.

"Are you okay?" His voice was low and breathy. I was in need—in need of him.

"Yes."

"I think you should be on top. Would that be easier with the baby?"

My pounding heart connected to my excited center and intensified when he mentioned the baby. We were all one now, and we were going to make love.

He stood, removed his clothes, and then helped with the dress. I was naked for the first time in six months in front of him, and I looked different. My belly invaded the space between us, and he bent down and kissed it. Tears ran down my face, and I thanked him over and over. I told him how much we needed him. How much I loved him. I waited to hear his love back, but I considered that this was how he said it through his emotions. He wasn't the type who could say it. But with his uncontrollable kissing and touching and crying, this was how he said it.

He sat me down on his erection and held my hips as he pushed up into me. He was inside me, and it had been so long. He breathed and moaned about how it felt so good. How he missed this, and I yelled out his name.

"Michael."

He held my belly as we moved into each other, and for once, I felt connected, loved—us. It was the most intense lovemaking we had ever had; for once, life made sense for why we cried and hurt. Why do we love and become so vulnerable? And that's when I realized I made him weak, which gave me power.

As our rhythm increased, so did our emotions, words, and breath, which filled the room. "Oh, God, Jill. I swear…it's never felt so good." As he came inside me, repeating my name, chemistry molded us together as one, and all the doubts of the past melted away. We kissed like we were scared, and only holding onto each other would ease the fear. Until now, we have broken each other apart and are now molded into one. It all made sense now.

He came hard, and I had already reached my third orgasm. We held each other close, fearing what would happen if we were to let go. He rolled me to the bed, and we morphed into one another. As our breathing slowed to shallow breaths, I heard Shania in the background, the lyrics of how we made it. And I knew then I would never stop fighting for us.

I never slept any better than I did that night, with Michael beside me, tracing circles on my belly. We had succumbed to our situation, turning us in a new direction. But little did I know chemistry came with an expiration date. And, the glue that once bound us together would only become something sticky, keeping us from moving on.

•   •   •   •   •

Michael had kept his promise to have our pregnancy portraits taken, and we were meeting Beth, the school photographer, at The Round Barn. The place was famous for senior portraits and weddings. It was a warm spring day, and things had been moving in the right direction for us. I had picked out a few casual outfits—a form-fitting T-shirt tunic and a loose button-up shirt. Beth showed me many pictures exposing just a hint of the naked belly. Michael also wore a white button-up shirt.

As I looked around the blooming spring day, I thought about how I would like to get married here someday. Then, I remembered…I was married. Maybe after the baby comes, I could convince Michael to let us renew our vows—have a real wedding.

The pictures we were taking today would also double as my senior pictures. I was so preoccupied with work, school, and Michael that I had never taken any of them. But to have Michael in my photographs and our unborn child, goosebumps pricked at the thought. I was hoping it wasn't just the chilling spring wind.

Due to the heavy spring rains, Beth posed us next to a creek that flowed deep and fast. The cherry blossoms were the perfect backdrop, with white and pink flowers. "Michael, I want you to place your hands on Jill's belly and kiss her forehead. Jill, look into Michael's chest, but close your eyes," Beth instructed us. "Perfect. Just let a slight smile form on our lips. Like you're both thinking about the baby."

I heard Michael give a slight huff and hoped the look on my face wouldn't show my disappointment. He hadn't said much since we arrived, and for him to start showing annoyance pained my heart. Yet, he was here—trying.

"That was great. If you want to change inside, we can do some open-belly shots." Michael furrowed his brows, and I explained what we would do.

"Not you, Michael. Me. It's something new, some of the new mothers are doing." He rolled his eyes, and I pleaded with mine. I felt everything was coming undone as I went inside and changed. I returned, and Beth posed me with my back snuggled into Michael, his arms around my belly and opened just a few buttons. It was just enough to expose my bump.

"Jill lay your head in the crook of Michael's neck. And Michael, look like you're whispering something in Jill's ear. Jill, I want you to smile like Michael said something romantic."

Just as Beth snapped the shot, Michael whispered in my ear. "This is silly and a waste of time. I would have picked something else as your birthday present."

As I started to cry, I was sure that the twitch of my jaw would exist in the picture. People say that a picture can say a thousand words. But for me, it only said one—*sorrow*.

CHAPTER 25

Now

As I drive to Ryan and Tammy's, I contemplate what I've been doing with Michael. Every day for the last month and a half, it's flowers, Love Michael notes, some special dinners, and sometimes just burgers on the grill. But whatever Michael does, it's laced with…love, romance…and sex.

I've yet to let him stay the night—though his pleading doesn't stop. After the great sex, I put on my mask and pretended it was all recreational. It's called survival. And survival is a tricky thing. You must remember where all things lead—what to expect. At seventeen, I knew nothing about survival. When the one-way-loveless-marriage escalated to unbearable levels, I had no emotional strength at twenty-two—the day life slapped me in the face. Denial is lost when survival skills don't exist. At the ripe old age of forty-two, I repeat my mantra daily. The best way to predict future behavior is past behavior.

Pulling into Ryan and Tammy's drive, I cut the engine, repeat my mantra, and clear out Michael's text: 'Have a good day, Jill. I love you.' I won't allow myself ever to say the words back and go inside only to find Tammy not ready for her chemo treatment today. She looks gaunt. Her hair has entirely fallen out, and recently she wears a terry cloth hat now. But today, she's not wearing it, and the life chemo has taken is fully showing itself today.

"Hey, honey. Is everything okay? I'm here to take you…" I don't finish the words because even though I'm happy to be taking her, it's killing her and me. Chemo is nothing but poison, taking you to the edge of death.

"I'm sorry, Jill. I thought Ryan called you."

"No. Ryan didn't. But it doesn't matter. I'm here now. You can tell me."

"I don't think I can make it today, Jill. I'm too weak."

"Well, I can see that, honey. Okay, do you want me to make you a comfy place on the couch or outside? Have you canceled your appointment?"

"Ah…I think Ryan did."

"Let's get you to the couch. Tammy, haven't they given you something to deal with the effects of chemo?"

"Yes, it's this patch," she says, lifting her arm where a patch is stuck. "But it doesn't seem to be helping."

"I will call the hospital and see if they have something stronger. This is ridiculous."

"No. Don't, Jill. I don't want any more chemicals in my body. It's draining the life out of me."

"I know. But I hate seeing you suffer. You know that."

"It's part of it." She walks to the couch, where I follow her and help her lie down.

"What can I make you to eat?"

"Nothing. Just smelling food makes me vomit. No offense, Jill," she says, thinking she can lighten the situation.

"You need something. You've lost too much weight."

"Good."

"Stop it. You *just* don't stop."

She looks at me. "I'm stopping now, Jill."

"Well, good. About time you… What do you mean you're stopping now?" I don't like what she is insinuating.

"Chemo. It's only making me worse."

"Tammy, we both know that's how it does the job. I know it must be so awful for you. But we'll get through this, and it will all be behind us. You are stronger than this. I'll take care of you. I'll do everything, so you don't have to lift a finger."

"Jill, you already are, and so are the girls and Ryan. I don't want to continue the treatment."

"Stop it, Tammy," I yell, and it shocks us both. My chest tightens, and I feel the burn behind my eyes. "You are going to finish this, and you are going to be strong. Beat this thing."

"Jill," her voice is hoarse, and I feel bad that I must upset her

"Let's get you some sunshine. Lots of vitamin D. I'll take you to our private spot. Just you and me. You'll feel better."

"Jill, I know what you are trying to do, and I appreciate everything you have done. But this is not about you. It's about me."

"No, it's not. It's about all of us. You would be doing the same thing if it were me. Remember how you lectured me, gave my ass a big kick, and told me to get my shit together? Well, get your shit together, Tammy. We're both going to kick this cancer's ass."

"Jill! Stop. The cancer has progressed. The treatment has had no effect on it. It's now about quality of life. The life I have left."

My body shakes, and all the survival tactics I had learned fly out the window. Denial invades that spot once again. "What? What are you saying?"

"Jill, we both have medical backgrounds. You know what I'm saying."

"No, I'm not listening to you. You're mistaken. You are tired and weak, and I understand and…"

"Dammit, Jill. Stop it and listen to me. I don't know how much time I have left. And I don't want to waste it fighting with you."

"Oh, my God. Tammy…"

"Jill…"

I don't have any words to offer—to her or myself. So, I hold her—and we cry…and cry and cry. I can't believe this. I don't want to think about this. How? What will I do without her? I don't know if I should be angry at her or myself. Nothing makes sense at this moment. Nothing is fair at this moment.

"It should have been me," I say.

Her chest heaves with cries and laughter. "Now, why would you say that? Think you're better than me?"

"Oh, Tammy. It's just that you have young girls and a wonderful marriage to Ryan. Me? No marriage. Monica has Jordan, so who would miss me?"

"Everyone, Jill. Monica would be devastated if something happened to you. She's going to have babies, and you'll become a grandmother. And what about me? I will miss you so much."

"Oh my God. Let's stop talking about this," I yell. Just the thought of her not seeing her girls graduate, marry, or have children only adds to this atrocious unfairness life loves to heckle upon us.

I kiss her cheeks and taste our mixed tears. I want to hold onto her for dear life, and maybe she will never be gone. Since the age of four, there has not been a day we have not spoken or been in each other's thoughts. Our lives began when my mom babysat Tammy, and we grew up together—had chickenpox together. We held hands as we started our first day of kindergarten together. We began our periods on the same day. My life coincides with hers, and I don't know how I'll go on.

"Jill. You know what I want to do…today?"

"Anything you want," I say, crying.

"Have you got the next book in Fifty Shades?" She smiles. Minutes after telling me she doesn't have long to live, she smiles. The least I can do is smile at her.

"Yes, I downloaded it this morning."

"I have to know what happens. I'm all in now."

"Then that's what we'll do. Let's get all comfy on the couch or wherever you want. The beach?"

"No." She looks out the back window. "Up there in the girls' treehouse. It will be like old times when we used to steal your mom's "True Romance" magazines and read them in your treehouse."

"Remember when we found Scott's "Playboy" magazines?" I say.

"Oh, God. We had him blackmailed for life. Your mom thought you and Scott had the best brother-sister relationship the way he took us wherever we wanted to go. She had no idea the hell we were putting him through."

"You go out to the tree house, and I'll meet you there. My purse and phone are still in the car." She thanks me with a kiss on the cheek and walks out the patio doors. I watch her weak body climb the ladder, but she does make it, and I run to my car. When I do, I see a text from Ryan.

Ryan: *Jill, I didn't call because I thought she might change her mind, or maybe you talked her out of it.*

Me: *I tried. But even now, your wife is more vital than me.*

I wait for his response, which doesn't come, and head to the treehouse. Tammy is all glassy-eyed and smiles. "You ready?" I ask.

"Yep. I need to know if Anastasia comes back."

We curl up under the open spot in the treehouse, where the sun shines in, leaving the phone behind our heads as we lay on the blanket and start chapter one.

'Fifty Shades Darker.'

•   •   •   •   •

Dear Jill, how was your day? I miss you. Please let me take you to the lake tonight as we watch the sun go down together. Love, Michael, the note on my car reads, along with a single red rose. Coming to work today was hard after learning Tammy has so little time left. I asked to be put on leave—to be there for Tammy and her family. The hospital said they would work with my schedule and give me the time needed.

I give Michael a quick text.

Me: *I'll be your guest.*

Michael: *Thank you. I love you.*

I read it, and I know he's waiting. But I won't let my defenses down. So, I drop the phone in the passenger seat and head home.

I change into a sundress and sandals when Michael rings the bell. I open the door to another bouquet and a kiss. "You are beautiful as always," he says.

I assess his attire—cargo shorts and a white T-shirt. He is handsome, but I'll only address his look. "You look…beachy."

"If that's a compliment, I'll take it."

"Have you eaten, or shall I make something?" I ask, taking the bouquet to the kitchen. Each day, a new bouquet—a patient gets flowers. If I kept them all, my house would burst at the seams.

"We'll get something in town," he says.

"Oh? Well, just let me put these in some water."

He waits and then holds my hand as we walk to his car. Maybe I shouldn't be with him tonight. But Tammy made me promise I would give him a chance. She doesn't know I'm only using him for comforting sex. And that makes me ashamed of myself.

In the car, he smiles differently at me. I can't place it and give my usual smile back. I told him about Tammy's decision, so maybe that's what the lake is all about. I tell myself I'm doing this for her—not myself or Michael.

He parks, and we walk hand in hand down to the beach. To all the watchers, we are a couple in love. Little do they know. I'm not going in blind this time; sooner or later, I will need to end this before the new wears off and the old Michael shines through. I know it will be coming. I just want to be in the driver's seat for a while.

The sun is still high, and it's early before the sun sets. He suggests we walk down the coast and find a spot alone to watch the sunset.

As we walk, I can't help but think of Tammy and how few sunsets she has left to watch. Michael senses my despair and pulls me in. "I'm truly sorry for Tammy. I know how much she means to you. Let me know if there's anything I can do. I might know a doctor she could call—seek more advanced treatments."

"You do? Yes, thank you, Michael. I'm still not ready to give up on her." He kisses my forehead.

"I know. Life is such a gift," he says, looking deep into my eyes.

We continue our walk along the coastline, ending with a sharp bend. "We better go back and grab something for dinner before we miss the sunset."

"It's right around this bend."

I crane my neck. "Around there? I think that's private property."

He looks back. "Yes, I believe you are right. However, that is where our dinner is waiting. Besides, they don't own the water's edge."

He takes me by the hand and leads me around, stepping over large driftwood of trees and roots. A small dam separates the beach from the other side, and he picks me up and carries me across the water. "Michael, I don't want to get yelled at for being on someone's beachfront property."

"There," he says, setting me to my feet.

Up ahead, I see a private cabana set with a table and chairs. A breeze blows the curtain, displaying someone's dinner and champagne. Closer to the water, a fire burns low in a pit.

"See, that's what I mean. This is someone's private property."

"Yes, I know—mine. Come on," Michael says, pulling me along in the sand.

I was right. Dinner has been set: lobster and corn on the cob. "How did you get this all set up?"

"Monica and Jordan are staying here. But tonight, it's ours."

"You bought this place?"

"Yes, it's ours. To use anytime."

I look up the steep stairs and see Monica and Jordan smiling down. I wave, and they wave back.

"Should still be hot, Dad," Monica yells down. Michael gives her a thumbs-up.

"You two—I don't believe this."

"You like?" I look around—private. Quiet waves move in and out on the sand. The sun sparkles down on the water, and I can't help but be amazed.

"Yes, Michael. It's all charming. But I hope you didn't buy this place to have dinner."

"I bought it for us, Jill. I know you always wanted a place on the lake—camp on the beach and listen to the waves at night." He recalls something from our past. Another request I had, only to be called dramatic and delusional.

"That was a long time ago, Michael. People change."

"Yes, I know. People do change. Stay with me on the beach tonight. We can talk about anything you want. You can cry in my arms for Tammy, and I'll cry with you."

"Why are you doing this, Michael?"

He gets down on one knee and takes my hand. "Because I love you." He reaches into the pocket of his cargo shorts and pulls out...a ring. He doesn't say a word and pushes the ring up my finger. I'm speechless—in shock. He then looks up, and his eyes are full of remorse.

"Marry me, Jill. Don't answer now. Wear the ring and think about it for a few days. I know you have a lot on your mind with Tammy. But...wear it, feel it on your hand, and know I love you and will always be here for you."

"Michael...I..."

"Shh," he says and kisses the hand with his ring. "Not now. Let's have dinner and enjoy the sunset."

CHAPTER 26

Then

June came, and I graduated from high school and was now enrolled in a community college where I would earn my degree in nursing. And…I was due any day now to have the baby. I would spend most of my summer looking for a babysitter when classes started in September. Though my mom said she'd help, her help came as an exasperated 'I suppose.' I'd rather have a flat on 'no.'

Despite Tammy's desire to enter culinary, she signed up at the same community college under the same nursing program. She used the excuse that nursing would ensure her a job after graduation. Whether it was the case or not, I was happy. I was going to need her.

Michael's newfound interest in wanting to try had already fizzled. He was back to no show most Friday and Saturday nights, traveling for business as he climbed the ladder at Whirlpool. But now that the baby was due any day, he did at least call in and check on me. I already had a backup plan—Tammy. She, after all, was my Lamaze coach. Michael showed no interest in taking the class with me.

The picture of us that Beth took was hung on a wall as you enter our apartment. Despite the words Michael spoke in my ear, it was a beautiful picture. Tammy was the only one who ever complimented on it. My parents felt no need to have one. To them, my marriage was just as much a charade as it was to Michael. And it didn't help that my parents wanted no part of Michael in their lives, which Michael used as an excuse never to come to family get-togethers. I doubt he'd go anyway.

Tammy and I had picked Monica for the baby's name. Another thing Michael had no interest in. As Michael's interest in his family dissipated more each day, I thought of ways to rekindle just an ounce of spontaneity. I knew Michael loved waterskiing and found a place on Lake Michigan where we could stay for free for the weekend. Tammy's uncle owned a resort, sometimes lending it out.

It was Michael's birthday, and I surprised him with a picture of the place. The caption read: *It's yours for the weekend.* "I don't understand," he said.

"I know you've been working hard, and it's time to relax and do some skiing. There's a boat there too we can use."

"When? This weekend?"

"Yes. Tammy's uncle said this was the only free weekend open."

He looked disappointed, and it didn't surprise me. He usually never came home on the weekends. I also knew now he had other girlfriends. They would call and be shocked when his wife answered the phone. We had many fights about it. It would lead nowhere, and Michael would only remind me of our situation. To him, he was a knight doing me a favor while I was only baggage.

"I already have everything packed," I told him. There was no getting around it. We were going, and he would stay the weekend with me—his wife. And hopefully, I wouldn't go into labor.

"Can I invite some of my buddies?" he asked.

"Michael, I don't think that's a good idea. Tammy's uncle is trusting us with his place, free of charge. I don't think we should take advantage of that." He rolled his eyes and started to walk away. "Well?"

"Fine," he said, annoyed. "We'll go."

I should have ended it right there. The more I fought for us, the more I felt ugly, unloved, and in the way around Michael. It was hard to find joy in my life, and I feared I wouldn't be a good mother because of this.

We took my car to the lake house that weekend because Michael refused to give up his Corvette even though we had a baby coming. He also suggested we drive separately—anything so he didn't have to be with me. I told him the sand whipping around might damage the paint on his car. That convinced him.

I pulled into the drive, and Michael appeared excited. "Well, what do you think?"

"This is pretty nice."

Maybe this weekend, I could get him to try again. Get him to show mercy and affection like he did a few months back. I would do anything to have him love me. And that's the funny thing about love. It doesn't work that way. It's either there or isn't. But why was it there for me? Michael never gave me a reason to love him. Yet, I did.

As we stood inside the big, open living room, the floor-to-ceiling windows showcased Lake Michigan. It was beautiful as the water sparkled for endless miles. I wrapped my arms around Michael. "Happy birthday. I love you, Michael. We have it all weekend, so maybe one night we can camp on the beach and listen to the waves as we sleep," I said, laying my head on his chest. "I hope you like it."

"It's really nice. Tell your friend's uncle thanks." Michael's arms were weakly held around me, and I could tell he was itching to get out of my embrace. So, I squeezed tighter. "So, where's this boat?" He broke our hug and went out the back door to the lake, finding the boat tied to the pier.

"Hey, I arranged for us to be here for your birthday and told you I love you. Are you going to say anything to me?" I was angry and tired of being ignored. I was tired of sounding jealous when all I wanted was his attention.

"Are we going to fight about it here? I thought we came here for a good time. If you want to fight, we'll go home."

"Why? So that you can leave and stay with your girlfriend?" I had had it. And maybe we could fight without all the apartment neighbors hearing by being here. "Michael, I'm still your wife despite how you qualify our marriage. I want a little respect and affection from you. Is it too much to ask?"

He stood up from the boat and placed his hands on his hips. "You know, Jill, maybe I would give you a little affection if you weren't such a bitch all the time."

"How can you say that? All I do is love you and take care of you."

"Oh, and I don't? Who pays for you? Who's paying for your college? Who gives you a place to live? Who's giving up four years of his life to help you? Who stuck by you when you got pregnant? Surely not your parents. Not your brother. Who gave you their credit card to buy baby shit? I don't see anyone else doing those things for you. And all you do is bitch at me."

"Stop it," I cried. "You know what I mean. Why can't you love me?" I was crying hard, and once again, my efforts were pointless. He twisted everything in his view to look like a martyr. He was the one sacrificing everything, while I stayed home and cried night after night, knowing he was with another woman. The mind games never ended with him. I didn't want to apologize, but I knew it would be like this the entire weekend if I didn't. I was out of fuel and had lost the ability to fight with him. I wiped my eyes. "I'm sorry. I'll go make dinner," I said and turned to walk back.

As I made dinner, the tears never stopped. I was waiting for a miracle that would never come—Michael running back to tell me he was sorry. Tell me he loved our unborn baby and me. Tell me, thank you for the weekend. But all he did was convince me that I had ruined his weekend.

I heard the boat take off, and I hoped he was only leaving to clear his head and that he would be back soon. The dinner I had prepared was ready, and he still wasn't back. The sun was about to set, and I wanted us to watch it go down over the water together.

I blew out the candles on the table, walked outside and down to the pier, and sat with my feet dangling in the water. Monica was kicking inside me, and I talked to her since she was the only one there.

"I'm trying, baby. I am fighting for us. I hope you don't hate me when you're born for putting us in this situation. But I promise I will love you enough for both of us. Your daddy may not be fond of me, but I bet he won't be able to resist when he sees your little face. I already love you. So, don't you worry about that."

I heard a boat coming in the distance, heading in my direction. It was Michael. I held my breath and prayed we would make up and salvage this weekend when he returned.

The boat slowed and drove into the wake, and I stood as I waited for him to cut the engine and tie off the boat. I didn't know if I should run to him or stay on the pier. He looked up once at me and still appeared to be angry.

"Michael, I'm sorry. Dinner's ready." He didn't say a word, and a jet ski drove into the wake. It was a girl in a bikini wearing a life jacket. She pulled up to the boat.

"You ready?" she said to Michael.

"Yes," he said and jumped on the back with her.

"The houseboat is just a few miles out. You'll need a life vest."

Michael climbed back into the boat, took one from the cabin, and then climbed back on with the girl.

"Michael, where the hell are you going?" He said nothing and looked at me with disgust. She pulled the jet ski around, causing rippling waves as the exhaust from the jet ski sprayed in my face. When I opened my eyes, I watched the two of them disappear under the sunset—the sunset I wanted to watch together—to a houseboat somewhere in the distance. I sat back down on the pier…and cried.

The sun had long set, and the water stilled like glass. Somewhere out there was my husband on a houseboat with another woman. This fight had to be the last straw because I wouldn't make it. I had a baby coming any day, and I knew Michael would never change, no matter what I did. I was going to file for divorce. And what made it worse—it's what Michael would want. The only thing that would make him truly happy.

I continued crying inside, curled up on the window seat while watching the moon reflect across the lake. I considered going home. He would need to find his way home when and if Michael returned. Which would constitute me being, once again, a bitch. I couldn't justify why my broken heart and shed tears made me a bitch. But that's what my actions had warranted. I was nothing but a bitch, according to Michael.

I thought I had shed the last tear when I got up, packed the car, and left around midnight. However, five miles down the road, I pulled over when I could no longer see. The dam broke, and I lay, crying hysterically, over the steering wheel.

I had failed. And now, my only choice was to move back home with my parents and have my baby. I had convinced them that Michael and I were happy and things had all worked out. Now, they, too, would see the charade.

I wiped my eyes and drove back to the house I grew up in—where my daughter would be raised now.

The door was unlocked when I quietly walked in and padded upstairs. Time had only shortly passed, but it felt like years when I stepped inside my childhood room. With its posters and school memorabilia, it still looked like a teenage girl who lived here. I wished to be a teenager again and do everything right this time. I would never let myself fall in love with Michael.

•   •   •   •   •

A week had passed, and I still hadn't filed for divorce. I told my parents we just needed a break. Mom seemed to understand. Dad, as usual, rolled his eyes and said, 'If you want to dance, you must pay the fiddler.'

Tammy and I visited the mall several times, but it was different. Instead of shopping for shoes or purses, we picked out a breast pump. I was now three days overdue and hadn't heard a thing from Michael. I wasn't sure if it was because he didn't care or was afraid to face my parents. It was both. Though I told myself I wanted to divorce Michael, each day, I feared having divorce papers served to me. Mom would keep her silence as to what I was going to do. But Dad would throw his opinion whenever he could.

"What are you waiting for? Either get divorced or don't. Decide. You wanted to be an adult. You can't go back to being a kid. It doesn't work that way."

"Dad, I'm not thinking that…"

"That's the problem. You don't think."

"Dad…I've been trying to make it work with Michael," I said, my voice strangled on the edge of crying.

"That's another thing a man doesn't want when he comes home. Fighting."

"I don't mean fighting, fighting. I mean…" It was useless. My dad would always be old-school to this and never understand how lucky he had it. "What makes it so hard for him? He carries on as he always did. Yet, I'm the one making his life hard? He's not exactly making my life a picnic. If anything, I've made life easier for him. He no longer has to feed himself, clean his home, shop for groceries, or write the checks for the bills. Deal with the cable guy when he can't get the ballgame he wants. Buy new underwear when his have holes. I pick up his suits at the cleaners, and I do everything. I gave the man more time to fly all over the country and party with his friends, whom he calls business associates."

"That's your job," Dad said, and it only made me more furious. He hated Michael, yet he had defended him over his daughter? "How do you expect him to get promoted and climb the ladder?"

"You just don't get it, do you?" He laughed, and it only made me appear childish in his eyes. Life was real now, and I wasn't ready to handle it. "Well, he was doing just fine before I came along. It would just be nice to be loved and appreciated. I…" A sharp pain tore through me, and I buckled over. "Aww!"

Mom rushed to my side. "Jill, are you okay? Arthur, don't be upsetting her," she said.

"Aww. It hurts Mom. I think I'm in labor."

"Oh, dear. Arthur, get the car ready. Is this your first pain, honey?"

"Yes. Mom…I'm scared. How bad will it be?"

She helped me to a chair as Dad went to get the car. "Honey, this will be the least painful of becoming a parent. Trust me." Another pain shot through me, and I couldn't imagine anything worse—had all the things Scott and I had done growing up become more painful than this?

"Come on, let's go," Dad said, popping his head in the front door. "She okay?"

"Yes, Arthur. She'll be fine."

"Mom...I'm scared. Don't leave me."

"Baby, I'll be there. Come on, let's go have this baby," she said and helped me to the car.

It was real. The *real life* of Michael and me, being married and having a baby, felt nothing like the fantasies I had only nine months ago. This real-life of Michael and me was broken and painful. We weren't together, and I no longer felt special in anyone's eyes. I was just another knocked-up teen about to have a baby—alone.

"Tammy," I cried out through another pain. "She has to be there. She's...aww...she's my coach."

"All right. I'm sure we have time to stop and pick Tammy up."

"Oh, hell, we do," Dad spat at Mom. "She's not having that baby in this car."

"Arthur, it's her first. It will be some time."

"What? No. I want it over with now!" I yelled.

"There you go, scaring the poor girl," Dad said.

"You two, stop!" I couldn't take their bickering. I just wanted the pain to go away. I wanted Tammy with me, and I wanted Michael. I wanted him to be there when our daughter was born. But I didn't mention his name. I was afraid Mom and Dad would start another fight, and all I wanted was some peace—somewhere.

Dad had us to the hospital in record time, and Tammy and I were now in the delivery room. Mom couldn't believe I was already ten centimeters dilated. As they told us in Lamaze class, the pains never came and went. My labor pains came and never let up. It was one big hurt, and I swore she would be an only child.

"Okay, Jill. It's time to push," the nurse told me, and Tammy held my back as I bared down. "Aww!"

"Breathe now, Jill. Breathe," Tammy said.

"Screw that breathing shit. Just get this baby out. NOW!"

"Push. Push, push, push, push, push, push," the doctor said as his fingers pulled down on my opening. "Here she is." Not a second later, my baby girl's cries came wailing out, and I never heard a more beautiful sound. They handed her to me, and she was pink and perfect…and mine. Everything I went through with Michael came down to this moment. She was meant to be here. She was meant to be mine. And…she was meant to be Michael's.

"Oh, Jill. Look at her," Tammy awed, and we were both crying.

"I know. Oh, my God. I'm shaking. I can't stop."

"That's normal," Tammy said. "Remember? They said that would happen due to the hormones."

Mom and Dad came in soon after, and whatever occurred moments before was now forgotten with this perfect baby. There was no way I could ever look at her and see her as a mistake. Mistakes didn't look this perfect. Mistakes didn't feel this wonderful. And it was as my mother had said. Giving birth to her would be the easiest thing about her. Because I realized I had created something that could destroy me—because I loved her so much.

I had survived her birth, and all I could think about was how I could ever survive if I lost her. Or to see her in pain or heartbroken. I would never let her know what it felt like all those months I carried her, as I knew her father never wanted us…*this*. She would be enough.

I was exhausted and had no idea how much time had passed. Mom kissed me on the forehead and told me how beautiful Monica was. Dad even said the same and called me pumpkin before they both left.

Tammy stood beside the bed, holding Monica when the door opened. Michael. She looked at me and then the baby. Michael looked…sunken. His face was unshaven, his eyes were lifeless, and he looked as if he lost weight. He was holding flowers, balloons, and a pink bear.

Tammy handed me the baby and said, "Call me when you're ready to be released. You can stay with me if you want."

"Okay. Thanks, Tammy." She kissed Monica's little head and touched my hand. Her eyes raised in an expression that Michael and I should talk. She turned and gave Michael a quiet hello before leaving the room.

"What are you doing here, Michael?"

"Scott said you had the baby. Wow, can I see her?" His eyes went to the bundle in my arms and then back to me. There was a sad reserve in them. Almost like the night, I told him she was a girl.

"When did you see Scott?"

"April…"

"Shut up, Michael. I don't want to hear about you and April." I looked away and began fussing with Monica's blanket.

"No, Jill. I wasn't with April. I ran into her at the grocery store. She congratulated me. Jen and Scott told her your parents brought you in. Why didn't you call me?"

"Are you serious? You've had a week to call me. Why didn't you?"

"I wanted to. I did. You know how it is with your parents. I've been here for almost three hours. In the parking lot—I was waiting for your parents to leave. I swear, Jill. After April told me, I bought you and the baby these," he says, setting the balloons and flowers on a table. "Here, I hope she likes it," he says, setting the pink bear beside Monica. "Can I hold her?"

Why's he doing this? I was ready to end this. I don't know if I can remain strong enough now. I will need my strength to raise this baby. "Michael…"

"Please?"

Against my better judgment, I handed her up to him. He took her in his arms like she was precious glass. "Oh, God. She's so tiny." He moved with small bounces and looked at her. "How was it? Is everything okay? Is she healthy?"

"Yes, Michael; she's healthy. Everything went okay…"

"I wanted to be here. I promise…I did."

"I don't believe you. What about that girl you left with on the jet ski?"

"Nothing happened, Jill. I promise. It was just a party boat. Once we got there…"

"What? What happened, Michael?"

"Nothing. It was just a bunch of people partying on a boat. I swear. Nothing happened with her."

"How'd you get back then?"

"Ah…I woke up, not remembering much. And someone brought me back to the house."

"Give me my daughter back. I don't believe you, nor do I want to hear it."

"Please, Jill. Hear me out. I felt like shit for what I did. I was going to make it up to you. I promise."

"You had a week to call me. You didn't. So, I still don't believe you." My hands reached for my daughter. He looked at her and then began to cry. I was confused and wasn't sure how to process it. Be mad? Be sad? Be Strong? I couldn't let him get my hopes up again. I couldn't fall in love with only the fantasy again.

"Jill," he said, and his voice cracked as he cried. "I'm going to get it right this time. Believe me."

"Michael," I said and looked away. My throat ached from the large lump forming. "I can't keep going on like this. It's not fair to me and now to her."

"I know. It's going to be so different. I will make you happy—I promise."

"But, Michael…do you love me?" I was mad now for asking. Because I knew he didn't. And now, I was going to hear the truth.

"I know I don't show it. But…I do, Jill." I waited for more. I expected, 'Yes, I love you, Jill,' but it only came as a, 'I do.' Would that be enough? He did love me, but couldn't say the words? He was here. That alone was unexpected.

"What do you want, Michael?"

"Don't go back to your parents or move in with Tammy. Come home, Jill. I want you and the baby home with me."

My heart was breaking. Michael wanted us home, but I was still afraid. I was crying, and the baby blues had already set in. I didn't need this on top of it. "Michael...I..."

"I've been thinking. The apartment is too small. Let's buy a house. A house to start our family. A house with a backyard and trees." All through his words, my tears never stopped. It was everything I'd ever wanted to hear from him. But would it last? Was he willing to try this time? "Please, Jill. You won't regret it—I promise."

He bent down and kissed my lips, still with Monica in his arms. "She's beautiful. Thank you for giving me such a beautiful daughter."

I cried harder. Michael's beautiful words ached deep inside me. It was as if my lungs were coming up for air, and I was breathing life again. The nightmare was over, and a new life was there, waiting for me. I just had to take it and believe him. It wasn't just about me anymore, and I was torn between giving my daughter a family with a mother and father or raising her on my own and never living in fear of what if.

And that's the thing about *fear and what-ifs*—no matter what side of the coin you choose, *fear and what-ifs* exist on both sides.

CHAPTER 27

Now

A ring? Now? What's he thinking? He was only to walk his daughter down the aisle and then leave. From my point of view, anyway. I haven't seen this man in over twenty years, and he shows up and proposes.

"Michael...I..."

"I said don't answer now. Let's deal with Tammy. I know you want to be there for her. I'll be here waiting, Jill. I'm not going anywhere." He's still on one knee, braced in the sand. He holds my hand with the ring. I look at it. I look at Michael. I look at Monica and Jordan at the cliff's top. Seagulls squawk and squeak in the background. The splashing of waves closes in, and the sun is about to set. He stands and wraps his arms around me. "Let's watch the sunset...together," he says, kissing me gently.

Turning around, Michael cradles me in his arms, and his chin rests in the crook of my neck. "I never want to miss another sunset with you, Jill."

So many emotions are running through me. The past, the present, Tammy, Monica, and Jordan. Michael. I can't process so much in such little time. But he said not to answer him. And Tammy is high on the list. Even if I wanted to enjoy this moment, I couldn't, with my best friend, who has such little time left.

"I promise to always be here for you. All you have to do is accept it," Michael says, and I close my eyes. I don't want to see the sunset because it's the end of another day and one day closer to Tammy's end. How will I ever enjoy another sunset again?

I break from Michael's embrace. "Michael, I can't do this."

"I know it's hard…with Tammy and all…"

"No. It's not just that. I can't do this with you. I can't put myself back through that again. I'm not the same person. There was a time whenever I saw you, I would get all jelly-like inside."

"And now?"

"Now, nothing." His eyes rim with redness and well with tears. "I had to learn to look at the ugliness you caused in our life. And now…that's all I see."

"You can't see any beauty in us?"

"Yes, I did, Michael. You didn't." I turn and head back down the beach. The sand makes it hard for a fast getaway, and he's on my heel.

"Jill, please don't leave. Just have dinner with me. Monica and Jordan went to a lot of trouble…"

"And that's another thing. What is it with you getting all involved with my friends and family?"

"Monica's my family too," he defends.

"Oh, don't start that. Just because you gave life to someone doesn't qualify you as family. That's a whole other level. You gave that privilege up."

He hesitates, sadly gazing into my eyes. "Yes…I know, and it was the worst mistake of my life. If only I could go back, I would change everything. Watch Monica grow up. Have more children…"

"Stop," I say and continue to walk away. I can't listen to the *what-ifs* or *should have*. Staying away from Michael was the best thing I could have done for us. Although I wanted more children to give Monica a sibling, Michael damaged my concept of ever having that. If a father couldn't love and want his *own* daughter and family, how could another man love us? The fear of making that choice and having another baby with Monica cast to the side as the outcome; I couldn't take that chance. I couldn't let another man destroy me like Michael had.

I see Monica watching us from the top of the cliff. Though I know she can't hear us, the situation is visible. Is she part of this, too? And now I'm guilty of protecting her too much. Maybe now is the time to lay it all out. I want to tell her about my sacrifices to give her an everyday happy life. But that would undo all my hard work—never allowing her to be affected. But even I know that no one is left untouched after divorce.

"Why do you involve her in this? It's not fair, Michael. Not to her or me. I kept all your shit quiet from her—you're welcome."

"I know. Thank you. When I met my daughter…" He stops and looks out over the lake.

"When you met her…what?"

"Have dinner with me, at least. There are some things I would like to tell you." Looking up, I see Jordan come and lead Monica back to the house, allowing us some privacy. But whatever is going on, I feel her involvement. And that alone hurts. "Please."

"Okay," I say. "I don't know what's going on with you two, but I don't want to hurt Monica's feelings—as she's made this wonderful dinner." He holds his hand, but I push past and walk back to the canopy. "And it's not fair. You are using her to make me feel guilty," I say when he pulls the chair out.

He bends down and kisses me on the cheek from behind. "No, it isn't. But thanks for staying."

Dusk has set, illuminating the lights hung around the canopy as we eat lobster, corn, and champagne. Afterward, Michael adds more wood to the fire, lays a blanket over the sand, and asks me to join him. "Come here," he says, patting the spot beside him. "Let's finish this champagne, and we'll talk about anything you want."

I grab my drink and sit on my knees so I'm not pressed against him. Holding out my glass, he tops it off. Through the light of the fire, I watch the bubbles swim through the crystal. "Tell me what's going on, Michael, with you and Monica and asking me to marry you. You started to say something earlier. What was it?" I sip my champagne and study his face. He looks out over the darkness of the lake. "When did she come to see you? I was under the impression that you two only connected on Facebook. There seems to be more going on."

He looks back and presses his lips. "Monica did come to see me in Seattle." I huff and take another swallow of champagne. "Don't blame her. It wasn't her reaching out to me. I reached out to her." Sadly, that feels like a lesser betrayal, and I shouldn't feel that way about my daughter. She is what I created—sweet, loving, forgiving. "I was going through a bad time, re-evaluating my life. I had already been watching her grow up on Facebook."

"Did she know? Were you two online friends?"

"No, she didn't know. I didn't know how she even felt about me. Or if she had taken another man as her father. I was never able to find you on Facebook."

"And there's a good reason why," I say.

"So I couldn't see you?"

"Yup," I say, but it's a lie. I was afraid that, if I joined Facebook, all the consuming over Michael and what he was doing would be like a reappearing cancer. Nowadays, it's so easy to check up on someone and spy legally. If only we had Facebook back then, I could have spared the degrees I went through. Seattle. But I knew Monica posted pictures of me on her Facebook. And all this time, I hoped maybe he was watching. He was.

"It was Father's Day, and all her friends posted stuff about their fathers. It hit me hard. Because I knew she didn't have anything to post about me. Anything good, anyway. Things to tell the world how much she loved her father. I had to turn it off. Fear of what I might see. It ate me up, and I logged back in, and there it was."

"What was it? What'd she say?"

"The picture you took of us in Florida. The one with Monica on my shoulders, holding her arms out and pretending to fly. And, captioned above, she wrote: To my long lost father. *I hope you're happy whatever and wherever you are or what you're doing. Happy Father's Day.*"

"She kept that picture beside her bed growing up. I told her about that day. That it was a happy day for all of us."

"Did she ever ask about us? What happened?"

I look away and sip the champagne. The waves are becoming louder as the dark sky filled with stars replaces the sunset. "Not too much. I think it just became the norm for her. You were gone so much when she was little. That's how she thought it was for married people." I laugh. "When she started school, she didn't understand why some dads live with their moms. It was something she never considered. And at times, she'd ask why we weren't together. I'd tell her our marriage wasn't meant to be."

He looks out over the dark water. "After that post, I messaged Monica. I thanked her for her post and said I wasn't happy. I asked if she would come to see me if I paid her way."

"When?"

"Two years ago."

She would have been in college. "She never mentioned…"

"I told her not to. I didn't want to cause you any more pain. I had done enough to you. So, she knows Jill. You did an excellent job raising her and keeping her from hating me. But I made sure she knew the truth about me."

"How long did she stay?"

"The summer."

"The summer! She told me she was taking extra summer classes and staying with friends from college. Now I find out you two were hanging out. I can see the lying apple doesn't fall far from the lying tree."

"Jill, she wanted to tell you. I told her not to. Please don't be mad with her."

I get up and walk toward the water. I stop when I feel the water rush to my feet. I'm not sure how to feel—betrayed, confused? Michael comes up from behind me. I'm shivering; my arms wrap around my body, and he holds me close. "Cancer…had just taken a friend, and it made me see how much I regretted my own life and what I had done. And how unhappy I was in my life. I didn't want to die like that."

I think of Tammy and understand his concern. Having such little time left, we see things in a new light. Tammy has chosen to see peace, goodwill, and the truth. The good in people. The good in Michael. I don't know what to think or how to feel. Denial? I pray that by some miracle, Tammy's life will be spared. Has Michael changed? Or is he only a wolf in sheep's clothing?

"What did you and Monica do that summer?"

"She…helped me to heal. She gave me purpose and a reason to go on. She talked about her wedding and Jordan. It made me so happy and sad at the same time. Because I saw what I never gave you as a young bride. The way her eyes lit up when she talked of Jordan and their life together. It was love, and I saw the same thing in a young girl I destroyed years ago. You." He lays his chin on my head. "I saw something bigger than anything I had been chasing—to be the sparkle in someone's eye and the reason for the smile on their heart. I saw you. I saw everything I ever wanted. And when cancer took my friend's life, I was unsure which pain was worse—the shock of what happened or the ache for what never will. Death hurts the most when the story is not finished. Death is the end for all of us. But if my death leaves no memories in someone's heart, it was the end of nothing. I saw my life as a beautiful lie and death as a painful truth."

He holds me tightly, and we listen to the waves crash in and crawl back out. The fire crackles beside us, and I don't want to think for once. "Just stay with me tonight on the beach. No promises. No commitments. Just you and I and a memory we'll have after one of us is gone."

"You want us to camp on the beach?"

"Yes. There's a tent inside the cabana. It might be a little hard putting it up in the dark." He makes a small laugh. "It will make it more memorable."

I look up and see the sparkle in his eyes from the campfire's glow. "You're serious. You want to put a tent up in the dark, on the beach?"

He pulls me in, wrapping his arms tightly around me. "There are lots of things I want to do with you. But now, putting up this tent is first on the agenda." The fire reflects in his eyes, and I see sad desperation.

"Alright, Michael. I'll camp with you on the beach. Besides, it's something I've always wanted to do. And… I do not promise anything." I say, and his ring sparkles when my hand touches his shoulder, reminding me I'm still wearing it. I remove it and hand it over. "Here."

"No, it's yours forever. Even if you never marry me, it's what I should have given you a long time ago." He slips the ring back on my finger and places a small kiss on top. "I'm just happy I got to give it to you…" He starts to say something else and then stops. "Shall we put up the tent?"

"What else were you going to say?"

"Nothing. It wasn't important." He walks to the cabana and returns with a bag containing the tent. "Let's do this," he says, smiling while unzipping the bag.

"Okay."

We laugh through most of the process, and it's maybe the release I need. I wonder if Michael thinks back to the last time we tried this. He made everything I wanted to do a hassle and a waste of time. My *delusional, romantic* thoughts, he would call them.

It takes some effort, but eventually, we have a small tent up. Michael holds up his palm for a high-five. "Great job, kid." *Kid.* He hasn't called me that since high school.

"So, are we sleeping on the tent floor…or do you have some more surprises stashed away?" He smiles—diabolically. "What's that smile for?"

"I do. One sleeping bag."

"Okay, that will do. What are you sleeping on?"

"You."

I can't help but match his smile before running down the beach. He chases after me, and the harder I run, the more the sand slows me down. As we run, our laughter fills the night sky. I feel young and silly. I needed this. I've needed this for a long time.

He's close, and I kick up more sand, racing down the dark beach. "I'll never let you get away again, Jill Danforth," he yells and grabs my arm as we both fall to the sand, laughing. He's on top of me, and through the dimly lit light of the moon, I see love in his eyes. "Oh, Jill. Why didn't I do these things with you before? I love you. Thank you for loving me once." His eyes admire my face, and then he kisses me. It's full of regret, remorse, sorrow, gratitude, and…*love.*

CHAPTER 28

Then

Michael had kept his promise, and we bought a house after bringing our baby girl home. Things were getting better for us, and Michael worked hard at Whirlpool, and the company promoted him to project manager. I was now in school, and Monica was in daycare all day between my mom and the daycare at Michael's work. It was hard leaving her, and she was growing so fast. She walked at ten months and said her first word at four months—Mama.

She would turn a year old, and I couldn't wait for her first birthday party. Our house was a modest ranch in a small subdivision in town. I was surprised Michael didn't want to change jobs and move away. But my parents began tolerating Michael, and we all had to work to become a family. My parents loved their granddaughter, but I sometimes felt their reserve toward Michael. Now that we had a baby, there would be Christmases and birthday parties where we all would be together. I hated being the only one in the room who loved everyone. I loved my parents, my baby, and Michael. My parents loved Monica and me. Michael showed that he loved us, yet he still had to say the words.

When we looked at the house, the realtor showed us the backyard. It was fenced in and had one large tree. Michael commented that he would build Monica a tree house someday. Often, I would mention it, but he would say he didn't remember saying it. I hoped his newly found interest in us was genuine. And that Monica and I had found a place in his heart.

He didn't play with her as much as I wished he would, but my mother said that was normal for men. I felt he missed his single life and didn't spend much time with his daughter. I was surprised he mentioned the daycare at Whirlpool. He had to take her to work on those days, and he couldn't stay late since the daycare closed at five. Eventually, he said it would interfere with his promotions. He wouldn't get another promotion if he weren't willing to stay late. I wanted to disagree and say spending time with his daughter was more important—even if it was only in the car there and back. He also couldn't take the Corvette on those days and had to drive my car. I would drive his Corvette to the community college and experience life as a real college student. Even though I couldn't imagine life without my baby girl, if only for a few hours, it gave me some breathing room. Between school, Monica, and Michael, I was busier than ever. And there would be no promotions with all my efforts—just a job after graduation.

Tammy and I had scheduled all our classes the same so we could still be together. She and Ryan were engaged now and were planning their wedding that summer. She tried not to make a big deal out of it, and I felt it was due to my lack of a wedding. Nonetheless, I showed great enthusiasm to her and Ryan.

Ryan was now working for his father's construction company, and the two of them hoped to build a house someday and move out of the little Cracker Jack house they rented. In such a short time, we were adults dealing with all life pressures—bills, work, and family. Life started early for me, and I was going to prove we would make it. Some days seemed more complicated than others, and life pulled me in every direction. I was on a leash, no matter what I did or where I went. Whether Monica was with my mom or Michael, I was expected to drop everything and apologize for getting out of class late, filling the car up, or stopping to pick up needed items at the store. Michael had yet to change a diaper. However, no one worried about coming home and helping me. My life was unimportant, and I never needed to rest or take a break and soak in the tub. And if I complained about it to my mom or Michael, I was reminded of my choice. What others saw as a choice, I saw as a sacrifice. And it would have been nice to have a little appreciation for it. But whenever I saw that smile on my baby's chubby little cheeks, and Mama came out of her mouth, my choice was golden. Though she took so much of my time, she made me feel special and gave me the validation I needed and lacked.

Monica's first birthday was coming, and I stopped after class to shop. I carried bags filled with balloons and *'baby's first birthday'* decorations in the house, which turned into a big fight. It was Michael's day with Monica. I walked in, and he gave me that exasperated look.

"Where the hell have you been?"

"Michael, I told you yesterday. I was stopping to get her birthday party stuff. Remember?"

"No, I don't fucking remember. All I know is the baby smells like shit. I'm hungry, and all you've been doing is running around in my car, shopping."

"Why didn't you change her?" I was angry, and for once, I would show it. "Don't talk like that around her. My God, Michael, are you helpless? I don't ever see you rushing home to help me. It would be nice to come home to some flowers and dinner. Do you ever get the ache in the pit of your gut when you're not home on time? No, you are so self-absorbed that you only care about yourself." I went and picked up Monica to change her diaper. She was crying from all the shouting.

"Jill, don't you bitch to me about having a kid. That was your choice."

I stopped but didn't turn around. Monica was in my arms, and I wanted to throw something at him. It would have to wait until after I changed her diaper.

I heard him throwing pans around in the kitchen as I changed her diaper. Placing her favorite toys around her, I kissed her head, told her I loved her, and returned to face Michael.

"Don't you ever say it was my choice to have a baby. We had sex. We conceived a baby for which we are both responsible. I just happened to be the one doing all the work."

"Fuck you," he yelled. I felt the tears stinging the back of my eyes. I didn't want to cry. I didn't want to show weakness as I tried to argue my point.

"You've been home, what…twenty minutes? Are you such a pussy that you can't handle a little girl in that short of time? Be a father, Michael. Change her diaper and start dinner—it's called parenting. What the hell!"

He walked abruptly to me and glared at me inches away. "Don't ever tell me what to be. *This*," he swirled his finger in the air, "is not what I wanted out of life."

My chest was caving in. I didn't know if I could hold back the tears. So many times, he referred to us as, *this*. And each time, my heart broke a little more. I knew I walked around with a fractured heart, and maybe someday it would heal. I just knew it wouldn't be Michael who would cure it. "You are the most ungrateful bitch I have ever known. I work my ass off to buy you this house, pay for your school, buy things for a baby who shits and pisses her pants. I would rather be driving a Porsche up the West Coast, getting drunk at some club, and being laid by as many women as I want. But no! I'm here raising you and your daughter—here in this shitty house in hillbilly haven."

"Stop it," I cried out.

"Trust me, Jill. I would love to stop *this*." He rolled his finger around again.

"Then why don't you leave?"

"Really? Why don't I leave?"

"Why do you stay…if you can't take…*this* anymore," I said, exaggerating my finger. "And by the way, Michael, I and your daughter are not this. We are your family."

"Don't tempt me, Jill. I'm ready to walk out that door."

"Then do it. Leave!"

"Then what the hell will you do?" he mocked. "How will you finish school?"

"Student loans. Tammy's getting loans. I'll do the same."

"And how will you live?"

"I'll work part-time or go to school part-time."

He glared at me as his eyes showed no remorse and laughed. "You're as trapped in this hell as I am."

"Why must you see it that way? Why can't you be happy with us? You're only miserable because you make it that way. I'm willing to be happy, but you fight me all the way."

"Happy! You're happy?" He screamed his response, and everything inside me was shaking. "How can I be happy when I never wanted this?" He stormed over to the wall, where a family picture of the three of us hung. Pulling it off the wall, he stormed back to me. "You want to see how sick I am of this family?" The picture went flying through the room, and glass shattered everywhere. I was crying and begging him to stop. It was the only picture I had of us. A coupon I had from Olan Mills after Monica was born. I had always wanted a family portrait because, growing up, we never had one.

"Stop it, Michael. Why do you have to be so cruel? You know I loved that picture of us."

He didn't stop there and took the picture from my birthday—the one of us together when I was pregnant and threw it across the room, breaking it as well. Next, he ran to Monica's baby picture, and I ran to stop him. He pushed me back, and I fell to the floor.

"No, please don't. Not Monica's picture, Michael." Please," I begged.

His eyes got a crazed, satisfied look as he broke the frame across his knee. I heard Monica crying in the doorway, terrified by Michael's outrage, and I went to grab her. She was shaking, and I feared what Michael would do next. I held her tightly, trying to comfort her. But I was crying and trembling as well.

"Please, Michael. Just go away."

"Are you kicking me out?"

"You don't want to be with us anyway. Go!"

"If I leave, don't expect me back," he said, walking over the broken glass.

"I don't expect anything from you, Michael. That's the problem," I said quietly. But he heard me and had to throw in more insults.

"Oh, don't worry, Jill. I've wanted to leave for a long time. Have fun paying for all of this. I know I will be—fucking anyone I want."

"Like you haven't been anyway," I said, turning to leave.

"That's right, Jill. It's nice to look at something other than someone lounging around in scrubs all day. I have to do something to keep me from going insane."

"I have to wear them for clinicals. You know that. Oh, poor Michael. Life is so rough for you." I heard him coming to the bedroom and froze when he grabbed my hair.

"What did you say?" Monica's cries were becoming panicked, and I begged him to stop.

"Nothing. I'm sorry. Just go away. Go be with whoever you want." He let go of my hair and left the room. I heard him slam our bedroom door, and I hoped he was packing. A few minutes later, he returned and was holding his suitcase.

"Kiss the daycare at work goodbye. You'll have to quit school or have your mom here every day. See what life gets you when you're such a bitch," he said and left.

I calmed Monica down and put her in bed with a bottle as I cleaned up all the glass. The pictures were unsalvageable. I sat on the floor of the living room and silently cried. Michael had destroyed all her baby pictures, and I would never have that time back. I hated Michael. I hated that I loved a man who could do that.

I took the pictures and placed them in a drawer. I still couldn't throw them away. The sack from the store containing Monica's birthday decorations was still on the counter. I took them out and cried some more. It hurt that these simple, precious things meant so much to me yet were hated by Michael. Nothing about us was special to him, and I had to escape. He would never change because we were something he never wanted. He never wanted…*this.*

•   •   •   •   •

Friday was Mom's day to have Monica, and I never mentioned the fight Michael and I had when I dropped her off before class. I wasn't ready to tell her, and I had been taking Monica to daycare at Michael's work. But I had to cut class early to drive an hour to pick her up. I saw Michael's car in the parking lot and wondered where he was staying. I was curious if he checked to see if his daughter was in the daycare, to see if I brought her anyway and would be waiting for me. He never was, and it didn't surprise me.

After classes, I picked my daughter up on time and rushed home to decorate for her first birthday party. Mom and Dad, Tammy and Ryan, and Scott and Jen were all coming over. I used the excuse that Michael had to travel for work and couldn't get out of it. Only Tammy knew that he was gone. I didn't know what I would say when they noticed all the pictures were gone from the wall.

The decorations were up—*The Little Mermaid* and Tammy made an Ariel cake. Though she was only turning one, Monica loved to watch "*The Little Mermaid*" for hours. The cartoon was a lifesaver when trying to finish my homework, as Michael never offered help when he was home.

I hadn't heard from him in four days, and I thought he would come by chance for his daughter's birthday. But deep down, I knew it was the last thing he wanted to do. And it hurt more than ever to know he was sleeping with someone else. I didn't know who and hadn't had time to find out. Soon, however, I would be consumed by Michael's betrayals and infidelities and miss out on life's little joys with my daughter.

Tammy and I both helped Monica blow out her candle. She was one year old, and Michael would never get this moment back. It was these special, little moments in life he found no importance in, and to think that anything was better than us came crashing down on my heart. I would have to give Monica enough for both of us.

"So, what are you going to do?" Tammy asked once everyone was off eating their cake.

"I don't know. If I get divorced, I must quit school and find a job. There's no way I could afford this house on my own, even with student loans. Michael may be an asshole, but at least he pays for my schooling with the help of the reimbursement program through Whirlpool. If we divorce, it goes away."

"Which is more important? Your degree or your sanity?"

"Ahh, it's so tough. Why can't he love us like he should? I was all ready to divorce him last year. Then, he suddenly had a change of heart. I thought it would last. But you're right. I can't go on like this. I should ask Mom if we can move back home and give Michael the house." It was the last thing I wanted to do.

"Well, if you're single, you may get better assistance with school and other stuff."

"Not with Michael's income and child support. It's strange. He's the one who hates being in this marriage, but I am the one who feels trapped. Maybe before I talk to Mom, I should talk to Michael. Maybe we could devise an arrangement if he wants out so bad."

"Like what?" Tammy asked, her eyes wide with unbelief.

"I don't know. Maybe stay married while I live at home…" I was starting to cry, and Tammy pulled me outside. We stood on the patio in the backyard, and I tried desperately to compose myself. "When we bought this house, Michael promised to build Monica a tree house in that tree," I said, nodding to the lone large maple tree.

"Well, she is a little young right now."

"I know. But I thought it'd be one of those things a father would do with anticipation. For example, when they buy their newborn son a baseball bat and hat, Maybe if she were a boy, he'd be different."

"No, not Michael. That's just the way he is, Jill. The sooner you realize it has nothing to do with you and Monica, the better off you'll be. He's just not the settling down type."

She was right. Guys like Michael would always live with the Peter Pan Syndrome. He denied growing old and never wanting the responsibility. I was the one-time chase he conquered before moving on to the next. I was the obstacle in his way, and he hated me for this reason.

After the party, I kissed Mom and Dad goodbye and told Mom I would like to talk in the morning. I could tell she knew something was wrong by the look in her eyes. Mother's always do. She also looked at the empty walls and commented that I must already be packing. I had no heart to tell her that Michael destroyed all our family pictures.

The house was empty of guests, and Monica was put to bed. Maybe I would stop in Michael's office after dropping Monica off and ask if he would talk. But instead, I called and left a message on his voicemail at work. I didn't know any other way to get a hold of him.

It was dark, and lightning flashed. A storm was coming, and I went around, closing all the windows as the rain began to pour. Before closing the blinds to the back door, lightning flashed again, and I saw the quick image of someone sitting on the patio step. My heart jumped, and fear shivered through my body. I locked the door and grabbed the phone to call 911. With my finger, I pulled down enough of the blinds to see if someone was still there. The rain was coming down hard, and he was soaked. When the lightning flashed again, I recognized him. Michael.

What was he doing in the backyard—in the rain?

I ended the call before it rang and unlocked and opened the door. "Michael?" He turned around. "What are you doing out here?" He stood and walked toward me. He was soaked and looked...strange. "Are you drunk?"

"No, Jill. I'm not drunk."

"Then why are you sitting in the rain?" The look on his face was full of sorrow. It was not like him.

"I was looking at the tree."

"Michael, you're being weird. Why didn't you just come in through the front door?"

"I was afraid."

"Afraid of what?" He was confusing me.

"Afraid you had the locks changed, and I wouldn't be welcome."

I didn't know what to say and wanted to enjoy the silence between us in the rain. It said more about Michael's feelings than he could have said himself. Was he going to say he was sorry? "It's your house too. But I did want to talk to you. I left a message on your work voicemail."

"I know. I called in and listened."

"Why didn't you call the house then?" I wanted to ask where he was staying but didn't want to ruin whatever this moment was.

"I was afraid maybe you changed the number." He handed me a folded piece of paper. It had become wet from the rain, and I told him to come inside. The paper was still in my hands, and even though Tammy and I talked about me divorcing Michael, I feared he already had filed, and this was the paper telling me so. As I unfolded it, I prepared myself for what it was and was willing to accept it. At least someone had started the proceeding.

I looked at the wet paper and saw the heading: Menard's. I looked back up at Michael. "What's this?"

"Read it," he said.

Through the wet paper, I could make out terms like 2x4 treated and buckles. "I still don't understand."

"Sorry, it's late. It's Monica's birthday present. It's the lumber to make her tree house. They'll be delivering it tomorrow. I wanted you to know."

"Michael…I don't know what to say."

"I want to start building it. Can I come home?"

I looked at him in shock. It was the last thing I ever expected. Would this be the turning point for us, and we would be together forever? This would be the one thing we would look back on and maybe laugh about someday. Tell others struggling in their marriage to hold on and work it out? As much as I wanted it to be, I thought about the pictures he destroyed.

"Michael, I don't know. It really hurt when you destroyed our pictures. Those are moments we'll never get back."

"I know, and I'm so sorry. Can we have new ones made?"

"I'm not sure. The studio's not even in town anymore. I don't know how I could contact them." Beth had long gone to a college out of state. "Why did you do it, Michael?"

"I don't know. I regret it. I was angry and wanted to hurt you."

"Why? Why do you want to hurt me? I don't understand."

"I don't mean to." He took a deep breath. "This isn't going to come out right. It makes me mad that I can't walk away from you and Monica."

"I don't know how to take that," I said and tried to see the good in it.

"I never saw myself as the family type. I saw one thing. Me, success, and freedom. I'm still trying to figure out where to put you and Monica."

My arms hugged around me as I listened to his declaration of his true feelings. It hurt me that he couldn't find a place for us in his heart, yet he was honest with me. I thought I should do the same.

"Michael, I never saw us married either. Yes, in my stupid, girly fantasies. But now that it's real, I can't imagine life any different. And...I wished I did. I wished I could stop loving you. I wish the things you did didn't hurt me so much. I wish I never met you—not so much for myself. But so that you wouldn't hate me."

"Jill, I don't hate you. I hate that I do love you. But, I don't know how to show it. All I do is fight it, and I know it isn't fair to you."

"You love me?"

He stared at me incredulously. "Yes, Jill."

I began to cry. "You want to come home?"

"Yes. I want to try."

"Michael..." He took me in his arms, and I cried in his chest. "What kind of marriage is this if we wished we didn't love each other?"

He picked me up, and my legs wrapped his waist. "You're a good wife, Jill. I'm just not a good husband. And I don't know if I'll ever be." He carried me to the bedroom, and we kissed as we took off the wet clothes. "I missed you," he said, picking me up again and laid me on the bed.

Even though I wasn't sure if I did, I said it too. "I missed you too, Michael."

As he made love to me, he repeated how much he didn't deserve me, and I knew it to be true. He told me again what a wonderful wife and mother I was, and even though marriage was never in his plans, he couldn't have picked a better wife.

I accepted Michael's apology and his passionate lovemaking. I was still torn between his hatred of loving us and his willingness to try. But as time went on, the word try would leave a lousy taste in my mouth. Because to love Monica and me was simple. To love Michael would become a challenge.

CHAPTER 29

Now

My cell rings and I see Ryan's name displayed. Panic rises from head to toe. Tammy is getting worse, and I've already scheduled a leave from the hospital. Each day I hate waking up, knowing it's one less day she has left. I take a deep breath and wait to hear that I'm too late and that she passed in the night.

"Ryan…"

"Hi, Jill. She had a better night last night. She's asking for you."

"Of course. I'll be right over. Please tell Tammy I'm on my way."

"I will. There's something she wants to ask you."

"Oh? Well, give me about twenty minutes. I'll hurry. Goodbye."

"Bye, Jill."

I end the call and rush to get to Tammy, wondering what she wants to ask. She knows I'll do anything. She knows I'll help with the girls. I am their godmother, and I'll always be there when they need me.

Ryan's standing on the porch when I pull in the drive. He looks very concerned, and once again, I fear I missed her. "How is she? Please don't tell me…"

"No, Jill. She's in the living room waiting for you."

I rush in and see her curled up on the couch sipping tea, wearing a pink, fuzzy robe with a pink terry cloth turban. Her face gets paler each time I see her.

"I'm here, Tammy," I say, desperation ringing in my voice.

"Calm down, girl. I'm not going anywhere…not yet anyway." How she stays so positive is beyond me. I sometimes wonder, if once you know it's your time to die, is it more acceptable? "Cancel all your plans this week."

"You got it." I almost ask what she has planned but knowing her, the word *dying* will come flying out of her mouth.

"We will spend the week at my uncle's beach house."

"Yes, whatever you want. Want me to start packing for you?"

"You can. I don't know how much I'll need. At least pick something out you can bury me in."

And there it is. Tammy's it-is-what-it-is philosophy. "Fine then. I'm packing the skimpiest bikini you have." She laughs, and I don't know how.

"Better grab one of the girl's suits. Unlike you, I stopped wearing bikinis after the girls were born. Oh, and when they embalm me, make sure they give me one of those spray tans."

"Alright, that's enough of this talk," I say and run upstairs to pack her a bag. I never asked if the girls and Ryan were coming. So, I busy myself throwing in anything I think she will need and run back downstairs.

"Hey, are the girls and Ryan coming?"

"Yes, Ryan will bring them up Friday. I want a few days alone with just us." She sounds severe and…I don't like what she's implying.

"Okay, like I said, whatever you want," I say, kissing her pale cheek. It feels cold, and I want to wrap her in my arms, warming her failing body and never wanting her to leave me. Ahh, this is going to be complicated.

Ryan kisses her on the lips and tells her he loves her and says he and the girls will be there soon. "Let me know if I need to bring anything else up when we come. You're sure you want to do this?"

"Yes, it's not like I'm going to get better. This is as good as it gets," Tammy tells him, and I pad outside, leaving them alone to talk. I put her bag in the car and wait as Ryan helps her out. She's brave and tough, smacking Ryan away and letting him know she can walk to the car alone. Oh, Tammy. What will I do without you?

She falls into the seat and demands, "Okay, Thelma, let's hit the road." I giggle and start the car. Ryan expresses his concerns through the open window as Tammy hits the close button, shutting his fingers in the window. She bats her hands for him to leave.

"Now, Tammy, that wasn't very nice of you," I tease.

"Hey, I'm dying. I don't have to be nice. Alright, if it makes you feel better." She rolls down the window. "Ryan, get out and enjoy yourself tonight. I'll see you in a few days." They kiss again and he backs up, placing his hands on his hips this time when I put the car in reverse.

Shifting the gear into drive, she notices the ring on my finger. "Holy Moly! Is that…?"

"Oh. Don't get excited. I'm just trying it on for size before giving it back."

"He asked you to marry him?" She grabs my hand.

"Yes. And said it's mine, even if we never marry. Said it's the one I should have had years ago."

"We've got a lot more to talk about. Hope I get an extension from upstairs," she says with her hands in a prayer position. I smile and shake my head.

We stop by my house, and I pack quickly and run out the door in record time. If only it was just another girl trip…and not our last.

Her uncle's cottage is five miles up Blue Star Highway, so we're there in less than twenty minutes. I tell her to go inside, and I'll bring in our bags. "I think I can carry one thing, Jill."

"Fine, carry the wine."

"Oh, thank you, God. I was afraid you wouldn't bring any. And…do not tell Ryan." I make the button-my-lip suggestion and grab the bags.

I haven't been here since the night of Michael's birthday—the night he left and partied with girls on a houseboat. I need these reminders, so I don't do anything stupid and marry him again. But for now, I'll enjoy the ring. Maybe I lose it in the lake.

Walking inside, I'm doubly reminded. The window seat where I cried all night, waiting for him to come back. The kitchen where I prepared a gourmet birthday dinner—that we never ate. And now, I'm here with Tammy—her last summer here. This will always be a place of bad memories for me.

"Oh, I feel better already," she says. "Being cooped up in the house all day. And Ryan on my ass every minute."

"You know he can't help it."

"I know. I'm grateful to have Ryan. I was going to suggest you two get married after I'm gone. But now that I've seen that ring."

I pick up a pillow and throw it at her. "Will you stop? I'm not marrying Michael, and I could never marry Ryan. No offense, but it'd be like kissing my brother."

"Would it help if you thought of Ryan as the hot step-brother? Those books are trendy."

I pick up another pillow from the couch and toss it at her. "No step-brother. No brother's friend. Think I've had my share. Now, stop this nonsense and let's unpack and head down to the beach. Are you ready for some wine?"

"Some? I'm ready for the whole damn bottle."

We toss our things in the bedroom and then change for the beach. I make sure Tammy has plenty of sunblock and grab the beach umbrella, leaning against the fence as we walk down the sandy trail. Once the umbrella is securely anchored in the sand, I unfold the beach chairs lying on the ground and pour her a glass of wine.

"Oh, thank you, thank you, thank you," she says. After my glass is poured, I sit next to her and watch her enjoy this moment in time— with so little time left. "It's so amazing, isn't it?" she says, holding her glass out to the lake.

"Yes, it is." Sipping my wine, I wonder what is going through her mind. "How are the girls doing?" This does make her start to cry. "I'm sorry. I shouldn't have brought it up."

"No. You should. It needs to be discussed. Casey's mad at me. Callie is in denial, and Hailee, I think, doesn't quite understand. Casey thinks I've given up and I don't want to be around."

"Have you talked to her? I can if you want me to."

"Yes, I have. But I think it's the only way she can cope. And…maybe it's better that way. Anger is easier to deal with than sadness. Especially loss."

I search my stupid brain for any response. "Tammy, I don't know what to say or what you want me to say. But I promise you I will always be there for the girls."

"Oh, Jill. I know you will. And I'm sorry to have to put you in this situation. It's not fair."

"None of it's fair. It pisses me off so fucking much and I…" She starts to laugh. "What? Why are you laughing?"

"Because you sound just like Casey. She uses my dying as an excuse to swear."

"Well…"

"I get it. It makes you feel better. It's strange, isn't it? How swearing out loud relieves tension. Let's yell at the top of our lungs, so loud they'll hear us Wisconsin."

"Sounds good to me," I say. "I'll start. Fuck you, cancer! Why don't you go find some piece of shit's life to take?" Tammy laughs as wine comes spraying from her mouth. "That felt good. Your turn."

"Fuck you, cancer and the cancer cells you rode in on." She laughs and gulps a large portion of wine.

"Yeah," I yell. "Fuck you, cancer-clopping horse."

"Cancer-clopping horse," Tammy says, laughing hard from her belly. "Oh, God. This is good. I haven't felt this great since…well, since I got cancer."

"Cancer's going to be sorry someday." I stand and yell out over the lake. "Just wait. She'll come back in another life and be the doctor who cures cancer. She'll look you in the face and know who you are." I pick up a handful of sand and throw it hard. "Fuck you. Your paths will cross in a lab someday, and you will go down." I fall to my knees and punch the sand. Somewhere between the swearing and yelling, I begin crying uncontrollably.

"Jill…Jill." Tammy drops to her knees beside me and holds my shaking body.

"Tammy, I'm sorry. It should be me holding you."

"Yeah, well, whatever," she carelessly says. She cleans my face and gives me a reassuring smile. "A doctor? Thanks, but I plan on returning as Marilyn Monroe and watching the Kennedys squirm. I'd be bored in the lab."

"What…?" I look at her incredulously, and we both laugh.

"Whew. That was great. I should have done that instead of chemo," she says, pulling my arm and directing us back to our chairs. "I think we're going to need more wine."

I sit back in my chair and look at her. "You're unbelievable, you know that?"

"I know," she says and toasts my glass. "Okay, no more talking about me. I'm dying, blah, blah, blah—you'll help Ryan with the girls. The end is near, so there's nothing left. You," she stresses, "have plenty of time and I want to know what you're going to do with it."

"What am I going to do?"

"Spill it, Jill. I'm dying, remember? Not much time left. Talk."

"About what?"

"Where and when are you going to marry Michael?" I choke on my wine.

"Ah…I'm not." She waves her glass to the ring on my finger, sparkling in the sun. "I'm just wearing it for a while. Soon I let him down and send him on his way crying. Hopefully before the old Michael shows up."

"I think you need to marry him here on this beach. I'll get it all arranged with my uncle before I die."

"Tammy, are you listening to me?"

"No. It has to be soon—before summer's over. Beach weddings on Lake Michigan don't go over well in the winter." She continues planning my wedding with Michael as I laugh and drink more wine. I love her.

The sun begins to set, and I run up to the cottage, grabbing another bottle of wine. When I return to the beach, she tells me she wants to walk the coastline. "Are you sure? You're not too tired?"

"I'm always tired. It's probably the last time I get to do this. Come on." I refill our glasses, and we set out down the coast. Not sure how far we'll get. My arm wraps around her for support, and we giggle when passing other walkers and lovers who have come to watch the sunset. I'm sure they consider us a couple, and Tammy doesn't help when she loudly talks about our wedding—the wedding she's planning for Michael and me.

"There it goes," she says. We stop and watch as the sun slowly sinks into the lake. A tear runs down my cheek. It's an end to another day, and one less day I'll ever have with her.

•   •   •   •   •

Adding morphine to her drip, I hear Ryan and the girls enter the cottage. Tammy did her best not to have any the last two days. She wanted to be alert. But eventually, the pain became too much. She says only to give her half, and so I do. Her IV is portable, and she hates for the girls to see her wearing it. I tell her it can't be helped.

"Hey, my pretty girls," she says when all three come to hug her on the couch. Casey shows some reserve, allowing her younger siblings to hug their mom first. "Hi, Casey. Come here and give me a hug." The moment is emotional and my eyes well up. Casey sits next to her mother and the two start to cry.

"Come on girls," I say to Callie and Hailee, "let's put your stuff away and give your sister some time." With both girls wrapped on each arm, we climb the stairs to the room they'll be staying in. As they unpack, I take a seat on the bed and ask both girls to join me. I struggle to get my words out. "I want you to know that I will always be here for you. I will never be able to take your mother's place. But that doesn't mean you can't come to me for anything. Anything you can't go to your dad about."

"How much time does she have left?" Callie says, tears in her eyes. I wipe her face as they begin to fall.

"You know, let's not focus on that and enjoy this time together with her. She's brave. So, we need to be brave with her. That is how she wants it to be. Okay?"

Hailee starts to cry and snuggles into my chest. "I don't want Mommy to die." I hold her tightly and smooth her hair.

"Oh, baby. None of us do. And…it's okay to cry." Callie leans in, too, and I comfort both girls as we cry together. Casey walks in. I look up at her torn face.

"Mom doesn't want us to cry," she says.

"Jill said we could," Hallie tells her big sister. Casey looks at me with daggers in her eyes. She's going to be the hard one. I just hope she lets me in when the time comes.

"Okay girls, let's have our cry and go down and have the best day we can have with your mom. She's been looking forward to you girls coming." The two younger girls wipe their faces and nod. We get up to leave, and I tell them to go on so I can talk to Casey. They leave, and I shut the door behind them. "Casey, I know it's hard, and it's so unfair. I know you're angry…and it's okay to be angry. I want you to know that I'm angry too. Last night, I yelled every curse word imaginable across the lake." She stands next to the bed, holding herself tightly. I walk over and touch her shoulder. "You want to curse with me tonight? I'm giving you a one-time pass."

She presses her lips; her chin quivers, and she finally nods. "If I start, I don't know if I'll be able to stop."

"Duly noted," I say and kiss her on the forehead.

When I reach the bottom of the stairs, Ryan is sitting next to Tammy on the couch—both girls cover his lap. Tammy looks up and smiles faintly. Her eyes are becoming shallow, and her skin is gray. The morphine doesn't help her lethargic state. "Come here," she says, holding out her hand. I walk over and take her hand in mine. "How's she doing?" Her eyes cast to the ceiling, noting upstairs.

"We've talked. It's rough."

"I know," she says with a deep sigh. "Hey, girls, let's get our suits on and head down to the beach. Jill's given me my cocktail," she says, lifting her arm with the IV. "So…I'm feeling pretty good about now."

"Why don't I take the girls down while you and Ryan get ready," I say, thinking they need some alone time.

"Thanks, Jill," Ryan says and prods the girls to move from his lap.

"Love you, girls," Tammy tells them as we go upstairs to change.

I take a deep breath and focus on how to even make this weekend…a joy. But I will. For Tammy's sake, I will.

CHAPTER 30

Then

I was in my third year of nursing school, and Monica turned three. Michael and I weren't perfect, but I thought things might have improved. He was becoming frustrated with his position at work and expressed wanting to move on. Seattle was where he wanted to be, and I recalled the conversation when we were dating. Suppose you would call it that. Sometimes, I felt Michael and I were doing better than expected. After our marriage, when we had known each other for only weeks, we were still together and raising a baby. More so, I was raising her. The tree house was built as promised, and now we had to watch her closely when we were outside. At two and a half, she scaled the ladder like a monkey.

Michael was no longer able to take Monica to the daycare Whirlpool provided because he had switched plants. And somehow, I felt it was done purposefully—so he wouldn't have to take her. However, the change came with an ultimatum—he had to spend Wednesday nights alone with her so that I could join a study group. I was on a fast track—hoping to graduate a year early and continued my studies through the summer. I was well beyond the need for a break. And needless to say, Michael still wasn't much of a help when it came to duties around the house. I looked forward to Wednesday.

My study group was meeting off campus, and I let Michael know the coffee shop where we intended to meet. Dinner was in the crockpot, and Monica was now well potty-trained. He had no excuses—I burned the oil at both ends, and my duties as wife and mother were above and beyond. Though, I got little praise for it.

I kissed Michael goodbye on the cheek and told him Monica was down for a nap. "Don't let her sleep too long. She'll be up all night," I told him as I gathered my books. "And…oh, please place the dishes in the dishwasher and not in the sink." He was removing his tie, looking over some reports he brought home from work. "Did you hear me?"

He looked up. "What?"

"Don't let her sleep much longer and put the dishes in the dishwasher. I'll be home around 8:00."

"Yeah, yeah, yeah. I heard you, Jill."

As I walked out the door, I breathed fresh air. "Ah…adult night," I mumbled, even if it was just to study.

Walking into the coffee shop, I didn't see Tammy or the other two girls in our study group. But I did see the new student—Drake Daniels. He was a transfer student from Michigan State and had recently joined our study group.

"Hey, where's everyone at?" I asked, joining him at the table.

"I don't know." He looked at his watch. "Shall we wait a few minutes?"

"Yeah."

"I'll grab us some coffee," he said, touching my arm as he passed by. Drake was good looking and single and was studying to be an anesthesiologist. There was no doubt that I was attracted to him. But it wasn't just his looks. He was kind and attentive to me. But then again, so was Michael back in the day. He would ask how Monica was and commented on me being a mother and student. He made me feel…*noticed.*

"Here you go. On me," Drake said, setting the coffee down and sliding into the booth across from me. "Well, it looks like everyone else is a no-show."

"Yes, it looks that way," I said, eager to see that it was only us. I convinced myself there was nothing wrong with us being together and alone at a coffee shop. It wasn't something we had planned, and we expected others to attend.

I pulled out my books and waited for him to do the same. Drake smiled sweetly at me, and I had to ask what he was thinking. "What's up?"

"If no one else shows up, let's go to my place to study."

I grabbed my cup, took a quick sip, and burned my tongue. "Ah…"

"You okay?"

"Yes, I just burned my tongue."

"So, what do you say we take this party to my place? It's just across town." As much as I wanted to, I knew I couldn't. What if Michael came looking for me? Yeah, right. But it was more than that. I knew Drake was attracted to me, but worse, I was attracted to him. I looked for any reason to accept his offer. I thought of the times I knew Michael was probably seeing other women. Only, I couldn't prove it and didn't want to give in on assumptions.

"I better not. My husband knows I'm here, and if something happens to Monica, he knows where to get a hold of me."

He reached out and touched my hand. I felt the electricity run through me. It felt good and dangerous at the same time and I knew I was dealing with fire. The temptation was too strong, and I fought the urge to take his hand.

"Okay, I understand," he said and continued to stroke the top of my hand. I didn't move it and savored his simple display of affection. It had been years since Michael showed any attention toward me. Those times usually came after a fight, and he would leave. Only to return when I had made the decision to leave him and take me to bed.

I looked up and saw the begging in his eyes. It was hard to look away, and hard to say no. I was about to pull my hand away when he took mine in his, pulling it into his mouth. As he kissed the top of my hand, he looked at me through his lashes. My chest heaved with excitement, arousal. What should I do? I didn't want to be attracted to him, but I was. Would I be this way if Michael were different? More loving with me? I couldn't decide and panted through my slightly parted lips.

"We really should get some studying done," I said, pulling away. Drake smiled with a sweetness that only intensified my urge to reach across the table and kiss him.

"I understand, Jill. But I want you to know, I'm here…in any way you need me." Had Tammy been talking to him? No, she wouldn't. Would she?

I pressed my lips with a smile and nodded. It wasn't a yes, but it wasn't a no, either. I pulled out my books and opened them to the chapter I had marked. As we studied, I became more comfortable being with Drake. But could I trust myself to be *alone* with him?

He made me feel wanted, desired, worthy and we laughed easily. I didn't feel as if I had to try to get him to enjoy being with me. He just did. Then I thought of Michael. Was this how he behaved at work? Did he display sweet sentiments to other women, making them feel special? I didn't want to make the same mistake I had with Michael. But at the same time, I enjoyed what he was giving me. Special or not.

The time passed, and I panicked while gathering my books. Drake stood and helped me with my sweater. It was nice, again, one of those things Michael would never do. As we left the coffee shop, he took my hand in his…and I let him. It was risky, and anyone could have seen us. The feeling of his hand in mine was too beautiful to let go. He walked me to my car, and before I got in, he kissed me. It was unexpected, and my actions told him I wanted it. He pulled me close, and I wrapped my arms around his neck. I loved the way his hands smoothed down my back and squeezed me into him. I was dizzy, and my body felt like I was floating away. It was hard to return to reality, and I forced myself to break the kiss.

"I…I need to go. It's already late," I stammered.

"Jill, I'm sorry. I didn't mean to upset you."

"It's not that. I…I'm married, Drake." He knew that and kissed me anyway. "I have to go. Goodbye," I said and struggled with the key in the ignition. He placed his palm on the window, and before I pulled away, I pressed mine over his from the other side. I then gave a weak wave and drove away.

I was still shaking when I walked in the front door. Michael was watching TV, and I was sure he could see the guilt written all over my face once he looked at me. "Monica in bed?" I asked but knew she was.

"Yep."

His answer was short, and I knew that meant he was angry because I was late. An hour late. Was he going to say anything? "Was she good?" I needed to know his demeanor.

"Yeah, she was pretty good." I took a breath. He sounded normal and not ticked off.

"Was the crockpot lasagna okay?"

"Yeah. There's some left. I didn't put it away." Of course, he didn't, but I was relieved he wasn't suspicious or upset that I was late.

"Thanks for putting the dishes in the dishwasher." I was looking for reasons to praise him. Though, to clean up after yourself after someone prepares your dinner should be a given.

"No problem," he said and then looked at the clock.

"Ah...sorry I'm late. The time just got away from us." As I walked past him, he looked up, and the panic on my face was palpable. I felt my face begin to scrunch up and before I knew it, I was crying.

"Jill? What's wrong?"

"Michael...something bad happened tonight. I'm so sorry."

"Did you wreck the car?" He stood up and went to the door.

"No, Michael. It was me. I did something...something I shouldn't have."

He turned around and furrowed his brows. "Okay, what?"

I looked at him, and even though this man deserved nothing but a kick in the groin most of the time, I felt guilty. There was panic and concern on his face. This I had never seen from him, and it elevated my guilt.

"I kissed someone. I kissed another man tonight."

He stood there with his hands on his hips and looked at me incredulously. What was going through his mind? Anger? Jealousy? I couldn't stand it and kept apologizing. "I'm so sorry. I didn't mean for it to happen. It will never happen again. I promise." I looked for ways to punish myself. "I'll quit the study group. I'll only study here, and you won't have to watch Monica." He continued to stare at me. "God, say something, Michael."

"Is that all?"

I wasn't sure of the meaning behind his question. Is that all, and did he not care? Or was that all that happened? Did he think no one would find me attractive?

"Answer me," he seethed. His anger began to show, and no doubt he wanted more details.

"No, that was all. We studied and when he walked me to the car...we kissed. That's all, Michael. I promise. I came straight home. Please forgive me."

His shoulders lifted on a heavy sigh, and he ran his hands through his hair. He stretched his neck, and I watched his jaw twitch. He was angry, and I wanted to defend myself and tell him this is how it feels. But I had no proof of his infidelity, and I had just confessed to kissing another man. And on some level, the fact he was angry about it gave me an ounce of satisfaction.

"Who?" he asked behind clenched teeth. I hadn't anticipated this part—he should only be mad at me. I didn't want to get Drake into any trouble.

"It doesn't matter, Michael. He's just some guy in our group." Drake was more than that, and I felt terrible reducing him to a cliché. "I won't be seeing him anymore anyway."

He picked up one of Monica's stuffed animals on the floor and threw it across the room. I was surprised he didn't throw it at me. "Please say you'll forgive me," I pleaded.

"Just leave me alone for now," he said, and I waited for more. He looked at me with hate in his eyes and walked outside. Was he leaving me? I walked over and slowly opened the front door. He was sitting on the front step.

"Michael, if it's any consolation, it made me see how much I love you and fear losing you."

"Just let me be for now."

"Okay, I'm going to shower," I said, slowly closing the door.

I was in the shower, feeling both relieved and scared. I had no idea what Michael would do, and now I feared he would use this as an excuse to sleep around…or leave us. What had I done?

The shower door opened and Michael stepped in…naked. "Michael," I quivered. He didn't say anything at first, and his eyes had a strange look in them. I couldn't place it.

He took my hands and placed them above my head, against the shower wall. "What are you doing?" I didn't know whether to be scared or…turned on. We hadn't been in the shower together since dating.

"Don't be afraid, Jill. I'm not going to hurt you." Not sure what was happening, I did feel as if I could trust him. He hadn't touched me in that way since our wedding night. And when he pulled my hair. "But I am going to fuck you—hard. I'm pissed, but not at you." His face was inches from mine, and as I stared into his eyes, I could still see his chest rise and fall from his heavy breathing. "You make me feel so many things that I can't explain it." I didn't understand. And how could he explain it to me if he didn't understand himself?

He let go of my wrist and picked me up. My legs wrapped around his waist and he entered me like he said. Hard. "Ah," I cried out and his mouth covered mine. I felt fear in his kiss. I felt him trembling, and he kissed me like he never had before; wild and crazy, and passionate. For the first time in this crazy moment, I felt the love he had for me and knew I had done the right thing in being honest.

"You're my wife, Jill," he said with heavy breaths. "I may not be a good husband, but you are my wife."

"Yes…I know." My words were strained through the excitement. Was he now claiming his ownership of me?

"Promise me there isn't any more. Promise me you won't be sneaking around and fucking this guy," he said as he pushed in and out of me.

"I promise."

Each time he slammed into me, my tailbone banged against the shower wall, and when I cried out, he cupped his hands around my bottom and turned me around.

"Is that better?" he asked.

"Yes," I breathed out. Michale grabbed my hips and guided me up and down on his erection. My arms anchored around his neck, and I held on tightly as the water poured over us, and our bodies became slick. I loved him so much right at that moment. He had never been this demanding or passionate, and I knew it was the fear of losing me. He could say all he wanted, but his actions told me differently. He loved me. He couldn't say it, but I knew he did.

As he said my name and made me promise it would never happen again, I felt the wave of an incredible orgasm growing inside me. I screamed out his name, and he moaned, "Yes. Yes," over and over. He was coming too, hard and there was no denying how much he desired me at that moment.

Michael held me, and we kissed like we would never see each other again. The lovemaking was intense, and through the tremors of coming down, I found myself crying. Michael held me close, and I never wanted to leave his arms. I felt his hand smooth over my back and I kept my head in the crook of his neck. I felt his pulse beat heavy in his jugular. The storm had passed, and in its wake, we had each other. Life for us would be different, and our journey together would be full of love and appreciation. I had finally won a place in Michael's heart. But winners don't always stay on top, and to stay the course, means sacrificing a little of yourself every day.

•　　　•　　　•　　　•　　　•

I was making dinner when Michael walked through the door. It was Wednesday, and a week had passed since our shower incident and my kiss with Drake. I was surprised to see him home this early. In fact, every day he'd been home early. Maybe by letting him know another man could be interested in me made him stop and think about what he had. He had also been a tad more attentive with me.

"Aren't you going to your study group tonight?" he asked, looking surprised.

"No, Michael. I promised you I wouldn't go anymore since…" I didn't finish.

"It's okay if you want to go. You told me, and I trust you."

"Really? You don't have a problem with me being around…" I stopped before I said his name. He picked Monica up and gave her a kiss on her head.

"Daddy can handle Mommy being gone for a few hours," he said in his baby talk to her. She laughed when he pretended to bite her fingers.

"Well…I just started dinner. I didn't plan ahead, because I didn't plan on going tonight."

"I can finish it," he said, and I was suspicious of his intent. Had he done a one-eighty?

"Are you sure?"

"Yes. You want to graduate early, right?"

"Yes."

"Then go. I got Monica and dinner."

"Alright," I said, gathering my books and kissing Monica and Michael before leaving.

Tammy was surprised to see me when I walked in—and so was Drake. I told Tammy about the kiss, and she said she wasn't surprised.

"Hey, guys. Sorry, I'm late. I decided to come at the last moment."

"Well, we're going over organs and the systems they make up." I pulled out my anatomy book and flipped the pages to catch up. Drake gave me a sweet smile and I hoped the night wouldn't be awkward for us.

We were twenty minutes into our studies when the door chimed above, and I looked up. Michael was walking in, pushing Monica in her stroller. What the hell? I was surprised he even knew how to unfold it.

"Michael? Is something wrong with Monica?"

"No, I just thought I would take her for a walk," he said and looked straight at Drake, who was the only guy at the table. He had his target.

"Oh, well, you want to pull a chair up?"

"No, I'll just sit at the table across. Come on, Monica, let's get us a muffin," he said, taking her out of the stroller.

"Yeah," she squealed with excitement and ran to the counter. Tammy then looked at me, and there was a smirk on her face. Drake's face was white. I was a jumble of nerves. One—Michael never took his daughter for walks. Two—he was only here to claim me in front of Drake. I liked it…and sort of didn't.

We went back to our studies, and Michael sat across from us helping Monica with her muffin. He then leaned back in the chair, arms folded and stared at Drake with a wicked grin. There was no doubt Drake or I couldn't concentrate on any of the studying. Michael knew what he was doing, and he was doing it well.

We would only last another thirty minutes when Tammy said we should call it quits for the night. I was thankful—as was Drake. As we gathered our books, Michael stood and walked casually over and placed his hands down on the table. His face was inches from Drake's and said, "You ever come near my wife again, I will kill you. You understand?"

"Michael! Stop it," I hissed.

He turned to me, and the look in his eyes was cold. "I'm defending what's mine," he said. My heart jumped, and I was scared and turned on at the same time. And…embarrassed.

"Yes, Michael, I get it. But not here."

"Especially here," he said and kissed me hard in front of the group. It pissed me off, but part of me liked his claim on me.

Everyone scurried around the table, gathering their books, and quickly walked out. I looked up to Michael and peered into his eyes. "I think I took care of him," he said, and I couldn't help but smirk.

"I guess you did. Now, grab your daughter and clean the icing off her face and hands."

He winked, and I felt I had the Michael who was trying back with me. But how long would I have him?

CHAPTER 31

Now

We help Tammy down the sandy trail, carrying her IV and set up to watch tonight's sunset. Ryan and the girls are all gathered, and it's a beautiful evening. It's Monday, and we've had three more days to have Tammy with us. Sadly, her health has declined dramatically since our arrival.

I wrap her in a blanket to protect her from the chilly wind coming off the lake. She's nothing but skin and bones now. Ryan sits next to her in the sand and holds her in his arms. The girls also sit by her side, and we all search for something to say. You can only say how beautiful the sun is a number of times before it starts to sound like an insult to the one person who has so few left.

"Come on, everyone, speak up," Tammy jokes. The girls are so strong, but I know it's tough. She has become so much closer to them in the last few days. And it hurts to know they won't have her much longer.

"Are you warm enough, Tammy?" I ask.

"Yes." Ryan pulls her close and rubs his hands on her blanket-covered arms. Casey holds her mother's hand and gently smooths her fingers along her pale skin. Callie massages her feet and asks if it feels good. "Yes, it does, Callie. It feels so good."

"Mommy, you want me to massage something?" little Hailee asks.

"I think all my parts are covered at the moment. But can you do me a favor?" Hailee nods her head. "Show me all the things you've learned in gymnastics. Can you do them here in the sand?"

"Yes, I can do that, Mommy."

"All right," I say as Hailee gets up and sprints through the sand. We clap as she completes three backflips and lands perfectly on her feet.

"Awesome, baby girl," Tammy says in a weak voice, and the girls help to cheer her on.

Hailee gives us an outstanding performance—walking on her hands, falling gracefully into a backbend, and then taking off down the beach, flipping her athletic body into several more backflips.

"Gosh, she's so good," I tell Tammy. "How long has she been competing?"

"I think we started her when she was…" She looks up at Ryan, "Two?"

"Yep. We couldn't keep Hailee in her baby bed, and she scared us with all her jumping and climbing." Ryan then kisses Tammy softly on the lips.

"Well, she is absolutely amazing. Monica took gymnastics for a little while. But she was never that good." It feels like a breath of fresh air to have something so simple and ordinary to talk about.

Hailee comes flipping back, and we all laugh and cover our faces as sand whips through the air. "How was that, Mommy?"

"That was amazing. I could watch you all day, Hailee," Tammy tells her and then reaches for her hand. "Come here." Hailee plops down in the sand and smiles at her mother. "Don't you ever stop. You're going to be a star."

"You think so?"

"I know so." Tammy hugs Hailee into her chest, and the girls continue to rub Tammy's hands and feet. "Oh, girls. I love you all so much." The tears come, and there's no stopping them. But somehow, they're comforting, like lifting off a little pressure to accommodate the pain.

"Look, there it goes," Ryan says as the sun begins to slip into the water. Will this be her last sunset? "Pssst." Ryan makes a sizzling sound as the sun sinks deeper.

We are all silent as the sun slowly disappears, ending another day. I reach over and rub Tammy's shoulder. "Are you still warm enough?"

"Yes." She smiles at me, and her eyes look peaceful. "You know what I want to do now?"

"I sure do."

"I want us all to have a slumber party in the living room. You think we can all do that?"

"I think it's a great idea," I say.

"I want to sleep with Mommy," Hailee says.

"I think we'll all sleep with Mommy." I pull Hailee into my lap and squeeze her tightly. "I can't believe how fast you've grown. I remember the day you were born."

"Me too," Tammy says, reaching over and pinching her cheek.

We make our way back to the cottage and find every blanket, sleeping bag and pillow that we can and arrange them all together. I pull the cushions off the couch and make a soft bed for Tammy. Ryan helps her to lie down, and I can tell her pain is back and she needs more morphine. She eyes Ryan, suggesting he find an excuse to grab the girl's attention. She doesn't like them to watch when she needs more.

"Hey girls, did you bring the s'more stuff?" Ryan asks.

"Yeah, Dad. It's in one of the boxes."

"Oh, s'mores. Girls, will you make me one?" I ask.

"I will," yells Hailee.

"Come on, girls. Grab the box, and let's go out on the patio." Ryan says.

Tammy squeezes my hand and looks at me when they are all outside. "Shoot me up." I unzip the bag with the regulated vials from the hospice and fill the needed CCs to subside her pain.

"Better?"

"Not yet. It seems to be taking longer now. Thanks, Jill." I quickly discard the empty vial back into the bag and then stash it in my suitcase. The girls come running in with a plateful of s'mores. "Ooo, just what I need," Tammy says, picking one up and licking the oozing marshmallow. I can tell the morphine is kicking in.

"Ah, perfect," I say and stuff my mouth full.

We cuddle in, and Ryan runs through the Netflix menu. "What do you girls feel like watching?"

"*Stranger Things,*" Hailee says with a mouthful of s'mores and crumbs fly out of her mouth.

"Sounds good, girls?" Ryan asks the other two.

"Sure," Callie says, and Casey shrugs her shoulders.

"Okay, *Stranger Things* it is." He starts the program and snuggles down next to his wife. I'm on her other side, and all three girls crowd around our feet. I watch Tammy and see the love that surrounds her. She squeezes my hand and then mouths 'thank you' to me.

"You're welcome," I whisper back.

The backlight of the TV illuminates the room, and we're six episodes in. Hailee has fallen asleep, and Casey and Callie play on their phones. Ryan is now on his sixth cup of coffee. Afraid of falling asleep, Tammy and I keep the night alive reminiscing our past.

"Remember when your mom used to babysit me?" She coughs and it's a struggle for her to continue.

"Take your time," I say and rub her hand.

"Remember the attic? Your mom was so creative—how she made it look like the Grand Ole Opry."

"We played up there for hours. It was the perfect playroom. Monica used to play up there too. You know, I think we were the kids in the attic long before that book. What was it?"

"*Flowers in the Attic.*"

"Yes. I loved that book." I quietly laugh. "Maybe Mom fixed the attic to keep us out of her hair."

"Oh, …it was the perfect place. I never forgot about that attic. Even as we grew older, we still loved to stay up there." Tammy says. There's joy in her voice, and it gives me comfort.

"I think we have some cigarettes still stashed up there. And remember when we stole Scott's *Playboy*s and would look at them?"

She takes a deep breath and laughs. "Oh my God. Why would we do that? We were girls."

"Yeah, but we were still curious."

I think about that room in my childhood house. A place where we played, told secrets, hid secrets, cried, laughed, and grew up in. Even today, it holds magic from the past. And when Michael first left me, I cried up there for a week. In some ways, the room grew up with us, and there was nothing we couldn't solve in that room. The place is a time capsule, filled with toys, teen treasures, things outgrown and things waiting to be used again.

"You know, I think Heaven will be like that room," Tammy whispers, not wanting the girls to overhear. "And…I'm okay with that. That's how I have it pictured."

My eyes well up and my chin quivers. "Yeah? I think you're right," my voice squeaks.

"Can you believe we never got caught doing the stay-over game? I just knew this was it every morning when I got home—we were busted," she says.

"Oh, I know. I wonder how many times Monica played that game on me." She squeezes my hand like she knows something. And I'm sure she does.

As I look at her through my teary eyes, I can't believe this is it. This is all there is for her. Yes, she's had a great life, but why does it have to end so early? I rub her cheek, and with my thumb, wipe the tear running down. She knows. She knows the end is near, and all I can do is keep her comfortable.

"How's the pain," I whisper. Ryan rubs her arms.

"I'm as comfortable as I can get. I want to stay sober for as long as I can. Please, no more morphine," Tammy whispers.

"Tammy, please let me know if you need more, if only to rest."

Her eyes slowly move to the corner of one side as she looks at me. I know that sad, painful look. She knows, once her eyes close, this is it. Oh, God. Should I keep her talking? Keep her alert? Or, let her pass on in peace. Peace knowing we're all here. Then something strikes me.

It's not up to me. I have no more power over her than I had over Michael. This is up to her. Up to God. Not that I'm happy about it. And for once, I wish I had all the control. I would keep her here with me forever. I would be stuck to her side, so much that she'd be sick of me. But I wouldn't care. I might not have control over her or when she goes, but I do have control over myself. And I will keep her talking.

"Do you remember the time we had that party at your parent's house when they left for the weekend?" Her lips form a smile—weak, but it's there. She knows that night. "We hid all the cars behind the barn so that when your brother drove by to check on us, it would look as if no one was there." Tammy's brother was older and married and lived just a few miles out of town. "If it wasn't for that damn plane taking aerial shots." Her chest heaves with a laugh.

"It was the perfect plan," she strains.

"I think your parents bought that portrait just to haunt us." Two weeks after we thought we had gotten away with the party, a salesman showed up with aerial portraits of their property. We were busted. There, plain as day, were the six cars parked behind the barn. "Your dad tried so hard to find out whose cars they were," I laugh.

"He wrote down every make and model and carried it everywhere. Every time he came upon a car that matched the description, he would drag the driver out of the car," Tammy says softly.

"All those guys sold their cars once the story got out."

"All but Ryan," I say.

She turns to look Ryan in the face. He cups her cheeks and says, "I wasn't afraid of your dad. I knew someday I would marry you." They look at each other, lost in the silence and holding onto this moment. And then, he kisses her softly on her dry, chapped lips. How utterly awful to know this could be your last kiss, your last gaze into your loved one's eyes, your last expression of love for each other. Maybe it's best to be alone; alone like me. I won't have to look into someone's eyes and know it's the last time. Or vice versa. No regrets of leaving them behind or being left behind. Is it better?

"Jill, remember when we told your parents we were going to the hayride?"

"Oh…yes. My first kiss."

"That's all we talked about in the attic that night. How you broke it down, piece by piece until the tongues touched." She struggles to laugh. And she is laughing. At death's door—she is laughing. "Oh my God. After that, you were the expert of French kissing and walked with merit. I was afraid you were going to do a term paper on you and Tommy Sommers, on how to properly French kiss."

"Oh, God, it seems like a million years ago," I say. Yet, time hasn't been long enough. Long enough for her. I look up at Ryan. "I remember the day you called and told me Ryan asked you to the homecoming dance." He smiles. "You were afraid I would be upset."

She turns to Ryan again. I want this moment to last forever for them. And somehow, it will. It will be one of their last memories they both share. "Well, I'm sure you would have if it weren't for Michael asking you to go."

"Pssst, please," I tease. "We all know what that was about." Although, after all these years, I don't. I don't think I will ever understand Michael. Looking down at his ring, I remind myself to give it back. I know it's wrong, but for just a short time, it feels good to have actually had an engagement ring. But I don't want to think about Michael and me.

She grabs my hand and brings it to her dry lips. As she looks at me with tired, half-closed eyes, she kisses my hand with the ring. She knows what she's doing. Her fingers brush over the ring, and she says, "Promise me you'll marry Michael."

I don't know what to say. I can't say no and feel I am betraying Tammy's dying wish. I can't say yes because I can't marry Michael. I just can't.

I brush her hair and kiss her forehead. "I only want to think about you and us and Ryan. Michael is not invited to this party." She gives a weak smile and her eyes close as she coughs. Ryan reaches for her water and helps her take a sip.

"Party," she mocks. "Lucky him. Who in the hell invited me here," she laughs, and her coughing returns.

"You're incorrigible, you know that? You need to concentrate on you. Not me."

"Why? What's the fun in that? My time is done. Kaput. No mas."

"Will you stop?"

"I will…I promise. Soon there will be no more words coming from my mouth. So, until then, I will just keep saying it. Marry Michael."

"I love you," I say and press my lips on her forehead. She squeezes my hand, and her eyes close. I look at Ryan, and although we are expecting it, our eyes capture that fear in each other. I check her pulse. "She's just resting," I whisper. I watch her chest slowly move up and down. I look at the girls, hoping they are engrossed on their phones or anything but this moment. But they're not. All three sit at the end of our makeshift bed on the floor, staring at me with glassy, scared eyes. Should they be seeing this? "Girls, it's up to you…if you want to leave the room. I'm here, and I will not leave her side. Neither will your father." They all three shake their heads, holding each other tightly. "Okay. Just know, she's in no pain. She is at peace…and she knows you are here. She can hear you. So, if there's anything you want to say, you can say it."

"I love you, Mom," Casey says, choking out the words, followed by Callie and Hailee.

I feel Tammy squeeze my hand and I smile up at the girls. "She heard you. She says she loves you too."

We all cuddle together, each of us touching Tammy and lay our heads as if we could just go to sleep. I listen to Tammy breathe. Each breath farther and farther apart…until…no more. I know she is now gone. But I want to keep this from the girls, if only for a little more time. Let them believe she is still with us.

I touch Ryan's shoulder and sadly nod. When he breaks out in a full cry, the girls know.

I have to be strong. I have to be there for the girls and Ryan. There are no words I can say to them. Nothing can take away this pain. All I can do is cry with them. And that's what we do. We hold each other. We embrace Tammy…and we cry.

CHAPTER 32

Then

Christmas season had just begun, and Michael's company was hosting their annual Christmas party. I was surprised he had asked me to go because he had gone by himself for the last two years, telling me it was all business and that I wouldn't enjoy it. This year, he told me to buy a lovely dress and asked if Mom or Tammy could watch Monica. Ever since the Drake incident, he had become more attentive toward me. I had now graduated from school and started my internship at the hospital. Michael didn't like the fact that I worked three twelve-hour night shifts. This meant he had to pick Monica up from daycare and have dinner ready when I walked through the door at 7:30. I felt things were moving positively for our marriage and family. I was now contributing to the household income, and Michael showed a bit more respect toward me.

Tammy and I were shopping at the mall, like we had in the old days, as teens. Now, here we were, married and employed. And to tell you the truth, I couldn't believe Michael and I were still together after three years. Maybe we had defeated the odds.

I wanted a dress that spoke, classy, elegant—that little black dress. I found exactly what I was looking for—short, sassy, yet sexy. It had a scalloped hem that was mid-thigh, tight waist to show off my slender curves and snug in the bust. It was perfect.

"Damn! Are you sure this is a Christmas party?" Tammy stated as I swung around stepping out of the fitting room.

"Too much?"

"Too perfect."

I glanced from every direction in the three-way mirror, swinging the dress side to side. It was perfect, and I couldn't wait for Michael to see me in it. Ever since Michael's scrub comment, I constantly changed as soon as I returned from work. I did my best to remind him continually of the lovely wife he had, even though he didn't mention it too often. But what man does? I hated when men could brag about another woman but feared their tongues falling out when complimenting their wives. This dress was sure to get his attention. I wanted him to know I was a woman, his wife, and not just the mother of his child. But I was pretty proud of that also.

Monica was three now. She was running and talking up a storm. She was everything I ever dreamed of as a daughter. Long, blonde curls. Golden, peachy baby skin from playing in the backyard all summer and the bluest of eyes you've ever seen. They were Michael's eyes. She was the poster child of the beautiful baby. Everyone complimented her wherever we went. I loved when Michael would smile at me and then tell them thank you. It made me proud that I gave him such a beautiful daughter.

"Are you sure Monica can stay with you and Ryan this weekend?"

"I'm sure. It will give us some practice." There was a little something in her voice. I looked at her, and her eyes widened.

"No way! Are you?"

"I think so," she said, and there were tears in her eyes. "I'm almost three weeks late but haven't taken a test yet. I want to make sure this time before I tell Ryan."

"Oh, my God. We must get one today." She took a deep breath and nodded.

"Okay. But if I am, you can't tell Ryan you already know."

I held up two fingers. "Scout's honor."

We quickly found shoes to go with the dress, paid, and ran to the drugstore. This was now the hot topic; to find out if Tammy was pregnant overrode my need to look sexy at the party. Maybe Michael and I could start planning another baby soon, and Tammy and I could be pregnant together this time.

We were in and out of the drugstore in record time and back to my house. Michael was feeding Monica lunch when we ran through the door. "Mommy," she squealed.

"You're back early. Did you find a dress?" Michael asked, cutting strawberries up for Monica.

"Yes, I did. I can't wait for you to see it," I said and kissed Michael. I loved him more than ever and hoped he was ready for another baby. "Hey, Munchkin. Daddy's giving you strawberries?" She picked one up and handed me a berry. "Mmm, good," I said, chewing the juicy berry.

"Hi, Tammy," Michael said as she stood in the doorway.

"Hey, Michael. Hi, Monica. You're gonna come stay with Auntie Tammy tonight?"

Monica smiled and handed Tammy a strawberry. "Yes," she said in her little, baby voice.

"I can't wait for you to stay. We're going to have so much fun. You bring some of your toys."

"Whatever toys you take, leave them at your place. Make sure they're the ones that make noise," Michael said as he placed the strawberries back into the refrigerator. "Thanks for keeping her tonight."

I wrapped my arms around Michael's waist and smiled into his eyes. He looked at me and questioned my look. "Tammy thinks she might be pregnant." He looked over at Tammy.

"Well, I hope this is what you want," he said.

"Of course it is, Michael," I said teasingly, slapping his chest.

"Well, congratulations then."

"Come on. I can't take it any longer," I said, grabbing Tammy by the elbow. "Let's get to the bathroom."

Michael took Monica from her chair and cleaned her face at the sink. "Now, you little girl, wait as long as possible before you start having babies."

"Babies," Monica repeated.

"No babies," he said.

"I want a baby, Daddy."

"No, you don't. Trust me."

"I want a baby," Monica said again.

"No. Babies." His finger tapped her little lips with each word. I hoped his comment was meant for her, and her only, for when she grew up—and not for us to have another baby.

We shut the bathroom door, and when I turned around, Tammy said, "You're not staying in here with me as I pee."

"All right. I just got excited. But hurry up. It's killing me." I handed her the box and stepped out. Sitting on the bed, I waited for her to come out. The door opened, and I jumped. "Well?"

"We will know in five minutes, Jill. Remember when we did yours?"

"Oh, yeah. The longest five minutes of my life."

We both sat on the bed and then couldn't stand it. We began pacing around the bedroom. "Has it been five minutes?"

Tammy looked down at her watch. "No, it's been one."

"One!" I began pacing some more. Finally, she got up and started toward the door.

"I can't. I'm too nervous. You look for me."

"Are you sure?"

"Yes." It didn't take me a second to run into the bathroom, spot the stick, and walk out with it covered in tissue. "Well?"

My smile was beaming. "Positive!"

•   •   •   •   •

We dropped Monica off at Tammy and Ryan's, along with her overnight stuff, horsey, and blankie. Since they just found out they were pregnant, I asked again if they wanted to be alone and celebrate and if I could ask my mom. They insisted it couldn't have come at a better time and were so excited to have Monica for the weekend.

Ryan whistled as I came through the door. "Why thank you, Ryan," I said.

"I was referring to Michael." I rolled my eyes and handed Monica over to Tammy. I had to admit: Michael was stellar in his dark suit. I was indeed a lucky woman. I only hoped he felt the same. His only remark about the dress was, 'It's nice.' And that was after I had asked him while helping with his tie. I thought of the suits he bought years ago at the mall; I was so fascinated with him the day Tammy and I were shopping and ran into him at the food court. The day he told me never to change. Had I changed? Was I what he still wanted?

We kissed our daughter goodbye and left for the car. Since it was December, winter covered the ground with snow, Michael had the Corvette stored away and took the newer family SUV to the party. I hoped he'd make an exception and we could take his corvette—no such luck. That was his summer car only.

We arrived at the president of Whirlpool's home, and my eyes fell back in my head. The place was a castle. Complete with a moat and bridge. We pulled up to the circle drive, where a valet waited to park our car around the back. Michael handed over the keys and lifted his elbow for me to take. "This place is amazing," I said as I smiled at my handsome husband. He winked and smiled back.

Jazzy Christmas music played as we walked through the grand entrance; my eyes went to the twenty-foot Christmas tree next to a winding staircase. Everyone wore tailored clothes for the occasion, and it was easy to see why Michael wanted me to buy a flashy dress. I hoped it was enough.

"Welcome," an attractive lady in her fifties greeted us as we walked through the parlor.

"Hello," I said.

Michael raised his hand to shake hers, but she kissed his cheek instead. "Nice to meet you. I'm Michael Danforth, and this is my wife, Jill." I loved to hear him call me his wife.

"Yes, I know. I make sure to know the guest list. Please, enjoy yourself with some cocktails."

"Thank you," Michael said and slightly bowed.

"Yes, thank you," I said, feeling like that shy schoolgirl again.

We walked around as Michael introduced me to several of his office friends. Everyone looked at me as if they didn't know he was married. I questioned Michael about it, and he said it concerned how young and pretty I was. They knew he was married. Though, Michael didn't wear a ring. We still hadn't bought any, not due to my lack of asking. And we still hadn't taken another family picture since he destroyed that one. I was waiting for him to take the initiative. I'd be waiting for a long time.

A man came over with a tray of champagne, and Michael grabbed one for me. I was six months shy from turning twenty-one, and standing next to Michael in that little black dress, holding a glass of champagne, felt like a fairy tale—my fairy tale. The one I dreamed me and Michael would have someday.

As I took a sip, I noticed a woman with her eyes fixed on Michael and then on me. She was with a man, but it didn't seem to matter. She was ogling my husband with an agenda. I couldn't spot a ring on her finger and wondered if she was who Michael had stayed with when we separated a few years back. Of course, every woman I encountered who stared at Michael was the one I thought could be. She eyed me up and down, sizing me up. I was going to play her game. I smiled at her and walked across the room. Looking back, Michael watched as I walked away. He looked nervous and then returned to the man he was talking with, turning his head again in my direction.

"Hello. Do we know each other?" I asked most pleasantly. "You were looking at me as if you may know me. I didn't want to appear rude. Have I forgotten that we have met before? Maybe college?"

She suddenly appeared guarded and gave me a nervous smile. "Ahh, I don't think so."

"Are you sure? I mean, college was so hectic, and I did graduate early. Did we run in the same circle?"

"Again, I don't think so."

"Where did you graduate…college?" I asked and took a sip of champagne.

"Um…I didn't." She looked around for the man that was with her earlier. Now that I was closer to her, she wasn't as pretty as I gave her credit for a few seconds ago. She was apparently in her thirties. Her face was dull with dry skin. The fine lines around her eyes and cheeks gave evidence of excessive sun and lack of elasticity.

"I'm Jill," I said and held out my hand. She looked at it as if it would bite and slowly gave me a puny shake.

"Denise," she said.

"Denise," I parroted, feigning my memory of a Denise. But I knew no Denise. "Sorry, maybe we don't know each other. Do you work with Michael—*my husband?*"

"I've…seen him around. He works on the upper floor," Denise said, still with a nervous edge in her voice. She was *definitely* the woman he stayed with, and I wanted her to know that I knew it.

"Oh, now I remember. Michael told me you helped him a few years back while we separated. Men," I exasperated, "Just don't like to give us credit. But when he came begging me to take him back—what could I do?" I smiled and glanced over at Michael. He smiled and walked our way. His arms wrapped around me, and I leaned into his chest.

"What are you ladies talking about?" he said, his eyes begging Denise.

"Wouldn't you love to know," I said, kissing his jaw and taking another sip of champagne. I felt his chest rise as he took in a breath.

"Jill, I would like to introduce you to my boss," Michael said, and I knew it was an excuse to get me away from Denise.

"Oh? Okay. It was nice meeting you, Denise."

Michael's eyes cast from me to her in a panic. Good. Let them know how it feels to be on the other side of the unknown.

As we walked away, his tight hold around my waist wasn't from his sudden urge to adore me. He was pissed, but I didn't care. "What the hell was that all about?" he asked.

"I was just being friendly." He eyed me surreptitiously, and I only returned his look. "She was looking at me like she knew me. So, I went over and said hello. I didn't want to be rude." I lifted my glass, but before I took a sip, I said, "She was rude by staring at me…and ogling you." When I brought my glass back down, I said, "She is the one, isn't she?" His eyes threw me daggers and then pleaded with me.

"Jill, please," he said, and just for a second, I felt pity for him. I didn't know why. He didn't deserve my sympathy. Just being in a room with another woman who slept with my husband elevated my boldness, and I felt my backbone come to life. But I knew it was long ago and I wanted to enjoy this Christmas party with Michael.

"I'm sorry," I said, kissing him on the cheek. "So, where's this boss you want me to meet?"

"Over here," he said, walking me across the room with his arm around me. I hoped Miss Denise was watching.

"Mr. Hayden, this is my wife, Jill." Again, I loved the word *wife* flowing from Michael's lips. I smiled and looked up at the gentleman.

"Hello, it's nice to meet you. Thank you for inviting us. This place is lovely." The man looked at me with a strange look on his face. At first, I thought maybe he was deaf or perhaps spoke another language, but I knew he didn't. His gaze was confusing. I looked up at Michael.

"I'm sorry, forgive me," Mr. Hayden said. "I wasn't expecting Michael's wife to be so young. You're just a child, my dear." I batted my lashes, suddenly feeling shy. I thought I looked grown up tonight; so much for the little black dress.

"Jill is a bit younger than me," Michael said. And as he talked to his boss, the man's eyes never left me. He was handsome in an Italian sort of way. Dark, thick hair glossed back, and his face appeared powerful and controlling. He stood a few inches taller than Michael, and his Armani suit fit his body like art. It was most likely tailor-made.

My eyes moved to the floor, and I bit my bottom lip. I was afraid I was embarrassing Michael. "It's a pleasure to meet you," he said, and I looked up at him. He offered his hand, and when I extended mine, he kissed the back of it. Instead of letting go, he held my hand throughout his conversation with Michael. I finally made a fake cough and pulled my hand from his. "Sorry," I said. Still, his eyes remained glued to me.

The man with the tray of champagne appeared, took our empty glasses, and offered us more. "Are you even old enough to drink, my lovely?" Mr. Hayden teased. But I thought he was serious and moved my hand away from the tray, holding my waist uneasily. "I'm only kidding, Dear. Here," he said, grabbing a glass for me, "please, take." I took the glass like an offering, and his fingers trailed over mine with the exchange.

"Thank you," I said and sipped while his eyes watched my mouth. As Michael talked, I looked around at the party, busy with the festivities, to avoid feeling the stare Mr. Hayden still had on me.

"Michael," a man hollered. Michael looked back at the man calling his name.

"Hey, what's up?" Michael said in that buddies-watching-football-together voice. He stepped away and began talking to the man. As the two men were engrossed in their conversation, slapping backs and shaking hands, I waited for Michael to call me over. I looked up at the man still ogling me. I smiled to excuse myself. But before I could get the words out, he took me by the arm and began walking me away.

"Let me give you a tour of the place. Have you ever been to the Whirlpool mansion before?"

"Ah…no," I said, my voice shaking. I looked back at Michael, still oblivious to the man walking me away.

"Well, let me give you the grand tour." He smiled, and his teeth seemed to gleam with his toothy white smile.

As we left the room, his hand went to my waist, and I felt the heat radiating off him. The man towered over me. "You like to read?"

"I do—when I have time. I have a three-year-old. So, most of my reading is for her. But I try to get a few books in for myself," I added to appear invested in the conversation.

"Let me show you the library. What do you read?"

"Fiction. Suspense and thrillers."

"What? No romance for such a beautiful young girl?" he asked as he opened a massive double door and waved for me to enter. I did read romance but didn't want him to know that. Michael made enough fun of me for reading them.

"I do read…romance," I said.

The door shut, and I was now alone with this vast Italian man who looked like he wanted to bed me. He was at least twice my age. I looked around the historic library, books from floor to ceiling. "How's the champagne?" he asked.

I looked down at my glass. "It's good."

"Something a bit stronger for my needs," he said, walking over to a cart with decanters filled with bourbon—I guess. I heard the pop of the decanter as he poured himself two fingers full into a small glass. "Would you like a bourbon?" I was right.

"No, thank you. The Champagne is fine."

Mr Hayden poured his drink and walked over with that look in his eye again. I swallowed and looked around. Couldn't he see he made me nervous? But maybe that was his plan. Where was my backbone now?

"Michael is a fortunate man," he said, sipping his bourbon.

"Thank you. I'm lucky too—to have Michael," I said, letting him know my devotion to my husband.

"Yes. Michael is quite the lady's man." I didn't like what he was referring to. "A player." All while he talked, his eyes lusted all over me.

"Excuse me; I need to get back. Michael is probably looking for me." He grabbed my arm. It was not hard, but enough to stop me.

"He'll find you. Trust me." He winked, set his bourbon down on a table, and pulled me to him, pressing me into his muscular chest. "You've met Denise?"

My eyes scanned across his face. What was going on? Was he and Denise in on something together? Was there more about Michael? "I think you should let go of me." I forced authority in my voice. But next to him, I still sounded like a lost fawn.

"You know, Michael likes his women. I see now why he has kept you hidden."

"Mr. Hayden, Michael and I have had our problems, and that was a long time ago. We have a child and are working hard to keep our family together."

"That's not what this is about, my Lovely. I would never bust up your family. I just would like to enjoy you for a little while. I can share, and I'm sure Michael is keen on the lifestyle."

"Stop it. Let me go." I struggled to get out of his hold.

"Or, we could keep this just between ourselves. Wouldn't you like a man to worship you? Trust me, I would worship every inch of your body." Was Michael into that lifestyle, which was why he brought me? If he was, then why was he upset when Drake kissed me? Michael displayed nothing but ownership over me in front of Drake.

"Please, let go of me. Michael and I are not like that. We love each other," I begged.

"Jill!" Michael's voice echoed in the room. I turned and saw him running toward me. Mr. Hayden quickly released me from his embrace. "What's going on?"

"I was just making Jill an offer. But maybe I should ask you. I want to sleep with your wife," he said, like I was a bike he wanted to borrow.

I ran into Michael's arms, and he looked confused and then angry. "What the hell are you talking about? No, you can't sleep with my wife."

"Oh, come now, Michael. Like you've been a saint in your marriage." I looked into Michael's eyes, and even though I didn't want to believe it, I knew it was true.

"You know nothing about me and my marriage. Come on," Michael said as he guided me from the room. "We're leaving."

Once in the car, I began to cry. Michael punched the steering wheel. "What the hell was that in there? How did you end up alone with that man?"

Was he accusing me? "You left, and he wanted to show me around. I didn't know things would end up like that." I wiped my face. The tears were streaming down, and I knew my mascara was running. My fairytale night with Michael was ruined. "Why did you want to introduce me, anyway? Was it a setup? Is this what goes on at work? Are men swapping their wives? How many women have you slept with—since we've been married?"

"Don't make this about me, Jill. I wasn't the one seducing an old man." I turned and slapped his face.

"How fucking dare you," I hissed. "All I wanted to do was make you proud. I did nothing to provoke your boss."

He pulled me over, picked me up and planted me on his lap. "Did you like it? Did you like him touching you? His eyes and hands all over you?" His eyes were crazed.

"NO!" I was crying even harder. I couldn't get control of my emotions.

"You're mine, Jill. You understand that?"

"I told him that. I told him I was lucky to have you." He pulled my dress up and yanked my panties to the side. Grabbing my face, he kissed me hard.

"Undo my belt," he breathed and kissed me harder. "I'm going to fuck you so hard, reminding you how lucky you are."

My hands trembled with excitement and apprehension as I unbuckled his belt and unzipped his pants. Within minutes, he was inside me, grabbing my hips and pushing hard. He held me tightly, and I felt his ownership once again as his emotions unraveled, and he repeated my name with demands. "You're fucking mine, Jill. You get that?"

"Yes," I breathed out.

"No man will ever have you. I may be a fuckup, but I can't give you up."

Please! Please say you love me. Michael's form of love came in ownership, his transgressions, and fucking me hard. And I accepted it as his love. He did love me, and this was his way of showing it.

"I want to take you back inside and fuck you in front of him. Show that bastard who you belong to." I knew I should have taken offense to the way Michael's love was displayed as ownership. But I didn't, and his *out-of-control* lovemaking would somehow shift and give me a sense of power over him. If only I could have controlled Michael's values of me and kept it alive during the grind of everyday life.

CHAPTER 33

Now

Here's the thing about attics. Time stays still. Our secrets, our past, stuffed away, waiting for us to return and rediscover them. An attic is like a time capsule. Old things are stored away because we don't want them around us, yet we dare to throw them out. Why is it that when we put something in the attic, we're relieved to find a spot for it? But when we see it again, we feel sad.

It's been three days since Tammy's funeral, and I've taken some time off work. Ryan and the girls seem to be coping much better than me. Walking into the attic at my childhood home, I somehow expected Tammy to be waiting for me. And maybe she is here—in the attic of our childhood home. Everything's the same. Nothing has changed. Time has only added dust and cobwebs. Tiger Beat posters, faded and frail, still hang on the walls. The blanket hung from the rafters, used as our backstage when Tammy and I performed as Tiffany, Paula Abdul, or Madonna.

I touch the blanket and move it to the side, pretending she's behind it and waiting for us to talk and laugh about growing up in this room. She's here. I can feel it.

My heart aches and feels comfort at the same time, if that's possible. Maybe that's why we put things up here. It's things that attach us to a specific time or particular person. This attic only has one time and one person for me. Tammy.

Looking around, I see a box in the corner and recognize my favorite macramé purse I used to carry in junior high. God, I loved that purse. I grab the wooden rings that make up the handles and peek inside—another time capsule. I pull out an old bottle of perfume—Sand and Sable. Oh, my God. This was Tammy's and my favorite perfume.

I open the cap and spritz some on my wrist and inhale. Memories come to life as my nose connects time with smells. The Christmas morning I pulled this from my stocking. Tammy and I had it both on our list. Everyone wanted to know what perfume we were wearing. But we would never tell them. It was our signature scent.

The first time we were dropped off at the mall and allowed to go alone. Oh, we felt so grown up, carrying our purses, this macramé one, wearing heels with jeans. My favorite pair were three-inch heel Candies. I loved those shoes. I wonder if they're still here somewhere?

I dig through the box and find an old, school pencil box. The kind we used to have in elementary that held our crayons, glue, pencils, and lift the lid. Inside, I find a photo strip of Tammy and me, taken at one of those photo booths. God, I remember this day like it was just yesterday. We slid two quarters in the slot and closed the curtain. The first shot we didn't know was being taken, because we're looking around. The second, we looked surprised. The third, we smiled, and the last, we were goofy with our tongues hanging out.

Digging through my pencil box, I find several notes folded into triangle football shapes. Wow, how I miss writing letters. Now, with texting, how will we ever go back to the attic and find the words that were so dear to us that we had to save them? I unfold one and feel my lips press into a smile. Tears begin to fill my eyes as I try to read.

Jill,

After the football game, let's say we are staying to clean the stadium. I heard Ryan will be at Pizza Hut tonight. That will give us an extra hour to stay out past curfew.

Love, Tammy

I open another folded note.

Jill,

Did you hear about Kim? They caught her and some other girls smoking in the bathroom. I mean, how crazy is that? You can't hide the smell. You've probably already heard, but study hall is boring today. Ryan isn't here for me to stare at and all my homework is done. Mr. Snyder looks hot in jeans. I love seeing him in jeans. I wish teachers could wear jeans every day and not just on Fridays. Let's hang out at Delanie's after school.

Love, Tammy

Jill,

Is something wrong? Are you mad at me? Sorry, I didn't come over last night. My dad took away my phone privileges for a week, and that's why I didn't call you. You seemed bothered by something in the first period. I just want to make sure you're not mad at me about not calling. Remember, you are my best friend forever.

Love, Tammy

I sniff and wipe the snot and tears dripping down my face. It's like Tammy is still here, tucked away in this attic. Another time capsule waiting to be opened. Though my heart is breaking, I unfold another note. After I read it, I look around the attic. It's her handwriting, but I don't remember this note or why she would have written this. It's a poem. "*A Light in The Attic.*"

There's a light in the attic.

Though the house is dark and shuttered,

I can see a flickering flutter.

And I know what it's about.

There's a light in the attic.

I can see it from outside.

And I know you're on the inside…looking out.

Is it possible she wrote this and hid it away, knowing I would find it? Her mention of this attic and that's what Heaven will be like. Is this attic her Heaven? Though I know it's not possible, I see her sitting on an old chest, smiling fiendishly at me. And…she's dressed as Marilyn Monroe.

"Well, are you going to say anything?" I hear her say in my head.

Taking a cleansing breath, I begin talking like she's here. "You knew I would come, didn't you?"

She looks at her nails and then blows on them like they're wet with polish. "Yup. But do me a favor. Don't spend too much time up here. Remember, I'm always with you. Please don't store me away in this attic. How's the wedding coming?"

Now, why would she say that? I huff a small laugh. "So, how are the Kennedys?"

"Guess what. No Kennedys," she whispers.

I chuckle. "Maybe you're in the wrong place."

"Ouch. Seriously, Jill—Wedding." And then, she disappears. I fall to my knees and bawl. I'm still crying when I hear the attic door open. I know it's Mom and she's checking on me.

"I'll be down later. I…I just want to…be alone and cry."

"Hello, Jill." It's Michael. I look up and see the sad expression on his face. "It's sort of hot up here. Why don't you come down and get some air?"

"Michael, I don't want to leave this place. I…I feel close to her here." He walks over and bends down.

"I understand, Jill. But seriously, it's too hot to be up here." He smooths my cheeks and wipes my tears and then runs his hands through my hair, lifting the back to get some air. "You probably don't even know you're sweating. You'll become dehydrated." He moves closer and kisses my forehead. "I know it hurts, Baby."

Baby?

Nothing feels real. Monica's a married woman. Tammy is dead. And Michael is back. It's too much to take all at once. I just wish my thoughts could go back to the way it once was—simple.

"You know, it was her that got me through when you left."

"And now I'm here to help you get through this. You're not alone, Jill. You have so many people who love you. Tammy was just one of them."

I give him a distasteful look. Just the way he said it like she was a dime a dozen. "She was special, Michael. We've been together since we were four. I don't know what life will be like with her gone. I know life went on after you. She taught me that."

"I'm here now, Jill. And as long as I'm alive, I will never leave you," he says, holding my face. I begin to feel the hot, sticky heat and see the beads of sweat on his upper lip.

"You know, I spent years hating you, wishing you still loved me. And the problem was, I never knew if you ever did. You never said it."

"I love you, Jill. Do you hear me? I love you." I want to believe him. I do. And it's those three little words I've waited to hear my whole life from him. But my heart refuses to accept him. What I have learned about love is, it messes with your head and plays tricks on you.

I look into his pleading and sorrowful eyes. If the eyes are the window to the soul, then he is genuinely hurting. But why? Why has this…a once wild and untamable man suddenly become…appropriate and…responsive to my needs?

"Why does it take a loss to make you realize what you had? This is one of life's injustices," I say. "I just thought she'd always be here."

"We all think we're immortal." He starts to say something, then hesitates. "Until something happens. And all we can think is what we didn't do and what we should have." Is he talking about himself? "You have nothing to feel guilty about, Jill. You were a best friend for her. Never left her side…right up to the end. How many people can say that?"

"When you left, Michael, I knew it was probably for the best. But still, it was like my heart forgot to work. I had to learn to breathe again. And it was Tammy that told me I just had to learn to think differently. I had to wash the Michael off me, she used to say. I don't want to wash Tammy off me, so I can go on."

"Come on, Jill. Let's go talk somewhere else. It's way too hot up here." He picks me up from the floor and carries me across the attic. Cradled in his arms, I feel the wetness of his chest on my face through his shirt. When he reaches the ladder, he sets me to my feet, and I climb down. Once he's down, his arm wraps my shoulders, and he leads me outside, and we walk across the street to a park shaded with large trees. The breeze coming off the lake feels good, and I realize now how hot the attic was.

We sit under a large oak, and I lean my head on his shoulder. The sun reflects off the engagement ring he gave me a few days ago. Tammy's words from the attic echo once again in my head. Or…were they my own words? "How's the wedding coming?"

He must notice me looking at the ring and holds my hand, running a finger over the ring. "You're still wearing my ring. Is that a yes?"

"Michael…"

"Yes?"

"Tammy wanted me to marry you. Even now, I hear her saying it."

His finger touches my chin, and he moves me to look at him. Those pleading eyes. "But, what does Jill want?"

Silence.

"I…I'm just afraid."

"Afraid of me, of marriage, of…"

"Of the unknown. To be optimistic. It's like I'm always hanging onto that scrap of hope. And there are always two sides—reality versus possibility. I just wish that for once, possibility would win." He kisses me tenderly on the lips. A quiet gesture that this is possible. Him and I. I study him—really take in his face and still see the man I fell in love with twenty years ago—the young Michael. And maybe that's what scares me—the young Michael. In this short time, we've been together, it's like I don't see the old Michael. Like a lifelong marriage would be. You look at the older version and still see the young version.

"Please, marry me, Jill, and let all your possibilities become your reality. We can't rewrite the past, but we can write the future. Our future."

•   •   •   •   •

The water is like glass—smooth and clear. I feel everything has stopped for this moment. The sun shines high in the sky, the breeze wraps me with a warm hug, and I can smell the sweet scent from the bouquet of flowers I'm holding. They're all looking at me. Monica, Jordan, Mom, and Dad. Ryan and the girls have smiles on their faces. It's good to see them happy. I'm happy. The sand on my bare feet feels soft and powdery. My veil whips around, and through the mesh, I see his face. "He has tears in his eyes, Tammy. Just like I always dreamed of," I whisper.

'See, I told ya." I see her sitting on the back of a chair, her feet on the seat, still disguised as Marilyn Monroe. Her smile, with those powder-pink lips refills the much-needed joy in my heart. She winks at me as I pass by, and I reach out and touch her open hand. I know she's here just for me; no one else sees her.

I'm that bride. That beautiful bride and he's looking at me with such longing in his eyes. I've never seen him look so handsome. As I walk to him on this beach, the beach Tammy spent her last day on, watching the sunset, I fill with such overwhelming emotions. Ends and beginnings. Rights and wrongs. Love and pain. But most of all...happiness. Happiness, because I know she is here, and she is happy.

I take Michael's hands and still, he gets down on one knee and kisses my knuckles. My ring glistens from the sun and shines in his eyes as he looks up at me.

"Jill, I used to think about the lucky man who got to have you as his wife. The man who got to see your beautiful smile each day when he woke up. The warm kisses on his face when he was sleeping. The beautiful soul he got to be around every day and wonder if he knew what he had. Today, I am that man, and I know the gift I have been given. You."

CHAPTER 34

Then

Michael surprised Monica and me on Christmas morning with a trip to The Gulf. He had a friend with a condo in Ft. Myers and asked if we could use it for the rest of the Christmas break. Although I was shocked and impressed, Michael needed to clear his head from what had happened at the Whirlpool Christmas party. He was more attentive to me, and I felt more was on his mind. And I hoped it was to have another baby. I hadn't yet brought the subject up and wished to discuss it over Mai Tais on the beach. He was ready to be all in. Buckle down and be the husband and father I needed. After all, we were still together, and no talk of divorce after I graduated from nursing school was brought up, which was his original plan for us. Therefore, he loved me and wanted us to remain a family.

Monica came running into the bedroom, wearing her new Christmas pajamas, and carrying her new baby doll and climbed into bed with us. Michael picked her up and sat her on his chest. "Hey, baby girl. How would you like to go swimming in the ocean?"

"But, Daddy, it's cold outside."

"Not where we're going. You want to get on a big airplane and fly to the ocean?"

"Yeah," she screamed, jumping on her knees and falling back onto his chest. She was excited, and I loved to watch him interact with his daughter. Would he want us to start trying for another baby?

I rolled over and kissed him on the lips and then lay my head on his chest. We were both still naked, and my leg brushed against his penis under the covers. When I looked up at him, he smiled and told

Monica to go pick out which toys she wanted to take on her trip. "And Daddy will come to check on you," he said. He picked her up, and she ran excitedly out of the room. As soon as she was out of sight, he picked me up and sat me down over his growing erection. It didn't take long for us to be joined together, bouncing the bed with our wild passion. Michael may not have been good with passionate words for me, but when it came to sex, I felt I was his everything. He was all I ever knew and all I ever wanted. But soon, I would learn Michael would need so much more than me…or his daughter.

We were packed and headed to the airport. One week alone with just Michael and our daughter was, to me, a ticket to forever, and this was just the beginning. As soon as we landed and set out for the beach, I would talk to him about having another baby.

Monica was fascinated with the airplane and wanted to know if we were riding on the clouds. Michael told her yes, and I watched the two of them become closer. Maybe now seeing how much she meant to him, he would want to do it right this time. Be involved and happy for a baby to be coming.

We landed and rushed to get through the airport and grabbed a taxi. The air was warm and balmy when we stepped outside, and Monica asked what happened to the snow. Michael laughed and told her it stayed home because we forgot to pack it. But here, all the snow turned into a big puddle of water, and we were going to swim in it. Michael held my hand and carried his daughter as we moved through the hustle and bustle, and it gave me a feeling of protection and belonging.

The car ride took only twenty minutes, and we stepped out again in the warm Florida air and walked up to the condo belonging to his friend. "This is so awesome of your friend to let us have this place for a week," I said.

"Sure is. However, this friend owes me for completing his project."

Michael tapped in the code for the door, and we walked into a beachy, inviting floor plan with whitewashed floors, cabinets, and paintings of palms and seascapes. The master bedroom was huge with an adjoining bath, complete with a large shower and garden tub. Monica's room was set up with bunk beds, complete with toys and her own bathroom. As I unpacked her clothes, she climbed up and down the beds, deciding which one she wanted to sleep in.

"I want the top one," she said. But it didn't have a rail, and she wasn't too happy when I told her she must sleep on the bottom bunk.

"What's all this crying about?" Michael asked, popping his head through the door.

"Mommy says I have to sleep on the bottom. But I want the top."

"You'll fall out and hurt yourself. Do you want to get hurt, and not be able to swim in the big water puddle?" Michael teased her. He then picked her up and gave her a bounce on the top. "Look how far down it is." She looked down, and her eyes did show a little fear.

"Get me down, Daddy." Michael laughed and told her she had to jump into his arms.

"No," I said.

"I'll catch her." It didn't take much persuading. She jumped into his arms like a flying monkey. I gave him a look, and he kissed me on the cheek. "Let's get to the beach."

"Yeah," Monica squealed, and we quickly changed into our suits, packed a beach bag and headed out the front door. Walking to the beach, I wore a wrapped skirt low on my hips and bikini top. Monica was covered in sunscreen, and I dressed her in a little red, polka-dotted sundress. She had on little white sunglasses, and Michael picked her up and carried her on his shoulders. He looked like a man who was proud to be with his family. And I was proud to be with him. He looked so gorgeous, wearing a white, long-sleeved shirt that was unbuttoned and his slim-fitting swim trunks. I watched the two of them as he walked ahead and they both held out their arms. "I'm flying, Daddy. I'm flying."

A flock of seagulls came screeching by, and Monica flapped her arms, pretending she was one of the birds. I'd never seen Michael so happy. Happy with us. And even as I watched this tableau of father and daughter, I held my breath. It was like some part of me knew this was the calm before the storm.

We reached the beach. Foamy waves rushed to shore, and Monica yelled with excitement. Michael continued to carry her on his shoulders, as he walked to the water and held out his arms. Monica did the same, and I quickly snapped a picture with my camera. A moment in time that I could have forever—for when someday, I would not have the real thing.

He lifted her from his shoulders and set her feet in the water. She giggled and splashed around. He picked her up by her hands and dipped her up and down. She would kick the water and laugh that innocent childish giggle.

"Is it cold," he asked her.

"No. Not like the snow is cold."

They continued to play, and I laid out our blanket on the sand. I unwrapped my skirt and stretched out on the blanket and rubbed on tanning oil. I was probably going to burn, but I didn't care. I was here, in the sunshine, with Michael and our baby. I was happy. I was in love.

Michael stripped his shirt, walked over, and sat down beside me. I kissed his cheek and thanked him for bringing us here. He rolled me over and lay on top of me. Giving a slight growl in his throat, he smiled and kissed me back. I was sure it all had something to do with his boss, Mr. Hayden, and how he tried to seduce me. Michael now took notice of what he had.

"You're welcome. But you will be paying me back," Michael said with a tease in his voice.

"Oh, yeah?"

"Yeah. I will be fucking you senseless while we're here."

I smiled and pulled his face to me and kissed him again. Though his use of the words was harsh, and I wished he could say 'make love' or even 'have my way,' that was how Michael expressed himself to me. And I had to take it for what it was worth. He did love me. He just couldn't say it.

We sat up, and I rubbed oil on his back as we both watched Monica shovel sand into her little bucket. "She's having such a good time," I said.

"She sure is."

Moving to my knees, I wrapped his shoulders and kissed his neck. I was working up the courage to ask for another baby. The moment was perfect. And by perfect, I meant perfect for us to be here at this moment, not praying for another baby. I didn't want to ruin this little moment in time. So, I took a deep breath and started to form the words when Michael began talking first.

"I think I have made a decision," he said, looking out over the water.

"Oh yeah? What?"

"I'm leaving Whirlpool."

"Leaving? You mean…quitting?" My stomach knotted, and I was afraid he was leaving us too. And this little vacation was goodbye.

"Yes, when we get back, I'm putting in my two weeks' notice."

"What will you do for a job?" Was he planning on my startup salary? I wasn't making much yet. And Michael was not the stay-at-home-dad type.

"I haven't said anything, but Boeing has contacted me for an interview. I think I'll take a week's vacation and check it out. See what they have to offer."

Boeing. Seattle. The place he really wanted to be. Before me. "And, what if they offer you something? Do you have a price in mind?"

"After what fuckin Hayden did at the Christmas party, the price doesn't matter." I now wondered if he knew he was being fired…because of me.

"Are you in trouble, Michael…because of the Christmas party?"

He looked at me bizarrely. "Hell no. I'm not in any trouble. At least, not that I know of. But, I'm ready for a change," he said, and I hoped his change was only as employment. And not me.

"So…if you take the job, we'll be moving to Seattle?"

"Kind of a long drive from Michigan. Yes, we'll be moving to Seattle."

My heart rejoiced. Michael's plans did include me. I knew now was the time to discuss growing our family. He was ready to make changes, and we were still involved. "Well, I've been doing some thinking also."

"Like what? You've just started at the hospital. Kind of early to be making career changes. You'll be able to find another nursing job in Seattle."

"No, not that. I've been thinking about us...having another...baby." I said it, and it was out. I couldn't take the words back. His eyes bulged as he looked at me like I said something so incredulous. He took a deep breath and remained quiet. And I took that as a good sign. He didn't yell NO.

"Let's just see what Seattle brings." I pressed my lips and nodded. It wasn't a yes, but it wasn't a no either. But deep down, I knew what Seattle would bring.

We decided to take a walk down the coastline, and the three of us held hands. Monica joined us in the middle. Every moment I could, I looked at Michael and fell deeper in love. I watched our shadow before us and loved how we were joined together. When the waves came in, we picked our little girl up, and she would scream and giggle. We were so happy. And at the moment, I knew it would be the happiest I'd ever be with Michael. I would be right.

The sun was dropping on the horizon, and I suggested we go back, and I'd make us lunch and put Monica down for a nap. With all her playing that day, I knew she wouldn't even make the walk home. As Michael carried her, I was right. Our beautiful daughter fell fast asleep, hanging over Michael's shoulder. She was out.

As Michael changed her out of her wet bathing suit and put on dry panties, she never woke. I made us a quick salad with the food Michael's friend had left for us when we arrived, and we ate it together on the patio that overlooked the gulf. Everything was coming along. But I was still afraid to breathe.

I was rinsing the dishes when Michael picked me up and carried me to the bedroom. "It's now time to pay me back for this vacation. You ready to fuck hard?" I was eager to make love to Michael and once again tried not to show the disappointment on my face with his choice of words.

"Yes, my handsome husband. I'm dying to make love to you," I said, waiting for his response.

"Ooh, make love. Why so fancy? Young people like us don't make love. We fuck. Hard," he said and threw me onto the bed. His clothes were off in a second, and he stroked himself as he came to me. "On your knees and make love to me with your mouth," he said. It wasn't quite what I was looking for, but I took it.

As I pleasured him orally, he praised me on my skills, and I did pride myself that I could so easily pleasure him that way. After all, he taught me how he liked it.

He was close and pulled himself away and told me to lay back and spread my legs. I did, and he pleasured me with his mouth. Michael was great at oral sex.

I was so close and couldn't hold off as his tongue so skillfully lapped around my sensitive bud. And I came, thrusting myself uncontrollably. He smiled approvingly at me and moved between my knees and pushed himself deep inside me. I came again, and it was the first time in a long time I came twice in our lovemaking. It had to be all the magic this place had brought us, and I would cherish this forever.

Michael moaned out his release while kissing me softly. It was so not like him to do this. He usually came hard and then fell over me. And I didn't mind those times either, as I would feel our hearts beat against each other.

He lifted his head and looked at me with concern. "Please don't tell me you already went off the pill."

"No, I haven't."

He turned his head and gave me a sideways look. "Promise?"

"I promise, Michael. I just wanted to talk about it."

"Like I said, let's see what Seattle brings."

Seattle was already a sour word in my mouth. Although I understood his reasoning, I felt Seattle took precedence over growing our family. But I had to trust him.

He still eyed me suspiciously. "I promise, Michael. I'm still on the pill."

"Okay," he said and moved from the bed. I could already feel the distance he was putting between us.

• • • • •

It had snowed six inches when we returned to Michigan, and I tried to keep the magic Florida had brought. I was determined to keep Michael's focus on us. And now back in the cold and snow, I knew his mood would begin to falter.

We found our car covered in snow at the airport, and Michael repeated every curse word in the book. "Michael, please," I said and threw my eyes at Monica, who was repeating, 'fucking snow.'

After throwing the suitcases in the back and I do mean, throwing, I helped him clean the snow off the car before we got inside. "Instead of being mad at the snow, let's make a snowman when we get home," I said, doing my best to enlighten the situation.

"Jill, I'm not building a fucking snowman."

"Michael," I seethed.

"Let's make a fucking snowman," Monica expressed proudly, sitting in her car seat.

"Now see what you've done? She's cussing like a sailor."

He rolled his eyes at me. "Jill, vacation is over. Reality is here, and you need to get these melodramatic notions out of your head. No adult wants to build a snowman."

"Oh, so I suppose we bundle up our three-year-old daughter and have her build one herself," I sarcastically said.

"She played on the beach by herself."

"We were there with her, Michael. Those are the things parents do. Can't you understand that?" We were already fighting, and once again, it had to do with me wanting more from him—being involved with his family.

We pulled into the drive, and the SUV became stuck in the driveway.

"Fucking son of a bitch," Michael said, and it was too late to begin chastising him now. The Michael I spent the last week with in Florida was gone. And back, was the Michael who didn't want to be here. Be part of this.

CHAPTER 35

Now

It has been six months, and I'm still holding my breath. Every day with Michael, now my husband, has been a complete paradise. I wake with kisses on my face, breakfast and coffee waiting for me when I leave the shower—and sweet notes inside my lunch bag packed by Michael. Some days, I feel I'm in the twilight zone, and it will all fall apart sooner or later. I don't want to think this way, and I fear my thoughts will keep me locked in the past. Michael says we can't rewrite the past, but we can write our future. Each day, the present is now our future. And I must remember this.

We live in my house—well, our house again. Michael says this summer we'll live at the beach house he bought. The place he proposed to me. And to tell you the truth, I'm looking forward to living on the beach. It's February now, and today is quite a snowy day. Even though there's enough room for both vehicles in the garage, Michael keeps his outside, giving me complete access. Strange from the old days—the old Michael. The old Michael kept his car in the garage, and parked beside his car was his covered Corvette. My car always remained outside.

He waits for me at the garage entry door, holding my lunch. And though there is no need, Michael has the garage door open with my car warming up inside. He also drives me to the hospital each day. It's kind of cute. While he drives, I catch up with Monica on the commute or talk to Ryan and the girls—checking in on things. It's been tough with Tammy gone, but Ryan says they are coping.

Michael pulls from the drive, and I put Monica on speakerphone. "Good morning, Sweetheart. How are you and Jordan?" I ask, and Michael also gives his greetings.

"Hi, Mom and Dad. We're great. In fact, we were going to invite you and Dad over for dinner tonight. If you don't have any plans."

"I don't think so," Michael says.

"It will have to be late. I'm working a twelve-hour shift."

"That's fine. Jordan won't be home until seven anyway. I'm taking the day off."

"Anything you want us to bring?" Michael asks, now that he's the stay-at-home husband.

"No, I have it covered."

"Great, we'll see you tonight. Love you, Sweetheart."

"Love you too," Michael says.

"Love you both. Bye."

"Bye," we both say, and I end the call.

"Hmm. I wonder what's up," I say, and Michael shrugs his shoulders.

"Maybe she misses us." He smiles over at me and then pulls up at the hospital door.

"Maybe." He leans over and kisses me before I get out of the car.

"I love you, Jill." This has become his mantra each day…and little text throughout the day. So not like the old Michael.

"I love you, too." Exiting the car, he pulls me in for one last kiss.

"See you for lunch?" I look down at my bag.

"But you already packed me lunch. But, yes…great. I'll meet you. Just text me, and I'll let you know where I'll be."

"Thanks."

Now out of the car, I wave before walking through the doors. It was hard coming back to work, knowing I would never see Tammy here again. It's hard knowing I'll never see her anywhere again. And she was right, I needed Michael for when she was gone. It's like she just knew. Maybe there is wisdom in death. One thing is for sure, it's non-negotiable. I shiver just thinking about it and how she was so brave.

Stepping into ICU, my new position, I grab the chart and run through the patients on my schedule today. Dorothy, Dotty she likes to be called, is first to have her meds administered through her IV. I reference the correct dosage through the hospital depository and set forth to her room. I feel my phone vibrate in my scrub pocket and give it a quick check. Michael. *Miss you already. I'm so happy, Jill. And so very lucky. I love you.* With my hands full, I will have to remember to text him back.

When I walk in, Dotty is sleeping, and I notice her pale skin, but her vitals are stable—a little on the weak side. She did go through surgery, and this can be rough for a seventy-eight-year-old lady.

Logging into the BCMA, I scan Dotty's wristband, and the system accepts her as a patient. I then scan her meds. All is good, and I administer it through her IV.

"Don't forget to text Michael back," I hear that whispery voice of Marilyn Monroe. There she is, sitting in the bay of the window. The morning sun glowing around her like an angel. Of course, she's an angel. She's my Tammy.

"It's good to see you," I say, logging out of the BCMA. "You've been quiet lately."

"I've been busy spooking around the Kennedys. The ones I can find, that is."

I laugh and finish recording Dotty's information for this morning. "I will text him back. Don't worry. Of all the places you could be, you came to work?" I tease her. But I'm glad she is here.

She hops down and straightens her white dress and walks over to Dotty's bedside. "She was always my favorite," she says. "I took care of her through both hip replacements." Tammy—Marilyn, rubs her fingers down Dotty's cheek. Dotty stirs a little and then opens her eyes. She looks at Tammy like she can see her and smiles.

"It's you," she faintly croaks out. Tammy looks at me.

"I thought you were just *my* imagination. Dotty sees you?"

"Yep. Dotty can. I'm here to care for her." And when she says this, her eyes turn sad.

"You…what? What are you? Some Marilyn Monroe angel of death?"

"Yes. I'm sorry, Jill. But Dotty's not going to pull through this one. She knows it, and she's ready."

My eyes swell with tears. "Oh, my God," I whisper. Poor Dotty, I think and look down at her. Her eyes are closed, and there's a smile on her lips. I hold her hand, and she gives a weak squeeze. She knows I'm here and she is telling me she is ready. I lean down and kiss her cheek. "You're in good hands, Dotty. In some ways, I'm jealous. I hope she comes when it's my turn," I whisper close to her face. Again, she smiles, never opening her eyes. I look up, and Tammy's gone.

I look back one last time before leaving her room, hoping to see Tammy again. But she's not there. But I do hear her whisper. *Text him back.*

•   •   •   •   •

Michael opens the car door as I exit the hospital. It's dark, and the snow is still falling. With a kiss on the lips, he smiles and tells me he misses me and loves me even though he was just here for lunch six hours ago. "I love you, too," I tell him.

"How are the roads?"

"Not too bad. The plows have been keeping up. It's beautiful though. Don't you think?" Michael asks, looking over at me.

I laugh. "You? You think the snow is beautiful? You hating snow was how Monica learned the word, fuck." Placing my hand over my mouth, I laugh and start to cry at the same time. He touches my leg.

"Hey, Baby. What's the matter?"

I shake my head, wiping under my eyes. "I lost a patient today. Dotty. Tammy and I were her favorite nurses. But she went in peace. I…I felt it happening and called her family in so they could be there. Otherwise, it would have been too late."

"I'm sorry. That must be hard."

Looking out the windshield, I watch the snow fall to the ground. It is beautiful and peaceful. "It never gets any easier."

"There comes a time when you realize there are two people on each shoulder. And one of them is death. That's when we hope we have become allies with death." He looks at me and then goes back to the road. Maybe I should ask about his friend who died.

I quickly change clothes, and Michael grabs a bottle of wine, and we head out across town to Monica and Jordan's. With the passing of Dotty, I need my family all around me, and I'm glad she called and invited us tonight.

The snow is still falling, and the roads are a little slick. Yet, Michael continues his love of the snow. "Tomorrow, since you don't have to work, we are building a snowman," he says, bringing my hand up to his lips.

I give him a skeptical look. "Who are you, and what have you done with Michael Danforth?" I tease.

"Here in the flesh, Baby." He winks, and my heart stirs.

We pull into Monica and Jordan's drive, and Michael parks the car and comes around to help me out—such a gentleman in everything he does. But still, I find myself holding my breath.

"Oh, my gosh, look at the snow," Monica says, meeting us at the door. Michael's and my eyes meet, and we share a laugh between them.

"Come in, guys. What's so funny?" she asks, shutting the door and taking our coats.

"Oh, your father and I were talking about the snow on the way over."

"Yeah, what about it?"

"The snow was how you learned the 'f' bomb."

"What?" she laughs. "Why would I say that because of snow?"

"Ask your father," I say and walk away. Jordan kisses my cheek, and I give him a big hug. "How's my favorite son-in-law?"

"I'm great, Jill. The roads are getting bad out there. You have any trouble getting across town?"

"Not too bad."

"It was a struggle getting home from work. I'm glad Monica stayed home today."

I turn to Monica, who is now laughing with Michael over the snow and f-bomb incident. "Did your company close today?" I ask.

"No, I just wasn't feeling well." She looks over at Jordan.

"Well, Honey, if you're not feeling well, we could have come a different night."

"No, it's fine Mom. I'm feeling better now. Let's move to the dining room. I have everything ready."

Michael wraps his arm around me, and we move into their dining room, where Monica has prepared a beautiful display of white dishes with miniature pink and white carnations centering the table in a vase. A card has been propped up against it that says: Mom and Dad.

"Your setting is gorgeous, Sweetheart. You need to start your own interior design."

"Thank you, Mom. You and Dad have a seat. Jordan will bring in the pot roast."

"Mmm, pot roast. Perfect on such a snowy night," Michael says and reaches for the envelope that has been addressed to the both of us. "What's this?"

"Well…just wait until Jordan's here and then you and Mom can open together." She smiles, a bit unsure and I look over at Michael.

"Ok. I can't wait," I say.

Jordan sets the dish with the pot roast, and they both take a seat. "Okay, now you can open it," Monica says, her voice ringing with excitement.

Michael pulls out a homemade card with pink and blue carnations and opens it up to read.

"Roses are red, violets are blue. August fourth, your first grand baby is due." My mouth drops. "Congratulations, Sweetheart,"

Michael says and stands to go kiss his daughter. He shakes Jordan's hand, braces his shoulder. "Congrats, man."

"Mom? Are you going to say anything?" I'm still sitting, and I'm in shock. "Are you happy for us, Mom?" Monica, Jordan, and Michael all look at me from across the table. She's pregnant. My baby is pregnant. I need to say something.

"Jill?" I hear Michael say.

"Ah…yes baby, I'm happy for you. But don't you think it's a little early to be having a baby? I mean, you and Jordan need some time. Time to be…just a couple." Why am I saying this? I should be jumping for joy. It's another blessing in Monica's life—my life. I'm going to be a grandmother. "I mean…you're so young."

"You were seventeen when you had me."

"Yeah, well, I didn't plan to have you at seventeen. Monica, I'm barely in my forties, and I'm still learning how to deal with…life…and motherhood."

"So…you're not happy for us, Mom."

"No, Honey, I didn't say that. Of course, I am. But have you thought this through? You work, and I still work. Who will be caring for your child?"

"I will," Michael states as a matter of fact.

I laugh. "You? Michael, it was like pulling teeth to get you to watch your own daughter. What makes you think you're even qualified?"

"Because I want to. It will be alright, Jill. I couldn't be happier to become a grandfather and to help raise and take care of them. It's a second chance."

"Daddy, do you really want to babysit?"

He takes Monica in his arms. "You bet I do, Sweetheart." He kisses her forehead. "Thank you so much for giving me a chance to become a grandfather. You know how much this means to me." I don't know if he's stating or asking.

"I would love that, Daddy," she says, and the two of them embrace again. What is all the Daddy talk? Have I been in a weird coma for the last twenty years, dreaming that Michael and I were divorced? And all along, I've been the one missing?

"This is unbelievable," I state. My family looks over at me, still waiting for my acceptance of this baby. I'm back in my old bedroom, reading the positive pregnancy test as Tammy rubs my back.

"This is happening, Jill. You're so lucky to be able to live and see the birth of your first grandchild." I hear Tammy say in her Marilyn's voice. Looking up, she's standing next to them, and I suddenly feel like a piece of shit. I'm once again letting my tragic beginning affect Monica's present. Something I swear I would never do. Tammy's right. How selfish of me to feel this way when she will never hold her own.

"Oh, Baby, I'm so sorry. Yes. Oh my God. Yes. I'm so happy." I rush over and take her in my arms. "I'm going to be a grandma. I can't believe it. My baby is having a baby."

She smiles with tears in her eyes, and I too have tears. "Thank you, Mom. I'm going to need you through this."

"Of course, Baby. I'll always be here. Oh, my God, I need a tissue…my nose is running…my eyes are running. Ahh," I shake with excitement. "You're having a baby."

I turn to Jordan. "I know you're going to be such a great father to my grandchild, Jordan. You take such good care of my daughter."

"Thank you, Mom. I can't wait to be a father. And I'm so honored to have your blessing."

"I guess you won't be having any wine that I brought tonight," Michael says.

"No, Daddy. But thanks. And…Daddy, thanks for wanting to help raise this baby," she says and puts her hand on her tummy.

I'm going to be a grandmother. Michael and I are going to be grandparents.

CHAPTER 36

Then

I was kissing Michael goodbye at the airport and hoping this would be the last time. "Tell Daddy bye-bye," I told Monica. Michael took Monica in his arms and kissed her cheeks, telling her to be a good girl for Mommy. He was leaving for Seattle once again. Six months ago, he was offered the position of lead research engineer for Boeing. Yet, I was still living back in Michigan. I asked several times to put the house on the market. But Michael said he wanted to give it a full year before moving for good. Monica was almost four, and Michael was missing out on her growing up.

I watched him leave through security and waved when he looked back. Each time it became more challenging, and I missed him so much. Not only that, but what closeness we built up again in Florida was now melting away. He used to call as soon as he arrived and when his workday was over. He would talk to Monica, and she couldn't wait for Daddy to call. Now, his calls were few and far between.

He was still staying at the hotel the company put him up in, and I asked if he started looking for a house. Occasionally, he would say he checked out a few, but they were overpriced. Tammy, Ryan, and their new daughter, Casey, were my only companions. And even then, I felt I wore out my welcome.

As much as I hated to ask, I needed Tammy to watch Monica for at least a week, so I could fly out and surprise Michael. She was a new mother now and putting a four-year-old in the mix wouldn't be easy. But when I returned home from the airport, I called her.

"What's up? Michael gone?"

"Yes. I just dropped Michael off at the airport."

"Are you coming over? I just put a pizza in."

"No. I won't bother you tonight." I cringed over what I was about to ask. "I need a favor, Tammy."

"Sure. What's up?"

"I hate to ask, but could it be possible to take Monica for a few days? I would like to fly out and spend a week with Michael. Maybe if I'm out there, it will push him to make a decision about moving or not."

"No problem. Monica loves playing with Casey. But I hope the decision is not," she said. Ever since Seattle was brought up, Tammy and I would discuss how we would handle our long-distance friendship. I didn't want to leave her behind. But I didn't want Michael to go on without us.

"Oh, thank you. I will call Michael's hotel and find out when would be a good time."

"Don't worry. We'll be fine."

I hung up and counted the hours until Michael's plane would land, and he'd be at his hotel. After four hours, I figured he'd be back and called. There was no answer, so I left a message at the desk.

"Hello, this is Jill Danforth. I want to leave a message for my husband, Michael Danforth."

"Yes, Mrs. Danforth. Let me check his room number," the man said. I waited for what felt like an eternity. Finally, he came back and asked. "Do you know his room number? I don't have a Michael Danforth listed here."

"Are you sure? He's been living there for the last six months. He's with Boeing…if that helps?"

"Ah yes," he said, and I felt relieved. "Mr. Danforth left the hotel three months ago." My heart dropped, and I began to shake.

"Well, that can't be right. I just took him to the airport. He should be arriving there anytime."

"Yes, Miss. I see where he was registered here with Boeing. But Mr. Danforth checked out on May the seventh. He hasn't returned, according to our records."

"Oh…okay. I see." I felt the phone slide in slow motion down my face and drop to the floor. I couldn't breathe, and my heart was banging against my ribcage. I could still hear the man on the other end as the phone dangled against the wall as I slid to the floor. I reached up and set the phone back into its cradle. Michael was somewhere in Seattle, and I had no way to get ahold of him. I would have to wait until he called—*If he called.*

My mind went to the darkest place, and Michael was gone on some faraway island with another woman. Maybe, he was not even at Boeing. However, wherever he was, he was still paying the bills. I would have to wait until Monday morning when the bank opened and find out where Michael's checks were being deposited from.

•   •   •   •   •

It was noon, and I was on my lunch hour walking into the bank. Michael and I had a joint account, so there should be no reason for me not to see activity on it. The credit card statements had all been ordinary transactions—clothes, dining. What wasn't expected was the number of guests that dined on his card. I hoped it was all business-related.

"Good day, Jill. What can I do for you?"

"Um…I need a printed-out statement of our checking account. A few things I can't remember if I recorded."

"Sure, no problem. Have your ID with you?" Mrs. Black, the bank teller, asked.

"Yes," I said and pulled out my wallet.

"Thanks." As she pulled up the account, I started making small talk to avoid sounding suspicious of my husband.

"Michael used to always run the checkbook. I want to make sure I'm not making any mistakes," I said. She smiled and excused herself.

"I totally get it. It's printing out. I'll have to go back and get that for you."

As I waited, I told myself I was paranoid, and all was on the up and up. But this was Michael I was dealing with. And I knew what he was capable of.

"Here it is," she said walking back. She handed me the printed-out copy and I folded it up and put it down in my purse. But I was dying to read it now.

"Thank you," I said and smiled politely at her. Once in the car, I pulled it out and scanned over the transactions. Men's clothing stores—seemed appropriate since Michael had to dress the part. There were lots and lots of dining. And then I saw a purchase for Bowers Jewelry. The transaction was long before Michael came home. If he bought me jewelry, why didn't he give it to me?

My hands trembled as I read the list, looking for any clues. According to the automatic deposits, Michael was still employed with Boeing. A transaction for seven thousand, six-hundred and eighty-seven dollars was deposited into the account each month. Michael was making more than he let on. But it was the withdrawal of half his pay the same day I questioned. Why did he withdraw half his paycheck, and where was it going?

He never called last night to check in, and I would now have to reach him at Boeing. But I had no extension—only his name. I wished I didn't have to go back to work. I wanted to call him now. No long-distance phone calls were allowed at the hospital. But then I remembered my phone card. I just had never used it.

Racing now to get back to work, I ran to the nurses' station and called information for Boeing in Seattle.

"Which plant are you asking for?" the operator asked. I didn't know there was more than one, so I asked for them all and wrote the numbers down. I thanked her and started with the first number.

"Hello, I'm calling for Michael Danforth's office." I could hear the shakiness in my voice.

"Do you know his extension?" Of course not. Why hadn't he ever given it to me? Why hadn't I ever asked?

"I don't. Sorry."

"Does he work in this plant?" Again, I didn't know.

"I'm not sure. Micheal is in research. Engineering?" Knowing so little of his job, I didn't want to say I was his wife.

"Okay, that would be building five, fourth floor. Do you have that number, or shall I transfer you?"

"Oh, that would be great if you could. Thank you."

"No problem."

A few seconds later, I was greeted by another operator from Boeing, and I asked for Michael Danforth's office again. And again, I didn't have his extension.

"Let me page him," she said and put me on hold. A few seconds later, Michael answered.

"Hey, Babe, what's up?"

Babe? He had no idea it was me because I had no way to get ahold of him. So who did he think was calling?

"Michael?"

"Jill?" There was a question in his answer.

"Yeah, Michael. Were you expecting someone else?"

A slight pause. "No, I figured it was you because I forgot to call home last night. I'm sorry. I left a message on the recorder. But you must have left for work. Is something wrong?"

Everything was wrong, but I didn't know how to begin. I didn't have any proof that Michael was doing something wrong. But I could ask why he wasn't at the hotel anymore, and why he left three months ago.

"I called the hotel last night. They said you moved out three months ago."

"Yes, that's correct," he said with no hesitation.

"Where did you go? Why didn't you tell me?"

"I'm sorry. I should have, but I guess it didn't seem like a big deal. Boeing is putting me up in one of their pilot hotels. They own this hotel and use it for pilots during layovers. It's all a budget thing. And, the accommodations are much nicer, I can tell you that." He was rambling on so smoothly that I couldn't accuse him of anything.

"Oh, well, you should have told me."

"I know, I'm sorry. How's Monica?"

"She misses you. So do I, Michael."

"I know. Shouldn't be much longer."

"Longer? Longer for what?" We hadn't ever put the house on the market.

"Longer until we decide what to do."

"Do you like the job? It seems to pay well." I now had a reason to ask why he withdrew half his paycheck each month.

"Yes, I do."

"Michael, I was balancing the checkbook, and I saw you withdraw half your pay each month. Why?"

"I've put it into a special savings Boeing offers its employees. It's to save for a house, Jill."

Okay. That was explainable. "Tammy's going to watch Monica, so I can come out and spend some time with you."

"That's not really necessary, Jill. I was just home last weekend. Don't be wasting your vacation time. I'll be coming home again."

"Michael, I want to. I want to check out the place. This decision involves me too."

There was another slight hesitation.

"Ah…you're right. But I can't promise how much time I'll be able to spend alone with you. I work late most nights so I can get my projects done and come home at times."

"I understand. I…I would love to see you, Michael. I love you."

"Baby, I know you do. Let me check with the hotel and see if it's okay for you to stay. If not, I'll get us a place of our own." He wasn't going to say he loved me back?

"Okay. Thank you. I'll let you know my flight schedule when I book it."

"Okay." I heard his hand muffle the phone and talk in the background. "Hey, I have to go. Let me know when you get here. Bye," he said and hung up. No 'I love you' back.

•   •   •   •   •

Michael was there, waiting for me at the airport when I walked through the terminal. It was hard to leave Monica, but I needed to find out some things for myself.

Michael was dressed for work: black slacks, white shirt, sans tie and black suit coat. As usual, he was devastatingly handsome, and my heart skipped a beat when I saw him. He was tanned, and I wondered where Michael had found time in the sun—since he worked so late. He smiled and waved me over, and when I walked up to him, I had visions of jumping into his arms and being swirled around. But no such thing. He simply pecked me on the cheek and said, "Let's get your baggage."

Baggage? I would have preferred the word luggage. But I was still on defense, and he didn't have a clue.

We grabbed my bag and headed out of the airport. Michael's rental car was parked not far, and we pulled from the parking lot. He hadn't said much of anything in the last five minutes we'd been together. "You look nice, Michael. Is that a new suit?" Recalling his shopping sprees.

"Yes, I've picked up a few new suits. Oh, we'll be staying at the Hyatt. I've got us a room for your time here."

"Oh? We can't stay at this…pilot hotel?"

"No. Even though we're married, it's for employees and pilots only. Sorry. But, this will be more private for us. No bumping into work colleagues." I wanted to see who his colleagues were.

"I've taken the rest of the day off so we can spend some time together. Is there anything in particular you want to do?" *See what you've been hiding for six months.*

I reached over and kissed his cheek. "Just be with you. Why don't you show me some of the sights and neighborhoods?" *And talk about putting our house on the market.*

"Alright. First, let's get your baggage put away and I'll drive you around." Baggage.

After we dropped off my luggage, Michael took me to a small court where food trucks were lined up. I found it an odd place for him to suggest lunch when I saw all the exotic dinner places on the credit cards. I wanted to ask but knew Michael would only give me a suitable excuse, and I wanted to appear to be here on true intentions. But Michael had no idea of my true intentions.

The view through the valley was quite picturesque with the snowcapped mountains and green hills as we sat on a picnic table enjoying our deli sandwiches. I noticed Michael was wearing a new watch. One I hadn't seen when he was back home a few weeks ago. I thought now would be a good time to ask about the jewelry purchase.

"Michael, is that a new watch?"

He looked at his wrist and then back to me. "Yes, my old one broke."

Sounds reasonable. "Did you just get it?"

"Yes. My old one broke on the plane coming back."

"Where'd you get it?"

He looked at me painstakingly. "Oh, I don't know. I can't remember."

He couldn't remember where he bought a watch two weeks ago. "I saw a purchase in our account from a Bowers Jewelry store. Would it be from there?" His face turned ghostly, and then he acted as if a light was turned on.

"Yes, that's where I brought it," he said. The purchase was from two months ago. I didn't want him to know I was fishing.

"I like it. I would like to buy my father one. His birthday is coming up. I think he would like a nicer watch. Could you take me there while I'm here?"

"Sure, no problem," he said while wiping his mouth with a napkin. As he chewed, he stared at me, and I was afraid he was reading my suspicious mind. I needed to play it cool. I planned to find something out. So, I kept the conversation at a level of reason.

"Michael, it's gorgeous here. I think I would like it. Maybe while you're working, I could look at a few houses? And…do you think it's time to put the house on the market? You never know how long it will take to sell."

"What about Tammy and your family? I wouldn't think you would want to leave them."

"Michael, you're my husband. I need to be with you. Monica needs to be with her father. Tammy and my family will come to visit. Why can't we put the house up for sale?"

He took a deep breath and appeared bothered. "I don't want to sell it. I haven't been here for a full year. I still only have my foot in the door. I need to make sure."

"Well, we could always just buy another house if we want to come back."

"And…be stuck with another house here."

He was stubborn, and I was not backing down on this one. "What if we rent our house out and rent a house here?" His eyebrow quirked at the thought.

"Yes, that's a maybe. We'll see." Finally, I had some movement where the house was concerned. But what about Monica and me?

We left, and I told him I wanted to see his place of work. I wanted to meet his co-workers and visit his office. "But, I thought you wanted to look at houses?" he asked. He was backpedaling, and there was a reason he didn't want me at his work.

"So, you want to check out some houses? Rent or buy?" He studied me as he drove, and his eyes went back to the road. "Michael, is there a reason you don't want me to see where you work?"

"Of course not, Jill. It's just…I've taken the day off. So, why would I want to go back? I'm here with you. Maybe before you go back." I watched his expression as he drove. Not once had he asked how I had been or how his daughter was.

The hotel had a hot tub, and I suggested we grab a few drinks and check it out. I brought a new bikini and some sexy lingerie and kept my hands all over him as much as I could. He seemed skittish, and I wanted to question him about it. Michael never lacked in the wanting-sex department, and I had to wonder why now. But now wasn't the time. I had my plans and must play it down.

I came out of the bathroom with the new bikini, turned around, and shook my ass at him. "What do you think?" I was relieved when his brow quirked and a smile formed on his lips.

"Nice," he said with a sexy, exciting voice. "Wow, sometimes I forget what a beautiful body you have." A chorus of angels filled my heart with song, and I felt that doubt shifting. Maybe it was my paranoia that only made things seem suspicious. But in a few days, I would know the truth.

After the hot tub and a few martinis, Michael made love to me. And it was different, passionate. Not his usual fuck hard and talk dirty. He seemed…scared, unsure, and maybe it was the long distant relationship finally taking a toll on his emotions. He kissed me hard, and I couldn't remember the last time Michael kissed me during sex. It was almost a goodbye like we would never see each other again. It was the first time Michael had shown a real passion for me… and it scared me to death.

It was my last day in Seattle, and I told Michael I had a taxi taking me to the airport and for him to go to work. It was an early flight. "Are you sure?" he asked.

"Yes, it's fine—I hate long goodbyes. You'll be home soon, right?"

"Yes." But his look told me differently. Soon, I would find out why. I wasn't going back to Michigan. I booked the last two days at another hotel. This was my plan. To make him think I was only here for five days when I was here for seven.

Instead of having the taxi take me to the airport or the hotel, I told the taxi driver to drop me off at Avis, where I had reserved a rental car. After claiming my rental, I checked in at my hotel. I paced the room, waiting for five o'clock when Michael got off work. He had driven me by Boeing, so I knew where it was. But he never gave me a tour.

At five o'clock, I was in position—parked two cars away from Michael's car. I watched him walk out of the building and to his car. I was expecting him to come out with another woman. But to my surprise, he was alone, and I prayed my intuitions were wrong. And Michael would never know that I mistrusted him and spied.

His car pulled out, and I stayed close behind, hoping he wouldn't see me in the car. He showed me the hotel where the pilots stayed but never took me there again. I thought this would be the route he would take. But he didn't, and twenty minutes later, we pulled into a housing estate with big, gorgeous homes. What the fuck? Why would he be coming here? But deep down, I knew why.

I was close behind him now, and he turned into a driveway. I watched the garage door open. No other car was inside, yet he pulled in to leave room for another. Who would be coming?

I drove past and turned around in the cul-de-sac at the end of the street. I slowed next to the curb when I reached the house and parked the car. My hands were wet with sweat, and I was shaking all over. I needed to go into that house.

Glancing in the mirror, I checked my appearance, saw the frightened look in my eyes, and exited the car. My legs felt like jelly as I walked to the door. I was about to ring the doorbell when I saw Michael walking through the house from the sidelight window. I checked the door, but the handle was locked. Peering through the window, I could see the patio door was open to the backyard, and I slowly walked around. Michael was nowhere around, so I padded in and looked around. What was this place? Had he already purchased a home and didn't want his family with him?

I looked around for a place to hide. I wanted to witness with my own eyes what I knew would kill me, and I saw a coat closet next to the entry door. Michael must have been in the shower because I could hear water running from the bedroom. I padded to the door and snuck inside. I was also grateful that the door was louvered and not paneled. I could see everything from the inside. I had a front-row seat if this show was to be taking place in the living area. But the floor plan was open to the kitchen and the downstairs. And…completely palatial. How could Michael afford this place while still making the mortgage back home? I would soon find out why when the utility door from the garage opened into the kitchen. In walked a woman—fortyish, professional, and…pretty.

She dropped her designer purse on the counter and bent down to remove her three-hundred-dollars Louboutin's. "Michael? I'm home, Babe," she yelled. My heart was thumping so loud. I knew for sure she could hear it. I was hyperventilating, and no matter how much I prepared for this moment, my blood was pumping iron. The thrashing sound through my ears sounded like waterfalls, and I was afraid I would go deaf and not hear what I needed to hear.

Michael came down the stairs—showered, with wet hair, and wearing only three-hundred-dollar designer jeans. "There you are, Babe," she said, pulling him to her tugging on his jeans. "God, I love the way you look in these. Could you pour me a glass of wine? I'm going to shower." She kissed his lips and then licked down to his naked navel.

"Red?" Michael asked.

"Yes. And…did you tell her?" Michael turned to get the wine, and she demanded. "Oh, God, Babe. Please tell me you told her so we can continue this."

This?

"Okay, not yet. But I told Jill not to sell the house. I'm still waiting to cash in my stock to pay it off."

He had enough stock to pay off our house? But why did he want to pay it off?

"She'll be well taken care of, Michael. My God, get it over with. Daddy said he would represent you pro bono. It will be the easiest divorce ever. I mean, what can she argue about? She'll have a home with no mortgage, child support monthly, and you can use her college debt you paid as leverage."

My God, I was just a case to them. How long had they been setting up my fate?

"Cami, we were married when I paid for her college. Most of it was paid by my tuition reimbursement from Whirlpool. She doesn't owe me a thing."

I stepped out of the closet and walked to where they were standing. "Hello, Michael." I turned to the woman who considered me a case. "Cami."

"How'd the fuck did she get in here?" she yelled.

"Jill? What are you doing here? I thought you went home?"

I smirked, forcing myself not to cry. "Well, I guess we were all wrong. And by the way, Michael, we are still married. But it looks as if you've forgotten." I looked at Cami and saw a necklace around her neck. "Did Michael buy you that necklace at Bowers?"

Her hand went to the necklace as her fingers smoothed the pendant on her throat. I wanted to rip it off and stab her in that soft hollow spot, the way I learned in self-defense. Michael never bought me jewelry—not even a wedding ring.

"Yes, he did."

I looked back at Michael. I hoped he recognized all the hurt and betrayal he had caused me all these years. What was so special about this woman?

"Well, enjoy it. I guess I paid for half of it." I turned to leave and walked toward the front door, but it was still locked, and I struggled with the handle. Turning the lock one way and then the other, I still couldn't open the door and slapped the wood. Michael's hand appeared above mine.

"I need to put in the code." That was it? The code? He flipped a panel next to the door, and after four beeps, I heard the door click. I opened the door and ran to the car. Michael chased after me. "Jill, you're too upset to drive. Let me call you a cab."

This was unbelievable. But then again, it wasn't, knowing Michael. "Oh, now you finally care about my well-being? What about my heart, Michael? What about our marriage?"

"Just let her go, Michael," I heard Cami yell from the front door. "She finally knows now. It's over."

I opened the door to the car and fell in. Michael held the door open and spoke his last words. "I'll be home soon, and we'll sort this out." I looked up at him incredulously. "The divorce."

"Looks like you two have it all sorted out." He stood back, and I slammed the door. I started the car, and even though I had no memory of returning to the hotel, I somehow drove through traffic and was parked in front of the building. I ran through the doors and pressed the button for the third floor—five times, dying for it to open. I needed Tammy. I needed her with me right now.

Struggling with the damn keycard because I was inserting it backward, I finally unlocked the door and ran to the phone.

"Hello? Jill?"

"Tammy," I cried. "I need you."

CHAPTER 37

Now

Today is Monica's ultrasound, and Michael, Jordan, and I are here. She's six months, almost seven. Although we are dying to know what gender the baby is, today will not be the day. She has planned to have a gender reveal party. And guess who is making all the arrangements and will know the sex today—Michael. The transformation is endless, and I'm slowly learning to breathe more comfortably.

We all watch in anticipation as the nurse spreads the jelly and moves the sonogram along Monica's swollen belly. As soon as the head and little hands appear, we all sigh. Tears come to my eyes, and I feel Michael squeeze my hand. I look up, and he embraces me in his arms. "I wish I were with you the day you had your sonogram. I missed so much," Michael says and kisses my forehead.

"I wish you were there too. But this is the future you spoke of, and we're all here now."

Holding Monica's hand, I look at how my baby has grown and now looking at her baby. Jordan makes comments that he knows it's a boy. Even though these sonograms have come a long way, I still can't tell the sex. But to be sure, Monica has had an NIPT to check for chromosomal conditions.

"This is unbelievable. Look at my precious baby. I can't even express how much I already love this baby," Monica says, admiring the screen. "Does everything look okay? Is my baby healthy?"

"Everything appears normal," the tech tells her. "But your GP will read the final results." She looks through Monica's file and smiles.

"Your NIPT came back normal negative. And who am I to give this to?" she asks, writing the baby's sex down.

"Me, the grandfather," Michael says proudly, holding up his hand.

She folds the paper up and hands it to him. Michael takes the piece of paper and shoves it down into his pocket. "Well, you won't look at it right here?" Monica begs.

"Oh, no, Sweetheart. It would be best if you didn't read into my facial expressions. But yes, I'm dying to know."

"You do have the Pinterest board I shared with you?"

"Yes, but I thought I was planning it?"

"You are, Dad. I'm just giving you suggestions."

"Okay, everything is good. You are free to go," the tech says, wiping the gel from Monica's tummy.

Jordan helps Monica off the table, and Michael suggests taking us all out for lunch. "Since we all took the day off, I know of a great place to have lunch. And don't even think I'll look or show you the piece of paper tucked safely away in my pocket."

•   •   •   •   •

Another perfect day. Another perfect Michael. *Breathe.* My days include love notes placed around the house, love texts whenever we're not together, and songs dedicated to me on social media. It must all be real because everyone tells me a gorgeous glow surrounds my smile. I feel I'm seventeen again and ported back when I first met Michael. In this life, I feel I'm the reserved one and waiting for the bottom to fall out. Sometimes, I want to ask what happened with Cami and what made him want me back. But each time I do, something inside me tells me to accept it and not argue with a good thing. Maybe someday I will know.

Walking into the kitchen as Michael pours our morning coffee, I look up to the whiteboard stuck to the fridge, where a love message from Michael is handwritten each day. But today, it's a little different.

Captioned above his message is the word jeopardy. He smiles at me when I take my coffee.

"That is the answer, and you must guess the correct question," Michael says.

"Oh, so now it's a game?"

"Yep. And you must answer in the form of *who is* or *what is*."

"Hmm. I've never been good at Jeopardy."

"Well, I'll give you a hint. The '*who is*' is always about you. That should narrow it down."

Taking a sip of my coffee, I read the answer. 'So fucking beautiful.' "Well, if the who is always me, then the answer is: Who is Jill Danforth?"

"Well, that's a given. But this has to do with time."

"Time?"

"Yes."

Grrr. "This is hard but simple. When Michael sees me dressed up? Now. You have never complimented me in the past."

His eyes blink with a hint of sadness. "True, and I'm so sorry. But, let's change this to things I was thinking but never said."

I reread the answer. "So fucking beautiful. Um…the Christmas party at the Whirlpool mansion. I mean, how did Jill look at the Christmas party?"

"Wrong, but right. You were drop-dead gorgeous that night. But here is the correct question to that answer. "When I first saw you sleeping in your brother's car. So fucking beautiful."

"Oh, Michael. You really thought that? I was so embarrassed. I thought I had drool running down my chin."

"I wish I would have told you, "he says, kissing me sweetly. "I wish I would have told you a lot of things."

I smile up into eyes full of love, desire, and regrets. "I love you, Michael. Even when I thought I hated you. I loved you."

"I will always love you, Jill, and still regret the twenty years I wasted when I could have been with you because there's so much I want to do with you. And tonight is one of them."

"Oh, yeah? And what are we doing tonight?" I ask, reaching up on my tiptoes and kissing his lips.

"Karaoke."

"What? There is no way I'm getting up and singing. No way. No, how."

"Not you. Me."

"Oh." I cock a brow and cover his cheeks in my hands. It takes me back to our first kiss. The abrasion of his beard and how it felt so manly. So grown up. "Really, who are you?" I tease.

"The man who will love you for the rest of his life."

We head to the patio for coffee and see Alan and Tyler working in their gardens. I wave when Alan looks up and, for once, feel as happy as they have always seemed to be. "Your garden is gorgeous as always," I holler over.

"We have tomatoes ready. I'll bring some over in a bit."

"Oh, that sounds wonderful. Thank you."

Michael smiles and then takes a sip of his coffee. "I got lucky your neighbors are gay. Or else, they would have been hitting on you. But, this time, I was willing to fight my competition."

"Competition? What are you talking about?"

"Drake. And I'm not talking about the night at the coffee house when you were in college." This time, he winks at me and takes another sip. How does he know about Drake? It was so many years ago. I don't have Facebook, so how would he know?

"How do you know about Drake?"

"I saw you two together. I saw you...happy. And though I intended to get you back, I didn't want to cause you more problems."

Oh, my God. I don't believe this. I move away from his stare, look at Alan and Tyler in their garden, and sip my coffee. "Yes, we were...happy," I say quietly.

"What happened?"

Is this the part where he asks me, and then I ask him about Cami? Do I want to know about her and relive the worst moment of my life? But he is asking.

"Me. I was what happened," I confess and hide my shame inside the coffee cup, taking a sip. "I…freaked out and called it off." Wow, admitting out loud still isn't comforting. "I was still in my dark years, unwilling to let go of the past, and…I don't know. I just felt I couldn't trust someone. It was wrong, and he didn't deserve it." I feel his gaze on me, and I don't know what he's thinking. Does he think I'll do the same to him to even the score?

"I see."

"Michael, if you think I'll do the same to you, I won't. I promise. At first, the thought was there in the far back of my mind. But as I saw the change in you, I started to trust you again. I love you, Michael. I do." I pause. "It was a few years after you left. He asked me to marry him—surprising me with a ring and the whole entourage in front of a crowd. What every girl dreams, right?" He presses his lips with shame, I can tell. "Right in front of the restaurant, he got down on one knee and said those words. 'Jill, will you marry me?' I was elated and said yes right away. Once he slipped the ring on my finger, it was what he said next once the clapping and cheering were over. He held my hands from across the table, looked into my eyes, and said something that changed how I felt about him. Everything inside me changed, and I felt once again like a second-class citizen. But maybe I jumped the gun and missed out. I should have talked more about it with him. Instead, I returned the ring and told him goodbye later that night. He was hurt, and I never gave him an explanation. But look, it worked out for the best." Should I ask about Cami? "Michael…what happened after I left? What happened to you and Cami?"

Taking a deep breath, he sets his cup down and searches the sky for words. A few seconds go by before he begins.

"You always think the grass is greener on the other side and I know that sounds cliché. But here is what you learn about that other grass. It still has to be watered and mowed. And some grass becomes…too high maintenance and you find yourself missing the grass you used to have. The grass that only wanted to love you, adore you and just simply…you."

Am I that grass?

"I went on, thinking I found love at first sight—many times. I feared being irrelevant to someone, so I never let anyone attach to my heart. The problem with youth is it's your penis falling in love at first sight. Then…when you finally figure out what true love is, it's left the building. You find yourself sitting across the room watching the love of your life being proposed to. That ship has sailed, and you're only a bad memory to her."

"You were there?"

"Yes, and I got what I deserved that night."

"Oh, my God. I had no idea."

"But to answer your question about Cami, in the end, we…just became friends and business partners."

"Do…do you still keep in touch with her?"

"Yes, I do. But it is strictly business. Please, don't ever worry."

How can I not?

•   •   •   •   •

Michael tells me to wear jeans and a tight T-shirt for tonight's date. He still hasn't told me where we're going, but I have a feeling it's not a place I would typically go—or he for that matter. He is dressed in tight jeans, cowboy boots, and a tight black T-shirt. He so reminds me of the young Michael in those jeans. And…he's put on a few pounds since we've been together. But only in the right places.

I laugh. "Oh, my God. Howdy partner. Michael, you've never been *country*. And I haven't listened to country music since high school. Are we really doing this?"

He walks over and scoops me up in his arms. "You bet, Gorgeous. Once the baby comes, our date nights might become limited."

"Yeah, but this is Monica and Jordan's baby."

"I know. But I want to make up for not being the father I should have been. I want my grandchild to know how special they are to me."

My insides burst with love when he talks like this. "Speaking of grandchildren…"

"Oh no you don't. My lips are sealed. You'll just have to wait." Still, in his arms, he rolls me forward and gives me another big kiss. "You ready?"

"As ever."

Twenty minutes later, we pull into the parking lot of Diamond and Denims, a country bar I've passed by several times but never went in. I never had a reason to. But looking over at the handsome man in the driver's seat, I sure do now. He's so gorgeous and loving, and thoughtful and I'm so afraid I don't give him enough credit.

"Michael, if I don't say it enough, I want you to know how happy I am because of you."

"Thank you. I have another *Jeopardy* answer for you."

I laugh. "Okay, hit me."

"Blondes are the prettiest."

"Oh, how easy. What was the caption on a T-shirt you bought me in high school?"

"Hehe," he says, sounding like a buzzer.

"No, I'm right."

"Correction. What was an excuse for Michael to come to see Jill?"

"Ahh. Really?"

He holds up two fingers. "Scout's honor. And how lucky I got, that Scott was gone, and you were washing your car in those tight, little jean shorts. I even remember the song that was playing on your car stereo."

"Really? Because I don't."

He places his finger under my chin and looks into my eyes. "This Kiss," he says and gently lays his lips on mine. "Maybe you'll sing it to me tonight."

"Ahh, no."

Stepping inside, it's what I expected and the last place I would expect Michael to be. And I tease him about it. "Okay, Mr. West Coast. What barrel shall we sit on?"

"The one closest to the stage."

We settle in on a high wooden whiskey barrel used as a table and slide our barstools in. The place is genuine country, with bowls of peanuts and shells all over the floor. The waitresses are dressed in denim shorts and shirts tied at the waist. And of course, country music playing—loud.

Michael orders us a few drinks—him a beer, me a diet, and Captain. "You still don't drink beer?" Michael asks

"No, it never appealed to me."

Our drinks are served, and Michael asks for the karaoke list to put his name on. He's really serious. The only time I recall him singing was when I delivered him a pizza, twenty years ago, and he sang to *"You're Still the One"* by Shania Twain as we danced.

He smiles over at me and hands the list back. There's a cheeky grin on his lips and a twinkle in his eye. "What did you pick to sing?"

"It's a surprise," he says, holding his beer for a toast.

A few singers go by, and Michael is called to the stage. I'm nervous—and I'm not the one singing.

"Hello, everyone. My name is Michael Danforth, and that stunning lady there is my wife. Isn't she a knockout?" The crowd whoops and whistles, and my face flushes. "Can you believe she is about to become a grandmother?"

"No way," I hear someone in the crowd say.

"Tonight," Michael continues, "I want to sing a song to my beautiful wife. I'm not much of a country person, but I heard this song once, and it hit my heart hard. And I said to myself, if I ever get the chance to sing this to her, I would. So, here goes."

The music starts, and I'm unsure if I know this song. But then someone hollers, "I love Blake Shelton, and I love this song."

Michael begins to sing, *Mine Would Be You,* and I've never heard something sound so full of love and regret at the same time. His eyes never leave mine with each word, and then he comes and takes me to the stage. On one knee, he sings the last chorus.

What's the greatest chapter in your book?
Are there pages where it hurts to look?
What's the one regret you can't work through?
You got it, baby, mine would be you.

He finishes the song, and with tears in my eyes and my hands shaking, he kisses me on stage and everyone in the bar claps. Slowly by slowly, I begin to breathe again.

CHAPTER 38

Then

You would think two years would have been enough time for me not to think about Michael and that horrible day when I found him with Cami. But more importantly, you would think I should be glad he was gone. And no more worries of distrust and betrayal. But here's the thing about suspicion and betrayal. There's only one victim, and while one goes onto the next victim, the victim sees everyone as their future reason for distrust and betrayal.

Monica and I decided to add a puppy to our two-person family—mainly her. She was five now and had started kindergarten. Michael was now a total void in her life. Once he came back and settled the divorce, we never saw him again. The puppy was more of a guilt present, but when I saw its sweet, little face in the window at the mall pet store, I couldn't resist.

Monica would ask about her father now and then, and at school, she had met little friends who had visitation time with their fathers. She even asked me once if it was true that some moms and dads live together. I then realized she hadn't much of a memory of Michael. And maybe that was a good thing. But then she would ask why she didn't have visitation with her father—like her little friends. I didn't have an answer for her, so we bought a puppy instead.

Financially, we were okay. That was the one thing Michael did set up for us. I'll never forget that day he walked through the door. I thought for sure Michael would change his mind. I stared at him with such loss in my eyes—and a part of me felt he had the same look in his eyes. And damn it, I should have been glad it was over. But that didn't mean it hurt any less.

"Jill," he whispered after standing in the doorway for ten minutes. "I'm sorry you had to see us. That's not how I planned it," he said.

"Planned it! Who plans a divorce, Michael? How long has it been going on?"

"That's not important, Jill."

"Oh, I know. I've never been important to you. I've never been a priority to you."

"That's not true. I've stayed with you longer than I planned."

"Oh, my God, Michael. Just shut the fuck up." He pressed his lips, placed his hands on his hips and looked around the house.

"The house is yours. I cashed in my Whirlpool shares and paid it off. So, don't plan on taking half my pension or retirement. I'm giving you the house, free and clear."

"That's right, Michael. Just throw money on it. Make us go away. That's where half your paycheck was going, wasn't it? To your new place...with her."

"Jill, I've never wavered from my responsibilities here with you."

"You've been fucking around, Michael. So, I say, you have."

"Financial responsibilities," he corrected me.

"Just because you pay the bills, Michael, is not a free card to cheat. And don't you forget. I, too, contribute to this household."

"And let's remember who paid for your education."

"Stop it. I'm tired of this being nothing but a business arrangement between us. I'm your wife, Michael. Not a contract you signed."

"Jill, you had to know it was coming. I had to end it now, especially with all your *having another baby* talk. That's when I knew it had to end. So, you kind of brought this on yourself."

My jaw dropped. Michael was unbelievable. "Then why didn't you tell me you didn't want another baby? You said: let's see what Seattle brings. Well, I guess that settles it. Seattle brought you Cami and brought me nothing."

"That's not true, Jill. This house is yours, paid in full. I've set the support for Monica to be automatically deposited into your account. I even had it set above the standard. You should be just fine."

"And my heart?"

He looked around and then back to me. "Jill, I can't do this anymore." *This.* Monica and I were…this thing he couldn't do. So, what was Cami? The one? I wanted to scream. I wanted to scratch his eyes out and then tell him I loved him. But how do you tell someone you love them when you shouldn't? And so…I didn't. I just stared at him. Tears dripped down my cheeks.

He walked to the bedroom, packed the last of his stuff and before he walked out the door, he said, "Take care, Jill." That was it. No…goodbye. No, I will miss you. No, I love you. And deep down, I knew he never did.

I watched his car from the window until it disappeared down the street. And my stupid, stupid heart thought he would turn around and change his mind. My eyes began to burn because I was afraid to blink. I think it was getting dark when I finally called Tammy, who stayed with me all night and let me cry myself to sleep.

We named the new puppy Molly, and I had scheduled to get her at a veterinary office that came highly recommended. Since I never had a dog before, I didn't know of a good one. I was shocked when we walked in and saw Drake walking out one of the rooms in a white lab coat. After the coffee house incident, he left the community college, and I never knew what happened to him.

"Oh, my God. Drake?"

"Jill? Look at you," he said and set down the clipboard he was holding as he reached out for me. "Wait, is Michael going to come storming in?" he laughed.

"No. We're divorced," I said, hoping I sounded sad.

"Oh. Well, sorry to hear that. But then again, I'm not."

My face blushed and I forgot about the puppy in my arms and Monica at my side. "So, you became a vet. Wow."

"Yes, it took another few years. But hey, time goes by whether we're in school or not. Right?"

"Ah…yeah. It sure does." Another moment of perfect silence when he finally spoke again.

"So, what do you have here?"

"This is Molly," I said, holding up the little cocker spaniel. "We just got her, and a friend at the hospital recommended your veterinary clinic." I then put two and two together. The recommendation came from Tammy.

"Wow, is this your little girl…Monica, right?" he asked, bending down to her level. She nodded shyly. "Last time I saw you, you were just a baby…with a muffin all over your face." Monica giggled and looked up at me. She reached for her puppy and petted Molly's little feet. "Well, let's take Molly back and have a look at her," Drake said, and we followed him to one of the exam rooms.

I set Molly on the metal table and watched as Drake handled the puppy with such care. I still couldn't believe he became a vet. "She looks very healthy. Do you have her papers?"

"Yes, here in my purse," I said and pulled them out. Handing them over, Drake looked through her pedigree and was a little concerned that she came from a puppy mill.

"I had no idea. The puppy's sweet little face was what sold me."

"Well, she'll be much better with you. I won't lie to you," Drake said, and for some reason, I respected how he said *won't lie to you.* "Puppies from these mills aren't always as healthy as those from private breeders. So, I will check for any lung issues, and I would like to do blood work and check for parasites."

"Yes, please. I want to ensure Molly's healthy enough to be around Monica and in the house."

"She should be fine," he said and got busy with Molly's shots. He gave Molly a treat, which she gobbled up and then gave Monica a balloon. "Here you go, Monica. You like balloons?"

"Yes," she said with her fingers in her mouth—her shy response.

Molly was finished with her shots and physical, and Drake said he'd call when her blood work was done. "So, are you…dating?"

I bit my lip and smiled like a stupid schoolgirl. "No. I'm not." Was he asking or just curious? I had been out of the dating scene since high school. In fact, I never even dated. Michael was my first. And after two years, I still didn't know what to call it.

I looked down at his hand and saw no ring. But then again, Michael never had or wore a ring. "So, I take it you're not married?"

"Nope. Guess I've been waiting for you," Drake said, staring into my eyes. I felt something in my chest and realized it was my heart—beating.

"And, adding a few more years to your education helped you pass the time?"

He laughed. "I guess you could say that." He bent down and petted Molly and handed Monica the leash. He stood and said, "I never stopped thinking about you, Jill. Or that kiss."

We both knew what he meant, and to me, it was the kiss that got Michael to notice me. After all these years, he still remembered that kiss.

"Yeah, that was pretty crazy, right there in front of the coffee shop. I wonder how many saw us that night from the café window."

"I was hoping everyone." He tilted his head, and his eyes looked so kind, full of something I wished I had seen in Michael's eyes. But he wasn't Michael. He was better, and I didn't want to keep comparing.

"Drake, I would love to go out with you, if you're asking?"

"I'm asking." He smiled slyly and wrote down his cell number and handed it to me. "This Saturday?"

"Yes, Saturday works. Um…do you want my number…in case things…change."

"I have it." He looked down at Molly's chart and repeated, "555-6469."

I threw my head back with embarrassment. "Of course. Duh," I said.

"You're still so cute, Jill."

A compliment and I didn't know what to do with it. "Um…thank you, I guess." He could tell I was becoming uncomfortable and walked us out of the exam room.

"I'll call you, Jill. About Saturday," he said and grabbed the next dog's file and headed to the next exam room. I looked at the receptionist who was smirking at me and tried to ignore her.

"We're old college friends."

•   •   •   •   •

I was back in high school, roaming through my wardrobe, searching for something to wear. Nothing seemed right. It was either too young or too old. And I was only twenty-two. I looked at the tiny, black dress I wore to the Christmas party. And then, thinking about Michael and me having sex in the car knocked on my head. Was he ever going to go away?

Unfortunately, the yellow dress hung on me. Since the divorce, I had lost weight, so I had to go with the black dress from the Christmas party. "Let's make a new memory in this dress, "I said aloud.

He picked me up at six and, once again, I was speechless from his compliments. "I saw these flowers, and they reminded me so much of you. All the colors and the sweet scent." He was holding out a bouquet of painted daisies, and I kissed him on the cheek.

"Thank you, Drake. It's been forever since I've had flowers. You look…great." Great? He wasn't an idea or a piece of furniture. "I mean…God, let me start over."

"It's okay, Jill. Take your time," he chuckled.

"Drake, I've always thought you were handsome, and…wow, you're a doctor and…you're just amazing. I was so attracted to you in college. But I was married, and…"

"Don't stop there," he teased and pulled me to him. "Let's finish that kiss."

Setting the daisies on the counter, he pulled me into his arms. The second his lips touched mine, I felt life inside me push out the dead, and for once, Michael was gone.

•   •   •   •   •

"So, I looked at him and said, seriously, 'There's a pencil stuck in your dog's anus?'"

"Oh, my God. You're kidding, right?"

"I wish I were," Drake said, grabbing my hands from across the table. He was funny and gorgeous and so easy to talk to. I couldn't remember the last time I had been part of a conversation. The whole night was filled with laughter and jokes, and I couldn't believe I was a part of it. Oh, the things I had been missing. Michael never made me laugh like this, nor did he care to involve me in his work or thoughts. Drake told me about his goals and dreams; as he shared them, he never made me feel I wasn't a part of them. He talked about marriage, family, and the vacations he would take his children on. And he looked me straight in the eye each time he said it. He was talking about me—us. Again, that distrust and betrayal began to chatter inside my head. They were warning me with laughter. Drake was my first date in two years, and it told me not to get too excited. I didn't want to listen to it. I tried to listen to Drake and focus on something good. Drake was good. He had to be. How could someone become a vet and love animals and not be good?

The magic of the night continued when we left the restaurant and had drinks at a local nightclub. For only one second did I think of Michael when we walked in. The place was classy, in that dark, Martini bar way and it felt like a place Michael would pick up women. But I was here with a good man, and he wanted to be with me.

As we sat in a red velvet booth, tucked away in the dark sipping our dirty Martinis, Drake kissed me, and the moment felt serene.

With so much laughter, I thought I'd lose my voice. His hand smoothed along my cheek, and we stared into each other's eyes. He touched my lips with his thumb and told me how beautiful I was. I was ready now and all the pain and hurt I went through with Michael was gone. I looked into Drake's eyes and said, "Drake, would you like to spend the night with me?"

He didn't answer, but only smiled and then kissed me passionately. And I took that as a yes.

CHAPTER 39

Now

Sitting outside, having coffee in the hospital courtyard, I breathe in and acknowledge all the beautiful blessings. The trees are a portrait of red, yellow, and gold. I could look at them all day. Fall is my favorite time of year. Not only with its golden beauty, but it takes me back to when I first fell in love with Michael. School had just started, and summer was still hanging on. Allowing me to wash my car on warm days in the drive—the day Michael took me for a motorcycle ride. For the homecoming dance and the night, I made chicken cacciatore for Michael. The first kiss we shared on his couch. The exact time of year I lost my virginity and made love for the first time—with Michael. I know a lot of bad things happened between that time and now. But I can't imagine life without him.

"There she is. There's Grandma." Twisting around, I find Michael coming into the courtyard, pushing a stroller. He kept his word, and Michael has been our granddaughter's caretaker since the age of twelve weeks. Bindi Michelle was born one year ago in this hospital with her entire family gathered around—a beautiful seven-pound, six-ounce screaming bundle of joy. I never saw Michael so happy. And there was some guilt there, too, on how he missed Monica's birth.

Men may struggle with age and becoming fathers and grandfathers, but if they only knew how this makes them even more attractive to us. I was never more attracted to Michael than when he was playing with his daughter, carrying her on his shoulders, or talking baby talk with her. The day at the beach in Florida, when she rode his shoulders and pretended to be flying. Never was Michael more gorgeous to me than that day. And just now, watching him push that stroller, is more captivating to my heart, than when he was on a motorcycle or his Corvette. Because this shows all the man can be. And it takes a tough man to raise and care for his family.

"Hey, Sweetheart. What are you and Grandpa doing today?" She reaches out her little arms, and I grab her up. "Hi, Michael," I say when he kisses me.

"Man, what a gorgeous day. You don't think it's too cold to have her out in the stroller, do you?" Michael—the over-protective grandfather.

"No. It's perfect. The sunshine is good for this little girl. I don't think she needs a heavy coat on, though. You have a lighter jacket in her bag?"

Michael ruffles through the bag and pulls out a small, lined windbreaker. "How about this?"

"That's better. It may be fall, but it's still seventy degrees today." He changes Bindi into the light jacket and then hands her back. I lift her up and down and listen to her sweet baby giggles. "Mmm," I say, kissing her rosy cheeks. "Grandma could just eat you up."

"Here, I brought you something. Bindi and I made you some potato soup."

"You did?" I coo to the smiling baby.

"Bindi likes it too," Michael says, pulling a container from the back of the stroller.

"Well, thank you. You too, Grandpa." I hand Bindi back to Michael and open the container. It's still warm, and the smell reminds me of cool fall evenings. "Oh, this is delicious."

"Hey, sorry to bring this up at the last moment. But I need to fly back to Seattle for a board meeting at the jet center. We are electing new members. I saw on your calendar that you don't work this Friday."

"No, I don't." Does he want me to go?

"I've booked my flight for Thursday night and scheduled the meeting for Friday. You'll be available to watch this little princess," he says, lifting Bindi to kiss her forehead.

I guess I was wrong. "Ah, of course. I'm not too out of practice."

"Great. That way Monica doesn't have to waste a vacation day." It's just business, Jill. Don't start getting those feelings back. Michael has shown and proved he has turned a *one-eighty*. He loves me and our family. Though this is swarming in my head, I smile and tell him it's no problem.

"How long will you be gone?"

"Not sure yet. That's why I booked a one-way ticket. Might come back on a run with one of our pilots if it's more convenient. We used to travel like this all the time. Flights were always going somewhere you needed to go." We? He and Cami? I dare not ask. I must remind myself; the past is in the past. *Seattle.*

"Okay. Keep me posted if I need to change my schedule here at the hospital."

"I will. Thanks for understanding."

I sip my coffee. "No problem." It leaves a bad taste in my mouth. Or is it Seattle?

I finish my soup, and Michael packs up Bindi and tells her to wave bye-bye. "We'll see grandma later."

"Bye-bye, Munchkin. Grandma loves you." I kiss her little hands and cheeks and then kiss Michael. "Tell Monica hello for me."

"I will, Baby," he says, and I watch him push the stroller down the sidewalk and out of the courtyard. Taking a deep breath, I tell myself not to worry. But yet, why do I?

"I'm just paranoid," I tell myself and head back to work.

•　　•　　•　　•　　•

Michael is packing when I get home, and I see a suit laid out on the bed. "So, this is not a casual meeting, I take it?"

He steps out of the closet, holding two ties. "Red or blue," he says, holding both.

"Tell me what's all involved, and then I'll tell you the best choice."

"What's that supposed to mean? It's just a meeting," he says, but his tone is a bit…defensive. Or is it just me?

"Is it an official board meeting or cocktail negotiations?"

"Both." He eyes me surreptitiously and drops both ties on the bed. I guess both will be needed. I watch him walk back into the closet.

"Michael?" I wait for him to answer before continuing to assess his mood.

"Yes?"

I'm still not entirely sure and ask. "Was there any way you could have scheduled it on a Saturday…so that we could have gone together? I mean…I've never seen your jet center."

Walking out of the closet, he holds two pairs of shoes and drops them into the suitcase set next to the bed. "No, Jill. Meetings aren't held on Saturdays."

"Yet, you have meetings after hours…in bars…with drinks."

"What are you getting at?" This is not going well. He's upset, I can tell.

"I just find it odd that, after all this time, you've never mentioned Seattle and…this jet center. And now it's a big deal."

"Jill, I have been off location and quite inactive with the business. Yes, I communicate through e-mails and web meetings. But my presence is needed for this." Now, his hands are on his hips and glaring down at me. I know I've hit a nerve." We stare at each other, waiting for the other to speak.

"Okay, I'm sorry. I know you've put us as priority…and babysitting Bindi. I guess I haven't given your company much thought. I'm sorry." I stand from the bed and wrap my arms around his waist, looping through his bent elbows. I'm a bit relieved when he pulls me in.

"You are my priority—always—another reason why I must go. I need to add you as the beneficiary to the company. I'll have my attorney draw up the request."

Breathing in, I smile and beg forgiveness, batting my eyes, waiting for a kiss. Kissing my lips, Michael holds me close and whispers in my ear. "You will always be the most important thing in my life. Please, don't worry." I pull away and look into his eyes. "I'll make sure to take you next time. I promise. I didn't want Bindi to be left with another sitter."

"You are a wonderful grandfather, husband, and father," I compliment him, but it's more of a reminder. For the rest of the evening, we have our dinner, watch our favorite shows, and lay in each other's arms without another word about it. But something still stabs at me. It's nothing, Jill. Michael is a wonderful, loving man. You have nothing to worry about.

With me lying in his arms, he falls asleep, and I watch him for a while before waking him and going to bed together. I study his perfect-to-me features. How different he looks from when I first met him all those years ago as a young twenty-something man. The minute I saw him for the first time in years, I knew the contour of his brow, the ridge of his nose, and the small cleft beneath his lips. I now see the lines around his eyes, his five o'clock shadow on his jaw, and his face has become leaner and more defined. But he's still Michael. Young or old, he is forever woven into my heart.

As much as I hate to wake him, I do. "Hey, sleepyhead. Let's get you to bed. You have a plane to catch in the morning." He cracks open one eye, and I help him up and to bed. When I return from the bathroom, I'm expecting him to pull me down and make love. However, walking in, I see he's fast asleep. Though I'm slightly disappointed, I kiss his forehead, turn off the light and climb into bed next to him.

We wake early, and I rush around, busying myself with positive actions while showing Michael my full support. "I have your breakfast ready," I say when he walks into the kitchen. Pouring his coffee, I notice how handsome he looks this morning. He looks handsome every morning. Why does he look so astronomical today? It's because he's leaving. "Shut up," I tell that devil in my mind. "You smell good," I say, bending down and kissing his smooth, shaven cheeks.

"Thank you."

"Are you sure you have everything you need? What about your wash bag?" I cringe and remember the condoms I once found. He looks up and cocks a brow. He remembers. "I mean, did you pack your pravastatin and vitamins?"

He reaches over and pulls me into his arms. Looking up at me, he smiles. "Jill, you have absolutely nothing to worry about. I understand not having your trust…"

"No, Michael. It's not that. I'm a nurse, and you know how we are about taking our meds at specific times. I just didn't see you pack them."

"Touché. Would you please pack them for me?" He grins, and I bend down to kiss the tip of his nose. "I love you."

"I love you, too."

We leave for the airport, and there's one more thing I want to ask. But I know what the answer will be—and it will only deepen my suspicions. "Is there a number at the jet center where I can reach you…if there's an emergency?"

"Just call my cell. It will be on me at all times." And there it is.

"Oh, I know. I didn't want to call and have your phone go off and interrupt your meeting."

"My phone is always on vibrate. If I don't pick up, leave a message." Always on vibrate. Good to know. Stop it!

He pulls up to the terminal drop off and parks. "Don't you want to park in the garage?"

"No, I'm going to get through security and start with all the emails and phone calls while I wait to board."

"But, Michael. Your plane doesn't leave for another hour."

"Exactly. It will take an hour to get caught up."

I can see there is no winning this one. "Okay. Well, please call me when you get in."

"I will. Thanks for watching Bindi."

"Of course. Bindi is my granddaughter, too." We kiss before getting out of the car and then again before I return to the driver's seat. He waves before walking through the doors.

He's telling the truth. It's business. It's...Seattle.

•   •   •   •   •

Five hours and still no word from Michael. I know, because I have watched the clock non-stop since returning home. I want to enjoy this day with Bindi and do all the grandma stuff. Bake cookies, go for a walk, go shopping and buy little, frilly dresses. But instead, I'm consuming once again over what I don't know is going on. Monica read right into my edginess when dropping Bindi off. I tried to convince her it was just the excitement of being with my granddaughter today. Damn it. I don't want it to be like this.

Looking outside, I feel guilty not taking her out on this gorgeous afternoon. Why not? I have my cell. Michael will call. He will. "Bindi-Roo, want to play outside?" She smiles and gives a big noddy-nod, her blonde curls bouncing around her head. "Okay, let's get your jacket and Grammy will take you." She toddles out of the room, knowing exactly where her bag is and comes running in just as fast as her little legs will take her.

Now bundled up, she runs to the patio door and points outside.

"Swing," she says.

"Yes, Grammy will push you on your swing." I open the door, and she beelines to the Little Tykes swing Michael hung from the tree. Just looking at the thing makes me feel guilty—all the things he does for his granddaughter and me. And I'm still not trusting him? Do I only trust him on a leash? Ah, I must stop this.

Bindi does her best to climb into the swing, but it takes one final push from Grammy to help her. "You ready?" Another big *noddy-nod* with a happy smile. "Is this what Grandpa does? Pushes you on the swing?" I give a slight push, and she giggles as the swing moves back and forth. "*Weeee.* Is that fun?"

"Yes," she says, followed by more giggles. I look across the yard at the treehouse Michael built for Monica, now with a fresh coat of paint intended for the next generation. Michael said Bindid had already climbed to the top step and to watch her when out back. He's entirely engaged this time, and I should stop worrying. I shake it off, breathe, and say, "He would never hurt me again. He loves us, and especially this little girl." Then, he commented about Cami and how they are still friends and business partners. And this is a *business* trip.

Damn it!

My phone rings and I am all thumbs retrieving it from my back pocket. Ah, yes! Michael's name lights up the screen. "Hey, Sweetie, Grandpa's calling. Let Grammy answer, okay?"

She nods. "Michael?" There's a pause, and then I hear a muffled sound, followed by breathing. Oh, God. Don't let this be a butt dial while he's having sex with someone else. Should I yell his name...or just listen?

"Hi...Jill."

"Michael...you there?"

"Yes, sorry. Just catching my breath." Why?

"So, you just arrived...or..."

"I got in about an hour ago." And you're just now calling?

"Ah...yes. Sorry. Just got tied up with things and...all." He doesn't sound right. He seems...preoccupied.

"Well...how was your flight?"

"Good. Good." More silence on his end. "I ah...I need to get checked in." Checked in? He's just said he got in an hour ago. What's he been doing?

"Are...are you at the hotel or...jet center?" *With Cami?*

"No, I'm...I went to my meeting first." Why does he sound so...distant...guilty?

"Did it go... good? The meeting?"

The sound of a deep breath, followed by, "No. Not really." Is this an excuse to have to stay longer?

"So...what now?"

"Hey, Jill...I have to make some calls. I'll call you later. I love you. Kiss Bindi for me."

"Oh, okay. I will. Bindi's on the swing you made. She misses you. I miss you."

"I miss you all too. Make sure my little granddaughter doesn't climb that ladder."

"I will watch her…"

"Bye."

"Michael?" He's already ended the call. That was quick. He seemed bothered by something. His conscience? Rolling the phone in my hand, I consider calling him back, saying I was concerned. He was too quick to get off the phone. Yet, he did say he loved me and went on to express his concern for Bindi. Maybe it's nothing. He did say the meeting went terribly. I'll send a text just to be sure.

Me: Sorry about your meeting. You sounded stressed. Is everything ok?

Michael: *Thanks. Yeah, a bit stressed. Talk when I get home. Kiss the girls for me. I love you.*

Me: *I love you, too.*

Talk? About what? Everything's fine, Jill. It's just a lousy meeting. He asked about his granddaughter. He said he loved you. Stop worrying.

"Swing! Swing," Bindi hollers, kicking her little feet back and forth.

"Yes, Baby. Grammy's sorry." Grabbing onto the rope, I kiss her cheek. "That's from Grandpa. He misses you." And I miss him. So. Much.

CHAPTER 40

Then

Drake and I were celebrating six months together, and I was the happiest I've ever been. He was such an ideal man, always opening car doors for me, helping me with my coat, allowing me to enter the room first while he held the door, and waited to eat until I sat down. Though Drake was good with Monica, I kept her at a distance from him. I was afraid of them getting too close and how she would feel if he left. She had already been abandoned by her own father. And to allow it to happen again, I would never forgive myself.

Drake was always…happy…smiling, whistling. And in those six months, never once had I seen him get mad. I know six months wasn't a long time to get to know someone and I was going to be cautious this time. In one month, I thought I knew Michael. But it took three years to discover I never knew him at all.

I tried not to think of Michael much and the sour taste he left in my mouth. I feared Drake would taste it each time we kissed. In bed, he was gentle and sweet. It was a different passion I had come to know. Michael's passion came with possession and flavorful words. Drake's passion came with extended foreplay and slow sex that lasted all through the night. The kind that put me at such peace and smiling in my sleep. I had never known such love.

As a mother, I was uneasy letting Monica see us sleep together in the same bed. But Tammy said what she was learning was love and how a man should love and treat her mother. I didn't want Monica to think it was okay just to crawl in bed with a man. Then I reminded myself, Drake wasn't any man. He loved me, and Monica loved him. And this alone scared me.

Drake would tell her of the horses he would get someday and how she could ride them. We stayed with Drake on the weekends on the farm he bought, hoping to fill it with unwanted pets. I'd never seen such a loving heart. The farm had five dogs and many cats. Every animal had a name and was friendly and affectionate. Molly also came with us when we stayed with Drake. I was glad Drake had them all spayed and neutered. I didn't want any more dogs in the house at home.

We spent a week at the state fair, and Monica was in Heaven. I think it was the best summer we ever had. Drake volunteered his services as a vet and cared for many of the livestock. But looking after horses was where he wanted to be.

Monica ate so much cotton candy, I thought she would become sick when she asked Drake to take her on the tilt-a-wheel. But the faster it went and the more it would spin, I could hear their shared laughter as I waited behind the gate.

We all three rode the Ferris wheel, and when we reached the top, Drake told me he was the happiest and luckiest man in the world. Monica and I gave him joy. And with that joy, I felt purpose and belonging.

When we rode the merry-go-round, Monica insisted that Drake ride on the horse with her. My heart was blissful, and I watched this man show my little girl such love and attention.

It was Saturday morning, and I was still lying in Drake's arms as he slept. This was another thing I loved about him. He held me all through the night as we slept. I couldn't recall a time Michael ever held me through the night. Granted, in the mornings he would wake with a considerable hard-on and would pull me to him, even if I was sleeping.

Moving up on one elbow, I watch the rise and fall of his chest. He was uniquely handsome in his own way. He was a country boy, and never tried to put on airs—even though he was a doctor. And I found it strange how attracted I was to him and his lifestyle. Never was I a country girl. I always thought it was Michael's city boy ways; traveling on planes and attending corporate parties made me feel so grown up. But it was Drake, who drove an old Ford pick-up, refurbished an old farmhouse, and slowly paid back his student debts, that made me appreciate being a responsible adult.

Tracing a heart on his chest, my fingers felt the hair that covered it. It always smelled like fresh soap at night and in the morning. But during the day, Drake still smelled like the vet's office—dogs and sanitizer. I loved to cook for him because he was always so appreciative and complimentary, and he got me to try new things. We would go horseback riding where he made house calls to a few equestrian farms, and he would tell me about the horses he wanted to raise on the farm. I looked forward to the weekends and staying at the farm.

He slowly opened one eye, and I watched the smile form on his sleepy face. I kissed his chest and looked up at his face. His arms came around me, and I felt his penis twitch on my leg. He was going to make love to me. Drake never used the word fuck, and his biggest pet peeve was hearing the word coming out of a lady's mouth. I respected that so much.

"Good morning, Peach," he whispered his nickname for me. Peach or Peaches, he would call me. I asked why peach. He said because my skin was that of a peach, soft and always glowing with perfect color. My hair, he would pet softly, telling me it reminded him of a palomino horse's mane—long and shiny. I loved to feel his hand brush down my hair and to the small of my back. His hands were always warm and had the touch of love—soft and caring, and I would think about all the puppies and dogs those hands cared for.

"Good morning, Doc." My nickname for him.

"Hmm," he purred. "Doc wants to play doctor." He rolled me over and lay on top of me. I felt how hard he was, and I felt my own sex flutter. His hands brushed the hair away from my face, and he put his forehead to mine. "You're so beautiful, Peaches. I can't believe you're here with me."

"You make me happy, Drake. You're such a good man." He kissed me tenderly on the lips as he held my face. This would go on for minutes and even longer. I would be aching for him to be inside me. But Drake took his time with my body. He said I was a creature who deserved to be worshiped. *Worshiped.* How I would love to hear this word.

"I love you, Peaches. I love this face, this hair, this body." He kissed each breast and then the center. "And I love this heart. You are unique and gorgeously made." No matter what Drake said, my heart and insides melted.

My hands explored his back, moving up and down, feeling his muscles grow taunt as he worshiped me. I, too, was learning how to take the time and discover a man's body—his body.

His knee pulled up and opened my legs. I moaned a sigh of relief when he entered me. "Open your eyes, Peaches. Look at me when I make love to you." His eyes would give the illusion that he was lost somewhere, lost in me. The more he moved in and out of me, the more his eyes would shine, and he would smile when I began to climax.

"Ah…Drake. God, yes."

"You love me, Peaches?"

"Yes, I love you, Drake." As soon as I said the words, his slow lovemaking heightened into a world of all things right, and sexy, and loved. He was so good, and I felt I was learning all over again. And in ways, I was.

When our lovemaking ended, he picked me up and walked us to the shower. I wasn't worried that Monica would walk in on us. She was spending the night with a little friend from school. However, Monica was straightforward when I dropped her off. She wanted me to pick her up early so she could spend the night on Drake's farm. She loved the large yard, the big trees, and the many barns she loved to play in. All the dogs would follow her every step, which helped with her whereabouts. Drake had a pond dug, and currently, we were stocking it with fish. We would spend evenings around the campfire roasting marshmallows and watching the sun go down. All the romantic things Michael heckled as melodramatic and silly were now coming to life. And this was proof that romance did exist and was alive and well. At least with Drake, it was.

As Drake washed my hair, like he would a horse's mane, I closed my eyes and basked in his worship of me. I was in heaven, and he spoiled me.

"My sister said she would stay here with Monica tonight when we go out," he said, wrapping his arms around me and massaging my breasts with foaming soap. Jenny was Drake's sister, who had a daughter the same age as Monica. Together, the two of them would play for hours on the farm.

"Monica loves to play with Skylar. She'll be excited. I'll need to pick her up soon. She didn't want to miss a minute on the farm."

"Okay. We can pick the *little sweetie* up on the way to the Miller Ranch. I wanted to check on the new colt."

"Oh, she'll love that." The Miller Ranch was one of the places we would horseback ride, and Monica loved the baby horses as she would call them.

We finished our shower and dressed in blue jeans, flannel shirts, and boots. Something I never thought I would ever be caught dead in. But with Drake, everything was in style.

• • • • •

Drake had made reservations in town at a bar called Clementine's. Walking in, the place was so him. With its mahogany, curved wood and ruined brick, the bar looked like something from the old west. It was classic-saloon chic. The place once held the bank of South Haven in the eighteen hundreds, and behind the bar still stood the brass bars that covered the opening to the bank's vault.

I felt Drake's warm hand on the small of my back as he took me over to the table reserved for us. While getting ready for the evening, he appeared nervous. Something I never saw in him. As I sat, I looked around the bar. We were once again tucked away in a booth to ourselves and I saw several men sitting at the bar with their backs to us. Something hit me inside, and a shiver ran through me. I didn't know why or what it was. But when Drake moved my face with his finger and smiled in my eyes, that weird moment passed, and I was back to all things Drake.

"This place is amazing. I can't believe I've never been here before."

"It's my first time too. A lot of my clients talk about this place. So, I thought we would check it out."

"Well, thank you. I'll have to tell Tammy and Ryan about this place."

He took my hands from across the table and lifted them to his lips. As he kissed me, he looked up through his lashes, and something was there. I was about to ask when the waitress stopped to take our drink order.

"I think we would like a bottle," Drake said and looked at me. "Jill, what kind would you like?"

"Cabernet. If that's okay with you?"

"A bottle of cabernet it is."

"Yes, sir," the waitress said and left. It wasn't long before she returned with the bottle and poured out two glasses. "Enjoy." She smiled and once again we were alone. Drake had that look in his eyes.

"What's that look about?"

"Okay, I can't take it anymore. It's burning a hole in my pocket." He stood up and walked around to my side of the booth and pulled me out. Drake pulled something from his pocket and got down on one knee. The bar went silent, and I felt all eyes on us. "Jill, Peach…will you marry me?"

A blanket of heat went through me, and my mouth fell open. Drake was asking to marry me in front of all these people. Everyone was waiting. Especially Drake. This type of proposal is what every girl dreamt, what I had imagined. And it was happening. There it was—a ring for me. I never had an engagement ring or a wedding ring, for that matter.

I swallowed and looked into Drake's scared expression. "Yes, Drake. I will marry you."

The bar filled with claps and cheers as Drake slid the ring up my finger. He stood and picked me up and swung me around. "Thank you, Peaches. You've made me the happiest Doc in town." We kissed and toasted our engagement with the cabernet, and each time I lifted the glass, my eyes went to the sparkle on my finger.

I had my first engagement at the age of twenty-three, and I had already been married and a mother to a beautiful girl. It may have been a bit backward, but it was ours, and now life was going to be what I had always wanted.

"I know it's early, Peaches. But I love you. You're not getting away this time."

"Nothing could ever take me away from you." Except the next thing he said.

"Now we can have our own children," he said, and the word "own" came out italicized in his voice. Not, 'we'll have more children,' or 'we'll fill the house with babies.' My stomach panged not from hunger, but from the fear Monica would be left out. Known as 'not his' or 'not ours together.' Her own father didn't want her, and I couldn't let her go through that again. I wasn't about to make her feel like a second-class citizen.

"Excuse me," I said and stood. "Where's the ladies room?"

"I think I see the sign over there," Drake pointed. "Are you okay?" There were tears in my eyes, which he thought were tears of joy. If only they were.

"Just need to freshen my mascara," I said and went in the direction of the restroom. My head was bowed as I walked by the bar. A man was getting up from his stool and bumped into me. "Sorry," I said, not looking up to the man.

"Sorry," he said, and his voice was very canny. "Congratulations." He threw some bills on the bar, and before I could get a look at him, his back was to me. My eyes were still blurred with tears. His voice sounded like Michael, or maybe it was all the bad omens from the past coming to warn me. Either way, I wouldn't let my daughter suffer just so I could have happiness. We would be happy together.

I found the ladies room and pushed through the door and locked it behind me. Looking in the mirror, I was anything but a happy bride to-be. I grabbed some toilet tissue and cleaned under my eyes the best I could. But I still looked red and swollen.

I returned to the table and forced a smile. "Are you okay?" Drake asked.

"Yes...just all the excitement." Michael's lousy taste filled my mouth again, and I grabbed the wine and tried to swallow it.

All through the dinner, I couldn't match Drake's excitement. I avoided eye contact as much as I could. And would only give short answers throughout the conversations. Drake sensed my reluctance and asked several times if I was upset. How could I tell him without seeming defensive? In Michael's eye, Monica is what destroyed our relationship. But it was him...and his unwillingness to be in a relationship. Somehow, I was going to have to end it.

He patted my arms on the drive home, and I thought about telling him then but felt telling while he was driving wouldn't be a good idea. The ring on my finger, the ring I always wanted, felt like a weight on my heart. I would have to tell him as soon as we got home.

Jenny congratulated us when Drake told her the good news. The girls were playing in the bedroom, and when she left, I took a deep breath. "Drake, I feel it's a little soon to be asking me to marry you." I began to pull the ring off when he stopped me.

"Jill," he said—not Peaches. "No, please don't take it off. I know it's soon. We can wait. I'll wait until you're ready." I began to cry because I knew I would never feel ready to let Monica suffer the consequences.

"No, Drake. You deserve a fresh start. A woman all to yourself. Not me."

"Jill. What are you talking about? It's you I want. It's you I've always wanted. Please, don't do this. I love you."

My heart broke for breaking his. I went into the bedroom and told Monica we had to go. She didn't want to and complained. "Monica, tell Skylar goodbye. You'll see her at school."

"But Mommy."

"Now," I commanded.

Drake looked as if the world had just ended. And it was all my fault. It pained me to pull off his ring and set it on the table. I couldn't look at him as I walked out. And when I shut the door, I closed the door to the best thing that ever happened to me. But then I reminded myself: Monica was the best thing that ever happened to me.

CHAPTER 41

Now

This has to be the worst weekend of my life. And sadly, it should have been the best. I asked Monica to let me keep Bindi for the weekend, and for her and Jordan to have some alone time. I wanted this weekend to be all about Bindi and me, doing Grammy things and spoiling her. Instead, I am obsessed with Michael's lack of calls, his demeanor when we spoke, and his inability to call a direct number at the jet center to check if he's really there. Something in his voice, or lack of that, is once again leaving that bad taste in my mouth and that punch in the gut feeling. What the hell is going on?

I've called a few times, and his cell goes straight to voicemail. Each time, I left no message. But maybe I should. Perhaps I should leave my concerns—as a good wife should. But I know the minute my mouth opens, all things accusatory will come flying out. Yet, he should have seen my missed calls. Not able to stand it any longer, I call again.

"Hi…Jill. What's up?" He finally answers and says…What's up?

"Did you get my missed calls?"

"Yes, but why didn't you leave a message? I figured you would call back."

"Well…how are things going? Better?"

Pause. "Ah…no, not really." He sounds really distressed.

"Oh, I'm sorry. Are you able to…fix whatever is wrong?"

"I…don't know. Hey, let's not talk about it. How's Bindi? Does she miss her grandpa?"

"Yes, she does. She's spent the weekend with me. Monica and Jordan, I thought, could use some alone time."

"Wonderful. That's important in a marriage. We should have done that."

I tried many times, but I don't say so. "I miss you too, Michael. So much."

"Oh, Jill…I just want to come home, and go back to the way things are."

The way things are? What's changed? "Michael…."

"Yes?"

"Has…has something changed…between us?" My heart is pounding against my breastbone as I wait for his response.

"No, Baby. Nothing's changed with us. Just a bad weekend for me." For You? I've been transported to the past Michael-hell years. "I'll be home tomorrow. Kiss Bindi for me."

"Yes, of course."

"I love you, Jill. Never forget that."

"I won't." Why would I? Unless he's been unfaithful again.

He ends the call, and I'm worse than before. There's something to be said about the unknown. It can't hurt you—until it's too late. But everything is fine. I'm just scared and jaded. Michael's just having destructive work-related issues, and we'll get through this. Oddly, since we've been together, he's never even spoken much about work and the jet center. Maybe his lack of involvement is the problem— granted, his main focus is here with me. So, I shouldn't jump to suspicion.

"Where's Tammy-Marilyn Monroe now?"

I take a deep breath and run over to pick up Bindi. Grabbing her up, I blow raspberries on her little belly. She giggles that perfect, baby laugh. Just like Monica used to. "Hey, Bindi Baby. Let's go for a walk. You want to?"

She gives her big noddy-nod and toddles over to her stroller. With all her might, she pushes it toward the door. I grab her sweater and tell her to come here. "Come here. Let's put this on." Another big grin and my heart melts. "Is this what Grandpa does? Takes you for stroller rides?" She nods. Unzipping the attached bag, I rifle through the contents Michael keeps stored inside—wipes, toys, snacks and I'm slapped with guilt. He loves this little girl and me. He has been the one to raise her this last year.

Now wearing her sweater with the Paw Patrol characters, she crawls into the stroller and gives me a look that says, 'let's go.' "Looks like you're all ready," I say and open the door.

Walking down these same sidewalks where I used to walk Monica, I envision the people who now watch Michael pushing a stroller down this same path. How far he has come from the man he used to be. As I think this, I decide to call and tell him how much I love him, even if it goes to voicemail.

"Hello, you've reached Michael Danforth. Please leave a message."

Err. "Hey, it's me. And…I was thinking about you. Bindi and I are on a walk. I want you to know how much I love and appreciate you, Michael. The wonderful husband you are. The amazing father and grandfather you have become. I hate you being this far away, and I miss you so much. Bindi misses you. I hope everything works out…at the jet center. Call when you can. Love you." Ending the call, I slide the phone back into my pocket, take a cleansing breath, and push the stroller down the sidewalk. *Why doesn't he call?*

•　　•　　•　　•　　•

Driving home from Monica's, I have a dreaded fear of being alone. I've just dropped Bindi off, and even though a one-year-old isn't much of a conversationalist, she did keep my mind preoccupied. The hospital did not schedule me to work in the morning, so I doubt Michael will be home tonight. And the fact that he still hasn't returned my message only elevates my fear. I asked Monica if she'd heard from her father. She said she hadn't and told me not to worry. I guess she saw right through me.

Now, pulling into my garage, I gravitate my focus on things to get done around the house, such as tidying up the front room, as Bindi left it a step hazard with all her toys. Walking into the house, I find a beautiful bouquet, a card, and two glasses of wine on the table. Michael?

I don't see him, but the toys are all picked up and returned to her toybox.

"Hey, Beautiful."

Turning around, Michael is leaning against the doorframe, smiling fiendishly.

"Michael." I race over, and he wraps me in his arms. "How'd you get here?"

"I took an Uber from the airport. I wanted to surprise you. I got your message…after I landed."

"Oh, God. I missed you." He kisses me and holds me tightly.

"I missed you too. So, glad to be home. How'd things go with Bindi?"

"I don't know how you do it all day. She's a handful."

"Says the woman who raised a little girl with no help from me," he says. He walks us toward the table and hands me a glass of wine. "To being home," he toasts.

I look over the glass, searching for any sign on his face. Is something there? He notices my suspicion and looks away. Is he not able to make eye contact with me? Stop it, Jill. He's here. He surprised me with wine and flowers. Or is this guilt?

"Open your card," he says, walking away.

Reaching for the card, I open it and read. *You will always be the one thing I will never have enough of. Love, Michael.* "Thank you. Do you honestly feel like this?"

He walks back, taking me into his arms. "Jill, I've wasted so much, and I know I will never have enough time to do everything I want to do with you."

Maybe it's just me, and I need to stop looking and acting accusatory. "Did you get everything squared away at the jet center?"

He releases me from his embrace and picks up his wine, clearly wanting to avoid the question. "I don't want to discuss it," he says, leaving the kitchen. I grab my wine and follow.

"Okay. Is there anything I can do to help? I mean…I don't know much about the company. But I'm willing to learn."

He turns around and has a faraway look. "I will need your signature on a few documents. My lawyer is drawing them up now." His statement is all business, like we've just entered a board meeting.

"Oh, what for?"

"It's for protection. Don't worry about it. I've already handled it."

Has he handled it? Is he protecting his assets? From what? "Do I need my attorney to look it over first?"

His head turns, and he looks at me with disbelief. "Why? I told you…It's taken care of."

"I'm sorry. I just thought…"

"Come here," he says, reaching out for me. "Let's finish this wine, and then I'm going to make love to you—no more talk of the jet center or lawyers. I've had enough of that this weekend. I just want you now."

"I'm sorry. I've just missed you so much."

"Really," he smiles. "I'm impressed."

We finish our wine and Michael does what he says—picks me up and carries me to our room. As he undresses me, my eyes shoot to his suitcase. Why do I think there's something in there?

His finger lures me back to his eyes. "You look miles away, Jill. I thought you missed me."

"Yes, I did. Sorry, come here," I say, wrapping Michael's neck in my arms. "Don't ever leave me." I feel him stiffen as he lays his head on my chest. I wait for him to say something. Something is bothering him. It's not my imagination this time.

"Michael?"

I feel him breathe in, and he braces up on his elbows, looking down into my eyes. Something's there. But I don't know what. I wait for him to speak, but he doesn't. He only begins with kisses down my neck as he unbuttons my blouse.

When he has my clothes entirely removed, he takes off his own and begins with his lovemaking. Michael's lovemaking has been passionate and full of love since reuniting. But this time, it takes me back. Back to Seattle, when he last made love to me before asking for a divorce.

Afterward, he falls asleep. But I lay awake staring at his suitcase.

•   •   •   •   •

I have no idea when I fell asleep. I wake, and Michael is in the shower—and his luggage is gone from the floor. Sometime this morning, he must have unpacked it. How did I not hear him?

I crawl out of bed and pad to the bathroom door. The shower is still running, so I walk to the closet, hoping to find Michael's suitcase inside—and not unpacked. I see it and slowly pull the zipper open, cringing when it makes a sound. Before flipping it open, I peek from the closet to see if the bathroom door is still closed. It is. Leaving the closet door cracked open enough for light to spill, I flip open the suitcase and find it empty. Crap. What am I expecting to see? I should be happy there's nothing here.

Michael walks out of the bathroom wrapped in a towel low on his hips as I walk from the closet. I fight not to have a suspicious look on my face. He alone would recognize it because he's the one who put it there years ago.

He must not notice and walks over to kiss me. "Good morning, Gorgeous. Sleep better now that I'm home?" Is his comment for my lack of trust or because I genuinely missed him?

"Yes."

"You sure? You seemed to toss and turn a lot."

"I did?" I thought I lay awake all night staring at his suitcase. "Do you need me to take your suits to the dry cleaners?"

He walks to the closet, grabs a pair of jeans, and puts them on. "You don't have to."

"Well, I need to take my wool coat in for a cleaning. Thought I might as well grab the suits you took to Seattle."

Pulling his head through his T-shirt, he says, "Alright, if you want." *Yes, I want.* Maybe I can smell some perfume or find a lipstick stain or… Stop it, Jill. What are you? A Harlequin Romance detective now?

His phone vibrates on the dresser, and we both look over. He grabs it up before I can read the name on the screen. After looking at it, he hits *ignore* and shoves it into his pocket. "I'll call back later. Let's have some coffee. I already made a pot while you were sleeping."

Damn it. Why didn't I think to check Michael's phone? My eyes gravitate to the phone in his pocket, and I bite my lip. I need to check that phone. "Wow, you've been busy this morning while I was sleeping. Why didn't you wake me up?" Because you were busy hiding whatever you were hiding? He senses my despair. However, I'm trying to sound legit.

He walks over and takes my hands in his. "Hey, why don't you take a shower? I'll make you breakfast. I've missed taking care of you."

"Michael, I'm fine…"

"I'm not taking no for an answer." He kisses my forehead and then guides me to the bathroom. "Want me to run you a bath instead?"

"A shower is fine. Thanks, Michael," I say and turn to kiss him.

"Okay. Your breakfast will be waiting." He smiles and leaves the bathroom. I quickly undress and shower in record time. Stepping out of the bathroom, I see he's laid his suit on the bed. I inspect the material for perfuming smells, lipstick, or anything I can find. They both smell like him—sage and citrus and earthy spice. I see a watery stain on the inside of his white dress shirt. It could be anything. God, I hate feeling like this. I'm twenty-two all over again. And not in a good way.

Reaching my hands down in the pocket of the sports jacket, I feel a piece of paper, and my insides are a trembling mess by the time I pull it out. My God, what am I going to see?

I unfold the paper and stare at a number with a woman's name. Cathy McGregor. No, no, no, no. Not this again. Why does he have a woman's name and phone number in his pocket? And it's not even his handwriting. The handwriting is loopy and neat—a woman's writing. Michael, what are you doing?

Throwing on a robe, I march out of the bedroom and head for the kitchen for some answers. I'm nervous when I hear him talking in the living room on his phone.

"Can I meet with you on Tuesday? I'll need to make arrangements with my granddaughter." There's a pause, and I wait behind the corner. "You come highly recommended." Another pause. "This must remain just between you and me. Thank you for understanding."

What the fuck? What's he involved with now? Sex for hire? Highly recommended? I squeeze the paper tightly in my hand and decide to investigate. Is he talking to her—*Kathy McGregor?*

"It's just…I'm married, and…Well, it's something I want to keep from my wife. I lost her once. I don't want to lose her again."

Then why the hell are you doing this, Michael? I want to run in there and scream, but I refrain and continue to listen.

"I'll have it all sent to you. Don't worry about the money. I have it covered."

Michael! No! He may have wanted me back, but he still wants that stranger on the side. How could I not see this? Nothing has changed. He's still the same old Michael.

"Look, I need to go. My wife will be coming at any moment. I'll call and get it set up." I walk in, and he quickly changes the subject. "Okay, I'll get those reports sent to the jet center. Thanks for letting me know." He ends the call and smiles. "There she is, my beautiful wife. I have my gourmet omelet for you."

I discreetly place the paper with Cathy's number into my robe pocket and feign a big smile. "Looks amazing. You are just full of surprises."

CHAPTER 42

Then

Breaking Drake's heart hurt more than Michael breaking mine. I was living with double heartbreak at the fault of my own hands. Drake didn't let me walk away that easily. That night, he showed up on my doorstep, pain in his eyes that I recognized as my own. To know I was the cause made me hate myself. I tried desperately to let him know it was all because of me. I was damaged, and he deserved better. *"We deserve each other, Peach,"* he cried. And it only increased the pain in my heart. The cards, the flowers, and the letters came daily. And when they finally stopped, all my hope stopped, too. I had now ruined the best thing ever happening to Monica and me.

"Why didn't you ever tell him how it made you feel when he talked of having children?" Tammy asked. We were finishing our shifts at the hospital, and it had been three months since I broke it off with Drake. Each day, she rode me. I didn't blame her. She knew how much I loved Drake.

"Because…because it's so complicated."

"Jill, it's so complicated that you don't even get it yourself."

She was right. I couldn't explain it. And that alone was all Michael's doing. "Tammy, please don't take this the wrong way, but you live in Disney World with Ryan and the girls." She and Ryan now had two girls, Casey and Cali.

She choked. "Disney World? How do you figure that?"

I took a deep breath and did my best to explain this. "Everything's perfect for you and Ryan…"

"Okay, first of all, everything is not perfect. And if perfect is what you're looking for, girl, you will be alone forever."

"I don't mean…perfect, perfect. I mean, perfect for you and Ryan."

"Well, today, I could have killed him. He called me a bitch, and I told him he was an asshole. He was mad because I was taking the weekend off. No girls. No husband. Just me and a book."

I laughed. "What if I call?"

"I might pencil you in. Ryan has golfed for the last three weekends, leaving me with a toddler, a newborn, and a house to clean. This time, it's his turn. Don't get me wrong. I love my girls and husband, but we all need a break."

"Yes, exactly. But when you say you need a break, Ryan has just as much invested in the girls as you. I mean, we all know how Michael was as a father."

"Yes, but you said Drake was great with Monica."

"He was. But here's what I have learned about being a single mom. First, you're considered baggage, second-class if you come with kids. Second, if you're a good mom and put your children first, you're not meeting his needs. And he will never understand this because there is no personal, vested interest. So, you're forced to be a neglectful mother to have a man. And there's nothing I hate more than a man who tries to use the Bible in his favor. For example, your husband comes before your children. Where does that put Monica and me?"

"Did Drake say this to you?"

"Not exactly, but I felt it, and a mother knows. You may get mad at Ryan and he at you, but when it comes to your girls, you will both ache for them. I will never have this, Tammy. Those moments when you both look at your children and have that smile on your face. That is Disney World."

She sighed. "Oh, Jill. I want you to be happy."

"I know. I'll get there. Someday."

We changed out of our scrubs, and I wished her a peaceful weekend as we left for the parking garage. She waved as her car passed by, and I thought of what she said. Maybe I should have explained more to Drake. Instead, I ran like a scared deer.

As I drove to my parents to pick up Monica, I was dealing with the fear of being alone versus never having what Tammy had. It's not that I coveted what she and Ryan had. It only showed me how it should be. Was I willing to settle for the next best thing? What was the next best thing? And I would never know because I never gave Drake a chance.

Dad was teaching Monica how to play checkers—more like how to cheat at checkers when I walked in. She was his pride and joy now, and all the backlash I took for getting pregnant at seventeen was now history. He could never deny his little granddaughter. Between Dad and Scott, Monica had two men wrapped around her finger.

"Hi, Mommy. Pappy is coming to Dad and Doughnut Day at school next week."

Mom hollered from the kitchen. "Tell your teacher not to let Pappy eat too many doughnuts. He's supposed to be on a strict diet." She walked out with a bowl of cut-up apples and set them in front of Dad and Monica. "I've been giving your dad Monica's snacks. Maybe he'll learn some healthier eating habits."

"How'd your check-up go, Dad?" Dad was now starting to have heart problems and would never tell Mom. Last week, he ended up in the ER when I was on duty.

"Oh, those doctors don't know crap," he said.

"Ahh…I think those doctors do, Dad. Your EKG showed you suffered a light heart attack."

"Light. It was probably acid reflux. You know your mother's cooking."

"No, I know your bad eating habits when you leave this house. You need to take this seriously, Dad. Your test shows early signs, and you can help reverse this."

"Okay, Doc Jill. But I'm still going to Monkey's doughnut day." Monkey was his nickname for Monica. She loved it now, but that would change as she grew.

"Pappy, we could give the doughnuts to Uncle Scott. He has a good heart." A good heart he did. Scott and Jen loved to have Monica, and many would take her on my weekend shifts. I had no problems getting a sitter now. And the fact that she was older helped. She was no longer a baby but growing up so fast. And Michael was missing it all.

Michael's name was dead in this household. No matter how I tried to make us work, I was left with all the repercussions of our divorce. Dad only made one comment: "I knew that boy would not stick around." And this time, I couldn't disagree with him.

Myspace was new, and I tried it out for a bit. But all I would do was online stalk Michael—trips to Aspen for Christmas. He and Cami would post pictures of them sipping wine by the fireplace. After that, scuba diving and snorkeling in the Caymans. Their captions would kill me. *This is what love looks like.* I had to believe it was Cami posting these captions because Michael had no idea what love looked like.

A year later, she was out of the picture—literally. Michael was with a younger woman in Hawaii, maybe younger than me. Cradled in his arms, wearing their swimsuits on a white beach, were Michael and some blonde bimbo. Captioned above this picture was—Our babies will be so beautiful. A week later, she was no longer in any of his photographs. I guess with that caption, he dumped her at the airport. Michael had a beautiful baby. And she was mine.

I wanted to post my great pictures of Monica and me, and hopefully, he would see them. But since my account was private, he would never see them unless he sent a friend request. Michael's account was public. If not leaving me and our daughter wasn't enough, he purposely posted stuff for me to find. And I did.

My need to stalk Michael's social media waned during my relationship with Drake, and I found myself happy and relaxed. Now, the media cancer was back, and I was once again the stalker. If I did not hate myself enough for losing Drake, I punished myself with Michael's happy life. Last night, Michael and Bambi had dinner at an oceanfront property. Bambi. Like, that's a name? I hoped Cami was also stalking him, and in thinking this, somehow, I felt a bond with her. I once found her Myspace page and came close to sending her a friend request. But then I didn't want to be considered part of the *jaded by Michael Danforth clutch*. When Myspace lost popularity, Facebook came to haunt me.

"Was she good?" I asked Mom.

"Yes, she was. Your father wasn't. He used the excuse that Monica wanted ice cream. But I knew what he was up to."

"And I didn't even say I wanted ice cream," Monica piped in.

"Dad," I scolded. He threw his hands up in surrender. "All right, Monica, get your stuff. We need to get home and let Molly out."

"Yes, Mommy."

Monica gathered her stuff, and I kissed Mom and Dad goodbye and thanked them for watching her.

On the drive home, Monica began asking questions about Drake, which threw me for a loop. "Mommy, since Uncle Scott is busy and Pappy can't eat doughnuts, how about if I ask Daddy Drake?"

My mouth fell open. "Why did you call Drake that?"

"Because that's his name."

"I know, honey. But why did you call him *Daddy Drake*?"

"He told me to," she rattled off and began singing a tune from one of her videos. "Mommy, why don't we see Daddy Drake anymore?"

"Monica, when did he tell you to call him Daddy Drake?"

"When we used to go there. I miss going there, Mommy. I miss the animals, and I miss him."

I had no idea Drake told her that. I didn't know she felt this way about him, and here I thought I was protecting her when she was missing him. No doubt I missed him too. "Sweetheart, why didn't you ever tell me this before?"

"It was a surprise. One day, when you were at work, Daddy Drake took me to the waterpark. He said he wanted to ask me something." I remember that day. But I thought Drake's sister took the girls to the waterpark. "He wanted to ask me if he could marry you."

Oh, my God. "He...asked you?"

"Ah, huh. And I said yes. Daddy Drake also asked if I wanted a sister or brother. And I did, Mommy. He said he would love me just as much as you do. And together, we would be a family. But it was a surprise, and I wasn't supposed to tell you." Oh, my God. It was like a punch in the gut. How dare I. How do I fix this? I could barely pull into the drive. Everything was a blur, with the tears welling in my eyes.

"Well, Sweetie, you were a good girl keeping your secret for...Drake."

"He said I could call him Daddy now. But I said I would wait until after you're married. Not to ruin the surprise." My tears were running, and I quickly wiped my face before Monia would ask why her mommy was crying. "So, why did Daddy Drake leave like Daddy Michael?"

I was the worst person in the world. Now she would think she had been abandoned twice. "Monica, listen to Mommy. Daddy Drake didn't leave you like Daddy Michael. It was Mommy's fault. Okay? Don't you ever be mad at him. Mommy made a huge mistake."

"What kind of mistake?"

"Deciding what is best for us," I mumbled under my breath.

I had Monica take her bath, and we worked on her spelling words before bed. My mind was at a loss, all I could think of was how to explain everything to Drake. I was going to beg him to take me back. But I didn't know how. But when Molly jumped up onto my lap after Monica went to bed, I had a plan.

•   •   •   •   •

After dropping Monica off at afternoon kindergarten, I practiced my begging for forgiveness speech over and over in the car. I was on my way to his vet's office. I thought about calling him, but each time I picked up the phone, I froze. I knew I needed to see him in person. After what I did, he deserved a personal apology. And I hoped I wasn't too late. I already missed the cards and letters, and maybe that was a bad sign. Perhaps he didn't care for me anymore. But this was Drake, and he had been crazy about me. And I now knew I was crazy for him.

I pulled into the parking lot and saw his old truck. I was shaking. I was excited to see him, and I was also a nervous wreck. I knew his schedule from when we were together. At twelve o'clock every day, he left for lunch to the farm. And I hadn't missed him. Hopefully, we would be having lunch together.

The familiar smell hit my nose when I stepped in—dogs and bleach. And strange as it was, it was the scent my mind connected to Drake. Nancy, his receptionist, looked up and smiled.

"Hey, Jill." She seemed guarded, and I didn't blame her. She was very loyal to Drake, and I had been the one to break his heart.

"Hi, Nancy…I…"

"Jill?" His voice was familiar, but the name he spoke wasn't. Peaches. I wanted to hear his pet name for me. But now, I was just Jill—the Jill who left him for no reason. I turned around, and my heart melted when I saw him there—jeans, a black T-shirt, cowboy boots, and his white lab coat. The panic on his face was palpable in my heart.

"Drake…hello."

He set his clipboard down, removed his lab coat, and hung it on the hook behind him. I saw the hard body I missed holding me. I saw the strong arms that used to wrap me, and I wanted to run to him immediately. Beg him to take me back.

"What are you doing here, Jill?"

Jill. "I…ahh…" I heard the chime of the door behind me.

"Hey, Drake. Are you ready?" I turned around and saw a young woman dressed in a business suit. She was pretty, and I instantly hated her for saying his name. "I thought we would go to Tossi's for lunch. I have a client coming in at one-thirty."

"Okay. Jill, was there something you needed?" The woman walked over and wrapped her arms around him. I was back in that closet again watching Michael and Cami. And this time, it was my fault. "Jill, this is Tawny…my girlfriend." The word seemed to hurt saying it as much as it hurt hearing it.

"Hello. Jill, is it?" She asked, offering her hand. I forced my hand to hers. "Oh…you're Monica's mother. Drake talks a lot about your little girl. She must be a sweetheart."

I wanted her to shut up and stop being so nice. "Yes, she's my daughter." I looked at Drake, and I knew he could see the hurt in my eyes. But his looked just as painful.

"Was there something I could do for you?"

Forgive me. Take me back. But I stood there, heartbroken and said, "I think Molly has infected ears again. I needed to pick up some medicine."

"Did you bring her in? I could check and see." God, even now he was being so sweet. I wanted to shout how much I loved him.

"No, I just dropped Monica off at school…and you were on the way home."

"Drake," Tawny said, looking at her watch. "We need to get going."

"Yes. Well, Jill…it was good to see you. Nancy will get that for you. But bring her in if she doesn't get better. How's Monica?"

Missing you—calling you Daddy Drake.

"She's good…"

"It was nice meeting you," Tawny said and pulled Drake gently by the arm.

"Yes, you too." I watched the two of them walk out together. I had lost again.

"Here you go, Jill," Nancy said, handing me the medicine. I paid her and walked out, feeling lost. I'd come here to get Drake back. But what I got was a kick in the heart.

I tossed the ear medicine across the car and hit the steering wheel. Fuck. I lost him. I saw his old truck still parked in his spot and knew they must have taken her car. Crying, I laid my head on the steering wheel. After everything I had been through with Michael, this hurt more than anything because I had let this man get away. I felt my future pass by and saw no happiness in sight. For the next several years, dates would come and go, but there was no one I would ever fall in love with. A year later, Drake and Tawny were married, and two years after that, I heard they had twin boys. Most of my weekends would be spent with Molly, sitting on the couch and having a glass of wine until she died at fifteen when Monica was in college. The next time I would be happy would be when Monica came home and told me Jordan had proposed.

CHAPTER 43

Now

I'm going insane. I'm not scheduled to work at the hospital, and Michael has been attached to my side, never letting me out of his sight. I need to get away and call that number. Cathy's number. But how? I can't even step out of the room, and he's on my tail. Usually, I would love the attention. But not today. It's taking every ounce of control not to become enraged and kick him out. I've bitten my tongue twice, only to swallow a smile and act as if all is peachy. I will have all the facts this time before I start my interrogation. He should know the best manipulator trained me—*Michael.*

Rummaging through the cupboards, I pick my brain for something I know I don't have. And damn it if Michael doesn't have everything in stock and perfectly organized. Maybe he's gotten better at this game. Hmm. Well, I better up mine.

"Hey, what about chicken cacciatore for tonight? My treat since you haven't had a nice home-cooked meal in a while."

"I don't think we have any tomato paste."

"Oh?" You know you don't, Mr. Organized. "Well, I'll run to the store and grab some."

"I'll go with you."

"No!" Crap. "I mean, you seem a bit wound up. I'll get it. It's fine."

"Are you sure? Maybe a walk to the store will help. Jill, I'm sorry if I seem edgy. The last thing I want to do is make you uncomfortable."

Too late. "You…don't seem yourself…since you've been home." I watch his expression, detecting any signs. There is a worried look on his face, and he walks over to me.

"I know, and I'm sorry. Come here," Michael says and holds me in his arms. "I must be making you a nervous wreck. You're trembling." He notices I'm a bundle of nerves. I should just come out and say it. 'Michael, I know you're cheating again.' But something tells me not yet.

"I guess I'm very concerned about you…and your business. You seemed a bit too preoccupied when we spoke on the phone."

"I know. I'm sorry. It's nothing to do with you. Just…something I feared would happen." Like ending up in bed with…Cathy?

"Michael, why don't you get some rest? Take a little nap or maybe go see Bindi. She was missing her grandpa. I'll pick up the items for the cacciatore and drop off your suits at the cleaners."

"You sure? I do miss my little girl. I'll give Monica a call and make sure she's home."

"Great. I'm sure Monica's home. Monday is usually her day off." He kisses my forehead, releases me from his arms, and pulls out his phone. I need to see inside that phone. If only texting had been invented when we were married before—investigating would have been much more accessible.

"Hey, Monica. You home?" He says, walking out and on his phone.

Quickly, I snatch up my phone, feel for the paper with Cathy's number in my pocket, and dress to head to the store.

Now in the car, I only make it to the stop sign and pull over. Michael left five minutes before me. So, he won't see me parked on the curb using my cell phone. God, this is crazy. I can't believe I'm going through this again.

My hands are trembling, and my lungs feel as if I have run a marathon as I press in the number. I don't even know what I'm going to say, or what I'm going to hear. If there's no answer, should I leave a message? I concentrate on my tone. *Concerned? Fishing?* Or, let the bitch out. Lord knows she's been hiding dormant for twenty years. Walked on for the three years we were married. And know we're married again. And it's happening…AGAIN! Okay, calm down, Jill.

Let's just start by being truthful. You're his wife, and you have the right to know why her number was in your husband's pocket. But, be the grown Jill. We are all adults now. I take in a deep breath, slowly let it out and hit send. It rings and on the third ring…she answers.

"Hello, this is Cathy. What can I do for you?" Her voice is…pleasant; professional. Well of course it is. She's probably a high-priced call girl.

"Ahh, hi. Um, I don't know how to say this…"

"Yes? Is there something I can do for you?" Stop seeing my husband for starters? I should just come out and say it. I'm sure she deals with this stuff all the time and has an already prepared speech.

"My name is Jill, Jill Danforth…"

"Jill?"

"Yes, I found your number in my husband's suit pocket. And I think he was talking to you this morning. Michael Danforth." Complete silence. I don't think she's even breathing on the other end.

"Jill, you said your name was?"

"Yes. Please, just be truthful with me. Michael was unfaithful in the past. And now we're married…"

"Look, Jill," she cuts me off. "I can't discuss anything about Michael with you. You will need to discuss this with him."

"But…please. I want the facts before I talk with Michael."

"I can't do that. Please discuss this with your husband. I'm sorry…"

"No, please…just tell me if he talked to you today." I hear her sigh into the phone.

"Yes, he called me today. That's all I can say."

"Okay…thank you, I guess."

"Goodbye," she says, and I hear the beeps when her call ends.

I drop the phone to my lap and cry with my head over the steering wheel—just like I did as a pregnant, married teenager years ago. And you know what? It feels no different than it did twenty years ago. What am I going to do?

"I'll tell you what you're going to do." Looking up, Tammy—Marilyn—sits in the passenger seat, blowing on her nails.

"Tammy. Oh, Tammy. It's happening again."

"Jill, dry it up. Be strong. We'll get through this."

"How? Why did you talk me into marrying him again?"

"Jill, I'm dead. So, you can't blame me. I'm just a figure of your imagination. And maybe this is too."

"No. It's not. I just talked to her—*Cathy McGregor.*"

"Who?"

"You know damn well who."

"Jill, I'm dead. I'm only in your head. So, stop thinking I have some magical powers."

"But you're always here in times like these."

"I was when I was alive. Now, I'm here in spirit. Your spirit. And here's what you're going to do. Drop off Michael's suits, pick up the list of items—that you forgot to write down, and then you're going to make Michael our chicken cacciatore."

"And then what?"

"Talk to him. Don't accuse him of anything. Maybe he'll open up."

"Open up? Hell no, he's not going to open up. You think he's going to say, 'Hey, Jill; by the way, I'm fucking around on you again.'"

"No, but he will know that you know something. Let's play it smart this time. I'll get you through this." And then…she disappears.

My phone rings and I jump. Michael's name lights up the screen. I look in the rearview mirror and wipe my eyes. Clearing my throat, I answer as calmly as I can. Play it smart.

"Hey, Michael. What's up?" Sounded convincing. Yeah, what's really up?

"I have someone here who wants to talk to you." Oh shit! Is it Cathy? Did Cathy call him right after I called her?

"Oh?"

"Gammy." Shew. It's Bindi.

"Hi, Baby Bindi. Are you with Grandpa?" I don't hear her answer, but I know she's nodding her head.

"It's me again. Hey, Baby. I got Bindi for the night. So, I hope that's okay with you."

How are we going to talk with a baby in the house?

"No, that's fine. Want me to pick something up for her?"

"No, she's had your cacciatore before. I just cut it up really small." God, Michael. Why are you doing this? You've become the perfect husband, father, and grandfather. Why do you want to ruin what we have?

"Okay, maybe some ice cream?"

"Bindi," I hear Michael say, "You want Grammy to get you ice cream? That's a big nod."

"Okay, I'm just leaving the cleaners." Lie. "I'll be home soon. Kiss Bindi for me."

"I will." I start to end the call when he says, "I love you, Jill."

"I love you too, Michael." And that's why it hurts so much.

•   •   •   •   •

It's been two days of biting my tongue into oblivion. Michael has been overly sweet, attentive, loving, and regretting the past. And maybe that's how older men have affairs. Kill their wives with kindness while having sex with other women. At the same time, the younger ones find fault with what they have because there's something different they want. I'm not too fond of both.

Today is my half-day at the hospital, and I've called Cathy's number six more times. Only to have it go to voicemail. She has my number now. Indeed, she's said something to Michael. If she has, he hasn't said anything. I do detect something in his demeanor. Last night before bed, he sat up and waited for me while I brushed my teeth. He looked like he wanted to talk when I walked in.

"Hey, what's on your mind?" I ask..

"You. Always you. Never doubt that." It was hard to accept his sweet talk, and I tried to get it out of him.

"Michael is…is there something going on?" He looked at me intently, about to spill something. He looked down and then pulled me to him.

"I just have a lot of regrets. That's all. Let's focus on what we have left."

"Left?"

"Now. Let's focus on us, our life and do all those things you talk about when we were young. Maybe you should quit your job. We could travel around."

"But, what about Monica and Jordan, and Bindi?"

"We'd be back. Maybe take Bindi on vacation with us." Did he want me gone, so as not to find him with Cathy?

"Michael, I can't quit my job. I love my job."

"Okay, but the offer still stands if you change your mind," he said and turned off the lights. As he slept, I watched his face in the moonlight and wished I could climb into his mind.

Pulling in, I park in the garage and see that Michael is not home. Perhaps he took Bindi to the park. But, it's pretty cold today. This will give me time to search for something. But what? All his expenses are paid through his business. How clever. I must be cleverer.

I throw my purse and bag of scrubs down and run to the computer. Tapping on Michael's expense account in the Danforth Jet Center file, it opens, and I scan my eyes down the columns. But everything looks legit. Of course, it's not like he's going to put a column for sex. Look. Look. It has to be here. And then I spot it. The travel log column. Where's his flight ticket? Nothing in here shows any expense, travel, or food for the last year. The previous travel expense was dated two years ago. Yet, everything else has dates of at least two days ago. Why wouldn't he add last week's travel expense?

I hear the door from the garage into the kitchen close. Michael. I minimize the excel spreadsheet and crane my neck to see if he's coming. "Michael? Is that you, Honey?" He doesn't answer, but I hear him talking to someone. He's on his phone. I wait for the screen to go dark before leaving and walk out to find him on the phone. He looks up, and his face changes expressions.

"Look, I can't talk right now." He seems very upset and ends the call.

"Is everything alright?" I ask.

"Just…some shit at the jet center," he says, running his hand through his hair.

"Michael, what's going on at the jet center? I'm tired of you keeping me in the dark." His head swings back, and his eyes show anger. "I think we should talk about it."

"Jill, I don't want to talk about it. I don't want to talk about anything." He is angry—and frustrated. At me?

"Don't bite my head off, Michael. Something is going on, and I have a right to know, don't I?"

"I'm sorry. I…it's just been a frustrating day."

Looking around, I notice I don't see Bindi. "Where's Bindi? Isn't she with you?"

"I dropped her off at home."

"With who? Monica and Jordan don't get home for another hour."

"Jill, will you stop badgering me?" A wave of panic runs through me. The room is dead silent as he looks at me with fear in his eyes. "I didn't mean that. I'm sorry. It's just been a bad day."

"Was Bindi being a handful today…."

"No, and I called Monica to see if she could get off early. I had to meet with associates from the jet center in town."

"Well, why didn't you call me?"

"Jill, I don't know." His voice is rough, and he's becoming angry again. We stare at each other, and I can't take it any longer.

"Who's Cathy?" He stares at me in disbelief; then, that anger rises.

"She's nobody," he says and begins to walk away.

"You think I don't know, Michael? I was trained by the best—you. I found her number in your suit pocket." He stops and turns around.

"What's this about, Jill?"

"I think you know. You're back to having your affairs again."

His smile is all too condescending as he shakes his head. "That's what you think. I'm sleeping around?"

"Why would I not think that?" He doesn't respond and walks away. "That's right, Michael, just walk away like you did before." Still no response as he shuts the bedroom door hard, and I jump. I'm about to run to the room when the doorbell rings. Shit, not now.

Moving the blinds, I see Casey standing on the porch and go to open the door. "Casey, what's up? Is everything okay?

"Yes, is Michael home?"

Why would she need to speak with Michael?

"Yes, he's in the shower," I say, and I see Bindi's favorite teddy bear in her hand. The one she naps with.

"I forgot this when Michael picked her up today. I know she can't sleep without it. And could you tell Michael that I switched my classes around? And I'll be able to watch Bindi next week as well?"

"You've been watching Bindi?"

"Yes, the last few weeks. It's not a problem. It's kind of a nice distraction with Mom gone and all."

I have no idea how to respond, so I take the teddy bear and thank her. "I'm glad, and thanks for bringing it over. I'll let Monica know we have it. And I'll let Michael know, too." Boy, will I ever, I think, squeeze the bear. When I look back at Casey, Tammy, not as Marilyn, is standing beside her daughter. Tammy strokes her hair, but I know she's only my imagination.

"Okay, thanks. Bye, Jill."

"Bye, Casey. Tell your dad and sisters I said hello."

"I will."

Shutting the door, I hear Tammy. "I miss them all so much. I can't believe she's in college. Looks like they're doing well. It's the best I can expect."

"Now, why are you here?" I say to a figure of my imagination. "It better be to offer me support." She's not looking at me but past me. There's a faraway look in her eyes. Then, I finally hear her.

"That's not why I am here, Jill," she whispers and walks away. I watch her move to the door, where Michael is on the other side. She looks at me, then disappears.

Get a grip, Jill.

I march to the bedroom and start to open it when I hear Michael speaking quietly on his phone. I carefully crack open the door and see him pacing and whispering.

"I can't do this anymore. I hate lying to her." A pause. "She called you? When? Fuck! She said she found your number. You didn't tell her anything, did you? Because she's been acting suspiciously." Cathy. He's talking to Cathy. I should bust in there and tell his ass to get out. But instead, I continue to listen. "Yes, I have a sitter for my granddaughter all of next week. God, this has got to work. I can't lose everything again."

I can't take it any longer and push open the door. Michael swings his head, looking at me with fear. I don't walk in but stand in the doorway, my arms crossed.

"Look, I have to go."

"No, you don't, Michael. Continue your talk with Cathy in front of me." He looks at the teddy bear in my hands. "Casey dropped this off." His chest heaves with defeat.

"She's here. Yes, right here in the room with me." Amazingly, I'm able to stand because I'm shaking so badly. "I can't tell her," he says, dropping the phone on the bed and walking into the bathroom. I walk over and pick up his phone.

"You'll have to talk to me now. Michael has left the room."

"Jill, can you please hand Michael the phone? I need to speak with him."

"No, you speak with me. And then, you can talk to Michael as much as you want. Because as of today, he's out of here." I stand in the bathroom doorway and look at Michael, who looks at me in the mirror. His look is total defeat.

"Jill, just one second. Let me speak to Michael, and then I'll have him return the phone to you."

"Here, you high-priced whore needs to speak with you," I say, handing Michael the phone.

He takes the phone and presses his eyes shut. "Yes, tell my wife everything." Handing the phone back to me, he walks out, and I put the phone back to my ear.

"Hello."

"Jill, I'm Michael's oncologist, Dr. Cathy McGregor. Michael has stage four cancer."

CHAPTER 44

Then

Monica was now in college, and my days were filled with lonely despair. If it weren't for Tammy and her girls, *now three*, I'd be a hermit. Molly died the week after Monica left for college, and she blamed herself. No matter how much I told her Molly died from old age, she was still convinced it was from a broken heart. But the only broken heart was mine. I worked more than my share at the hospital, working many hours. What else did I have? I had no husband or daughter at home. And no dog, either. I sipped wine and stalked Michael's Facebook. I never got over Drake, and five years after that day in his vet's office, I ran into him and his twin boys. I saw everything that could have been mine.

I had just dropped Monica off for her piano lessons. My parents' neighbor gave lessons and stressed that I must sign Monica up. She was ten then, but Barb said it was never too early.

I was to have a date that night with a new doctor who had just come on staff at the hospital—another one of Tammy's fix-ups. I wasn't enthusiastic about the date and decided to cancel and stay in. After dropping Monica off, I thought I would order us a pizza and went to my old high school hangout, Delanie's.

Walking in, the smell of onions and pizza sauce hit me, and I was transported back to the first dance I shared with Michael—the night I delivered his pizza. My whole life pivoted on that night. I sometimes wondered if I would be here now if I had stayed in the kitchen instead of delivering pizzas. It's strange how things work out.

As I stood in line waiting to order, the door behind me opened, and I heard a man talking to his children.

"Okay, guys. What kind of pizza are we getting?"

"I want cheese. Just cheese on it."

I turned to smile at the cute little voice, and my eyes stared into Drake's. The same eyes that loved me once. I stared at the mouth that kissed me and called me Peaches. I looked down at the hands that used to touch and hold me, now holding the hands of two little boys—twins.

"Jill. Hey, it's good to see you," Drake said.

"Hi, Drake. Oh my, are these your boys? They're adorable."

"Yep. This is Cody," he said holding up his right hand, "And this is Jody. Boys, Jill is an old friend of Daddy's." The word, old friend, hit like a punch in the gut. I was downsized from all his pet names to just an old friend.

"Hi there," I said, bending down and meeting their faces. They were at least four or five, with Drake's brown eyes, and all I could see was what was supposed to be mine. "Oh, Drake. They are adorable. You must be so proud."

"Yes, I am. I wasn't expecting two at once, but I wouldn't change having my boys for the world." He bent down and squeezed both boys into him. Drake was a father that was so happy *to be a father*. Once again, it was something I never had but could of. If only I wouldn't have walked out that night.

"How's Tawny?"

"She's good. She's away on business with her real estate company. So, the boys and I are roughing it with pizza."

"Well, that's what Monica and I are doing tonight."

"How is she? I bet she's grown so much."

"Yes, she has. She's currently at her piano lessons. So, I stopped in to get us a pizza." Though I knew it was wrong, and with his wife out of town, I suggested. "Hey, maybe we could all go to the park and have a pizza party."

"Yeah!" one of the boys yelled.

Drake's brows furrowed, and his smile looked weak. "Jill, I don't think that's wise—with my wife out of town." And once again, I fell deeper in love with him. He may have been breaking my heart, but he was loyal—a good husband.

"You're right. I wasn't suggesting…"

"No, I didn't think you were. I just don't think it's appropriate for me—as a married man. And…you? Are you married?"

"No, I'm not. Guess I haven't found the one." Though I had and let him go.

"Miss, what can I get for you?" I heard the girl behind the counter ask.

"Hey, it was nice seeing you," Drake said, and I suddenly had no appetite for pizza.

"Yeah, you too. Your boys are gorgeous." *Just like you.*

He smiled and nodded for me to order my pizza as the girl waited. I turned around, made my order, and left to stay in my car. Outside, I saw Drake's big truck parked in the lot and missed everything we had. He had a perfect family with two perfect boys. And even though it was what I wanted for him, I couldn't be happy. And I hated myself every day for it.

I poured myself another glass of wine when my cell phone rang, and Monica's face smiled at me. Setting the glass down, I accepted her call.

"Hey, Monica."

"Hi, Mom." She sounded giddy, and I hoped she wasn't tipsy. I had a stern talk with her before leaving for college. And even though she swore she wouldn't drink and party, I still worried. I couldn't say, because I remembered myself at twenty-one. I was busy being her mother—and living the Michael hell years.

"Monica, are you drinking? You sound a little silly."

"No, Mom, I'm not. I hope you're home. Because Jordan and I are in town and coming over."

I jumped from the couch with excitement. "Of course. This is a great surprise. How far away are you?"

"Um…I'm looking at your garage. We are just pulling in."

"Ahhh," I screamed and ran to the door. Jordan's pickup was just pulling in, and I ran to the drive. She came running from the truck, and we embraced. I'd missed her so much and just to have her in my arms again was a blessing. Last summer, she didn't come home and traveled for a project to complete her thesis. This was the first I had seen her in almost a year.

"How long are you home for? Are you staying here? Of course, you'll stay here. This is your home." I was bombarding her with questions and not allowing her time to talk. But I was so happy to see her. "Jordan, come here," I said, giving him a big bear hug. He was the perfect boyfriend for my daughter. They had met her sophomore year in college, and though they had a few hiccups, they managed to work things out and have been happy and together ever since.

"Mom, we have a surprise for you," Monica said.

"Yes, I know. You're here."

She held out her hand. "Jordan asked me to marry him. I said yes, Mom." I stared at the jewel shining on her tiny fingers and couldn't believe she was not a baby anymore. We screamed and held each other as we jumped up and down. We were like two schoolgirls.

"Jill, I wanted to ask for your permission. May I marry your daughter?"

"Oh, Jordan. I couldn't have picked a better man for her. You have my blessing." He smiled big and kissed my cheek as he thanked me.

"I promise that I will be a good husband. Never worry."

"I'm not, Jordan. I'm so happy." I grabbed both of their hands. "Come on in. I want to hear all the details. Like where and how he proposed and how you reacted. Everything. I want it all."

We went inside, and I opened a new bottle of wine to celebrate. This was the best news in a long time. And I couldn't recall the last time I'd even had good news. If everything I went through was to put Monica here at this moment, then it was all worth it.

"Who all knows? Can I call Tammy? Oh, my God. She'll just be tickled."

"You're the first Mom." She looked at me, and there was something there. She then looked at Jordan. "Well, someone else knows." She was still looking at Jordan.

"Jordan's parents? Well, that's understandable. Your parents are wonderful people, Jordan. Monica is so lucky to be joining your family."

"Ah, no. We haven't told my parents yet," Jordan said.

"Mom. Please don't be mad. But Dad knows."

"Dad? Michael?" I was shocked. He had been out of our lives for years. How could this be? "How would Michael know?" I couldn't even bring myself to call him her father.

"He…friended me on Facebook about a year ago."

I had no idea they were friends. The many times I stalked his Facebook, it never occurred to me to look at hers. But, why would I? I saw her post and approved of the ones she posted of us together. And truthfully, I stopped checking his Facebook about a year ago. Tammy made me promise to stop and focus on my life, and not Michael's.

"Mom? Are you mad at me?"

What could I say? I had taught her to love and forgive. But I was a hypocrite because I didn't practice what I preached. "Of course not, Honey. He's your father."

"Well, there's more."

More? "What do you mean?"

"Jordan and I want to marry right after we graduate. That's three months away."

"Honey, planning a wedding takes time." What was I talking about? My wedding happened in a week. Though, I would never call it a wedding. Or a marriage.

"It's all been arranged and paid for."

"How?"

"Dad has paid for everything. The Round Barn, the reception, the dress, food, drinks, and…and the honeymoon."

"Wow," was all I could say. I couldn't even feel my glass of wine and feared it would fall from my hand. "Even the honeymoon?"

"Yes, Paris. Mom…please tell me you're not mad."

"No. I'm in shock, Monica. He…he's paying for the entire wedding?"

"Yes. And the photographer. It's like thirty grand, Mom."

"Oh, I imagine it is. One thing. What's the catch?"

"Well, you know how we always said Uncle Scott or Grandpa would walk me down the aisle one day?"

"Oh, no. Don't tell me."

"He wants to give me away, Mom. That's all he asks. How do you think Grandma and Grandpa will react?"

I took a deep breath because I knew exactly how they would react. The same way when I told them I was pregnant. Michael was coming back, and I had to prepare my parents and Scott. I picked up the bottle of wine and topped off my glass. I was going to have to prepare myself.

CHAPTER 45

Now

No! This isn't happening. Not again. She—Cathy, is still talking, but I don't hear a word. It's all a blur as she rambles on. Make her stop. Please! Somebody make her stop.

"Jill? Are you there? You need to be strong. Michael is going to need you."

"What? No, I don't believe you." Now, I wished she was just a call girl or an affair. I could maybe deal with that. But not this again. Death is final.

I hear someone whisper my name and look up to see Tammy as Marilyn again, standing across the room.

"What are you doing here?" I curse at her in anger.

"I think you know, Jill."

"What I know is you can't stand the fact that I'm still alive, and for that, you're taking Michael away from me. Wasn't it enough that you left me?"

"Jill, not everything is up to us."

"No. I refuse to believe you. None of this is real. You're not real," I scream and throw the phone at the *Tammy-Marilyn ghost*. It only hits the wall because she's not there. I run out the door, screaming Michael's name. "Michael? Where are you?" Running through the living room, I see him sitting on the patio through the glass door. I can't get to him fast enough and forcefully swing the door open. It hits the back wall, and he looks up at me with red, swollen eyes.

"Michael. I'm here. I'm so sorry for everything I said."

"Jill, I'm so, so sorry. This is not what I planned. You have to believe me." He pulls me in with a crushing hug. "I love you so much. I never wanted this to happen. If I knew the cancer would come back, I never would have done this to you."

Grabbing his shoulders, I push back and look into his crying eyes. "What are you talking about? Come back?"

He reaches for my face and wipes my tears. I cup his and kiss his tears. "I've been in remission for almost three years. I was diagnosed with Non-Hodgkin's Lymphoma. After a year of chemotherapy and stem cell treatment, we thought we had it beat."

"We'll do it again. We'll beat this thing. Together."

"Jill, please forgive me. Forgive me for everything. I wanted to be with you for a long time."

"Michael, you will be. It's always been you and me." Even in Michael's absences, it's always been about him and me.

"Jill, the test came back. It's fast-growing this time and has spread to other areas. It's back, and it's back with a vengeance."

"I'm not giving up, Michael." My voice trails off. "I never have."

"I know, Baby. You're the best thing that ever happened to me. And I wasted twenty years of it. If I had it all to do over again…"

"Michael, you do. That's why you're here."

Somewhere through all the tears and heartache, he smiles. "That's right, Jill. That's exactly why I came. I thought I had another shot at life, and I wanted it with you."

"Oh, Michael."

I hold him tightly as the chilly fall air whips around us. Leaves fall to our feet. No longer is this a season of beautiful changes and colors. It's cruel and heartless, and I hate everything about it. How will I ever look up to the sky and see the golden and red canopy of trees without thinking of this moment? The sky is no longer blue but dark against the orange leaves. November will be just as ugly, leaving these trees bare and lifeless—an empty portrait of what once was. It's a reminder that life and nature are not always up to us, but we must decide what to do with it.

"Jill, please believe me. I thought I was cured. I thought I would never have to tell you. I never wanted you to think that it was death knocking on my door, leading me to your door. I wanted you back long before I was first diagnosed. But, I thought you had found happiness with Drake."

"How would you know that?"

"I was there that night, Jill—at Clementine's. You were so beautiful, so perfect, and so in love. I watched the way you looked at him. The way your eyes would light up, and I wanted it back. I wanted those eyes to see me that way again. Though I never earned a look like that from you, you unconditionally gave it to me, and I took it for granted."

"Michael, I swore I heard you that night. I thought it was all part of what made me doubt Drake's love for us."

"And that, I'm so sorry for. You should have been with Drake from the beginning. Not me. I never deserved you."

"But then I wouldn't have Monica."

He chokes on his cries, forcing his words out. "You would have had a beautiful baby with anyone, Jill. But you chose to have my baby. How'd I ever get so lucky?"

"Michael, stop this past talk: this doctor, Cathy McGregor. I heard you say she was the best. She will cure you again."

"She would if she could. But it's too far advanced, and more treatment and chemo will only leave me with no quality of the life I have left."

My eyes search his face in massive disbelief. "No. No. I refuse what you are saying. You can't; you can't just give up."

"I'm not giving up. I've just gone as far as life has allowed me. And guess what?" Tears run down his cheeks, and I kiss them, tasting the love leaking from his eyes. "It allowed me to be with you. I can't think of a better way to go." I fall into his arms and cry, allowing him to comfort me.

"I love you so much, Michael," I cry into his chest. I should have picked up on all the things he said. He had a friend dying from cancer.

His concern for Tammy. Our daughter's wedding and the look on his face when he saw us. I saw a deep appreciation when he bent down and let the water run through his hand after our photo shoot. It was all there. His second chance of life was with me, and he wanted it. "How are we going to tell our daughter?"

"Monica knew. But she doesn't know it's back."

"How did she know?"

"She came and took care of me. Something she learned from her mother. Unconditional love. Forgiveness. Respect and loyalty. Everything her mother is. Can I have this day for ourselves before we need to tell her?"

"Michael. I have *nothing* and *everything* to say. Things I don't want to ask and *things* I want you to know." The wind blows my hair and wraps around our faces. I want to keep him here. Tucked away and never to leave. Everything passes by momentarily as Michael holds me in his arms, gently rocking us in a wordless song. Each time I gasp with another cry, his lips press to my forehead, followed by a shush. I learned to live without him, not knowing he was always there. There in my heart, my soul, my anger, my love—he was still there. No matter how much I thought, I walked away from his memory. But that's what memories are. They're ours to hang on to. Cherish. It's only how we want to remember them. I have him here right now. And even this memory will be cherished—as hard as it is.

I squeeze him with all my might, wishing to crawl inside and go with him. Always be with him. "How long, Michael?" Don't answer. "No, I don't want to know."

"It doesn't matter how long as long as it's with you. That's what I want us to focus on. Let's not mark my life with time, but with who."

"I'm here, Michael. I'll never leave your side."

"I know. I've always known."

CHAPTER 46

Then: Michael

The sun beamed down a guided path as I trailed along Highway 2, taking the Great Northern Road trip. I drove over the volcanic Cascade Range, climbing above sea level. I took in all the wonders along my way. The Columbia Plateau, the Grand Coulee Dam, and the Idaho Panhandle before climbing into western Montana. I was on a journey to claim a life I didn't deserve, a life I took for granted, and a life I was going to beg to get back. I didn't need music or company on this extended trip. My regrets sat along for the journey. Soon, I would walk my daughter down the aisle and give her to a man to love and cherish her. A man much better than myself.

I rolled down the window and held my arm out, enjoying the feel of the wind. It was early May, and everything was blooming. I hadn't missed it and would never take another moment for granted. Remission was the word my oncologist said just five days ago. I was cancer-free. And I was going to get my wife back.

I took pleasure in making this a long country road trip. Sure, the freeways would have been faster, but I had almost a month before Monica's wedding, and I wanted to use this time to focus on life. I was blessed with another chance, and this time, I would slow down to appreciate everything in this life that was here for me. Things I discarded and never saw the beauty of. Jill was one. A young girl I used for pleasure and to feed my selfish ego. The limits I put her through, never giving her the love or desire she deserved. I wanted her back long before the cancer started. But I was too late.

It was a few years after Jill found me with Cami. Though my business was booming, my life was spiraling downhill, and I needed to grow up. I thought chasing the corporate dream and women would satisfy all my desires. I was only fooling myself.

Each night, I felt empty when I put my head down to sleep. My mind roamed back to my time with Jill and my baby girl. I would lie awake wondering what they were doing, how they would now look, and who the lucky guy was to have Jill as his own—a woman with youth and beauty and a mature woman's heart. I had found that this quality was lacking in every woman I met. But the problem wasn't always them. I was with the female version of myself. Taking and never expecting to give. I thought since I had plenty, I would give when I chose. Only to find I had nothing because of my unwillingness to give. They say when a woman sleeps with a man, part of her soul goes with him, leaving less for the next man. But what does that say for the man who took it? Thinking he has the right to damage her for the next. I hated to think this was what I was doing, and I did it to the woman who gave me everything. The woman who saw me as perfect in her eyes, and I was far from it.

One night, I jolted up in bed, determined to get her back. In the middle of the night, I booked a flight to Michigan and landed when the sun was rising. I rented a car and drove around the little town, where I was once a husband and father. I couldn't believe how much I missed this place and the little nest Jill had made for us.

I drove past my old home, now her house, and I wanted to run inside. I wanted to smell and touch the good memories I had there. The memories I never knew I had until they were all gone. I wanted to pick her up, spin her around in my arms and promise her a life of happiness and promises. I would never break her heart again.

After the second day, she never came home. So, I went and waited at the hospital. There she was, leaving in her car and I followed her. She didn't go home. She didn't go to her friend Tammy or her parents. But we ended up outside of town at this farm. I pulled back, careful not to be spotted, and watched as she ran into the arms of another man. God, it hurt, and I deserved every bit of that pain. I then recognized the man as Drake Daniels. I soon discovered he had become a Doctor of Veterinary Medicine. Monica followed behind them, running down the porch steps with a slew of dogs chasing after her. After Drake held and kissed Jill, Monica jumped up in his arms, and I saw the happy family I could have had.

I drove back to my hotel and stared at the ceiling until I could no longer count another spot on the tile. I showered, went down to Clementine's, and ordered myself a round of bourbon. Maybe tomorrow I would send flowers and meet her at the hospital.

I shot the bourbon down when my eyes fell on them walking in. Oh, Jill was even prettier than the day I met her. And she had aged to perfection. She wore the black dress the night of my Christmas party, and I wondered if she saved it to remember me by. But the only thing I gave her was terrible memories. The dress gave me hope. Until I watched Drake get down on one knee and ask my wife to marry him. She had gotten the proposal she had always wanted—and deserved. Jill said yes, and the two of them looked so happy. I took another shot when she came walking right towards me. Her eyes were full of tears, and for a moment, I thought there was recognition in them. I turned when she bumped into me and apologized. She hadn't recognized me—and I had lost. I walked out and wished her the best because she deserved it.

Now, here I was, twenty years later, driving home with one last chance life had given me. I thought back to the first day of chemo and the letter I began writing to Jill. I poured myself into that letter with all the words I never said. I had no idea how I would get it to her and wondered if she would even care.

Another week, more chemo, and I would add to that letter. I was the only one there who didn't have a spouse or friend with me. And…that was my own fault. An elderly lady who was scheduled for chemo on the same days befriended me and she told me of a long and wonderful life she and her husband had before he passed away five years ago. I thought of Jill as an old lady and what she would have to talk about when it came to me. I knew what that would be.

"Let me tell you this, son," Ruth, my chemo companion, would say. "Those first years of marriage are tough and sometimes not so good. That's because while we learn who our spouses are, we still don't know ourselves. And we can do a lot of damage in the process. Let me tell you." She would laugh, and it would shine a little light on our dark days. I thought I knew it all as a young man, but I didn't know anything next to Ruth. Her talks and tiny pearls of wisdom helped me craft my letter to Jill, especially regarding love. She asked me once if I had any children. I didn't know how to respond. Monica was now in college, and I hadn't seen or spoken to her since she was three. I wanted to talk about her. Show her pictures of my beautiful daughter, but I had none. And then I thought about the photographs I destroyed.

I began to cry when my phone pinged. I hoped it was the jet center, looking for an excuse to hide my shame. It was a miracle, and when I looked up at Ruth, she smiled and pointed to my phone. "I bet that's her."

How she would have known will always be a mystery. It was a friend request from Monica Danforth. My daughter wanted to meet me. At that moment, I had someone honest in my life. I accepted and read her message.

Hi, Dad. In case you don't recognize me, I'm your daughter. I don't remember much about you or that you and Mom were married. I'm in college now and hope to meet you this summer. I don't want anything, so don't worry if I'm asking for money. I want to meet you.

Your daughter, Monica Danforth.

My fingers trembled as I accepted and messaged her back. As soon as I accepted her, I was able to open and look at all her pictures. Years and years I had missed. She was beautiful, just like her mother. And then, there she was; Jill. The two of them on a beach having a *mom and me day*, the caption said. Jill was still so young looking, and the two of them looked like sisters.

I scrolled through more and smiled at all the silly Jill and Monica together pictures. They had gone on, were happy and I wished I was part of it. There was no mention of a stepfather, Drake. Nothing in her post or pictures suggested Jill had remarried. I messaged her back and asked how soon she could come and that I would pay all her expenses.

"Here's my daughter," I said, showing Ruth the pictures. "She's coming to see me." My words had all the proudness of a father, and for once, I felt something I had been missing all my life—*belonging*.

"She's gorgeous," Ruth said.

"Yes, she sure is. Just like her mother."

"Are you two no longer together?" I shook my head. "Oh, what a shame."

"It sure is. But if I had the chance…" I looked up at my chemo drip, now almost empty and silently prayed. "I'm going to get her back."

"Good for you," she said and patted my hand.

I was still in my chemo treatment when Monica came to visit. The thought went through my mind of having her come after my chemo was over. But I had wasted enough years of not seeing my daughter. I couldn't believe my eyes when she stepped off the plane. Like she always knew me, she ran into my arms with a big hug.

"Hi, Dad. It's good to see you. How've you been?"

"We'll talk about me later. I want to hear everything about you." Maybe I would not tell her about the cancer.

She told me all about college and her boyfriend, Jordan. The years she was growing up in Michigan with her mom. "Mom never remarried," she said out of the blue.

"I thought I heard once she was engaged." I wanted to know what happened. But Monica said she didn't know. She told me she loved the man and he was kind to her and Jill but never knew what happened. I let it rest there, but later, I would ask more questions.

The week turned into a few more weeks, and I hated to see her go. That's when I told her about the cancer. After that, she stayed all summer and cared for me, taking me to treatments and holding my hand. She met Ruth, and the two of them talked of young life and old life. I could see so much of Jill in her. I had indeed been blessed with a wonderful daughter. And I had left her behind.

By the end of summer, she had to get back to school, and we made a pact: I would live to walk her down the aisle. She said, "Dad, you'll live to do a lot more."

I kissed her before she boarded the plane, and I made her promise not to tell Jill. I wanted to do it my way. I wanted Jill to fall in love with me—*the new me.*

Ruth had passed away before I left for Michigan. I attended her funeral and met her wonderful family. When I was handed a book at the funeral, I asked what it was for. Her daughter asked if my name was Michael Danforth. I told her it was.

"My mother instructed this cookbook to be given to you. I'm not really sure why. I'm just granting her last wish."

"Thank you," I said. When I opened the book, there was a spot marked with a note.

Son, when you get your wife back, make her this plum pot roast. There's nothing a pot roast can't fix.
Take care.
Love, Ruth.

And so there I was, heading down Highway 2 in my Toyota 4Runner—no more little boy toys. I popped in my go-to-song, rolled down the windows and sang at the top of my lungs, '*All in*' with Lifehouse. Because this time, I was all in. I only hoped she would take me back.

CHAPTER 47

Now

Each day becomes more precious. Another day Michael is alive. Sleep doesn't come, at least not for me. Michael's cancer is winning the battle, but I refuse to acknowledge the evil growth slowly taking away another life. Michael does his best to put on appearances, but I know he's in pain. He limits pain medication to only the days when it's too intolerable. These days, he has two choices—take something for the pain and sleep or pretend he doesn't hurt and carry on as if all is well.

It's February, and I'm thankful to have had a few more months with him. There is no pain medication for my heart, but only the love and unselfishness Michael gives me. He's lost so much weight, but I pretend not to notice. He is and always will be the strong man who gave me his heart. He will always have mine.

Once again, I have taken a leave from work to care for Michael. And together, we get through the day with tears, laughs, and watching our granddaughter together. I know Bindi wears him out, but he will never say so. I see the determination in his eyes, though his body is weak. *Today is a good day*, he tells me. I don't argue. Because, as a nurse, I know there are no good days when dying from cancer. There are only days.

Christmas was extra special this year, and we celebrated like there was no cancer. Michael refused to let us think or talk about it—If it were that easy. The house was decorated to the gills. We all laughed when Michael flipped the switch, lighting up all the outside lights, and reenacted the scene from *"Christmas Family Vacation."* The neighbors all came over and stood around for the big reveal. The cancer hadn't yet taken its toll on him, and I prayed that, by some miracle, the cancer would disappear. Sometimes, I wonder if it was as bad as now, and Michael refused to let us see it. However, there's no hiding it now. His jeans, which once hugged his perfect body, now hang. He's cold most of the time and wears flannels over his T-shirts. I make sure to keep the heat set higher than usual. It's so sad what cancer does. Not only does it take away your loved ones, but it degrades one's worth as a man or woman—the broad shoulders, the bulky biceps, the square masculine profile, all bony and sunken. I tell him he looks like a burly lumberjack in his red-plaid flannel shirt, and I see appreciation in his eyes for still seeing him as the man I always have.

When he holds me, I feel bones where I once felt muscle. It's all so sad, but we refuse to let it ruin our days together. We talk of the future as if he will still be here. Who will be president when Bindi grows up? Where she'll go to college and what she'll be. Monica and Jordan will have a boy next when they decide to have more children.

I carry a plate of Michael's favorite cookies into the living room and watch him looking out the front window. "What are you looking at?" I ask, setting down the cookies. "Chocolate chip, your favorite."

He turns around and gives that supportive smile. "The snow. It's so pretty when snow first falls."

"Says the man who cursed the snow and taught our daughter to swear."

He laughs and comes to take me in his arms. "My job was to teach our daughter the bad things. Your job was to teach her the good things. And…I say you've done a pretty good job at that." After he kisses me, he reaches down and grabs a cookie. I love to see him eat and enjoy whatever he can. "Mmm, it melts in my mouth. Here," he says, sharing the cookie with me. I chew and smile into his eyes. His eyes still hold that shine and love he had when he first returned. I understand it all now. How much he has taught me.

"Hey, grab your coat. We're going to make a snowman," Michael says.

"But…"

"No buts. Today is a good day. And...I want to build a snowman with my wife. Go grab Bindi and bundle her up."

"Michael..."

"Shh. I want this more than anything."

I take in a heavy breath and know there's no arguing with him. And it's these things that are hard for him to do, which make him feel better. It's hard to watch, but I know I must do it if it is his wish.

"Okay. Bindi is finishing her cookies in the kitchen."

"Thank you," he says and slowly moves to the bedroom to bundle up.

I find Bindi at her kid's table, enjoying her cookie with chocolate all over her face. "Looks like someone likes cookies." She looks up and shoves more cookies in her mouth with the palm of her hand. She then holds out both hands to show me the chocolate all over them. "You want Grandma to clean you up?" A big nod. Picking her up, I take her to the sink and clean her face with a warm cloth. "You even have it in your ears."

Now clean and cookie-free, I ask if she wants to go outside. She shrills with baby happiness and wiggles to get down. "Go get your coat and boots." She pushes her little legs to the door where her bag lies. Michael grabs her up, and she screams with more giggles.

"Grandpa has his warm clothes on. Let's get yours," he says and bundles her up. I grab my coat and step into my boots. When I open the back door, the wind whips in, blowing snow inside. I look to Michael once more, but there is no stopping this. He wants us to make a snowman.

With Bindi between us, both holding a gloved hand, we step down from the patio and take giant steps through the snow. At least six inches that have fallen. Bindi drops to her knees and gathers snow in her tiny hands, and Michael begins with Snowman Building 101.

"Press it together like this, see?" He presses snow into a ball and hands it to her. "Roll it in the snow, and it will grow." Snowball rolling lasts about three minutes until Bindi decides the snow is more fun to eat than to roll.

"Looks like it's up to us, Grandpa," I say, and I help Michael with the snow. Once the ball grows to our knees, Bindi gives it another shot and pushes the snowball around.

"Yeah, like that. You're doing it," Michael cheers her on as he prepares another snowball. As I watch the two of them playing in the snow, I don't see cancer and all the pain that comes with it. Michael wants us to see only this—he and I and the life we've created. And that's how it should be. *Don't give cancer a minute's thought*, he always says. Today belongs to us.

I gather pine cones and sticks for the arms and face of their snowman, now layered with three giant snowballs. "Wow, did you do this?" I say, bending down to Bindi. She nods and rubs the snowman's belly. "Wait until Mommy sees it."

Michael picks her up, and I hand her the pinecones to push in the snow for his eyes. "Perfect," he says and kisses her big on the cheeks. "Brr, you got cold little cheeks. How about we go in, and Grandma makes us some hot chocolate? She smiles big with a nod. Wrapping his arm around me, we kiss and carry Bindi back to the house together.

We leave our clothes in a pile to dry next to the door, and I gather the cups and cocoa mix. Michael hugs me from behind and rubs his cold nose on my neck.

"Thank you. That meant a lot to me."

"Me too, Michael." I know he won't like it, but I need to ask. "How are you? Do you need me to get a blanket?"

"Only if you come and lay inside with me," he teases like there is no cancer.

"You have got yourself a date because I am freezing, and to curl up with this lumberjack is the only thing that can satisfy me."

He laughs under his breath. "You bring the hot chocolate. I'll grab the blanket."

I pour cocoa into Bindi's sippy cup and set her at the little table. "Here you go, little Miss Snowman Maker. She reaches for the cup, and I know she'll be down for a nap soon.

Michael is lying on the sofa with the blanket open, waiting for me as I set two mugs on the table. I quickly snuggle down and curl into his chest. "Mmm, I love snuggling with you," I say and tip my head to kiss his chin.

"I love you, Jill. Thank you for making me feel like a man."

"You are a man, Michael. And an awesome snowman builder." He squeezes me in, and I feel his ribs in my back. "Are you getting warm enough?"

"Mm-hmm."

I find his hands, cold and bony fingers, and lace them with mine, bringing them up to my lips. "I love you too, Michael." A slight squeeze of his hand lets me know he's heard me. I then cover our hands up and nestle down into him.

I watch the snow come down outside through the gap in the curtains and think about the years I've spent looking out that window. *Michael leaving, and Michael coming back.* Monica going on dates and walking in at night, sometimes a little late. I try to fill in the gaps from our voided years, but time has stitched together, allowing us time.

I feel Michael's chest move in and out, and I'm thankful for each one. Until they become smaller and farther apart, I squeeze his hand again. A faint squeeze back, and then it goes limp, and his last breath lands on my neck. He's gone.

Tears run down my face as I watch the snow come down outside, and I think how, only moments ago, we all built a snowman together. I silently thank him for making me forget that, for a short time, he wasn't dying.

Bindi walks in with her blankie and teddy and crawls beside us. I don't speak and pull her into me until she falls asleep. Maybe it's better this way—too young and not knowing she will never see her grandpa after she wakes from her nap.

When I feel she's deep in her nap, as much as I hate to, I slowly lift us, take her to the bedroom, and lay her down. I walk back to Michael, who looks so at peace. Like he's sleeping and will wake to smiles and kisses on my face. I sit down beside him and rub his chest, and see a note poking from his shirt pocket. Pulling it out, I open the worn paper and read what Michael has written. It's a list with things crossed off. It's his bucket list.

One, walk my daughter down the aisle—crossed off. Two, Jill loves me again; crossed off. Three, marry Jill—crossed off. Four, become a grandfather—crossed off. Five, live the rest of my life with Jill—crossed off. And six, die with Jill in my arms.

Through the tears, I see Bindi's crayons spilled along the coffee table and pick up a pink crayon. I cross off the last thing on Michael's list. I fold it back up, tuck it inside his pocket, bend to kiss him, and then whisper. "Go in peace, Michael. Your list is complete."

•   •   •   •   •

I stand next to Michael's coffin and prepare to speak. I don't know how to get through this, but I know I will somehow. Monica and Jordan are in the front row, next to Mom, Dad, Scott, and Jen. Ryan and the girls are behind. I don't recognize the faces in the back, but many have expressed their condolences and introduced themselves as Michael's friends from the jet center. All the other faces I remember from Monica's wedding. I remember that day, the first time I had seen Michael in over twenty years. It seems like a lifetime ago. I dab my eyes again, take a deep breath and begin.

"Michael came into my life when I was just a girl...and my life hasn't been the same. Things weren't always easy, and at times, I thought we'd never last. And...we didn't.

"Many of you know that Michael and I divorced twenty years ago. It was Michael who gave me a beautiful daughter." I look at Monica, tears heavy in her eyes. Jordan holds her close, and on her lap sits Bindi. "Michael left to find himself, and I know how cliché that sounds. But I think it was meant for us. Because once we found each other again, we learned how never to take love for granted and to hold on for dear life."

I brace myself, trying to talk over the lump in my throat and continue. "A few years ago, I lost my best friend, Tammy. She was my anchor through all the bad Michael years. And when she passed, Michael was there for me. That's the Michael I want to tell you about today."

I glance down at the note in my hand—Michael's bucket list. "There are three things I know about Michael. One, how much he loved me. Two, that he wanted to be a grandfather. And three, he died in peace. Michael would tell me about his regrets in life, but what he didn't know was that he had outlived them. Even dying young, he left no regrets."

Wiping my eyes, I look at the people sitting and see Tammy as Marilyn sitting next to Ryan. She smiles and blows me a kiss, and I feel the strength to go on.

"Michael was the husband who would open my car door and hold my hand publicly. He was the husband who surprised me with flowers for no reason and a hot bath waiting when I got home from work. He loved to care for his granddaughter, and for the first year of her life, he raised her while we all worked. He even planned her gender reveal party." I laugh and recall the day. "We were all to meet at the park here in town. Michael had tables set with food and cakes. We were all in suspense and had no idea what his plan was. All kinds of baby stuff were on the tables, which we thought would reveal if she was having a boy or a girl. Michael began talking when an officer came into the pavilion. He asked if anyone drove a white Honda Civic. Monica said it was hers. He told her that there had been an accident, that her car had been damaged, and she needed to fill out a police report. We followed her to her car when a parade of fire trucks and police cars surrounded the area. We thought a raid was going down when, over a loudspeaker, an officer said, 'Monica and Jordan, you are having a girl.' Every police officer and fireman came out with pink roses and began singing *"My Little Girl."* Not as good as Tim McGraw." The crowd laughs, and it's the air I need.

"I think as we all get older, we realize that growing old together is the real fantasy, not the one we daydream about as young teens and adults. As young girls, we think love is a first kiss, first sex, dates, dances, hearts, and flowers. But it's not. Those are things we do because we don't know what love is. Love is the crying babies, the dirty diapers, sleepless nights, and having that one person hold you as you experience it together. Love is discovering what life is all about together—being someone's anchor and light after a hard day. Love is watching someone slowly deteriorate away but still only seeing him as the hot guy who kissed you on his couch when you were seventeen. It's seeing the storms and sunshine together. The hills you climb to see the horizon, knowing it wasn't easy, but you did it together. Love is knowing you have moments to live, and you spend it building a snowman with your wife and granddaughter."

With tears running down my cheeks, I fold Michael's list, turn, and place it in his suit pocket. "Love is having the best husband I could ever ask for. Thank you, Michael. I love you."

CHAPTER 48

After

The snow is gone, replaced with fresh, green grass, and the trees are bursting with leaves. It's the end of May—Memorial Day—as I drive into the cemetery. Bindi is in the back, buckled in her car seat, taking a thousand pictures of me with my phone. Later, I will need to purge the stream of photos. But occasionally, she captures one that grabs my heart. A moment in time I was unaware of.

Michael has been gone for three months, but his beautiful spirit is alive all around us. Not a day goes by that I don't talk to or talk about him. We keep many pictures around, and Bindi is learning to say Pappy. She will know and remember her grandpa.

Several cars are parked here in St Joe Cemetery, placing flowers on loved one's graves, and I pull up first to Tammy's. Before getting out, I asked Bindi if Grammy could have her phone back. She hands it over, and we then exit the car. "You want to put flowers on Tammy and Pappy's grave?"

"Pap—py," she says.

"Very good. You know who Pappy is, don't you?"

A big nod, followed by, "Pap—py."

"Oh, you're getting to be such a big girl," I tell her, carrying her to the back of the car before setting her down. I pop the trunk, take out the flats of flowers I bought, and reach for Bindi's hand. "Come on. Give Grammy your hand, and we'll play in the dirt."

"*Durt.*"

"Yep. You like dirt, don't you?"

"Durt. Pap—py," she sing-songs as we walk to Tammy's grave. Ryan and the girls have planted Tammy's favorite flowers—painted daisies. I add a few more and a couple of small sunflowers to their arrangement. A garden stone with the caption *Mom, always loved and missed,* centers the flowers.

"Okay, ready to plant flowers on Pappy's?"

"Pap—py." She helps by picking up the half-empty flat, and we walk to Michael's grave. The grass has not yet grown over where he rest for eternity, so I sit down on my knees and plow the soil with my hands to prepare to plant the flowers. Bindi wastes no time jumping in and squeezing the dirt. "Yeah, like that."

"Durt," she says, picking it up and letting it sift through her tiny fingers.

"Can you hand Grammy a flower?" She shuffles over, picks up one flower with both hands and returns it. "Very good. Now, put it right here in this hole." She drops it in, and I tell her to get more while I make more holes. Soon, we have the entire plot planted with an arrangement of colorful annuals. "Now, let's give the flowers a drink." Gathering the empty flats and small spade, we take them back to the car, and I grab the sprinkler can that luckily hasn't tipped over. She holds my hand as we stroll back to Michael's grave. "Here, you hold this side while Grammy tips the water out." It takes a bit, but soon, all the water empties, and I sit on the ground and hold Bindi on my lap. "Now, who is this?" I say, pointing to the picture I put on Michael's stone.

"Pap—py."

"That's right."

"Jill? Jill Danforth?" I hear someone behind me say.

Twisting around, a woman stands behind me. A woman I recognize from years ago. "Yes, I'm Jill."

"Do you remember me? It's been…"

"Yes, You're Cami." She looks at Michael's grave and then to Bindi and me. "What are you doing here?"

"First, let me say I'm sorry for your loss."

"Thank you." I think. Why is she here? Michael did once tell me they were still friends. I can't remember seeing her at his funeral.

"This might seem strange. Is there somewhere we could talk?"

Curious, I lift Bindi from my lap, then stand to brush the dirt from my pants. "What's this about?"

"It's about Michael."

"I don't think there's anything to discuss. As you can see, Michael is gone."

"It's something from Michael. Please, is there a coffee shop or park we could go to?" she says, smiling at Bindi.

Curious, I tell her to follow me to the local coffee shop and buckle Bindi back in her seat. I climb into the driver's seat. She waits in her car behind mine, and I put the car in gear. "Let's find out what this is all about, shall we?" I say, looking at Cami in the rearview mirror.

Ten minutes later, I pull Bindi back out, and we walk into the coffee shop. I find us an isolated table, pull up a high chair, sit Bindi down, and hand her some crackers from her diaper bag. Cami returns with two coffees and hands one over. "Thank you," I say and try to steady my hand.

"So, is this Michael's little granddaughter?" she asks, shaking one of Bindi's tiny hands.

"Yes, this is Bindi." I take a sip of the coffee and set it down. "Cami, why are we here?"

"The board was cleaning Michael's office a month ago, and we found this." I tremble and grab my coffee as she pulls something from her purse. Through the tremors, coffee splashes over the rim, causing the hot liquid to run down my fingers. But I'm too nervous to reach for a napkin and begin with slow sips.

She hands me the envelope, and I freeze when I see my name scribbled across the paper. "I think you should read what is in this letter," she says.

Setting the cup down, I wipe my hands on my jeans and reach for the envelope. My heart races, and I slowly tear open the seal and pull out the letter.

Dear Jill,

As I write this letter, I don't know if you'll ever get it. And if you are reading this, please know that I have passed. A few weeks ago, I was diagnosed with non-Hodgkin's Cancer, and currently, I'm receiving chemotherapy. But that's not why I'm writing this.

I'm writing this letter to beg for your forgiveness. I regretted my past with you and wished I could have been a better husband and father. Each day, I'm haunted by the way I treated you and left you and Monica. I'd do anything if given another chance; I would do everything differently. I hate to think you will look back and see me as the worst thing in your life.

I know it's too late now to tell you this. I love you, Jill. I always have. I know you won't believe me, and I understand. You made me feel so many things, and the problem was, I didn't know what to do with it. So, instead of learning from you and accepting your love, I destroyed the best thing that ever happened to me. I hope you're happy with Drake and that the two of you live the life I wish I could have had with you. He loves you, Jill, and you deserve to have his love. Please know it wasn't about you when I left and said I couldn't do this anymore. It was about me not wanting to hurt you anymore. I was always in my own way, and now it's too late. If there's one thing life has taught me, it's this. In the end, we're all just stories. And I wished mine could have ended with you. I love you, Jill. Take care.

Love, Michael

Epilogue

Five years later

Never does it get easy. *Death.* Not even when a long, loved pet dies from old age. I think back to Molly, our little cocker spaniel, and how she got me through Monica's college years. That dog became just as good a friend as Tammy. Even though she only listened and let me have all the wine. I miss Molly and her furry body snuggling against me on the couch. I'd talk, she'd listen. Her sheepish eyes looked up from her brows each time I spoke. I miss petting her head, rubbing her ears, and listening to her quiet moans when it felt good on a tender spot. The day I finally had to put her to rest gutted me from the inside out. No longer could she eat, and when she smelled food cooking, she would find someplace to become sick, though there was no food in her belly. No longer could she go on walks, and she had to be carried to go outside to potty. That's when I knew she no longer had any quality of life, and it was too cruel to expect her to go on.

I'm no longer a nurse at the hospital, but I still use my skills as an office manager. Today is a day I'm not fond of because as I said, it never gets easier. We have lost a long-loved patient, Booker—a seventeen-year-old golden retriever. I never got the privilege of meeting Booker as a puppy but as an overweight, hard-of-hearing, gray-faced dog.

I stare at the blank piece of paper before me, waiting for the words to come. I want each letter to be personal and reflect the lives of these unique pets that held their owners' hearts. I know I'm on the right track when I begin to cry. But today is a little hard for me because Booker died next to me, his eyes looking up in appreciation as he took his last breath. The end was near, and I held his paw until there was no more heartbeat. And now, I'm writing a letter to his owners, who have already buried him in their pet cemetery. We do this for comfort and peace and to let them understand that they made the right decision. And the right choices are always the toughest.

"Awe, aren't you just the cutest thing."

Looking up from the paper, Tammy, as Marilyn, holds a kitten in her hand. It's good to see her on these challenging days. She softly strokes the tiny kitten's head as it meows quietly.

"Where have you been these days?" I ask her.

"Around. You haven't needed me as much."

"I always need you." I smile at her powdered face and red lips. "I miss you, you know."

"I know. So, we've come to help."

"We?"

"Hello, Jill." It's Michael.

"Hi," I whisper and look into his blue eyes. He's dressed in jeans and a Ball State T-shirt. Like the day I first saw him. He's sitting in a chair in the waiting area. It's good we're closed because I wouldn't have time with them. "What are you here to help me with?"

"Your letter. Are you ready?"

I pick up my pen and look up. "Yes."

"Jot this down," he says, and I begin to write.

Dear family,

Remember when you first saw me as a puppy, all cute and fuzzy? That was the first day I saw you, and I wiggled with excitement, hoping you would pick me. Through the years, I wasn't always such a good puppy. But no matter what I did, you would always welcome me with open arms. As we grew together, we built beautiful memories. And even though I'm gone, those memories will keep me alive forever in your heart. We had good times and not-so-good times. But that never stopped you from loving and taking care of me. I want you to know that my life was good because of you. When it came to love, you were all I ever knew and wanted. Though I ran off a few times, I deserved the swats on my behind. But after that, I was back in your arms and heart. So, please go on and know that though you may find another dog, I'll see that I was always unique to you. I want you to be happy and think of me without tears. Think of me each time you laugh and are loved because you deserve it.

I finish the letter and look up. "It sounds like you're talking about yourself."

"Maybe I am. But I'm not really here, Jill."

"Maybe you are."

He gets up, walks over, and sits at my desk. "I'm here because I'm always here." His finger touches my heart.

"Yes, you will always be."

I reread the letter, make a few changes, and add our company's condolences at the bottom.

Your love and unselfishness for your beloved pet was the kindest thing he knew. We are all so sorry for the loss of Booker and are also saddened here, for we, too, will no longer see him come in. Please take care and know we are here for you.

Love, Michael

A honk outside tells me my ride is here, so I get up and lock the office. Looking around once more before stepping outside, I say goodbye to Tammy and Michael. They both smile and fade into thin air.

I watch the truck pull up the lane and lean on the porch rail. Crossing my legs, I smile down at my cowboy boots, recalling the night Michael took me to a country bar and sang to me. Maybe he was preparing me back then. As Michael and Tammy were preparing for their deaths, I think both were preparing me for life.

The truck parks and outjumps Bindi, followed by her little brother, Michael Julian. They both run up and give me big hugs. "Did you guys have a good time?"

"Yes, we did," little Michael says. He's three and will talk your leg off.

"Grandma, you should have seen it. It was amazing," Bindi says, full of excitement.

I hear the truck door shut and watch him walk toward me in blue jeans, cowboy boots, and a ragged T-shirt. "Everything locked up?"

"Yes. Letters all written and ready to send."

Wrapping his arms around me, he looks into my eyes and kisses me with love. "I love you, Peaches." Peaches. I'll never tire of it.

"Sounds like the grandkids were pretty amazed watching a colt be born."

"Yep. And…," Drake says, pulling me into his arms, "They're ours for the weekend. I asked Monica if they could stay with us at the farm."

"Really? Thank you. You're such a wonderful man, Doc. How'd I get so lucky to have a husband like you?"

"Luck had nothing to do with it. I've always been yours, Peach. Time has a way of moving in many directions. I've always been drawn to you. That tells me you are connected to my path."

He's right. You may not see it today or tomorrow, but you will look back in a few years and be utterly puzzled by how everything added up and brought you somewhere beautiful—or where you always wanted to be. And you might even be grateful that things didn't work out how you once wanted them to. As for Michael, he will always be part of us. After his death, I was the sole beneficiary of the Danforth Jet Center. Now, Jordan runs it remotely from home. Monica now runs a preschool in her home and is expecting baby number three in a few months.

"All right. Let's load Grammy in the truck and head out to the farm," Drake says, swinging little Michael around and giving him a piggyback ride back to the truck.

"I get to ride Honey first," Bindi yells, making a beeline to the truck. Honey is one of the horses on the farm.

I look back once more and read the big letters on the side of the building. *Michael Danforth Animal Hospital.* I did this with Michael's inheritance, and together, Drake and I run the hospital. Drake had no problem letting me use Michael's name, so we signed each letter of condolence. *Love, Michael.*

Drake and Tawny divorced right after the twins left for college. Tawny said she needed a long-needed break and went on a cruise to find herself. She found herself in cabin 214 in bed with another man. Once Tawny returned, she asked Drake for a divorce. We have no idea if she and this man are still together.

The twins are both in graduate school to become veterinarians like their father, and currently, they live together in Michael's and my old home. Drake says once they are on their path, he would like to use the house for college students studying to become doctors. I couldn't agree more.

Now that I'm much older and wiser, I look back and see my fears differently. When Michael and I were younger, the fear of losing him scared me. Because I had given so much of myself to him in pieces, when he left, I feared losing myself. And that's when I learned that you must change yourself if you can no longer change a situation. Because your mind will believe everything you tell it. So, feed it with faith, truth, and, most of all, love.

Tammy and Michael will always be part of my heart and soul. Together, we're all woven into a tapestry of memories, good and bad, laughs and cries. But that's life. It's how we choose to remember someone. Don't hang on to the bad memories. Always think of them as part of you. Everyone you love will reflect on you. Life is only preparing you for what's next. So, be ready, embrace it, and enjoy it fully.

It was hard, so hard, losing Michael. People ask me how I deal. Would I have been better off if he'd never come back? And it's a fair question. I did lose him again. But this is what I tell them.

Michael and I were married till death do us part. It was the one vow he never broke. I would have never known if I had never become a seventeen-year-old mother and wife to Michael Danforth.

The End

ABOUT THE AUTHOR

Gina A. Jones is an Indiana-based, award-winning author who weaves tales of romance, mystery, and second chances into her books. Her characters are flawed yet unforgettable, seeking redemption in the hearts of readers worldwide. She began writing in secret then took a chance at publishing her first novel that became a three-book series. *The Secret Series* debuted in 2017 winning best moments in a book with Audiobook Obsession. When not writing, she loves spending time with her husband and grandkids. Gardening is a must because she's a vegan, and CrossFit is her guilty pleasure.

NOTE FROM GINA A. JONES

Word-of-mouth is crucial for any author to succeed. If you enjoyed *Love, Michael*, please leave a review online—anywhere you are able. Even if it's just a sentence or two. It would make all the difference and would be very much appreciated.

Thanks!
Gina A. Jones

www.ingramcontent.com/pod-product-compliance
Lightning Source LLC
Chambersburg PA
CBHW051313190726
48290CB00001B/138